# SOMEONE ELSE

*She Had Many Faces. One of Them Was a Killer.*

HUMAN
AUTHORED™
Ac Authors Guild
9088992

by

# Aurealia Nelson

ISBN 979-8-89778-061-7

# Staten House

# Please Be Advised: Content Warning

This novel is a psychological thriller that delves into mature and potentially distressing themes. It contains explicit content and explores sensitive topics that some readers may find disturbing. These include:

- Graphic Violence and Murder: Detailed descriptions of a murder, its aftermath, and body disposal (including the use of lye and a freezer).
- Abuse: Depictions and recollections of severe childhood trauma, including physical, emotional, and sexual abuse, as well as domestic abuse (spousal abuse, manipulation, gaslighting).
- Dissociative Identity Disorder (DID): Explores themes related to DID (formerly Multiple Personality Disorder), including the experiences of alters and fragmented memory.
- Self-Harm: Includes descriptions of cutting.
- Substance Abuse: Depictions of alcohol abuse as a coping mechanism.
- Mental Health Themes: Explores PTSD, OCD, anxiety, depression, and the stigma surrounding mental illness.
- Grief and Loss.

Reader discretion is strongly advised. If you are sensitive to any of these topics, please proceed with caution. This book aims to portray the complexities of trauma and mental illness with realism and sensitivity, but the content may be intense for some readers.

# Contents

# TABLE OF CONTENTS

## Dedication

This book is dedicated to the countless women whose voices have been silenced, whose stories have been buried under layers of societal expectation and personal trauma. To those who have endured unspeakable horrors, whose resilience in the face of unimaginable adversity remains a testament to the strength of the human spirit, even when that spirit is fractured and fragmented. It is dedicated to the survivors, those who fought their way back from the brink, who found the courage to reclaim their narratives from the clutches of their abusers and the insidious whispers of their own fractured selves.

This is for the Eleanor Vances of the world, the ones who, despite their silent screams and the invisible scars that marked their bodies and souls, somehow managed to build lives, however fragile, upon the foundations of their shattered pasts. It is for the Janes, the Lillys, the Evelyns—the many facets of a single woman struggling to find coherence amidst the chaos of a mind torn asunder. It is for their struggle to piece back their fragmented lives into a whole. Their resilience, courage, and determination serve as a beacon of hope to those still trapped in the darkness.

Their fight for survival is an echo of a silent battle, a relentless struggle against the ghosts of their past, and it is precisely that unseen battle that this story endeavors to make visible, to give voice to. This is a recognition of the complexities of trauma, the subtleties of mental illness, and the enduring power of the human spirit to survive, even when survival means bearing the indelible marks of a past that refuses to be forgotten. It is a testament to the complexity of the human experience; the delicate balance between sanity and madness, the darkness and the light within us all. This is for them – may their stories finally find a voice and bring solace to those who have endured a similar, unseen pain. For them and those who seek to understand. For the quiet ones, and for the loud ones, whose quiet cries for help were never heard.

# CHAPTER 1: THE FROZEN ECHO

The air in the attic hung thick with the scent of dust and forgotten things. Sunlight, fractured by the grimy windowpane, illuminated motes dancing in the stillness. Sarah Vance, her face etched with a weariness beyond her thirty years, ran a trembling hand over the worn wooden trunk. It was her mother's, a relic from a life she thought she knew, a life that now felt as distant and unreal as a half-remembered dream. Eleanor Vance, the picture of poised elegance, the trophy wife, the seemingly perfect mother, was gone. Unexpectedly. Suddenly. A heart attack, the doctor had said, a swift and silent end to a life that, from the outside at least, seemed impossibly charmed.

Inside the trunk, nestled amongst yellowed photographs and moth-eaten shawls, lay a diary. Not a pristine leather-bound volume, but a battered thing, its cover cracked and faded, its pages brittle with age. The spine was barely holding, threatening to surrender its secrets to the dusty oblivion surrounding it. The simple, almost childish, script on the cover suggested the diary belonged to someone quite young, a sharp contrast to the sophisticated woman Sarah had known as her mother. The leather was worn smooth in places, the result of countless hours spent holding the book close, confiding its secrets, whispering its anxieties. A faint, almost imperceptible scent clung to the aged pages—a melancholic perfume of vanilla and something else, something subtly acrid, like old fear.

Sarah hesitated, her fingers hovering over the clasp. A tremor ran through her, a premonition of the darkness that likely lay within. She knew her mother had her eccentricities – the compulsive tidying, the sudden, inexplicable mood swings, the unnerving detachment she sometimes displayed. But none of these quirks had prepared her for this. For the tangible weight of unspoken secrets, for the palpable presence of a pain she had never sensed in her mother's composed demeanor.

The thought of confronting the unknown filled her with a chilling dread. What horrors lay concealed within those fragile pages? What untold stories would shatter the image of her mother, an image so carefully crafted, so meticulously maintained? She had always admired her mother's strength, her ability to navigate life with effortless grace. Now, staring at the diary, that image felt like a carefully constructed illusion, a fragile façade built on layers of deceit and unspoken pain.

She opened the clasp, the sound a tiny, almost inaudible click in the otherwise silent attic. The brittle pages rustled like dried leaves under a winter wind. The first entry was dated twenty-five years ago, a date that sent a shiver down her spine. The same year as the unsolved murder – the murder of a young woman found encased in black plastic bags, a macabre tableau in a domestic freezer, the victim's body surrounded by lye and tied with red scrunchies. A detail that had become chillingly notorious in local police circles, a gruesome puzzle that had never been solved. A horrifying detail Sarah hadn't dared to think about in years, her memories blocked and hazy, leaving an unexplained unease in the pit of her stomach. It was a crime that had cast a long shadow over her family, a silent specter that always seemed to linger at the edges of her childhood memories.

Sarah's breath hitched in her throat. Could there be a connection? The possibility felt absurd yet terrifyingly plausible. The diary, with its worn cover and cryptic script, felt like a key, a key to unlocking a hidden chamber of the past, a chamber filled with secrets so dark, so shocking, that they threatened to consume her entire world.

She began to read, her eyes scanning the faded ink, her mind struggling to process the childlike script. The words were simple, almost innocent, yet they spoke of a world far removed from the idyllic suburban life Sarah had always known. The entries were fragmented, disjointed, as if written by someone struggling to make sense of a fractured reality. There was Jane. The first alter to reveal herself within the brittle pages of the diary.

Jane's world was a kaleidoscope of confusion and fear. Her descriptions were innocent, her understanding of events limited by her childish perspective. She spoke of a beautiful house, filled with shiny things, of a mother who sometimes laughed and sometimes cried, and a father who was often distant, his presence a mixture of looming fear and absent affection. Jane's entries were filled with a strange mix of wonder and apprehension, describing a world of baffling cruelty and unexplained pain. She wrote of noises in the night, of hushed whispers, of fleeting glimpses of violence that she couldn't quite comprehend. Her words painted a picture of a family in which love and hate, safety and terror, existed in a terrifyingly close proximity. She wrote of a red scrunchie, a symbol that seemed both ordinary and terrifyingly significant. Its recurring appearance in Jane's childish observations suggested an event of deep significance, an event she didn't quite grasp but clearly recalled with a chilling sense of unease.

The diary entries weren't linear, jumping erratically between seemingly unrelated observations and emotions. One entry depicted a lavish birthday party, a scene of vibrant colors and forced merriment, followed immediately by a chilling description of a locked door, the sound of muffled sobs, and the acrid smell of something burning. The stark contrast between these two scenes hinted at a reality far more sinister and complex than anything Sarah had ever imagined.

The more she read, the more the pieces of the puzzle began to fall into place. The seemingly perfect façade of her mother's life, the whispers of her eccentricities, the unsolved murder—they were all interconnected threads in a tapestry of profound psychological trauma. The diary was a map, a disturbing roadmap to the shattered psyche of a woman consumed by her fragmented self. As Sarah read further, the feeling of unease transformed into a profound sense of betrayal, and a growing terror at the implication of her own hazy memories and the knowledge that many things weren't as they seemed. The idyllic world she thought she knew was disintegrating around her, replaced by a chilling truth that threatened to engulf her in the same darkness that had consumed her mother. The red scrunchies, previously mere childhood trinkets, now felt like sinister symbols of a brutal past, tying together seemingly unconnected events and leaving a trail of horrifying clues. The seemingly innocent entries, childish in their simplicity, revealed a depth of abuse and trauma that defied understanding and slowly chipped away at the carefully constructed image of Eleanor Vance, the woman she thought she knew. Each page turned was a step further into a world of darkness, and each entry was a fragment of a shattered mind. The revelation of this dark past, hidden so effectively from the world, began to unravel the very fabric of Sarah's reality. The seemingly ordinary details from her childhood, now interpreted through the horrifying filter of the diary, began to take on a sinister new meaning. She looked at the worn leather of the diary, and she knew that her life would never be the same.

Eleanor Vance was the picture of grace. A vision in silk and pearls, her smile effortlessly captivating, her laughter a melodic chime that seemed to brighten even the dreariest of days. She moved through the world with an understated elegance, a quiet confidence that bordered on ethereal. Her home, a sprawling colonial nestled in the heart of Willow Creek, was a testament to her refined taste. Every detail, from the antique furniture to the meticulously arranged floral displays, spoke of wealth, sophistication, and a life lived in effortless luxury. Her husband, Richard, a prominent lawyer, was the embodiment of success – handsome, charming, and powerful. Their two children, Sarah and her younger brother, Thomas, were the golden children, seemingly blessed with intelligence, beauty, and a natural ease that made them the envy of their peers. To the outside world, the Vance family was everything a community could aspire to – the perfect picture of the American dream.

Yet, beneath the polished veneer of perfection, whispers circulated. Subtle murmurs that spoke of an unsettling undercurrent, a darkness that lurked beneath the surface of Eleanor's seemingly flawless existence. These whispers weren't malicious gossip, but rather observations, shared in hushed tones, exchanged with a mixture of curiosity and unease. There were the sudden, inexplicable mood swings –

moments of vibrant energy and infectious laughter that would abruptly shift into periods of unsettling quiet, of a chilling detachment that left those around her feeling vaguely uneasy. Then there were the eccentricities – the obsessive tidying, the meticulous organization of everything from her spice rack to her sock drawer, a compulsion that bordered on the pathological. She had a precise system for everything, each item having its specific place and order. Disturbing this order brought about a sharp, almost violent, reaction. There were tales of unsettling rituals, performed with a quiet intensity that defied explanation.

Mrs. Henderson, their next-door neighbor, recounted Eleanor's ritualistic watering of her prize-winning roses. Not a casual sprinkle, but a meticulous process, each drop measured, each plant treated with an almost reverential care. There was something unnervingly intense about it, a devotion that crossed the boundary between horticultural enthusiasm and a deep-seated compulsion. Mrs. Henderson often confessed to a growing feeling of unease watching this ritual, a silent, unnerving performance enacted with a strange intensity. The contrast between the serene beauty of the rose garden and the intense focus in Eleanor's eyes was stark, almost unsettling. The flowers seemed to be the focus of a strange reverence.

Even Sarah, despite her adoration for her mother, remembers instances that, in hindsight, appear deeply disturbing. There was the episode of the burnt dinner, a seemingly innocuous incident that turned out to be a turning point. The kitchen had filled with acrid smoke, the smell of burning so powerful that it permeated through the house. The event seemed insignificant, a simple cooking mishap. But the intensity of Eleanor's reaction, the wild-eyed fear and subsequent anger, left Sarah with a memory that was both chilling and completely inexplicable. There was no visible reason for this overwhelming emotion, and yet it was undeniably palpable. The incident was swiftly swept under the rug, dismissed as a temporary lapse in judgement, the episode seemingly fading from collective memory. But Sarah would carry the memory with her, the unsettling experience a silent, ever-present reminder of something hidden, something far more than a simple cooking mistake.

The local librarian, Mr. Fitzwilliam, a man known for his keen observation and quiet wit, recalled an incident in which Eleanor had become inexplicably agitated by a misplaced book, a seemingly trivial detail that triggered a cascade of fury. The episode left him with an abiding sense of unease, a feeling that Eleanor's anger was far more than a simple reaction to a misplaced item. Her fury felt displaced, the intense emotion disproportionate to the event.

These whispers, these subtle observations, were dismissed as eccentricities, as the quirks of a high-achieving woman under immense pressure. But the underlying tension, the persistent unease, remained. It was as if an invisible current of anxiety pulsed beneath the surface of Eleanor's seemingly perfect life, a darkness that hinted at a fractured reality, a chilling disharmony between the outward image and the inner turmoil that consumed her. The whispers were a subtle chorus, a haunting counterpoint to the idyllic melody of the Vance family's public persona. They were a prelude, a foreboding hint of the profound and disturbing truths that lay concealed beneath the surface of Eleanor's carefully curated life. The rumors were a shadow cast upon the bright sunshine, a premonition of the darkness that the family's facade concealed. The disturbing details, dismissed as minor oddities, hinted at a deeper, more troubling reality, a disharmony within Eleanor that would eventually unravel the perfect picture the family presented to the world.

The contrast between Eleanor's public image and these unsettling whispers was stark. It was the contrast between a perfectly manicured lawn and the weeds that grew hidden underneath, between a flawless performance and the dissonant notes in the background that hinted at the depth of the dysfunction. This dissonance, the gap between the idealized exterior and the darker undercurrent, is what fueled the mystery surrounding Eleanor Vance, creating an atmosphere of suspense and foreboding that would continue to deepen as the narrative unfolded. It was the chilling undercurrent that would steadily escalate, foreshadowing the violence that was about to surface from the depths of her fractured psyche. The idyllic life was a mask, a carefully constructed façade designed to hide the turmoil within, a turmoil that would eventually erupt in violence, shattering the image of perfect family life and leaving a trail of unspeakable horror.

The diary, discovered by Sarah, would ultimately expose this terrifying duality, revealing the devastating truth behind the seemingly perfect façade, the shocking reality that lay hidden behind Eleanor Vance's captivating smile. The diary would expose the extent of her suffering, the layers of trauma that contributed to her fragmented personality, and the chilling manifestation of her inner turmoil. The contrast between the public perception of Eleanor Vance and the hidden reality revealed in the diary would only serve to enhance the unsettling nature of the story. It was a dark mirror reflecting the truth about her life, a counterpoint to the picture-perfect image she presented to the world. The diary, in its rawness and honesty, is a stark contrast to the carefully curated exterior, emphasizing the disharmony between the two worlds, adding to the intensity and emotional impact of the story. The unraveling of Eleanor's life would be a slow, chilling process, as Sarah delves into the diary entries, piecing together the fragmented story of her mother's tortured existence.

The biting wind howled a mournful dirge around the dilapidated farmhouse, its icy fingers clawing at the peeling paint and rattling the frost-covered windows. Inside, Detective Miller shivered, the chill seeping deep into his bones, a stark contrast to the stifling heat emanating from the freezer in the center of the room. Twenty-five years. Twenty-five years since the discovery of that freezer, its steel door a metallic tomb guarding a horrifying secret. Twenty-five years since the case had gone cold, leaving behind only a trail of unanswered questions and a lingering sense of dread that clung to the small town of Willow Creek like a shroud.

The image seared itself onto Miller's memory, an indelible brand etched onto his soul: the body inside, encased in multiple layers of black plastic bags, meticulously tied with an unsettling array of crimson scrunchies. The bags were so tightly bound, the suffocating effect evident, like a grim, macabre cocoon. The sight had been a grotesque tableau, an unsettling performance in death. The victim, a young woman named Clara Bellweather, lay submerged in a caustic bath of lye, her features obscured, her identity initially unknown. The lye had begun to dissolve her flesh, a gruesome process of decomposition that had rendered identification initially impossible.

The freezer itself was an ordinary appliance, a commonplace item transformed into a chilling instrument of death. Its white enamel surface, once pristine, was now marred by grime and frost, its cold heart beating with a silent rhythm, a constant reminder of the life it had cruelly extinguished. The scene held a meticulousness that disturbed Miller to his core. It wasn't the brutality of the act that haunted him; it was the chilling precision, the deliberate, almost ritualistic nature of the crime. The neatly tied bags, the careful placement of the body, the chilling choice of the lye – it spoke of a mind that was both calculating and profoundly disturbed.

The initial investigation had yielded little. There were no clear witnesses, no apparent motive. The farmhouse itself was abandoned, a decaying relic of a forgotten past, offering few clues. Clara Bellweather's life, pieced together from fragments of information, painted a picture of a vibrant young woman with a bright future, a future cruelly snatched away in the darkness of that winter night. Her social circle offered no immediate answers, her friends and family baffled by the randomness of the crime. Her life seemed utterly unremarkable, devoid of any apparent enemies. The lack of a clear motive was as baffling as the meticulously staged crime scene. The case, therefore, became a haunting symbol of the department's failure, a chilling reminder of the darkness that could lie hidden beneath the veneer of normality.

The police had explored every possible avenue, every conceivable lead. They had interviewed neighbors, friends, and acquaintances, scouring the town for any shred of information that might crack the case. They had sifted through evidence, painstakingly analyzing every detail, every object at the scene. But the killer had left no trace, no discernible footprint that could lead them to justice. The only clues were the black plastic bags, the red scrunchies, and the chilling presence of the lye – details that were as perplexing as they were disturbing. These seemingly insignificant items haunted the investigation like phantoms, their presence casting a long shadow over the case.

The red scrunchies, in particular, fascinated and disturbed Miller. They were cheap, mass-produced items, easily available in any supermarket. Yet, their vibrant crimson color stood out in stark contrast to the chilling bleakness of the crime scene, a disturbingly incongruous element. Were they a calling card, a perverse signature of the killer? Or were they simply a random detail, a trivial element in an otherwise carefully orchestrated crime? The question remained unanswered, lingering like a shadow.

The local media, initially frenzied in its coverage, had eventually moved on to other stories, leaving the Bellweather case to gather dust on the shelves of forgotten headlines. Yet, for Miller, the case remained an open wound, a constant reminder of the unsolved crimes that continue to haunt law enforcement. The cold facts of the case were chilling enough, but it was the elusive nature of the killer, their carefully planned methodology, their complete lack of remorse that made this case stick with him even after so many years had passed.

Over the years, various theories had been put forward. There were whispers of a serial killer, a phantom figure lurking in the shadows, preying on innocent victims. But there was no evidence to support this theory, no pattern that could link Clara Bellweather's murder to any other crime. The case remained isolated, a chilling enigma, its secrets locked away in the cold, dark silence of the freezer. The mystery was further complicated by the lack of any clear motive and the seemingly random selection of the victim, turning this into an unsolvable puzzle. It was a case that preyed on the minds of the investigators and left a deep scar on the town of Willow Creek, becoming a legend in itself.

The lack of progress in the case only added to the unsettling atmosphere, fostering speculation and fueling the rumors that circled around the town. Was it a crime of passion, a random act of violence, or something far more sinister? These questions echoed in the minds of the residents of Willow Creek, a subtle reminder of the darkness that could lie beneath the surface of their seemingly peaceful community. The unsolved crime had become a part of the town's history, a chilling legend passed down through generations.

Years later, after the death of Eleanor Vance, the chilling truth would finally emerge, a truth so dark and disturbing that it would leave everyone who knew the Vance family reeling in horror and disbelief. The details that were available to the police during the initial investigations paled in comparison to the truth that the diary would finally reveal, leaving even Miller awestruck and horrified at the depth and cruelty of the crimes committed. The diary would paint a haunting picture of a woman fractured, a woman consumed by a fractured psyche, a woman capable of unspeakable acts of violence.

The diary, a collection of fragmented narratives penned by Eleanor's multiple personalities, would expose the layers of trauma that had shaped her, that had unleashed the monstrous violence that had ended Clara Bellweather's life. It was a journey into the heart of darkness, a descent into the abyss of a tormented mind. The diary, a collection of fragmented narratives penned by Eleanor's multiple personalities, would expose the layers of trauma that had shaped her, that had unleashed the monstrous violence that had ended Clara Bellweather's life. It was a journey into the heart of darkness, a descent into the abyss of a tormented mind. The unsolvable puzzle would eventually find its terrifying answer, hidden within the pages of the diary, a chilling testament to the power of psychological trauma and the devastating consequences of untreated mental illness. The shocking revelation would leave a lasting scar, forever changing the lives of those who knew Eleanor Vance, proving that appearances can be utterly deceptive and the darkness within a person can manifest itself in the most unforeseen and terrifying ways. The diary entries would uncover a chilling tale of abuse, betrayal, and a struggle for survival within the fractured mind of Eleanor Vance, a story that would ultimately shatter the idyllic picture of the Vance family. The unsettling truth, hidden for twenty-five years, was finally unveiled, revealing the terrible secret behind the meticulously staged crime. It was a revelation that would send chills down the spines of all who came to know it.

The diary fell open to a page filled with childish scrawl, the ink a faded, almost translucent blue. The handwriting was uneven, the letters tilting at precarious angles, some barely legible, as if the hand that held the pen trembled with an unseen fear. The date, scrawled in the corner, was illegible, lost to time and the relentless march of decay. But the name, penned at the top of the page in bold, childish lettering, was clear: *Jane.*

Jane's entries were a disorienting blend of innocence and disturbing observation. They lacked the chronological coherence of a typical diary, jumping erratically between seemingly unconnected events, reflecting a fractured perception of time and reality. She described the house as a place of shifting shadows and whispers, a place where laughter and screams danced a macabre waltz. The world, as seen through Jane's eyes, was a kaleidoscope of confusing sensory experiences, a fragmented tapestry woven from threads of fear, confusion, and fleeting moments of childish joy.

"The sun made the dust motes dance," one entry began, the words childlike in their simplicity. "They looked like tiny fairies, swirling and twirling. Mama laughed, a real laugh, not the tight, pinched one she usually wears. Daddy was there too, smiling. He smelled of…something nice. Like sunshine and woodsmoke." The shift in tone was abrupt, the idyllic scene jarringly juxtaposed with the following sentence: "But then Mama cried, and Daddy's smile turned hard. The fairies disappeared."

Jane's perceptions were fragmented, her understanding of events clouded by a child's limited comprehension. She witnessed violence, but lacked the vocabulary to fully grasp its horrifying reality. Instead, she described it through the lens of a child's imagination, transforming acts of brutality into distorted, almost fairytale-like scenarios. A broken vase became a fallen star, a spilled glass of wine a crimson flower blooming on the carpet. The adults' emotional turmoil was refracted through her innocent eyes, transforming into a confusing narrative of good and bad, joy and sorrow, without a clear understanding of the underlying causes.

"Daddy's hands were red," she wrote in another entry. "Red like the berries Mama used to pick in the summer. But they weren't sweet. They hurt Mama. Mama screamed, a bird caught in a cage. Then she was quiet, and Daddy's red hands went away." The lack of detail, the avoidance of explicit description, was both heartbreaking and chilling, hinting at a carefully constructed defense mechanism, a child's attempt to shield herself from the overwhelming horror of her reality.

The recurring motif of red was striking. Jane seemed drawn to the color, associating it with both beauty and violence, mirroring the duality of her own experiences. Red berries, red hands, red stains on the carpet - these fragmented images were like pieces of a shattered puzzle, each hinting at a larger, darker picture that remained hidden from her understanding. The repetition suggested a deep-seated psychological association between the color red and trauma, a subconscious link forged in the crucible of her abusive childhood.

She often described a feeling of being watched, of unseen presences lurking in the shadows of the house. These weren't specific people, but more like unsettling sensations, a constant feeling of being observed, judged, and even threatened. This implied a constant state of hypervigilance, a survival mechanism honed by years of living in an unpredictable and unsafe environment. The feeling of being watched wasn't limited to the confines of the house; it followed her outside as well, into the seemingly innocent world of children's games and playground fun. This constant state of anxiety and fear highlighted the pervasive nature of her trauma, affecting every aspect of her life.

There were moments of fleeting happiness, fleeting glimpses of normalcy that punctuated the darkness. Jane described playing with dolls, drawing pictures with bright crayons, and imagining herself in fantastical worlds far removed from the harsh reality of her home. These moments, however, were always ephemeral, easily overshadowed by the looming presence of fear and anxiety, serving as a stark reminder of the fragility of her innocent world. These precious moments were like fragile islands in a sea of trauma, providing temporary respite but ultimately failing to offer lasting peace.

The diary entries revealed a profound disconnect between Jane's perception of reality and the objective truth. She described events in a way that lacked depth, nuance, and a proper understanding of causality. This was characteristic of a child coping with severe trauma, a coping mechanism that manifested in emotional dissociation, a detachment from the full emotional impact of her experiences. Her ability to compartmentalize her experiences was both a strength and a weakness, protecting her from immediate psychological collapse but hindering her ability to fully process her trauma.

"Mama sang a song," one entry read. "A sad song about a bird with broken wings. The bird flew away. I want to fly away too." This simple sentence held a wealth of unspoken pain, a yearning for escape, for a world free from the shadows that haunted her life. The recurring motif of birds suggested a longing for freedom, a desire to escape the confines of her abusive environment and soar towards a world of safety and happiness. But the broken wings symbolized her helplessness, her inability to escape her reality on her own.

Jane's entries offered a glimpse into the complex tapestry of Eleanor Vance's fractured mind. Through her innocent eyes, a world of unseen horrors unfolded, a world of abuse, violence, and unspeakable acts cloaked in a veneer of normalcy. Her childlike perception, though fragmented and incomplete, was a crucial key to unlocking the mystery of the frozen echo, providing a disturbing insight into the origins of the darkness that would eventually culminate in Clara

Bellweather's gruesome murder. Jane's narrative served as a poignant reminder that even in the most innocent of hearts, the shadows of trauma can linger, casting a long and dark shadow that will shape her future in ways that are both devastating and unimaginable. The diary, through Jane's eyes, presented a chilling testament to the insidious nature of abuse and the enduring impact it had on the vulnerable mind of a child. It was a chilling chronicle of a life lived in the shadows, a child's desperate attempt to navigate a world that was both beautiful and terrifying, a world that she struggled to comprehend, yet one that she was forced to endure. The fragmented narratives painted a portrait of a young girl, lost in a labyrinth of fear and confusion, seeking solace in the fleeting moments of joy that offered only a brief respite from the harsh reality of her existence. The entries hinted at a deeper, darker story, one that would only be revealed as the diary unveiled the other fragmented personalities that inhabited Eleanor Vance's mind. The sheer innocence of her words, juxtaposed with the horrific realities she witnessed, created a powerful and disturbing contrast, leaving a lasting impact on the reader. The entries would serve as a chilling reminder of the lasting effects of trauma, and the desperate need for healing and understanding.

The discovery hit Sarah like a physical blow, a seismic shift that rearranged the tectonic plates of her reality. One moment, she was holding a fragile piece of her mother's past, a faded diary filled with childish scribbles; the next, her carefully constructed world was crumbling around her. The initial shock gave way to a nauseating wave of betrayal, a bitter taste coating her tongue, leaving her gasping for air, struggling to process the enormity of what she'd just read. It wasn't the violence itself that initially stunned her – she'd always known her mother had a troubled past, a darkness she'd kept meticulously hidden. It was the sheer scale of it, the systematic, brutal nature of the abuse, the chilling details that painted a portrait of a childhood spent in the shadow of terror.

Eleanor, the elegant woman with the perfectly coiffed hair and the subtly ironic smile, the woman who'd taught her to bake perfect chocolate chip cookies and who'd patiently helped her through teenage angst, this woman didn't exist. Or rather, she existed only as a carefully constructed facade, a mask worn to conceal a horrific reality. The elegant woman was a mirage, shimmering over a landscape of unspeakable horrors. Underneath the polished surface lay a fractured psyche, a collection of shattered selves struggling to piece together a coherent existence.

Sarah felt a deep, visceral sense of violation, a betrayal not just of her mother's trust but of her own perception of reality. The narrative in the diary hadn't just revealed a darkness; it had shattered the foundation upon which her understanding of her mother, her childhood, and even her own identity was built. The vibrant memories she held dear were now tainted, filtered through a lens of newly discovered pain. Sunday afternoons spent in the garden, the smell of freshly baked bread, family vacations to the coast – these once cherished moments were now imbued with a chilling undercurrent, a sense of pervasive unease. Each seemingly happy memory felt like a cleverly staged performance, a deception carefully designed to conceal a profound and deeply disturbing secret.

Her hands trembled as she reread the passages describing the abuse, the words blurring before her eyes. A torrent of conflicting emotions washed over her: anger, sorrow, confusion, disbelief, and a profound sense of loss. The loss wasn't just of her idealized image of her mother; it was the loss of her own innocence, the shattering of the safe, predictable world she had always believed she inhabited. Her carefully curated world had been an illusion, and now she was left confronting the grim truth – a truth that was both unsettling and intensely personal.

The detailed accounts of physical and emotional abuse left her breathless. She found herself reliving the scenes, feeling the weight of her mother's pain, her terror, her desperate struggle to survive. The vivid imagery – red stains on the carpet, broken toys, the child's desperate attempts to make sense of the senseless violence – left an imprint on her soul, forcing her to grapple with the implications of her mother's suffering. Sarah's own childhood trauma, long suppressed, surfaced unexpectedly, surfacing as a chorus of echoes mirroring the pain described in the diary.

The fragmented nature of Jane's writing added another layer of complexity. The diary wasn't a linear narrative; it was a disjointed collection of memories, sensory impressions, and fragmented thoughts. It was a kaleidoscope of emotions, shifting from innocent observations to horrifying descriptions of abuse. This lack of continuity mirrored the fractured psyche of Eleanor, reflecting the complex nature of her multiple personality disorder.

As Sarah delved deeper into the diary, she began to understand the profound impact of the abuse on Eleanor's life. The violence wasn't merely a series of isolated incidents; it was a systematic pattern of cruelty, woven into the very fabric of her childhood. The trauma had left its indelible mark on Eleanor's psyche, shaping her personality, her relationships, and even her perception of reality. Sarah began to understand the origins of her mother's aloofness, her erratic behavior, her tendency to withdraw into herself. The pieces of the puzzle began to fall into place, revealing a disturbing picture of a woman wrestling with the demons of her past.

The diary entries detailed not only the physical abuse but also the psychological manipulation and emotional neglect that Eleanor endured. The constant fear, the uncertainty, the feeling of being unloved and unwanted – these were just as devastating as the physical wounds. Sarah found herself questioning everything she thought she knew about her mother. Was the woman she knew real, or was she simply another mask, another persona crafted to conceal the pain and suffering hidden beneath the surface?

The diary entries also revealed a hidden strength, a resilience that allowed Eleanor to survive the unimaginable. She may have been broken, but she was not defeated. There were moments of hope, flashes of defiance amidst the darkness. The occasional glimpses of joy, the moments of childlike innocence, served as a testament to her indomitable spirit. These moments provided Sarah with a newfound respect for her mother, a realization of the depth of her capacity for endurance and survival.

Sarah was faced with a devastating truth: her mother's life wasn't what she thought it was. Her carefully constructed perception of her mother as a strong, elegant woman was replaced with a chillingly different picture – that of a fragile, traumatized soul battling a multitude of personalities born from abuse. The realization shook her to her core. Her mother's past wasn't a footnote in her life, but rather a gaping chasm that had shaped every moment of her being, right down to her deepest fears and insecurities. Sarah's own understanding of her life, her identity, her family, was cast into turmoil. She was not merely piecing together her mother's shattered past; she was grappling with the reconstruction of her own reality.

The diary, however, didn't just detail the abuse; it also hinted at the complex interplay of psychological disorders that Eleanor was wrestling with. Hints of obsessive-compulsive tendencies, attention deficit hyperactivity disorder, even possible traits indicative of autism spectrum disorder, were subtly woven into Jane's narrative. Sarah found herself searching for a connection between her mother's struggles and the disorders that she herself had been diagnosed with. This realization opened a new dimension of empathy and understanding that transcended the pain and confusion, offering a glimpse into the intricate web of psychological complexities that Eleanor's fragmented mind represented.

The diary's narrative wasn't a straightforward timeline; it jumped from one emotion to the next, from one sensory experience to another, creating a disjointed, chaotic tapestry that mirrored the fractured nature of Eleanor's psyche. Each entry was a snapshot, a fragmented piece of a larger puzzle. Sarah felt a surge of guilt, realizing that she hadn't ever looked closely enough at her mother's struggles, at the subtle signs of her inner turmoil.

Sarah now held a dark secret in her hands—a secret that revealed the truth about her mother's identity and the depths of her pain. The diary's narrative did not simply unveil the abuse, it also opened a window into the world of multiple personality disorder, a condition she hadn't known existed, a condition that now served to explain her mother's unpredictable behavior. It was a revelation that shook her to the core, shattering the image of a strong, composed woman, and revealing a life spent navigating a labyrinth of internal conflict. Sarah was forced to confront the unsettling truth that her mother's struggles had significantly influenced her own life, and the lives of those around her. The diary offered a rare and chilling insight into the mind of a victim, not merely of abuse, but of a deeply fragmented self. Sarah's journey into her mother's past had only just begun. The discovery had set in motion a chain of events that would shake her to her core, forcing her to confront not only her mother's history but her own identity as well. The past was no longer a closed chapter, but a living, breathing entity that would forever alter the course of her life. The weight of the revelations hung heavily on her shoulders, leaving her with a sense of profound sadness and a chilling understanding of the lasting impact of trauma on the human psyche. Sarah's journey of discovery had just begun, a journey into the dark heart of her family's past, a past that promised to haunt her long after the last page was turned.

# CHAPTER 2: FRAGMENTS OF A SHATTERED MIND

The diary entries shifted abruptly. The childish scrawl gave way to a bolder, angrier hand, the words sharper, more urgent, laced with a bitterness that chilled Sarah to the bone. The voice was different, raw and untamed, a stark contrast to the hesitant, almost childlike entries that preceded it. This was Lily.

Lily's entries were a torrent of rage, a furious outpouring of years of suppressed pain. Unlike the fragmented memories and sensory impressions of the previous entries, Lily's narrative possessed a chilling coherence, a focused intensity that painted a disturbingly clear picture of the abuse Eleanor had endured. There was no innocence here, no hesitant questioning, only a burning, unyielding anger that crackled from the page.

The sexual abuse was described in stark, brutal detail, leaving Sarah gasping for air. The words were blunt, devoid of euphemism, a stark depiction of violation and terror. Lily didn't shy away from the specifics, recounting incidents with a horrifying clarity that left Sarah feeling violated, as if she were experiencing the abuse herself. The descriptions weren't merely graphic; they were visceral, imbued with a chilling immediacy that transcended the written word. Sarah felt the cold, clammy touch, smelled the stale air of the room, heard the strangled cries. It was a brutal assault, not just on Eleanor's body, but on Sarah's soul as well.

Lily's narrative was punctuated by vivid imagery: the flickering gaslight casting long, distorted shadows across the room; the metallic tang of blood; the rough texture of the carpet beneath her trembling body. These sensory details weren't merely decorative; they anchored the narrative in a terrifying reality, bringing the abuse vividly to life. They were the tools Lily used to convey not only the act itself but the overwhelming terror and helplessness that accompanied it. Each image was a brutal hammer blow, shattering any remaining vestiges of Sarah's carefully constructed reality.

But Lily's anger wasn't directed solely at her abuser. It extended to the world at large, to the adults who failed to protect her, to the system that allowed such atrocities to occur. Her resentment spilled onto the pages, a corrosive acid that ate away at any attempt at understanding or forgiveness. She railed against the hypocrisy of the seemingly perfect life her family presented to the outside world, contrasting it with the horrifying reality behind closed doors. The elegant dinners, the carefully orchestrated social events, the perfect suburban facade – all were revealed as elaborate charades designed to mask the unspeakable horrors occurring within their home.

Lily's rage was not merely an emotional outpouring; it was a form of self-preservation, a desperate attempt to maintain control in a world where she had been utterly powerless. It was a weapon forged in the crucible of trauma, a shield against the overwhelming pain and humiliation she had endured. Sarah understood, with a gut-wrenching clarity, that Lily's anger wasn't a sign of weakness but a testament to her survival. It was a defiance, a refusal to be silenced, a refusal to be broken.

Interwoven with the descriptions of abuse were glimpses of Lily's resilience, her stubborn refusal to be crushed by the weight of her trauma. There were moments of defiant defiance, acts of small rebellion against the overwhelming powerlessness. She described petty acts of sabotage, instances of silent resistance that offered a glimmer of hope amidst the darkness. These tiny acts of rebellion, however insignificant they might seem, were evidence of her will to survive, her capacity to fight back against the suffocating grip of her abuser.

Lily's entries also revealed her attempts to make sense of the abuse, to find some meaning in the senseless violence. She questioned her own worth, her own sanity, grappling with the conflicting emotions of shame, guilt, and rage. Her self-doubt was palpable, echoing the insidious whispers of her abuser, the persistent undermining of her self-worth. Yet, even amidst her confusion and despair, there were moments of fierce self-assertion, brief bursts of hope and determination.

The writing style shifted drastically, reflecting Lily's emotional volatility. One moment, her words were precise and controlled, almost clinical in their description of events; the next, they were a chaotic torrent of rage and despair, the ink seeming to bleed onto the page, mirroring the intensity of her emotions. This stylistic inconsistency mirrored Lily's own fractured state, her struggle to reconcile the horrifying reality of her abuse with her desire for control and normalcy.

Sarah found herself deeply disturbed by the intimate details Lily unveiled. It was a violation not only of Eleanor's privacy but of Sarah's own sense of reality. The diary entries weren't just words on a page; they were a direct line into the heart of a trauma so profound, so deeply rooted, it threatened to consume her. She felt a strange mixture of anger, empathy, and guilt, as she realized the extent of her mother's suffering and the depths of her own ignorance. The idealized image of her mother had been shattered, replaced with a raw, disturbing portrait of a woman broken by abuse.

The weight of Lily's narrative was immense. It was a testament to the enduring power of trauma, its capacity to shape not only an individual's life but the lives of those around them. Sarah understood, with a chilling clarity, that the violence described in the diary wasn't simply a historical event; it was a living, breathing force that had shaped Eleanor's entire existence, influencing her relationships, her behavior, her very perception of reality.

As Sarah continued reading, the chilling details revealed a pattern of abuse that extended far beyond Lily's experiences. Lily's narrative frequently alluded to other personalities, hinting at the complex, fragmented nature of Eleanor's mind, foreshadowing the emergence of even more alters, each bearing their own unique burdens and perspectives. The diary suggested a complex web of interconnected trauma, a kaleidoscope of fractured identities struggling for control, all within the confines of a single body. This realization plunged Sarah into a deeper abyss of confusion and despair, a sense of overwhelming unease that gnawed at the edges of her sanity.

Lily's entries revealed not only the severity of the abuse but also its lingering effects on Eleanor's life. The trauma was not a singular event; it was a pervasive force that permeated every aspect of her being. It was evident in her unpredictable behavior, her strained relationships, her tendency to withdraw into herself. Lily's words provided a missing piece of the puzzle, shedding light on the origins of Eleanor's struggles and offering a chilling explanation for the events that had shaped her life.

The diary wasn't just a chronicle of abuse; it was a testament to Eleanor's resilience, her stubborn refusal to be defeated. Despite the horrifying experiences described by Lily, there were subtle hints of hope, glimpses of defiance woven into the narrative. Lily's rage wasn't simply blind fury; it was a potent force that fueled her resistance, giving her the strength to survive. These moments, although few and far between, provided Sarah with a newfound respect for her mother's strength, her capacity for endurance in the face of unimaginable horrors.

The entries also hinted at the possible presence of other mental health conditions alongside the multiple personality disorder. There were subtle indications of OCD, possibly ADHD, and perhaps even traits suggestive of autism spectrum disorder. These observations weren't explicitly stated; instead, they were woven into the fabric of Lily's narrative, reflected in her impulsive behavior, her intense focus on certain details, and her struggles with social interaction. Sarah couldn't be certain, but the implications were unsettling, suggesting a complex interplay of psychological factors contributing to Eleanor's fragmented psyche.

The emergence of Lily marked a significant turning point in Sarah's journey of discovery. It was no longer just about piecing together her mother's past; it was about confronting the devastating reality of a life shaped by unimaginable trauma. Lily's voice, raw and unrestrained, resonated deep within Sarah, shattering the idealized image she had held onto for so long. The revelation left her shaken, questioning everything she thought she knew about her mother, her family, and even herself. Sarah's personal narrative, already intertwined with her mother's journey, was now inextricably linked, the past casting its long shadow over her present and future. The diary was more than just a record of trauma; it was a window into a soul fractured beyond repair, a testament to the enduring power of trauma and the complex tapestry of the human mind. And as Sarah turned the pages, she knew that the journey was far from over, that the truth held within those pages had only just begun to unravel.

The diary entries shifted again, the furious scrawl of Lily fading into a neat, almost elegant cursive script. This was different; calmer, more measured, yet laced with a chilling detachment. This was the voice of Eleanor herself, or at least, the Eleanor Sarah had known—the composed, collected woman who had always maintained an air of serene control. But even in this seemingly placid narrative, Sarah detected a subtle undercurrent of unease, a hint of something lurking beneath the surface.

Eleanor's entries described her life with Robert, her husband. The initial descriptions painted a picture of domestic bliss; romantic getaways, laughter-filled evenings, the image of a loving, devoted husband. Robert was depicted as the supportive rock Eleanor leaned on, the strong, silent type who provided her with the stability she craved. He was the pillar of strength that contrasted sharply with the tumultuous inner world described in Lily's entries. Photographs surfaced —carefully preserved in a separate compartment of the diary —depicting a seemingly perfect family: Eleanor, radiant and beautiful; Robert, handsome and charming; Sarah, a happy child nestled between them.

Yet, as Sarah delved deeper into the entries, inconsistencies began to emerge, cracks appearing in the carefully constructed facade. The perfect image started to crumble, replaced by subtle hints of something sinister, something deeply disturbing. Eleanor's descriptions of Robert became less effusive, the details more guarded, more carefully worded. There were mentions of late nights at work, unexplained absences, and an increasing reliance on alcohol. The idyllic portrayal began to fray at the edges, revealing glimpses of underlying tension, simmering resentment. Sarah noticed the way Eleanor's descriptions of their physical intimacy shifted from loving embraces to cold, empty encounters, devoid of passion, devoid of connection.

One entry stood out, a single sentence tucked away at the bottom of a page, seemingly insignificant at first glance: "The red scrunchie...he always liked red." The words sent a shiver down Sarah's spine. The red scrunchies. The ones used to tie the black plastic bags encasing the murder victim found frozen in the old icebox all those years ago. The same type of scrunchies Eleanor had always favoured. This was not a mere coincidence; it was a chilling piece of the puzzle, a link connecting Robert to the horrific crime.

Sarah's gaze drifted to the photographs again. She examined them closely, noticing details she hadn't seen before. Robert's smile seemed forced in some images, strained and unnatural, and his eyes held a glint that seemed unsettlingly cold. The more she looked, the more she saw, or perhaps, the more she wanted to see. She began to perceive a pattern in the photographs, subtle shifts in Robert's demeanor, a subtle change in his gaze—a flicker of something dark, something hidden just beneath the surface.

The next entries detailed a subtle shift in Eleanor's behavior. She described becoming increasingly withdrawn, spending more time alone, her anxieties escalating. She started experiencing vivid nightmares, punctuated by sudden episodes of intense fear and paranoia. These incidents were vaguely described, shrouded in ambiguity, yet a chilling pattern emerged—her fear seemed to be connected to her husband's actions, or rather, his inactions, his absences. The more she isolated herself, the more Robert seemed to disappear, leaving her alone to grapple with the turmoil of her fragmented mind. She described the growing feeling of being watched, of a silent, ever-present threat that clung to the shadows of their home, and Sarah instinctively felt it was Robert.

The diary entries revealed a subtle campaign of control; not outright physical violence, but a more insidious form of manipulation. Eleanor described instances where Robert would minimize her feelings, dismiss her anxieties, gaslight her into questioning her own perceptions. He would subtly twist her words, making her doubt her sanity, her memory. He was like a puppeteer, pulling the strings of her reality, leaving her feeling increasingly isolated, increasingly vulnerable.

There were no explicit confessions, no blatant admissions

of guilt, but a series of carefully veiled hints, subtle implications that painted a disturbing picture of Robert's potential involvement in Eleanor's trauma. Sarah felt a sense of dread creeping into her heart, a chilling understanding dawning within her. The idyllic image of her parents had been shattered, replaced by a more sinister reality. Robert, the seemingly supportive husband, was emerging as a deeply unsettling figure, a man capable of inflicting pain on a far more profound level than physical abuse.

The diary entries became increasingly cryptic, fragmented, filled with allusions to events that remained shrouded in mystery. Eleanor's narrative jumped from one memory to another, her thoughts and feelings intertwining in a chaotic stream of consciousness. The vivid imagery returned—the same flickering gaslight, the metallic tang of blood, the rough texture of the carpet—only this time, it was interspersed with fleeting images of Robert, his presence always looming, always threatening, always just beyond reach.

One entry described a particular incident; Eleanor was confined in a room, her movements restricted, her voice silenced. The room was dimly lit, the air thick with fear. There was no explicit mention of Robert, yet the description evoked a sense of confinement, of imprisonment, a sense of being trapped and controlled. This incident mirrored the descriptions in Lily's entries, the pattern of abuse weaving through the different personalities' experiences. Sarah felt the pieces connecting, forming a more complete, and terrifyingly clearer picture of Eleanor's past.

The diary's final entries were disjointed, fragmented snippets of memories, like shards of glass reflecting a distorted reality.

The last few words, barely legible, seemed to be addressed directly to Robert, a whispered plea for help, a desperate cry for forgiveness. The abrupt end of the diary left Sarah with a deep sense of unease, a feeling that some vital piece of the puzzle remained hidden, a secret yet to be uncovered.

As Sarah closed the diary, the weight of its contents settled heavily upon her shoulders. It wasn't just the horrific details of Eleanor's abuse; it was the realization that the man she had always considered her father, the man who had smiled for all those family photographs, might have been complicit in her mother's suffering. This realization was a betrayal on a deeper level, a shattering of her childhood, of her sense of security, of her own reality.

The diary entries had revealed the devastating impact of trauma on a single life, but it also illuminated the hidden currents within her family's seemingly perfect facade. It had unveiled a truth far darker and more disturbing than she could have ever imagined. The case of the murder, the frozen body in the icebox, the red scrunchies—the entire mystery now seemed intrinsically linked to the secrets held within those pages.

The evidence was circumstantial, fragmented, yet undeniably unsettling. Sarah knew she needed to investigate further, to seek answers to the questions that haunted her. She had to confront the possibility that the man she had known as her father was not the man he appeared to be. She had to unearth the truth, no matter how painful, no matter how devastating the consequences might be. The diary had opened a Pandora's box, unleashing a torrent of secrets and suspicions, leaving Sarah to navigate the treacherous waters of her family history, a path fraught with danger and uncertainty. The journey toward understanding her mother's fragmented mind had led her down a path that threatened to unravel everything she thought she knew about her family, about herself, and about the darkness that lurked beneath the surface of even the most seemingly idyllic lives. The weight of the truth, heavy as a tombstone, rested on her shoulders. And the journey had only just begun.

The diary shifted again, the elegant script of Eleanor giving way to a childish scrawl, the letters tilting and uneven, sometimes barely legible. This was Jane. Sarah felt a pang of something akin to pity, a raw ache in her chest as she deciphered the childlike handwriting. Jane's entries were a stark contrast to the controlled narratives of Eleanor and the furious outbursts of Lily. Jane's voice was small, fragile, a whisper from the depths of a shattered psyche.

Jane's memories were fragmented, snapshots of terror and confusion, often devoid of context or clear chronology. One entry described a recurring nightmare: a dark room, the air thick with the smell of stale cigarettes and something acrid, something metallic that Jane couldn't name but that always made her stomach churn. In this nightmare, a shadowy figure loomed, its face obscured by darkness, its presence suffocating. The figure never spoke, but its silence was more terrifying than any scream. Jane felt the pressure of a hand on her mouth, stifling her cries, silencing her screams. She described the pressure, the suffocating weight, the fear of not being able to breathe, of being swallowed whole by the darkness.

Another entry depicted a memory of a cold, hard floor, the rough texture against her cheek. Jane recalled the stinging cold of the floor, the dampness seeping into her thin nightgown. She felt a sharp pain in her shoulder, a searing agony that made her gasp. She couldn't see clearly, her vision blurred with tears and fear. The words "bad girl" echoed in her memory, a cold whisper that chilled her to the bone, the words haunting her more than any actual punishment.

There was a recurring image of a red scrunchie, a bright splash of color against the otherwise bleak monochrome of her memories. Jane described the way the red fabric would sometimes be near her, brushing against her skin, a tangible reminder of the unseen presence in her life. It wasn't just a material object, it felt like a symbol, a chilling reminder of something she couldn't comprehend.

The entries were filled with descriptions of isolation, of being alone in vast, echoing spaces. Jane described feeling lost, adrift in a sea of fear. She often mentioned feeling like a tiny boat on a stormy ocean, tossed and turned by unseen forces that were beyond her control. The entries were peppered with small, seemingly insignificant details, a detail of a chipped teacup, the way sunlight fell through a dusty windowpane, the texture of a worn rug - details that seemed to evoke a sensory tapestry of fear and insecurity.

These details, though fragmented, formed a disturbing pattern. Jane's memories lacked specific dates or times, making it difficult to piece together a coherent narrative. The abuse was implied, not explicitly described, leaving Sarah to fill in the terrifying blanks. Jane's simple, unadorned descriptions were all the more horrifying for their innocence, their childlike inability to fully grasp the horror of what was happening to her.

One entry described a game, a cruel game played in the dark. Jane referred to it as "hide and seek," but the childlike simplicity of the phrase belied the horror of the experience. She spoke of being hidden away, locked in a small, dark closet, the silence punctuated only by the heavy thud of a door closing, a sound that echoed her growing despair. She felt the darkness pressing in on her, the overwhelming sensation of being trapped, alone, abandoned. The game wasn't a playful pastime; it was a chilling method of control, a sinister reminder of her helplessness.

Another entry detailed a seemingly mundane event: a family dinner. Jane described the elegant table setting, the gleaming silverware, the delicious aroma of roast chicken. But beneath the surface of this seemingly idyllic scene, a current of unease ran deep. Jane remembered a tense atmosphere, hushed tones, the adults whispering behind their hands. She felt the weight of their unspoken words, the unspoken accusations that hung heavy in the air. Even the delicious food felt tainted by the pervasive sense of fear. She focused on the shiny surface of a silver spoon, the reflection distorting her tear-filled eyes, the reflection a stranger looking back at her.

The descriptions often ended abruptly, leaving Sarah with a sense of unfinished business, a feeling of being left hanging on the edge of a precipice. There were mentions of pain, of fear, of a pervasive sense of dread that clung to Jane like a shroud, but no explicit details. The fragmented nature of the entries made the abuse all the more chilling, leaving Sarah to fill in the blanks and imagine the unseen horrors.

There were drawings interspersed with the text; crude, childish sketches depicting shadowy figures, dark rooms, and recurring symbols – the red scrunchie appearing again and again. The drawings were a visual manifestation of Jane's unspoken fears, a visual representation of the terror that lurked within her memories.

The frequency of the red scrunchie in both Eleanor's and Jane's entries struck Sarah as a chilling coincidence. It wasn't just a fabric; it was a recurring motif, a dark thread woven through the tapestry of their trauma, a horrifying symbol of the abuse. Sarah began to understand the depth of the connection between the red scrunchie and the crime – a gruesome link that tied everything together, a haunting clue that spoke volumes about the horrific nature of the events it symbolized.

As Sarah continued reading, a chilling pattern emerged. Jane's memories seemed to focus on specific instances of emotional and psychological abuse – isolation, manipulation, gaslighting, and the constant feeling of being watched, of being judged. The physical abuse, while implied, was never explicitly described, replaced by a constant undercurrent of fear, a pervasive sense of unease that hung over every memory. It was the unspoken, the implied, that made Jane's entries so incredibly disturbing.

Jane's entries became less frequent towards the end, the scrawls growing fainter, the words more spaced out, less frequent. The last entry was a single word, barely legible: "Scared." The simplicity of the word, its utter vulnerability, was more powerful than any explicit description of abuse.

It encapsulated the entire narrative, the underlying tone of terror that permeated Jane's experience. It was the final, chilling testament to the trauma she had endured, a final whisper from the depths of her fractured mind.

Sarah closed the diary, the weight of its contents pressing down on her. She had glimpsed the horrors of Jane's childhood, the devastating impact of abuse on a young, innocent mind. It was an unsettling experience, one that shook her to her core. The childlike innocence of Jane's descriptions made the abuse all the more horrific, the implied violence even more terrifying than any explicit account. Jane's memories were not just fragmented accounts; they were windows into the soul of a child struggling to survive the unthinkable, a child battling her way through a nightmare she didn't understand, couldn't escape.

The diary revealed not only the details of Eleanor's abuse but also the profound and lasting impact on her fragmented psyche. Each personality, each alter, was a manifestation of the trauma she had endured, a testament to the resilience of the human spirit in the face of unimaginable horror. And Sarah, armed with this newfound knowledge, was ready to confront the truth, no matter how dark, no matter how painful the journey ahead might be. The pieces were starting to fit together, revealing a picture far more complex, far more disturbing, than she could ever have imagined. The path to justice, to understanding, was a winding road, fraught with danger, but Sarah was determined to follow it to the very end. The weight of responsibility, of the truth revealed, settled on her, heavy as the frozen body in the icebox, the red scrunchies, a cold, haunting reminder of the years of silence that had preceded her discovery. The unraveling of her family's secrets had only just begun.

Lily's coping mechanisms weren't pretty. They weren't the quiet, introspective methods Eleanor favored, nor the childlike, almost surreal escapes of Jane. Lily's methods were raw, visceral, a brutal rebellion against the suffocating weight of her existence. They were a scream trapped in a throat too choked with fear to fully unleash itself.

Her diary entries, initially a chaotic jumble of angry scribbles, began to coalesce into a pattern of self-destruction. She didn't shy away from graphic details, her words a brutal honesty that painted a stark picture of her inner turmoil. Alcohol became her anesthetic, a temporary reprieve from the gnawing pain that never truly subsided. The cheap whiskey burned going down, a fleeting fire against the icy chill that settled deep in her bones. She described the taste, the raw burn in her throat, the numbness that followed – a temporary escape from the crushing weight of her memories. It was a self-medicating ritual, a desperate attempt to silence the screaming echoes within her mind.

But the alcohol only dulled the edges, it never erased them. The memories, sharp and jagged, would still pierce the haze, their icy grip tightening whenever the alcohol wore off, sending her into spiraling fits of rage and self-loathing. She'd lash out, her words sharp as shards of glass, capable of slicing through the carefully constructed facades of those around her. Her fury wasn't directed at any specific person, but rather at the unseen force that had shaped her reality. It was a rage born of helplessness, of being a pawn in a game she didn't understand, a game whose rules were cruel and unforgiving.

She detailed nights spent wandering the city streets, the anonymity a thin shield against her profound loneliness. The neon lights blurred into streaks of color, the sounds of the city a symphony of chaos mirroring the storm within her. She'd lose herself in the crowds, becoming a ghost among ghosts, a nameless face swallowed by the anonymity of the urban landscape. She'd stand on rooftops, the wind whipping through her hair, a sensation both exhilarating and terrifying. The city spread out before her, a labyrinth of lights and shadows, a vast, indifferent landscape reflecting the emptiness within her.

Sex became another form of self-medication, a desperate attempt to fill the void, to find a fleeting connection in a world that felt utterly alien. She described the encounters with a detached clinical precision, her body a vessel devoid of emotion. It wasn't about pleasure, it was about obliterating the pain, temporarily silencing the voices, pushing the memories into the darkest recesses of her mind. Each encounter was a fleeting escape, but the relief was always temporary, always leaving her feeling emptier than before. She'd feel the same raw nothingness after the encounters, as if she had just become more fractured after each interaction. She'd be left in the desolate vacuum, feeling like she'd traded one kind of emptiness for another. The feeling was hollow, and she knew she'd never truly feel whole.

Cutting became her ritual. The sharp sting of the blade against her skin, the rush of adrenaline, the blood a visceral reminder of her pain – a tangible manifestation of the invisible wounds that plagued her. It was a form of self-punishment, a twisted act of self-control in a world where she felt utterly powerless. She described the precise movements, the meticulous placement of the cuts – scars etched into her flesh, a map of her suffering. Each cut was a testament to the overwhelming pain, an attempt to claw her way back to some semblance of control.

She meticulously drew intricate patterns onto her arms and thighs, the blood forming perversely beautiful designs that echoed the darkness within. These patterns were her method of self-expression, a silent scream etched onto her skin.

The entries detailed vivid descriptions of the sensation: the sharpness of the blade, the hot rush of blood, the numb ache that followed. She spoke of finding a peculiar sense of satisfaction in the act, a perverse sense of control in inflicting pain on herself. It was a way of reclaiming agency in a life where she felt perpetually victimized. But this temporary sense of control did not last long.

She documented her attempts to cope with her intense emotional volatility. She'd describe the panic attacks, her breath coming in ragged gasps, her heart pounding like a drum against her ribs. She wrote about the feeling of being trapped in her own mind, the world around her blurring and distorting. Her writing during these moments was frantic, the words cramped and almost illegible, mirroring the turmoil within her. She described the struggle to breathe, the feeling of suffocating, of being swallowed whole by her own anxieties.

Yet, amidst the chaos and self-destruction, there were glimmers of something else. She described moments of clarity, of lucidity, where she would momentarily break through the fog of her pain and see the world with a fierce, almost desperate intensity. These moments were fleeting, like shooting stars against the vast darkness of her mind, but they were there, a testament to her resilience, a stubborn refusal to succumb to the darkness that threatened to consume her. In these moments, her writing would become calmer, more reflective, almost poetic in its description of the world around her.

Her descriptions of nature, oddly juxtaposed with her accounts of self-harm, hinted at a longing for something peaceful, something that resonated with the chaotic turmoil inside. She would write about the stillness of a moonlit lake, the gentle sway of trees in the breeze, the vibrant colors of a sunset. These images were stark contrasts to the raw, graphic depictions of her self-destructive behaviors, but they were there, a quiet counterpoint to the symphony of self-destruction playing out in her fragmented mind. It seemed that there was something inside Lily that wasn't destroyed; something still held onto hope and beauty, however dim it might be.

She documented attempts to find external help, which usually ended in anger and frustration. She was distrustful of authority figures, wary of anyone who might try to "fix" her. The idea of surrendering her control was horrifying, a vulnerability she couldn't afford. Each interaction was a battle for her autonomy, a desperate attempt to maintain the semblance of control she felt slipping away. These failed attempts at seeking help left her feeling more hopeless than before. She would end up more alone, more deeply entrenched in her self-destructive behaviors. She lacked the trust in others necessary for therapy to be effective.

The diary entries ended abruptly, the final entry a single, defiant sentence: "I won't break." This, Sarah realized, was perhaps the most chilling entry of all. It wasn't a hopeful statement, but a declaration of war against herself, a vow to keep fighting, even if it meant continuing her self-destructive patterns. It showed a woman who was desperate to reclaim herself, to escape the tyranny of her fractured identity. The ferocity, the raw, unbridled determination, mirrored her earlier frantic writing. It was a defiant whisper, a testament to the strength and fragility of a soul trapped in a violent storm. It was an ending that only served to fuel Sarah's growing determination to unravel the mystery of her mother's fragmented mind, and to finally understand the trauma that had led to the horrific murder 25 years ago.

Sarah traced the faded floral pattern of her grandmother's teacups, the ceramic cool beneath her fingertips. The chipped rim of one cup, a small, almost imperceptible imperfection, sparked a memory. A fleeting image, a sliver of a moment, like a photograph caught in the periphery of her vision: Eleanor, her mother, her face etched with a weariness that belied her usual composed façade, her hands trembling as she cleaned up spilled tea, a red scrunchie lying discarded on the ornate carpet. The scrunchie. The same color as the ones found at the murder scene. The same detail that sent a shiver down Sarah's spine, a thread connecting the present to the seemingly impenetrable past. This was more than just a coincidence; this was a clue.

The diary entries offered fragmented glimpses into Eleanor's life, but they were insufficient. They were the pieces of a shattered mirror, each reflecting a distorted, incomplete image. To understand the whole, Sarah needed more. She needed context. She needed to fill in the blanks. Her investigation began quietly, subtly, like a shadow moving in the dark.

She started with her childhood memories, sifting through the hazy recollections of her early years, searching for anything, anything at all, that might resonate with the horrors detailed in her mother's diary. It was like trying to assemble a jigsaw puzzle with half the pieces missing, the image obscured by time and deliberate obfuscation. She had blocked many childhood experiences, the result of a well-crafted defense mechanism, an ability to shut out the most intense, disturbing memories; to build a wall to survive. The thought of shattering that wall terrified her, but she had to try. There was a murder to solve, and a mother to understand.

Her first step was to reach out to old family friends, individuals who had known Eleanor before her marriage to Richard, before the carefully crafted image of the perfect family had been formed. These were the people who might have seen the cracks in the façade, the subtle hints of the fractured personality that lay beneath. The first call was to Mrs. Albright, a woman whose name echoed through Sarah's childhood as a symbol of unfailing kindness and warm apple pies. Mrs. Albright's voice, now frail and weathered by time, sounded hesitant at first. But as Sarah explained her quest, a subtle shift occurred in her tone, a cautious openness replacing the initial reticence.

Mrs. Albright remembered Eleanor as a vibrant, artistic young woman, full of life and laughter. But she also remembered a sadness, a deep-seated melancholy that occasionally clouded Eleanor's bright spirit. She spoke of moments of intense quietude, periods when Eleanor would withdraw into herself, becoming almost unreachable. These weren't fleeting moods; they were episodes, prolonged periods of emotional absence. These periods increased in frequency as the years progressed.

"She was a talented artist, Sarah," Mrs. Albright recounted, her voice filled with a touch of wistful sadness. "Her paintings were…intense. Dark, even. But beautiful, breathtaking in their own way." This confirmed an observation Sarah had already made from the diary entries - art seemed to be a way for Eleanor to express the suppressed emotions, a canvas for her fragmented self. Mrs. Albright's recollections were crucial, for it added another piece to the puzzle. Eleanor's art could be a window to her tortured mind.

Next, Sarah reached out to Mr. Henderson, Eleanor's former art teacher. He remembered her as a naturally gifted artist, but with a volatile temperament. "She could be angelic one minute, and a tempest the next," he recalled, his voice laced with a certain measure of awe and fear. He described how Eleanor's artwork often mirrored her moods, ranging from serene landscapes to disturbingly chaotic abstracts. He mentioned that towards the end of her studies, the paintings became increasingly dark and visceral, almost nightmarish. He had tried to offer counseling, but Eleanor refused. He recalled Eleanor's intense dislike of authority. This refusal would be echoed in the diary entries, adding weight to Sarah's understanding of Eleanor's character.

Each conversation unearthed a new detail, a tiny fragment of the shattered truth. Sarah pieced them together like fragments of a shattered mirror, carefully studying each reflection, attempting to construct a more complete image of her mother. She uncovered instances of Eleanor's emotional outbursts, her sudden shifts in demeanor, her unpredictable behavior. She heard accounts of her isolative tendencies. It wasn't just a case of multiple personality disorder, but it involved a complex interplay of trauma, abuse, and an almost superhuman capacity for self-preservation.

The more Sarah dug, the more disturbing the picture became.

Whispers of incidents, hints of aggression, snippets of unsettling behavior—all previously dismissed as eccentricities or mere coincidences—now took on a sinister new significance in light of the diary's revelations. She discovered that Eleanor had a reputation for being fiercely protective of her family, a reaction she now understood as an overcompensation, a desperate attempt to shield them from the pain she had endured.

Sarah's investigation extended to her own childhood. She painstakingly sifted through her memories, hunting for the faintest traces of her mother's alters. She recalled moments of confusion, instances where her mother seemed to change personalities without warning. She remembered snippets of conversations she didn't fully understand, sudden shifts in mood, and terrifying episodes of unexplained anger. These were all hidden behind the carefully constructed normalcy she had been taught to believe in. These repressed memories now took on a new significance; they weren't just random occurrences but clues left behind by the fractured mind.

Through the fragmented memories and the testimonies of others, a chilling pattern emerged. Sarah started to discern a timeline, an outline of her mother's life marked by periods of intense turmoil and inexplicable shifts in behavior. This timeline correlated directly with the diary entries, painting a disturbing portrait of a woman struggling to survive the psychological wounds of years of abuse and trauma. It became clear that Eleanor's "alters" weren't just personalities; they were survival mechanisms, fragmented aspects of a self trying desperately to cope with unbearable pain.

As Sarah delved deeper into the mystery, a sense of unease

settled upon her. She felt a growing dread, not only for the crime but also for what she might uncover about her own life. The more she learned, the more she realized that her understanding of her family and their past was not just flawed but deliberately obscured. The veil of normalcy had been expertly crafted to hide an unbearable truth, a truth that now threatened to shatter her world. The weight of the past pressed heavily upon her shoulders, the fear that her carefully constructed life was built on a foundation of carefully buried lies, a lie so dark it was almost beyond comprehension.

The fragments she collected, the pieces of the puzzle, began to converge. The image, once blurred and indistinct, started to come into focus. It wasn't just a murder she was investigating; it was a family secret, a legacy of trauma that spanned generations. Sarah realized that unraveling the mystery of her mother's death was inextricably linked to understanding her own life, her own identity, and her own carefully suppressed memories. The investigation was no longer just about solving a crime; it was about confronting a truth so profound and horrifying that it threatened to tear her apart. And that, Sarah knew, was only the beginning.

# CHAPTER 3: THE WEIGHT OF SILENCE

The diary fell open to a new section, the elegant script a stark contrast to the frantic scrawl of previous entries. This was different. This was controlled, precise, almost... elegant. The handwriting suggested a different hand entirely, one accustomed to wielding a pen with practiced grace. The entry began: "The others are...unpredictable. Chaos incarnate. Their outbursts, their childish tantrums, threaten to unravel everything I've so carefully constructed. It's exhausting, this constant vigilance, this perpetual battle for control. But it's necessary. For their sake, and for mine."

This was Evelyn.

Sarah traced the words with a trembling finger. Evelyn's narrative immediately set itself apart. Where the previous entries had been raw, emotional outpourings, stained with the tears and fury of their authors, Evelyn's words were carefully chosen, each syllable placed with deliberate precision. There was a chilling detachment, a clinical observation of the self, that sent a shiver down Sarah's spine. Evelyn wasn't just an alter; she was an architect, a puppeteer pulling the strings of Eleanor's fractured psyche.

"They see me as the enemy," Evelyn continued, her words dripping with a subtle sarcasm that sent a cold dread through

Sarah. "The stern guardian, the controlling force. They resent my discipline, my insistence on order. But without me, they would destroy themselves, and everything they hold dear. They don't understand the fragility of our existence, the delicate balance I maintain."

Evelyn's entries revealed a complex strategy of manipulation, a calculated game played to maintain a façade of normalcy. She described the elaborate routines, the carefully crafted lies, the subtle manipulations used to control the other alters and keep them in check. She spoke of her role as the "mediator," the one who smoothed over the rough edges, the one who prevented the others from exposing their true nature to the outside world. She was the architect of the perfect family, the carefully constructed illusion that hid the fractured reality beneath.

"Richard," Evelyn wrote, her words laced with a chilling disdain, "is an unwitting participant in this charade. He's blind, oblivious to the storm raging within his wife. He sees only the polished exterior, the charming façade I so diligently maintain. He's a fool, easily manipulated. And I use that to my advantage." The casual cruelty in her words was jarring, revealing a level of manipulation that went far beyond mere survival. This was cold, calculated control. This was power.

Sarah read on, a growing sense of unease settling upon her. Evelyn's narrative wasn't just a chronicle of her actions; it was a confession, a chilling revelation of her manipulative nature. She described her methods in detail, laying bare the intricate web of deceit she had woven around Richard and Sarah, a web designed to maintain the illusion of a normal, functional family.

Evelyn's entries detailed her meticulous planning, her precise execution of routines designed to prevent the other alters from surfacing. She described the medication schedules, the carefully constructed social interactions, and the subtle strategies she used to manipulate Richard and control the flow of information within the family. It was a masterful performance, a display of calculated control that bordered on the surreal.

"The others crave attention," Evelyn wrote. "They seek validation, yearning for recognition. I use that against them. I feed them scraps of approval, just enough to keep them docile, to prevent them from disrupting the carefully constructed order. It's a delicate dance, a precarious balance. One wrong step, and the whole facade could crumble."

Evelyn's narrative painted a picture of a woman trapped within a fractured self, a woman who used her intellect and manipulative skills to survive, to control the chaos within. But the entries also revealed a growing sense of weariness, a hint of exhaustion beneath the polished surface. The constant vigilance, the relentless effort to maintain control, was taking its toll.

"Sometimes," Evelyn confessed in a rare moment of vulnerability, "I feel the weight of it all. The burden of responsibility, the constant fear of exposure. The fatigue is relentless. But I can't afford to falter. Not now. Not ever." This small crack in her carefully constructed façade offered a glimpse into the immense pressure she faced, the constant struggle to maintain the illusion of normalcy.

Further entries detailed Evelyn's strategies for manipulating situations, twisting narratives to her advantage, and subtly controlling the flow of information within the family. She was a master of deception, a skilled manipulator who used her intelligence and charm to create an elaborate web of lies that hid the truth from everyone, including herself.

She discussed her interactions with Sarah, detailing the specific ways in which she carefully crafted Sarah's perception of Eleanor, presenting a version of Eleanor that was both loving and reliable, whilst actively suppressing the emergence of other, more volatile alters. She meticulously recounted events from Sarah's childhood, highlighting how she strategically controlled the narrative to protect the illusion of a stable family.

As Sarah read on, she began to understand the extent of Evelyn's control. It wasn't just about managing the other alters; it was about shaping reality itself. Evelyn had created a world where her version of Eleanor was the dominant force, a world where the chaos of her multiple personalities was carefully contained, hidden behind a mask of normalcy.

There were even instances where Evelyn described her interactions with the police, subtly guiding investigations away from any suspicion of Eleanor's true nature. She recounted her skill in manipulating individuals, deflecting questions, and steering the narrative towards seemingly innocent explanations.

Evelyn's detached perspective offered a chilling insight into the mind of a master manipulator. She described her actions with a clinical precision, devoid of any apparent emotion. There was no remorse, no regret, only a detached observation of her own manipulative behavior.

But as Sarah delved deeper into Evelyn's entries, she started to detect subtle shifts in her tone, hints of weariness, even cracks in her carefully constructed composure. The constant effort to maintain control, the unrelenting pressure of keeping the other alters in check, seemed to be taking its toll.

As the entries progressed, Evelyn's descriptions became increasingly fragmented, the narrative less controlled, revealing a growing sense of desperation. The meticulously planned strategies started to falter, the carefully constructed facade showing signs of wear and tear. Evelyn's control, it seemed, was beginning to slip. The weight of her carefully constructed world was becoming too much to bear. The meticulously crafted illusion was cracking, revealing the fractured reality beneath. And Sarah, armed with Evelyn's own chilling account, was beginning to understand the true horror of her mother's secret.

The diary entries shifted, the elegant script of Evelyn giving way to a spidery, almost illegible hand. This was a different voice, raw and filled with a barely suppressed rage. It was a voice Sarah hadn't encountered before. This was...Robert's voice.

The entries weren't a continuous narrative, more like fragmented memories, snippets of conversations, visceral snapshots of moments long past. They spoke of Eleanor's fear, not just of him, but also of herself. The fear was palpable, resonating through the worn pages like a chilling echo. He was more than just a husband; he was a controlling force, a predator cloaked in normalcy.

One entry was particularly chilling. It described a night, Eleanor's trembling hands barely able to hold the pen, recounting an incident where Robert had forced himself on her. The words were sparse, almost reluctant, as if Eleanor's other alters were trying to suppress the memory. But the raw emotion, the underlying terror, was undeniable. It was a story of powerlessness, of a woman trapped in a cycle of abuse, her spirit slowly being crushed beneath the weight of her captor's actions. The details were horrifyingly vague, leaving the reader to fill in the blanks, making the experience all the more visceral and unsettling.

The next entry, though fragmented, spoke of Robert's charm, his ability to manipulate and deceive. He wasn't merely a brute; he was a master of psychological manipulation. He could switch from tenderness to rage with terrifying speed, leaving Eleanor unsure of what to expect, living in a perpetual state of fear and uncertainty. This entry revealed the insidious nature of his abuse, the way he eroded Eleanor's sense of self-worth, the insidious ways he twisted her perceptions of reality. His charm was a weapon, just as devastating as his physical brutality.

A series of short entries detailed seemingly innocuous events: a birthday party, a family vacation, a casual dinner. Yet, woven into these seemingly ordinary moments were subtle hints of Robert's controlling nature. The way he'd subtly demean Eleanor in public, making her feel insignificant, or the sly remarks designed to erode her self-confidence. Each entry built a picture of his manipulation, chipping away at the illusion of a happy family, revealing the dark undercurrent of fear and control that dominated their lives.

Then came a series of entries that spoke of secrets—secrets Robert kept, secrets he guarded fiercely. They were brief, cryptic references to business dealings, to shady connections, to deals made in backrooms, shrouded in an aura of intimidation and fear. The exact details were never explicitly revealed, but the implication was clear: Robert was deeply involved in something sinister, something that went far beyond the confines of their domestic life. These entries hinted at a far-reaching web of deceit, a network of corruption that cast a long shadow over Eleanor's already fractured life.

The entries suggested that Robert's manipulative behaviour extended beyond his own family, hinting at other victims, other lives he had touched and damaged. This expanded the scope of his cruelty, leaving the reader to wonder about the full extent of his depravity. These subtle hints of a larger, darker world only increased the sense of dread and uncertainty.

Sarah found a particularly disturbing entry hidden between other pages, nearly overlooked. It was a series of seemingly random numbers and letters, jotted down in a hurried, panicky scrawl. It looked like a code, a cipher designed to conceal something crucial. The words "must protect," "danger," and "they know" were scrawled in the margins, adding to the unsettling nature of the cryptic message.

Further entries described the financial control Robert exerted over Eleanor. He managed their finances with an iron fist, controlling every aspect of their lives, ensuring that Eleanor was entirely dependent upon him. This financial control was another tool of manipulation, trapping Eleanor within the web of his abuse, increasing her reliance and dependence. This financial dependence was yet another layer of his systematic control, preventing her from escaping her abusive situation.

Then came a series of entries that recounted events from Sarah's childhood. These were particularly disturbing, revealing episodes of emotional manipulation and neglect. Robert's role, though never explicitly stated, loomed large; his absence, his silence, his casual cruelty toward Eleanor seemed to have a direct impact on Sarah's experiences. His silence was a form of abuse, too, his passive complicity a form of tacit approval. The casual cruelty he inflicted was mirrored in his actions towards Sarah.

As Sarah deciphered the diary entries, Robert's role became clearer. He wasn't just a perpetrator of domestic violence; he was a master manipulator, weaving a web of deceit, control and fear. He was a puppeteer pulling the strings of Eleanor's life, manipulating her, exploiting her, crushing her spirit. He created a situation where Eleanor, with her fractured psyche, was especially vulnerable to his abuse. He ensured that no one would believe her if she were ever to speak out.

The last few entries were a jumbled mess, the words bleeding into each other, the handwriting shaky and uneven. It was as if Eleanor was writing with trembling hands, her desperation clawing at the edges of the pages. It was a desperate attempt to record everything before her inevitable demise.

The fragmented entries hinted at a final confrontation, a last act of rebellion. It suggested that Eleanor, or one of her alters, may have attempted to fight back against Robert's control, leading to a violent altercation. The entry hinted at a battle between Robert and Eleanor, the chaotic nature of the writing mirroring the struggle between them.

Sarah closed the diary, the chilling weight of its contents settling upon her. The seemingly perfect family portrait concealed a nightmare, a dark secret hidden behind a façade of normalcy. The idyllic life had been a meticulously constructed lie, a carefully crafted illusion concealing a horrifying reality. The weight of the silence, the years of suppressed truth, now hung heavy in the air. The revelation of Robert's role deepened the mystery, casting a sinister shadow on the already tragic narrative. The questions it raised were far more disturbing than the answers she'd found so far. Robert's secrets were only just beginning to unravel, and with each new revelation, the truth grew more terrifying. The implications of his involvement were far-reaching, potentially extending far beyond the immediate family, extending to a larger conspiracy. Sarah found herself trapped in a chilling game of cat and mouse, the truth elusive, the danger ever present. The weight of the years of silence was slowly crushing her, yet the determination to uncover the whole truth spurred her on. The next chapter would need to delve further into these chilling secrets to discover the truth behind Eleanor's death.

Evelyn, the meticulous record-keeper, was a stark contrast to the raw, untamed fury of Robert. His entries were jagged, explosive bursts of anger, punctuated by chillingly calm descriptions of violence. They were like snapshots of a storm, capturing the terrifying intensity of his rage before it subsided, leaving behind only the wreckage. He wasn't just angry; he was consumed by it, a raging inferno trapped within the confines of Eleanor's mind.

Between Robert's entries were glimpses of a personality Sarah hadn't yet encountered, a quiet observer named Clara. Clara's entries were sparse, minimalistic sketches of the other alters' actions. She was the silent witness, the one who observed everything without judgment or intervention, a passive spectator to the turmoil within Eleanor's psyche. Her entries were devoid of emotion, mere factual accounts of events, as if she was documenting a scientific experiment, a detached observer charting the chaos. Yet, in her detachment, there was a chilling coldness that hinted at a deeper pain, a profound sense of isolation. Her silence screamed volumes.

Then there was the child, a fragment named Lily. Lily's entries were simple, childish drawings and fragmented sentences, conveying a child's innocent perception of the horrific events unfolding around her. Her innocence was a poignant counterpoint to the brutality documented by the other alters, a stark reminder of the innocence lost within the broken mind of Eleanor. Her drawings were unsettling, filled with dark colors and disturbing imagery, showing a child's attempt to process unspeakable horrors. The simplicity of her entries was profoundly disturbing.

The dynamics between these alters were complex and ever-shifting. Evelyn, the outwardly perfect wife and mother, appeared to be the dominant personality, but her control was precarious, constantly threatened by the other alters' demands. Robert's rage was a constant threat, capable of erupting at any moment, overwhelming the others and seizing control. Clara's silence was a pervasive presence, an ever-present reminder of the trauma and the inability to escape the darkness. Lily's innocence was a fragile island in the stormy sea of Eleanor's fractured psyche, a constant source of vulnerability.

There were instances of cooperation between alters, primarily between Evelyn and Clara. Evelyn would often meticulously record Clara's observations, creating a record of the other alters' actions, a fragmented history of the trauma they endured. This collaboration was a testament to the resilience of Eleanor's fragmented mind, the ability to find order and structure even amidst the chaos. But these moments of cooperation were rare, far outweighed by the conflicts and struggles for dominance.

The entries revealed a brutal power struggle between Robert and Evelyn. Robert's need for control extended beyond the physical. He manipulated Eleanor's thoughts, emotions, and memories, twisting her perceptions of reality. He planted doubts and insecurities, eroding her self-esteem, making her dependent on his approval. He used his physical dominance to gain control, suppressing her other personalities, but Evelyn fought back, desperately seeking to maintain order and preserve her fractured identity. The conflict between them was a desperate battle for survival, a struggle to assert control in a mind already shattered.

Evelyn's meticulous records, however, sometimes revealed hints of the other personalities' existence, even when those personalities themselves weren't writing. Subtle shifts in tone, slight changes in handwriting, and even unintentional slips of the pen, hinted at the underlying conflict within Eleanor's psyche. These subtle clues, almost imperceptible at first, provided a glimpse into the constant, underlying struggle between her alters.

Sometimes, a sentence would abruptly shift in tone and style, a jarring interruption that revealed a momentary shift in control. A sentence begun in Evelyn's elegant script would suddenly veer into Robert's jagged, angry scrawl, before snapping back to Evelyn's controlled style. These interruptions were like tectonic shifts in Eleanor's consciousness, brief glimpses into the turbulent landscape of her inner world. The abrupt transitions between voices created a sense of unease, mirroring the chaotic nature of Eleanor's inner world.

There were moments of terrifying clarity, moments when the alters seemed to be aware of each other's presence, even communicating in cryptic ways. A sentence started by Evelyn would be finished by Robert, their voices blending in a twisted duet of anger and control. These moments were like fragments of a conversation, a glimpse into the complex web of communication within Eleanor's fractured consciousness. The fusion of voices, the blending of personalities, illustrated the deep connection between the alters, a poignant testament to the interconnectedness of the fragmented self.

The diaries also revealed a disturbing pattern: a cycle of abuse, a constant repetition of traumatic events, echoing through the different personalities. The abuse was not a singular event but a pervasive pattern, shaping the very fabric of Eleanor's existence. Each alter carried the weight of the past, trapped in an endless loop of trauma, their memories intertwined, their identities intertwined. The constant repetition of traumatic memories underscored the pervasiveness of the abuse, highlighting the impact it had on Eleanor's fragmented psyche.

The entries also spoke of escape, of attempts to break free from the confines of their shared existence. Evelyn's meticulous planning, Clara's silent observation, and even Robert's moments of unexpected vulnerability all hinted at a longing for freedom, a desperate desire to escape the pain and the trauma. The longing for freedom, the repeated attempts at escaping the traumatic experiences, highlighted the determination of Eleanor's fractured mind to overcome the adversity it faced. These attempts at escape showed a flicker of hope amidst the pervasive darkness.

However, these attempts were always thwarted, a recurring theme of helplessness woven throughout the diary. Their fragmented identities prevented them from forming a united front against Robert, against the abuse, against their shared trauma. The inability to form a united front against adversity highlighted the vulnerability created by their fragmented identities. Their fractured identities reinforced their victimhood, preventing them from effectively combating the trauma they faced.

The diary entries revealed a horrifying truth: the murder wasn't a single act of violence, but a culmination of the years of abuse, of the struggles between the alters, of the failure to escape their shared trauma. The fragmented memories, the conflicting accounts, painted a picture of a horrific crime, a chilling culmination of years of suffering. The diary entries revealed the extent of their shared trauma, the extent of the psychological damage inflicted by Robert, and the manner in which that psychological damage had culminated in a horrific act of violence.

The weight of this collective trauma, the burden of the shared past, and the failure to escape it, culminated in an act of unspeakable horror. The murder was not the act of a single person but a collective failure, a chilling testament to the destructive power of untreated trauma and the devastating consequences of unchecked abuse. It wasn't merely the act of a single personality but a culmination of years of conflict and trauma within Eleanor's fractured psyche. This realization was chilling, leaving Sarah overwhelmed by the enormity of her mother's suffering and the complex, dark world hidden beneath the surface of her seemingly normal life. The weight of silence had finally been broken, but the revelation was far more terrifying than she could ever have imagined. The path to unraveling the truth had only just begun.

Lily's world was a kaleidoscope of fractured images, a chaotic swirl of vibrant colors and unsettling shadows. Her entries, unlike the others, weren't neat and organized. They were a chaotic explosion of childish drawings, fragmented sentences, and disturbingly vivid descriptions that hinted at a burgeoning darkness far beyond her years. She drew pictures of figures with exaggerated features, their eyes wide and vacant, their limbs contorted into unnatural angles. These figures were often surrounded by swirling, ominous black clouds, their bodies punctuated by jagged lines that seemed to represent both wounds and the barbed wire fences she saw in her fragmented memories. The colors were stark, violent – harsh reds, deep blues, and a pervasive, suffocating black.

One drawing, in particular, stood out. It depicted a figure encased in a black plastic bag, its limbs bound tightly, its face obscured. Around the figure, Lily had drawn small, meticulously crafted red scrunchies. Sarah recognized them instantly – the same scrunchies used to tie the victim's body.

The image was chillingly accurate, a disturbing premonition of the horrific crime. It wasn't a child's drawing of a scary monster; it was a blueprint, a horrifyingly precise visualization of the murder.

Accompanying the drawing was a simple sentence, scrawled in childish handwriting: "Make them sleep." The simplicity of the sentence, the casualness of its wording, belied the chilling implication. It wasn't a simple plea for sleep; it was a death sentence, delivered with a child's detached innocence. The phrase echoed through Sarah's mind, a haunting reminder of the innocent yet monstrous mind behind the murder. This was no accident; this was a planned act of violence, meticulously envisioned in the mind of a child.

Other entries depicted acts of violence, though less specific. There were drawings of figures being stabbed, burned, and suffocated. The details were fragmented, but the intent was clear: a profound desire for revenge, a burning need to inflict pain. Lily's fantasies were not merely childish games; they were visceral expressions of rage, a desperate attempt to process and understand the unspeakable horrors she'd witnessed. The recurring motifs – the black bags, the red scrunchies, the stark, violent colors – pointed towards a disturbing premeditation, suggesting that Lily's fantasies were more than just imagination; they were rehearsals, a meticulous planning of an act of vengeance.

The entries became more graphic as the diary progressed, mirroring the escalation of Lily's anger and resentment. She detailed her fantasies of torture, her imaginings of inflicting pain on those she perceived as her tormentors. These weren't random acts of violence; they were targeted, deliberate, meticulously planned. Lily seemed to know, on some level, who she wanted to punish, who she deemed responsible for her pain. This knowledge, this focus, suggested a level of awareness and planning beyond what one would expect from a child. The increasing graphic nature of her fantasies pointed towards a disturbing evolution of her mind, a gradual descent into violence.

Lily's descriptions were often laced with a disturbing blend of childish innocence and adult brutality. She would describe acts of violence with a clinical detachment, as if narrating a story, yet her drawings and accompanying words revealed a raw, unfiltered rage simmering beneath the surface. The contrast between her childlike language and the horrific nature of her fantasies created a disturbing juxtaposition, highlighting the profound psychological damage she had suffered. This unsettling combination of innocence and violence created a chilling portrait of a child trapped in a world of unimaginable horror.

The diary entries also revealed a growing obsession with specific objects. The red scrunchies became a recurring motif, appearing in almost every drawing, as if Lily was fixated on them, almost ritualistically associating them with her violent fantasies. She also drew pictures of lye, depicting it as a bubbling, viscous substance capable of dissolving anything in its path. The significance of these objects wasn't immediately apparent, but their repetitive appearance suggested a deep-seated connection to her plans for revenge, hinting at a methodical planning that belied her age. The symbolism of these objects pointed towards a deeper, subconscious connection to the eventual murder, underscoring the chilling premeditation involved.

There were entries that hinted at a plan, a carefully crafted strategy for revenge. While the details were fragmented and obscured, there were clues – cryptic messages, coded drawings, and seemingly nonsensical phrases – that suggested a coherent plan was slowly taking shape in her mind. The entries became more cryptic, more coded, as if Lily was trying to mask her intentions, even from herself. The veiled nature of these entries heightened the sense of suspense and danger, foreshadowing the ultimate act of violence.

Sometimes, Lily's entries were interspersed with fragmented memories of abuse, often depicted through disturbingly simplistic drawings. These memories weren't clear or coherent; they were flashes of images, snippets of scenes, and fragments of conversations that revealed a horrifying reality of sexual and physical abuse. These fragments, interwoven with her violent fantasies, underscored the connection between her trauma and her desire for revenge, highlighting the cyclical nature of abuse and the way it fueled her violent impulses.

The more Sarah read, the more she realized that Lily wasn't merely fantasizing; she was planning. Her drawings and writings weren't merely expressions of anger; they were blueprints, meticulously crafted plans for an act of retribution. The red scrunchies, the lye, the black plastic bags – these weren't random objects; they were tools, instruments of revenge carefully chosen and meticulously depicted. The disturbing reality was that Lily's fantasies weren't confined to her imagination; they were a chilling foreshadowing of the heinous crime to come.

The entries culminated in a particularly disturbing drawing, a detailed depiction of the murder scene itself. It was remarkably accurate, mirroring the crime scene photographs Sarah had seen. The figure in the black bag, the red scrunchies, the lye – every detail was precisely rendered, revealing a level of awareness and precision that was both terrifying and deeply disturbing. This final drawing served as a chilling testament to Lily's role in the horrific crime, a culmination of her violent fantasies and carefully crafted plan for revenge. It wasn't just a child's drawing; it was a confession, a meticulously detailed account of a premeditated murder.

The diary entries offered a chilling glimpse into the mind of a child consumed by rage, a child who had witnessed unspeakable horrors and who was plotting her own brand of chilling retribution. Lily's violent fantasies weren't just the ramblings of a disturbed child; they were a terrifying prelude to a gruesome murder, a stark reminder of the dark, twisted path that years of abuse can pave. The weight of the silence was broken, and what followed was a horrifying revelation: the murder was not an isolated incident, but the culmination of a decades-long cycle of abuse, carefully planned and executed by a fragmented mind. And at the heart of it all was Lily, the innocent child whose violent fantasies foreshadowed the unspeakable horror.

The air in Sarah's small apartment grew thick with the weight of unspoken horrors. Each entry she read was a fresh wound, reopening the festering sores of Eleanor's past, and, disturbingly, mirroring unsettling echoes within Sarah's own life. The diary, once a source of morbid fascination, had become a chilling mirror reflecting her own anxieties and buried fears. The rhythmic scratching of her pen against the notepad, a futile attempt to organize her thoughts, was punctuated by the frantic thump-thump-thump of her heart against her ribs. She felt a growing unease, a creeping dread that coiled around her like a venomous snake, tightening its grip with each passing page.

The fragmented memories interspersed with Lily's violent fantasies started to feel less like disconnected fragments and more like a disturbing puzzle slowly revealing a horrifying picture. Sarah began to see patterns, connections she hadn't noticed before. The recurring images of barbed wire fences, the specific details of the abuse, the chilling precision of Lily's drawings – they all seemed to resonate with something deep within her own subconscious. It was a haunting sense of déjà vu, a chilling familiarity that left her breathless and disoriented. The unsettling feeling wasn't merely a product of Eleanor's trauma; it felt intimately connected to her own.

Sarah found herself constantly reliving moments from her childhood, flashes of images and sensations previously buried deep in the recesses of her mind. The scent of bleach, the metallic tang of blood, the chilling silence before a storm – these fragmented memories, once dismissed as trivial, now held a terrifying significance. They were pieces of a puzzle, fragments of a horrifying narrative that she hadn't consciously remembered, but that the diary was painstakingly reconstructing. It was as if Eleanor's trauma was seeping into her own being, awakening dormant memories and triggering suppressed emotions.

One entry, written in Lily's shaky hand, described a game they played called "Hide and Seek." It was a chillingly twisted version of the child's game, where the hiding places were dark, confined spaces, and the seeker was a figure cloaked in shadows, his face obscured by darkness. Sarah felt a jolt of recognition. This "Hide and Seek" echoed a disturbing memory of her own childhood – a recurring nightmare where she would hide in the dark recesses of the house, desperately trying to escape a shadowy figure she couldn't clearly see. The game's chilling details – the darkness, the confinement, the fear of discovery – mirrored the same feelings of dread she experienced in her recurring nightmare. This wasn't just Eleanor's trauma; it was a shared experience, a chilling link connecting their lives across generations.

The diary entries weren't just recounting Eleanor's past; they were also revealing a terrifying connection to Sarah's present. The recurring motif of red scrunchies, previously dismissed as a random detail, now held a new significance. Sarah realized with a jolt that she owned several red scrunchies, the same style as those used to tie the victim's body. They were a forgotten relic from her childhood, a seemingly innocuous item that now held a sinister weight, a chilling connection to the past. This unsettling realization sent a shiver down her spine, the cold fear gripping her with an icy hand.

The lye, another recurring symbol in Lily's drawings, also held a disturbing relevance. Sarah recalled a time, years ago, when her mother had used lye to clean the kitchen. The memory was vague, fragmented – a fleeting image of a white powder dissolving in water, the acrid smell clinging to the air. But now, in the context of the diary entries, the memory took on a new, terrifying meaning. It wasn't just a household cleaner; it was a tool, a weapon, a terrifying symbol of destruction and death. The seemingly ordinary household item was now imbued with the sinister meaning from the diary, a horrific reminder of Eleanor's violent act.

Sarah's sleep became fractured, disturbed by recurring nightmares that mirrored the violent imagery in the diary. She found herself waking up in a cold sweat, her heart pounding, the chilling images of black bags and red scrunchies seared into her memory. The line between reality and dream blurred, the weight of Eleanor's trauma pressing down on her, threatening to consume her. The vividness of the nightmares, their unsettling resemblance to Lily's drawings, further strengthened Sarah's unsettling belief that these weren't mere coincidences; they were echoes of a shared trauma, a horrifying legacy passed down through generations.

The diary entries became increasingly disturbing, detailing the escalating abuse Eleanor endured, the gradual erosion of her sanity, and the emergence of her fractured personalities. Each alter had their own distinct voice, their own unique perspective, but they were all bound together by the shared trauma of abuse. Sarah felt a growing sense of empathy for Eleanor, a recognition of the pain and suffering she had endured. This empathy, however, was laced with a chilling fear – a growing awareness that the trauma wasn't confined to the past; it was a living, breathing entity that continued to haunt both Eleanor and Sarah. The past refused to remain in the past; instead, it stretched its tendrils into the present, threatening to engulf Sarah in its dark embrace.

As Sarah delved deeper into the diary, she began to see herself reflected in the pages – not just in the shared memories and symbols, but in the fragmented nature of her own identity. She started questioning her own perceptions, her own memories, the very fabric of her own reality. The line between herself and Eleanor became increasingly blurred, the sense of her own separate identity fading into the unsettling realization that the shared trauma had indelibly marked both of their lives. This sense of blurring identity left Sarah feeling unmoored, lost in a labyrinth of fractured memories and unsettling realities.

The diary's narrative wasn't simply a chronicle of Eleanor's past; it was a cautionary tale, a chilling testament to the lasting impact of trauma and its ability to permeate generations. Sarah's growing fear wasn't solely the product of Eleanor's story; it was a deeply personal response, a visceral reaction to the uncovering of long-buried truths that resonated with her own suppressed memories and unresolved anxieties. The weight of silence had been broken, unleashing a torrent of disturbing revelations that not only illuminated Eleanor's fragmented past but also unveiled the dark, unsettling connections to Sarah's own present.

Sarah started keeping her own journal, a parallel to Eleanor's, filled with her own fragmented memories, her own growing fears, her own attempts to unravel the tangled threads of her past. Each entry was a step towards confronting the darkness, a desperate attempt to understand the horrifying connections between her life and Eleanor's. The act of writing became a form of self-therapy, a way to process the overwhelming emotions that threatened to consume her. In her journal entries, Sarah mirrored Eleanor's style; the raw emotions, the fragmented memories, the sense of disorientation and confusion, were vividly described, highlighting the deep psychological impact of Eleanor's diary.

The weight of the silence had been lifted, but it had been replaced by a new weight, the oppressive weight of truth. The truth was a horrifying beast, its claws digging deep into Sarah's psyche. It was a truth that was not confined to the past; it was a truth that lived and breathed in her present. The unsettling realization of a shared trauma, a shared legacy of abuse and violence, left her in a state of profound anxiety and distress. The diary had done more than just unearth Eleanor's dark secret; it had cracked open the foundations of Sarah's own world, revealing a horrifying reality that she had never dared to confront. And as the darkness closed in, Sarah knew that the real horror was just beginning. The weight of the silence was gone, but the weight of the truth was far heavier, far more terrifying, far more deeply entrenched in her life than she could have ever imagined.

# CHAPTER 4: ECHOES OF TRAUMA

The diary entry was dated February 14th, 1998. Sarah traced the date with her fingertip, a cold shiver snaking down her spine. Valentine's Day. A day meant for love and affection, yet this entry spoke of nothing but chilling hatred and a brutal, calculated violence. The handwriting was spidery, frantic, unlike anything she'd seen before. It was Lily's, but a Lily consumed by a tempestuous rage, her usually precise script dissolving into a chaotic scrawl.

"The ice clung to my skin," the entry began, "cold, like his touch, cold like his heart. He deserved it. He deserved everything. He deserved to feel the slow, chilling embrace of death, just like he'd made me feel for years. He deserved to be... frozen." The words were raw, visceral, laced with a frightening intensity. The entry went on to describe the scene, not as a detached observation, but as a visceral experience, a brutal dance between predator and prey.

But then, another voice emerged, a subtle shift in the tone, a different handwriting layered upon Lily's frenzied scrawl. This was Evelyn. Evelyn, the pragmatic one, the one who always sought control, even in chaos. Her words were stark, concise, almost clinical. "The lye...it was necessary. It ensures... efficiency. Eliminates...the risk of...identification." Evelyn's voice, even in the diary, maintained a chilling detachment, a cold calculation that sent a shudder through Sarah.

The entry continued to flip between Lily's raw, vengeful perspective and Evelyn's meticulous planning. Jane's voice, the timid and fearful one, only surfaced sporadically, a whispered counterpoint to the violent narrative. "No...please...stop...I'm scared..." Jane's fear acted as a gruesome soundtrack to Lily's rage and Evelyn's cold efficiency, highlighting the terrifying dissonance within Eleanor's fractured psyche.

The entry described the meticulous planning, the selection of the tools, the precise movements. It was a chilling narrative of premeditated murder, devoid of any emotion except the cold, calculating precision of Evelyn's planning and Lily's unbridled fury. They were two sides of the same coin, two facets of a deeply fractured psyche, working in terrifying synchronicity.

"The bags...black, like the night he stole my innocence," Lily's frantic scrawl continued. "And the scrunchies...red, like the blood...his blood...flowing like...a river of...justice." The scrunchies again. The recurring motif, a chilling detail linking the past to the present, echoing Sarah's own unsettling discovery. The image seared itself into Sarah's mind, a vivid tableau of violence and cold-blooded revenge.

Jane's desperate pleas for mercy were scattered throughout Lily's narrative, like faint whispers in a hurricane. "It's wrong... this is wrong...we'll all pay...we'll all..." Her words trailed off, lost in the storm of Lily's rage and Evelyn's cold, calculating efficiency. The fragmentary nature of the entry, the jarring shifts in perspective, reflected the fractured state of Eleanor's mind, the chaotic interplay of her different alters working in horrific unison.

Sarah stopped reading, the chilling details settling upon her like a shroud. The image of the victim encased in black bags, bound with red scrunchies, and surrounded by lye—the description was so vivid, so visceral, that it felt like she was reliving the murder herself. The cold dread that had been a constant companion since she began reading the diary now intensified, a suffocating weight in her chest. It wasn't just reading about a murder; it was witnessing a disintegration of the self, a terrifying spectacle of fractured identity and unspeakable violence.

The entry continued, depicting the aftermath, the meticulous cleaning, the disposal of evidence. Evelyn's voice dominated this section, detailing the steps taken to ensure anonymity, to erase any trace of their violent act. It was a chilling testament to the level of planning and control that existed within this fractured mind, a horrific dance between rage and calculation. The efficiency was terrifying, the cold precision leaving Sarah breathless with fear.

But interspersed between Evelyn's methodical descriptions were fragments of Lily's lingering rage, bitter pronouncements, whispers of satisfaction mingling with the unsettling awareness of the repercussions that were inevitably coming. The violence was not just a release; it was a curse. A curse that seemed inextricably linked to Eleanor's fractured state, a chilling reminder of the destructive power of unchecked trauma.

Sarah reread the entry, slowly, deliberately, trying to make sense of the chaos. Each line was a piece of a terrifying puzzle, a fragmented glimpse into the minds of the alters, their individual motivations, and their horrifying collaboration. The contrast between Lily's primal rage and Evelyn's methodical efficiency was unsettling, showcasing the different facets of Eleanor's personality and the terrifying power of her fragmented psyche.

She closed the diary, her hands trembling. The events described in the entry were not just a cold-blooded murder; they were the culmination of years of abuse, the horrific manifestation of a shattered soul. Sarah felt a profound sense of pity for Eleanor, yet also a chilling recognition that this violence was not an isolated incident but a logical progression of years of suffering.

The entry highlighted the horrifying interplay between Eleanor's alters, their individual motivations, and the devastating consequences of their actions. The seemingly disparate personalities had coalesced for this one specific act of violence, their differing traits contributing to the effectiveness and horror of the murder. Lily's rage provided the motive, while Evelyn's control ensured the careful execution. Jane's fear was a haunting counterpoint, a silent scream amidst the storm of violence.

Sarah reached for her own journal, the blank pages mocking her with their empty silence. She needed to process what she had just read, to make sense of the chilling narrative and its implications. But the words eluded her, the weight of the story pressing down on her, choking her with its intensity. The room seemed to shrink, the walls closing in, the air thick with the unspoken horrors of the night.

She picked up her pen and started to write, the rhythmic scratching a fragile counterpoint to the echoing violence of the past. But her words were fragmented, mirroring the chaos of Eleanor's diary. The words came in fits and starts, mimicking the disjointed narrative of the night of the murder. "Ice...cold...black...red...lye...fear...rage...control..." The words were scattered, incomplete, reflecting her own disorientation and the overwhelming nature of the information she was processing.

This wasn't just about understanding Eleanor's past; it was about confronting her own, unearthing the buried memories that were stirring within her, awakened by the echoes of trauma. The chilling parallels between Eleanor's life and her own were becoming increasingly undeniable, tightening the connection between them, forging a horrifying bond.

Sarah wrote about the images that haunted her: the black bags, the red scrunchies, the chilling image of lye dissolving in water. These images, once insignificant, were now charged with a sinister meaning, imbued with the horrors of that Valentine's Day. They were more than just symbols of the crime; they were symbols of the trauma that had shaped both Eleanor's and Sarah's lives, creating a disturbing continuity between generations.

The night of the murder, as revealed through the fragmented perspectives of Eleanor's alters, was not just a single event but a culmination of years of suffering and abuse. It was a brutal, horrifying act, but it was also a chilling symptom of a deeper, more insidious illness—the shattering of a human psyche, the terrifying consequences of untreated trauma. And Sarah, as she delved deeper into the diary, was beginning to realize that this trauma wasn't confined to the past; it was a legacy, a haunting inheritance passed down through generations, whispering its dark secrets in the echoes of fear, rage, and chilling control. The night of the murder was not just a single night; it was a culmination of a lifetime of suffering, a violent climax to a horrifying narrative stretching far beyond a single date on a calendar. And Sarah, in the wake of this horrifying revelation, knew that her own journey of discovery was only just beginning. The truth was unfolding, but with it came an overwhelming sense of dread, a deep, visceral fear that extended far beyond the confines of the diary itself.

The diary entry shifted again, this time to a voice Sarah hadn't encountered before. It was hesitant, almost apologetic, a stark contrast to the chilling narratives of Lily and Evelyn. This was Clara, Eleanor's childlike alter, her voice a fragile whisper amidst the storm. "It was so cold," Clara wrote, her childish scrawl barely legible. "So very, very cold. And then…there was blood. So much blood. I didn't understand. I just wanted to be warm." Clara's perspective offered a horrifying glimpse into the innocence lost, a childlike horror juxtaposed against the calculated violence of the other personalities. The jarring shift in tone, from the cold precision of Evelyn to Clara's naive terror, highlighted the fragmented nature of Eleanor's psyche, the terrifying dissonance between her various selves.

The subsequent entries focused on the aftermath, each alter wrestling with the repercussions of their shared act. Evelyn, ever the pragmatist, meticulously documented the cleanup, the disposal of evidence, her clinical descriptions betraying a chilling lack of remorse. She detailed the precise steps taken to erase any trace of their crime, a chilling testament to her meticulous nature and terrifying efficiency. The chilling precision of her actions, her focus on the practical aspects of the post-murder cleanup, contrasted sharply with the raw, visceral emotion still lingering in Lily's fragmented memories.

Lily's entries, however, were filled with a simmering rage, a dark satisfaction mingled with a growing fear. Her fragmented recollections were filled with vivid sensory details—the icy grip of the freezer, the metallic tang of blood, the acrid bite of lye. These weren't simply memories; they were sensory experiences relived, the visceral impact of the crime lingering in her fractured consciousness. She expressed a perverse sense of justice, yet beneath the surface, a deep-seated terror threatened to consume her. The dissonance between her satisfaction and fear created a terrifying internal conflict, a reflection of the fragmented psyche that was Eleanor.

Jane, the timid alter, offered a harrowing counterpoint. Her entries were filled with guilt and overwhelming fear, a silent scream trapped within the violent narratives of Lily and Evelyn. Her fragmented memories were nightmares, chaotic and disorienting, her words a fractured echo of the events, conveying a sense of overwhelming dread and helplessness. She couldn't fully recall the details, but her sense of guilt and terror was palpable, echoing in the broken sentences and frantic scrawls that filled her diary entries.

The fragmented memories of the alters created a disturbing puzzle, pieces scattered across the pages of the diary, each offering a different perspective, each highlighting a different facet of the crime and its aftermath. Sarah struggled to assemble the complete picture, to understand the interplay between these different personalities, their motivations, and their individual roles in the horrific event. The diary entries were not a linear narrative; they were fragments, shards of memory and emotion, reflecting the shattered state of Eleanor's psyche.

One entry, attributed to a previously unknown alter, revealed a chilling detail. This personality, identified as Iris, described the moment of discovery, the chilling silence that followed the crime's completion. Her narrative spoke not of guilt or remorse, but of a profound emptiness, a terrifying void where humanity should have resided. Iris observed the scene dispassionately, detailing the arrangement of the victim's body as if it were a work of art, reflecting the unsettling combination of aesthetics and destruction that had marked the crime. Iris's voice was unnerving, highlighting a profound detachment and a lack of emotional connection, suggesting a terrifying level of dissociation that seemed to reside at the heart of Eleanor's fragmented psyche.

Sarah found herself struggling to comprehend the implications of what she was reading. She was confronted not only with a brutal murder, but with the complexities of the human psyche, the devastating effects of untreated trauma, and the terrifying reality of multiple personality disorder. The diary provided a horrifying glimpse into the mind of a woman whose life had been shattered by abuse, where trauma had manifested itself in the form of violent rage, meticulous planning, and chilling detachment.

Days turned into weeks as Sarah immersed herself in Eleanor's diary. Each entry was a chilling piece of a larger puzzle, a fragmentary snapshot of a life consumed by trauma. The narrative was not simply a chronicle of a crime; it was a descent into the fragmented mind, a disturbing exploration of the internal conflicts, and the devastating consequences that can emerge when the self is shattered. The diary was not a simple story, but a complex psychological portrait, a terrifying reflection of the human capacity for both immense cruelty and profound vulnerability.

The diary entries revealed not only the intricacies of the murder, but also offered disturbing glimpses into Eleanor's past, detailing years of abuse and suffering. The fractured narrative offered a haunting testament to the resilience, and the destructive power of the human spirit, highlighting the complexities of trauma and its impact on the formation of identity. Sarah started to notice patterns, recurring symbols, and motifs that connected the events of the murder to Eleanor's past experiences. The red scrunchies, initially presented as a chilling detail, seemed to represent a twisted connection to her childhood, the color symbolizing a suppressed trauma associated with a specific childhood memory. The black bags, initially symbolic of death and concealment, became increasingly connected to feelings of shame and isolation, mirroring Eleanor's long history of emotional and psychological isolation.

As Sarah delved deeper into the diary, she began to find parallels between Eleanor's life and her own. She started to unearth buried memories, repressed feelings, and unresolved traumas, which were stirred by Eleanor's story. This unsettling realization reinforced the unsettling bond between them, an eerie connection that echoed across generations, a grim inheritance of trauma passed down through familial lines. Sarah's own journey of self-discovery became intertwined with Eleanor's, as she grappled with the disturbing implications of her mother's fractured psyche and the horrifying legacy of abuse that haunted her family.

The diary's final entry was particularly disturbing. It was brief, almost cryptic, written by an alter Sarah hadn't yet encountered. This personality, simply identified as "The Watcher," offered a chilling, detached perspective on Eleanor's fragmented existence, observing the internal struggles as if watching a play unfold. "The pieces shatter, reform, and shatter again," this alter wrote, "a perpetual cycle of destruction and rebirth, forever trapped within the confines of the fractured self." The words were bleak, devoid of emotion, yet imbued with a chilling understanding of Eleanor's psychological torment, suggesting the presence of a profoundly dissociative aspect within Eleanor's fractured psyche, adding another layer of complexity to the already terrifying narrative.

The diary ended abruptly, leaving Sarah with a profound sense of unease and an overwhelming feeling of incompletion. The unanswered questions, the fragmented memories, the chilling echoes of trauma – all contributed to a lingering sense of unease, a chilling reminder that the consequences of Eleanor's actions, and her fractured psyche, extended far beyond the confines of the single crime. The unsettling revelation that her own life echoed that of her mother's intensified her sense of dread. The finality of the diary's abrupt end only intensified her sense of foreboding, leaving her with an uneasy feeling that the story was far from over. The echoes of trauma, the fragmented memories, and the unresolved conflicts within Eleanor's psyche resonated with a chilling intensity, creating an unsettling feeling that her own past was inextricably intertwined with Eleanor's, and that the trauma extended beyond the bounds of a simple murder investigation. The weight of the past, the chilling legacy of Eleanor's actions, and the disturbing similarities to her own life all contributed to a profound sense of fear, uncertainty, and a haunting realization that the story was far from concluded.

The diary entries shifted again, this time to a voice that felt less like a scream and more like a carefully constructed dam holding back a raging torrent. This was Evelyn, the pragmatic organizer, the one who cleaned up the mess, both literally and figuratively. Her entries weren't filled with raw emotion, but with meticulous detail. She documented the routines she established to manage the other personalities, a chillingly efficient system born out of necessity and honed over years of desperate struggle.

Evelyn's coping mechanism was control. She meticulously charted the emergence of each alter, noting triggers, durations, and behaviors with the clinical precision of a seasoned researcher. Her diary entries resembled case studies, each personality analyzed and categorized, their strengths and weaknesses cataloged as if they were variables in a complex equation. She described rituals, designed to appease or suppress the more volatile personalities—specific songs played at precise times, particular foods consumed to regulate mood swings, and carefully planned activities to distract from potentially triggering situations. These weren't haphazard attempts at self-soothing; they were strategic maneuvers, calculated to maintain a semblance of order in her chaotic internal world. She even devised a complex system of coded signals, subtle gestures or phrases, used to communicate with the alters and subtly influence their behavior, preventing unwanted outbursts or disruptive shifts in personality. This intricate system was both a testament to her remarkable mental fortitude and a chilling reminder of the profound fragmentation within her psyche.

One entry described a particularly challenging period, where Lily's rage threatened to overwhelm the others. Evelyn detailed her strategy: a carefully constructed sensory deprivation chamber, essentially a soundproofed, dark room where Lily was "contained" until her fury subsided. She didn't express remorse or guilt; her focus remained on the practical aspects of managing the crisis, documenting the length of the confinement, the effectiveness of the sensory deprivation, and the subsequent return to a more manageable state. This clinical detachment, while unsettling, highlighted the level of control Evelyn exerted over her own fractured self, a testament to her desperate, yet effective, coping mechanisms. She treated the other personalities not as integral parts of herself, but as separate entities requiring management, almost like a demanding, unruly household.

In contrast to Evelyn's clinical approach, Lily's coping mechanisms were volatile and self-destructive. Her entries were filled with furious scrawls, chaotic bursts of rage interspersed with periods of crippling depression. Her methods involved reckless behaviors—risky sexual encounters, substance abuse, and acts of vandalism—attempts to self-soothe and express her bottled-up rage. Her coping mechanisms were not calculated strategies, but desperate attempts to alleviate the overwhelming pain and anger that consumed her. She wrote of using alcohol and drugs as a blunt instrument, seeking oblivion as a temporary reprieve from the constant internal turmoil. The destructive spiral was clear, a clear consequence of untreated trauma.

Jane, the timid alter, employed a different strategy – complete withdrawal. Her entries were short, filled with trembling, hesitant scrawls, her coping mechanisms consisting of self-imposed isolation and avoidance. She sought refuge in silent spaces, retreating into her own inner world, creating a safe haven from the chaos of the other personalities. She used repetitive motions, counting objects, or tracing patterns, forms of self-soothing that hinted at obsessive-compulsive tendencies, a common manifestation of trauma. She described her attempts to create order in her internal chaos, clinging to routines and repetitive actions in a desperate bid for control, a tiny island of stability in the tumultuous sea of her mind.

Clara, the childlike alter, relied on fantasy and escapism. Her entries were filled with whimsical drawings and childish stories, an attempt to create a world separate from the pain and confusion of her fragmented reality. She described playing make-believe games, crafting imaginary friends and worlds where she felt safe and protected, a clear defense mechanism against the overwhelming horror of her experiences. Her coping mechanisms were simplistic and inherently childlike, reflecting her age and the nature of her trauma.

The diary revealed another personality, Iris, whose coping mechanism was complete dissociation. Her entries were chillingly detached, observing events without emotion, describing scenes with the clinical detachment of a scientist. She didn't participate in the rituals or engage in self-destructive behaviors. Instead, she seemed to exist outside the fray, an observer trapped within her own mind, her ability to distance herself from the pain a chilling defense against the trauma she experienced. She documented the others' coping mechanisms as if studying a foreign species, highlighting the unsettling degree of dissociation within Eleanor's psyche.

As Sarah continued to delve deeper into the diary, a disturbing pattern emerged. Each alter's coping mechanism, while unique, was directly related to the nature of their trauma. Evelyn's control stemmed from a need to manage the unpredictable aftermath of abuse. Lily's self-destruction was a manifestation of her unexpressed rage. Jane's withdrawal was a consequence of years spent in silence, afraid to speak out. Clara's escapism was a childish attempt to overcome the terror and helplessness she felt. And Iris's dissociation represented a complete detachment from the pain that she might have struggled to process.

The diary also highlighted the interconnectedness of their coping mechanisms. Evelyn's structured routines provided a measure of stability, preventing the more chaotic personalities from overwhelming the system. Yet, these tightly controlled systems also served to suppress unresolved trauma, preventing healing and contributing to the cycle of destruction and rebirth described by the Watcher.

Sarah began to understand that Eleanor's coping mechanisms weren't simply isolated strategies, but complex, interwoven responses to her overwhelming trauma. They were a desperate attempt to navigate the shattered landscape of her psyche, a fragile system holding back the torrent of pain and suffering that threatened to consume her. These mechanisms, while seemingly effective in maintaining a semblance of order, also reinforced the very fragmentation they sought to control. They were a testament to her resilience, yet also a chilling indictment of a system that failed to protect her and provide appropriate care. The diary entries served not only as a chronicle of a gruesome murder, but also as a disturbing case study in the complexities of trauma and the desperate, often self-destructive, ways individuals cope with its devastating effects.

Sarah noted that the diary entries themselves acted as a form of coping mechanism for Eleanor. Writing, for each alter, was an act of catharsis, a way to process the unbearable weight of their collective trauma. Each entry served a different purpose —Evelyn's meticulous documentation providing control, Lily's furious scrawls releasing rage, Jane's trembling confessions expressing guilt, and Clara's fanciful stories offering escape. Even Iris's detached observations may have served to process the overwhelming experience without emotional engagement. The act of writing itself became a form of self-therapy, a distorted, fragmented method of confronting the unspeakable horrors they had endured and perpetrated.

The final entry, penned by The Watcher, served as a chilling summary. It wasn't a coping mechanism, but an observation. A detached, clinical account of the perpetual cycle of shattering and reformation, a reflection of the unending trauma and the desperate, unsuccessful attempts to find peace within the fragmented self. The Watcher's narrative highlighted the self-perpetuating nature of Eleanor's coping mechanisms—the desperate attempts to control the chaos had become part of the chaos itself, trapping Eleanor within a perpetual cycle of trauma and self-destruction. The very act of documenting the struggles had become a component of the struggle itself.

Sarah closed the diary, the weight of its contents settling heavily upon her. Eleanor's coping mechanisms, meticulously documented, were not merely strategies for survival; they were a harrowing reflection of the devastating impact of untreated trauma and the intricate, often self-destructive, ways in which the human psyche attempts to navigate unimaginable pain. The diary offered a terrifyingly intimate glimpse into the fractured mind, revealing the complexities of survival, the resilience of the human spirit, and the ultimate, tragic failure of a system that failed to protect Eleanor from the horrors she faced. The story ended, but the echoes resonated long after the final word. The unsettling implications of the case lingered, leaving Sarah to grapple with the chilling parallels between her own life and her mother's, the inheritance of trauma, and the uncertain future that lay ahead.

The diary slammed shut, the sound echoing in the oppressive silence of Sarah's apartment. The weight of the revelations pressed down on her, a suffocating blanket of horror and disbelief. She hadn't just discovered a gruesome murder; she'd unearthed a lifetime of unspeakable trauma, meticulously documented in her mother's chillingly detailed diary. Eleanor, the woman Sarah had known – the elegant, composed wife and mother – was a ghost, a carefully constructed façade concealing a fractured psyche, a battlefield of warring personalities battling for control. The image of her mother, serene and smiling, was shattered, replaced by a kaleidoscope of fragmented selves, each bearing the scars of unimaginable abuse.

The initial shock gave way to a creeping dread, a chilling realization that her own life, her own identity, was inextricably linked to this dark legacy. Eleanor's trauma wasn't just a historical event; it was a living, breathing entity, its tendrils reaching across the years, wrapping themselves around Sarah, suffocating her with its insidious grip. The diary was more than a chronicle of murder; it was a roadmap to Sarah's own subconscious, revealing unsettling parallels in her behavior, her anxieties, and her own struggles with self-destructive tendencies.

Sarah found herself staring at her reflection, a stranger staring back. The familiar face, once a comfort, now felt alien, a mask hiding the turmoil within. She saw glimpses of Eleanor in her own eyes, the same haunted look, the same underlying tremor of unease. The diary entries had become a mirror, reflecting back not only her mother's fragmented self, but also the hidden shards of her own fractured identity. Was she destined to repeat the cycle, to become another victim of the same devastating legacy? The question hung heavy in the air, a chilling premonition of a future she couldn't yet comprehend.

Sleep became a battlefield. Nightmares plagued her, vivid recreations of the scenes described in the diary, the chilling details rendered with such horrifying accuracy they felt almost real. She relived the abuse Eleanor endured, feeling the icy grip of fear, the searing pain of betrayal. She saw the rage of Lily, the despair of Jane, the childlike innocence of Clara, all reflected in her own fragmented dreams, her own unconscious fears and anxieties. She woke in a cold sweat, heart pounding, the echoes of trauma clinging to her like a second skin.

Days blurred into a monotonous cycle of anxiety and denial. She tried to function, to maintain a semblance of normalcy, but the world seemed distorted, viewed through a lens clouded by grief, guilt, and the ever-present fear of what she might discover next. The vibrant colors of her life had faded, replaced by a muted palette of fear and uncertainty. Simple tasks became monumental struggles, the weight of the past dragging her down, making even the most mundane activities feel like an insurmountable obstacle.

Her relationships suffered. Her close friends, initially supportive, began to withdraw, unable to cope with the intensity of her grief and the dark secrets she was unwilling or unable to share. Her partner, initially understanding, grew increasingly distant, unable to comprehend the depth of her emotional turmoil, the constant shadow of her mother's trauma. Sarah felt increasingly isolated, trapped in a silent prison of her own making, her pain both a burden and a shield, driving a wedge between herself and the people she loved.

Therapy became a necessity, a desperate attempt to navigate the treacherous terrain of her emotional landscape. She poured out her heart to her therapist, detailing the horrors revealed in the diary, the chilling parallels between her mother's experiences and her own struggles. The therapist, a seasoned professional, listened patiently, guiding her through the labyrinth of her emotions, helping her to untangle the complex threads of her inherited trauma. The sessions were intense, draining, but they provided a lifeline, a sense of hope amidst the despair.

But the therapy also unearthed a disturbing reality: the cycle of trauma could extend beyond Eleanor. Sarah discovered suppressed memories of her own childhood, fragments of experiences that had been buried deep within her subconscious, now resurfacing like ghosts from the past. These were not explicit memories of abuse, but unsettling patterns of self-harm, instances of self-destructive behavior, and an overwhelming sense of anxiety and emotional instability, all mirroring the coping mechanisms documented in her mother's diary. It was a chilling confirmation of the intergenerational trauma, the inheritance of pain and dysfunction that had been passed down through generations.

The therapist diagnosed Sarah with complex PTSD, a condition characterized by chronic anxiety, intrusive memories, and emotional dysregulation, directly linked to the trauma she'd experienced both vicariously through her mother and through her own repressed memories. The diagnosis provided a framework for understanding her struggles, but it didn't alleviate the pain. It was a grim acceptance of the reality of her situation, a harsh reminder that her journey to healing was long, arduous, and fraught with uncertainty.

The discovery of the diary had thrown Sarah's life into chaos, shattering her sense of self and leaving her grappling with a legacy of pain and trauma. The seemingly idyllic life she'd led, the comfortable reality she'd believed in, had crumbled, revealing a foundation built on secrets and lies, on the unspoken horrors concealed within her family's history. Her struggle was not just to understand her mother's fractured psyche, but to confront her own, to confront the shadows that had haunted her for years, and to finally begin the long and difficult process of healing.

The diary, a symbol of both horror and revelation, became her constant companion, a source of both agony and understanding. Each entry was a painful reminder of her mother's suffering, but also a testament to her resilience. Sarah began to see Eleanor not just as a victim, but as a survivor, a woman who had fought tirelessly against the crushing weight of her trauma, finding ways to cope, to survive, to create a semblance of order amidst the chaos. This realization, while not minimizing the horrific details of her mother's life, provided a small flicker of hope, a sense that healing was possible, even in the face of overwhelming pain.

Sarah's journey was far from over. The road to recovery was long and winding, filled with obstacles and setbacks. But armed with the knowledge gained from the diary, the support of her therapist, and a growing understanding of her own inherited trauma, she began to take the first tentative steps towards reclaiming her life, towards rebuilding her sense of self, and towards breaking the cycle of pain that had haunted her family for generations. The echoes of trauma lingered, but they were no longer suffocating; they were a reminder of the past, a source of strength, a motivation to forge a future free from the shadows of her mother's legacy. The fight was far from over, but Sarah was finally ready to face it, head-on. The diary, a grim testament to the horrors of the past, had become, paradoxically, a guide to her future.

The initial police investigation had been a frustrating dead end. Twenty-five years ago, the discovery of the body – a young woman, frozen solid in a domestic freezer, encased in black plastic bags tied with distinctive red scrunchies and surrounded by lye – had sent shockwaves through the community. The brutality of the crime, the calculated nature of the disposal, had baffled detectives. There were no witnesses, no clear motive, and no discernible leads. The case grew cold, filed away alongside countless others, a chilling reminder of unsolved mysteries.

Sarah's discovery of her mother's diary, however, changed everything. The detailed, chilling accounts not only revealed the identity of the likely perpetrator – one of Eleanor's alters, a personality named Lily – but also offered a window into a world of unspeakable trauma, a lifetime of abuse that fueled

Lily's violent act.

Detective Inspector Davies, a seasoned veteran with a reputation for solving seemingly impossible cases, was assigned to re-open the investigation. He was a man known for his meticulous attention to detail, his unwavering patience, and his ability to connect seemingly disparate pieces of information. He knew this case was unique, unlike anything he'd encountered in his long career. The challenge wasn't just solving a murder; it was understanding the complex psychology of a perpetrator with multiple personality disorder.

The diary became the centerpiece of the investigation. Davies painstakingly read each entry, meticulously noting dates, times, and the descriptions of the alters' experiences, their interactions, and their emotional states. He consulted with a team of forensic psychologists, experts in dissociative identity disorder, to decipher the cryptic entries, to understand the triggers and motivations behind Lily's actions.

The psychologists explained that multiple personality disorder was a complex condition, a manifestation of severe trauma often stemming from childhood abuse. Each alter represented a distinct personality, a coping mechanism developed to deal with overwhelming pain and stress. Lily, they theorized, was a manifestation of Eleanor's rage, a personality born from years of unimaginable suffering.

The team also examined the physical evidence from the original crime scene. The red scrunchies, a seemingly insignificant detail, became a crucial piece of the puzzle.

Forensic analysis revealed traces of Eleanor's DNA on the fabric, providing a concrete link between the victim and Eleanor. Further investigation into Eleanor's life revealed a pattern of seemingly minor obsessions and compulsions – consistent with obsessive-compulsive disorder (OCD) – interwoven with stretches of erratic behavior suggestive of Attention Deficit Hyperactivity Disorder (ADHD) and traits that indicated autism spectrum disorder. These disorders, the psychologists explained, often co-occurred with dissociative disorders, creating an exceptionally complex psychological profile.

The investigation delved deeper into Eleanor's past. Interviews with family members and acquaintances painted a picture of a woman who led a double life. To the outside world, she was the perfect wife and mother – demure, elegant, and seemingly serene. But behind this façade lay a fractured psyche, a secret history of abuse that had shaped her personality and ultimately led to the tragic events of twenty-five years ago.

Davies discovered that Eleanor had been subjected to brutal physical and sexual abuse as a child and later in her marriage. Her husband, a man who outwardly appeared charming and successful, was a master manipulator, a domestic abuser who systematically controlled and abused her for years. The trauma was deeply ingrained, creating a fractured identity, with different alters assuming control at different times, each acting as a defense mechanism against the overwhelming pain of her past. The diary entries detailed the abuse in harrowing detail, documenting the physical and emotional wounds, the constant fear, the desperate attempts to survive.

The diary also revealed the intricate relationships between

Eleanor's alters. There was Jane, the docile, submissive personality who bore the brunt of the abuse; Lily, the raging alter fueled by pent-up anger and resentment; and Clara, a childlike personality who represented Eleanor's lost innocence. Each alter had its own unique memories, experiences, and coping mechanisms, creating a complex and often conflicting inner world.

The forensic psychologists helped the police to understand the triggers that might have caused Lily to emerge and commit the murder. They theorized that the victim might have unknowingly triggered a particularly violent response by Lily. This was compounded by the documented obsessive-compulsive tendencies of some alters, which could lead to specific rituals and actions.

The investigation was far from easy. Dealing with the complexities of multiple personality disorder presented unique challenges. Statements from witnesses were often inconsistent, memories fragmented, and perceptions distorted. The police had to carefully sift through contradictory evidence, separating fact from fiction, reality from the fractured perceptions of a deeply traumatized mind.

The team faced numerous setbacks. Some witnesses proved unreliable, their memories clouded by time and trauma. Others were unwilling to cooperate, fearing retribution or simply unable to confront the painful memories associated with Eleanor and her husband's actions. The case was emotionally draining, demanding both intellectual rigor and deep empathy.

As the investigation progressed, Davies and his team pieced together the fragmented narrative, slowly unraveling the mystery of the murder. They found connections between Eleanor's alters, the victim, and the specific details of the crime – the red scrunchies, the lye, the use of a freezer. The seemingly random details were, in fact, imbued with significance, reflecting the internal struggles and coping mechanisms of Eleanor's fragmented personality.

Through painstaking research and careful analysis, the team reconstructed the events leading up to the murder. They learned that Lily had emerged at a crucial moment, a moment when Eleanor felt the most vulnerable and helpless. The victim, it turned out, was connected to Eleanor's abusive husband. Her presence, her association with the source of her trauma, had unwittingly triggered Lily's rage.

The investigation ultimately concluded that Lily, driven by a lifetime of repressed trauma and rage, had committed the murder. While Eleanor herself was not directly responsible for the act, she was a victim of circumstance, a woman consumed by her fragmented self. The case was closed, a chilling testament to the devastating consequences of severe childhood trauma and the complexities of the human psyche. The prosecution, however, faced the challenging task of presenting a case built on the fragmented memories and accounts of a woman with multiple personality disorder, a case that relied heavily on the interpretation of a diary that served as both confession and chronicle of unimaginable suffering. The trial that followed was a difficult and emotionally charged affair, a reflection of the complexities of the case and the lingering questions surrounding Eleanor

Vance's fragmented life and the dark legacy of trauma she left behind.

# CHAPTER 5: UNRAVELING THE TRUTH

Evelyn, the alter known for her meticulous nature and sharp intellect, played a crucial, insidious role in the cover-up. She wasn't the perpetrator, but her actions ensured Lily's crime remained hidden for a quarter of a century. Unlike the other alters, whose memories were fragmented and emotionally charged, Evelyn possessed a chilling clarity. Her diary entries revealed a methodical mind, coldly assessing the situation and implementing a strategy to protect Eleanor's carefully constructed facade. The entries weren't filled with the raw emotion of Lily or the childlike innocence of Clara; instead, they were precise, calculating, and devoid of sentimentality.

Her first step was to erase any trace of Lily's involvement. The diary meticulously documented this process. Evelyn meticulously cleaned the freezer, disposing of the evidence in a series of calculated actions. She explained how she'd researched methods of decomposition and removal of traces of DNA, spending weeks scouring scientific journals and online forums, her chilling dedication to this task a testament to her obsessive tendencies. The process was described with the same detached precision one might use to detail a complex scientific experiment. She wasn't driven by guilt or remorse, but by a need for order and control, a need to preserve the image of the perfect family.

The red scrunchies, those seemingly insignificant details, received special attention. Evelyn's entries described how she carefully collected and disposed of them, piece by painstaking piece. She'd burned some, dissolving others in acid, leaving no trace but the faintest, undetectable residue that advanced forensic techniques eventually managed to recover. She considered every potential angle, every possible flaw in her plan, demonstrating a level of foresight that belied her outwardly demure personality. This methodical approach extended to every detail, from the disposal of potentially incriminating items to the manipulation of witness accounts.

Evelyn's manipulative skills extended beyond the immediate aftermath of the murder. She had carefully cultivated relationships, maintaining a network of acquaintances and associates who could provide alibis and deflect suspicion. Her diary entries detailed how she'd subtly influenced others, planting seeds of doubt and misinformation, skillfully guiding the narrative to protect Eleanor's pristine image. She strategically employed charm and intellect to shape perceptions, expertly weaving a web of deceit that effectively concealed the truth. The entries mentioned specific individuals, sketching portraits of their vulnerabilities and how Evelyn expertly exploited them to her advantage.

Her control over the other alters also played a crucial role in the cover-up. She was adept at suppressing their memories, a calculated form of psychological manipulation that kept them from unintentionally revealing the truth. Her diary entries revealed her methods, a detailed catalog of subtle psychological tactics that kept them subdued, their recollections blurred, and their personalities fragmented further. She'd use hypnotic techniques she'd learned from obscure books, employing a mixture of suggestion and coercion to maintain her control.

The manipulation wasn't solely focused on the other alters. Evelyn's entries showed a keen understanding of psychology, specifically the power dynamics within the family. She manipulated Eleanor's husband, subtly guiding his actions and behavior to deflect suspicion. She knew his weaknesses, his reliance on control and his inherent arrogance, using these to her advantage. The diary entries described detailed strategies, illustrating how she subtly shifted blame and manipulated his behavior to support her narrative. This wasn't brute force; it was strategic maneuvering, a silent chess game played out over years, preserving the façade of normality.

Evelyn's mastery extended to managing the external environment. She meticulously controlled Eleanor's public persona, ensuring she maintained her image of a demure and unassuming housewife. The diary detailed the intricate strategies employed to keep up appearances, creating a compelling illusion of normalcy. She meticulously organized Eleanor's life, scheduling social events and maintaining a facade that deflected attention away from any potential scrutiny.

Her meticulous approach was not limited to the immediate aftermath. Over the years, Evelyn meticulously monitored developments in the case, always one step ahead. Whenever a potential lead emerged, she carefully manipulated the situation, redirecting attention or planting misinformation. She used her knowledge of the investigative process to anticipate and neutralize any threats to her carefully constructed deception.

But even Evelyn's control wasn't absolute. The diary entries revealed moments of doubt, fleeting cracks in her composure. There were entries detailing sleepless nights, the weight of the secret crushing her, the constant fear of discovery. These moments of vulnerability, however, were quickly suppressed, overshadowed by her unwavering determination to maintain control.

The diary also hinted at the underlying psychological conflict that fueled Evelyn's actions. Her obsessive need for order and control stemmed from a deep-seated fear of chaos and instability, a fear deeply rooted in the trauma that had fractured Eleanor's personality. It was a complex interplay of trauma and control, an intricate dance between protecting the fractured self and maintaining the illusion of normalcy.

As Detective Davies delved deeper into the diary, he uncovered the terrifying extent of Evelyn's involvement. Her entries weren't just a record of her actions; they were a chilling testament to her manipulative genius, a disturbingly detailed account of a mind capable of planning and executing a deception that lasted for a quarter of a century. Her role wasn't simply that of an accomplice; she was the architect of the cover-up, the mastermind behind the meticulous strategy that shielded Lily and Eleanor from justice.

The discovery of Evelyn's calculated role added another layer of complexity to the investigation, making it more than just a murder mystery. It became a study in the dark recesses of the human psyche, a chilling exploration of the lengths a fractured mind would go to maintain its meticulously constructed illusion of normalcy. The narrative, once focused solely on Lily's actions, now expanded, incorporating the chilling contributions of Evelyn, the alter who ensured the truth remained buried for so long. Her role was not merely a footnote; it was a crucial element that shaped the entire narrative, highlighting the insidious nature of trauma and the chilling efficiency of a mind driven by control and a relentless need for order. The investigation was no longer simply about bringing a killer to justice, but about understanding the intricate web of manipulation, the profound psychological complexities that lay at the heart of Eleanor's fractured identity and the lingering questions about the interplay between the different alters and their roles in the events that transpired 25 years ago. The diary became a roadmap into this complex psychological landscape, revealing the intricate layers of deception and control, forcing those who investigated Eleanor's life to grapple with the chilling reality of a mind broken and expertly manipulated.

The red scrunchies. Such a seemingly insignificant detail, yet they clung to the edges of Detective Davies' mind like burrs. He'd initially dismissed them as a bizarre quirk of the killer, a macabre flourish in an already horrific crime scene. But Evelyn's diary entries painted a different picture, imbuing those simple hair ties with a chilling significance. They weren't merely random accessories; they were a key, unlocking a hidden chamber within Eleanor Vance's fragmented psyche.

Evelyn's entries described finding them, tucked away in a dusty box in the attic, alongside other remnants of Eleanor's past. They were a collection, a vibrant assortment of reds – crimson, scarlet, ruby, and even the faded rose of a once-bright pink. Each one held a memory, a fragment of a life Eleanor had tried desperately to bury. The entries meticulously detailed the specific events associated with each scrunchie, each a tiny thread woven into the tapestry of Eleanor's trauma.

One crimson scrunchie, almost impossibly vibrant despite its age, was linked to a childhood birthday party. Eleanor, a shy, withdrawn child, received a single, bright red scrunchie as a gift. The memory associated with it wasn't the joy of the present, but the chilling realization that she had been seen, not as a person with her own intrinsic worth, but as an object, a thing to be adorned and manipulated. The scrunchie became a marker, a visual representation of the objectification she experienced in those early years, a recurring theme that surfaced in disturbing ways throughout her life.

Another, a deep scarlet, was connected to a moment of intense emotional distress during adolescence. The diary entry described the scrunchie as a desperate attempt to maintain a sense of control amidst the chaos of her turbulent teenage years. It was a tangible symbol, a grounding object she clung to as her world fractured around her. Yet, ironically, that same scrunchie was later used as a tool of subjugation, taken from her and used in a way that reinforced the powerlessness she felt, adding another layer to its complex symbolism.

The entries didn't just describe the scrunchies; they portrayed them as active participants in Eleanor's narrative. They were objects of both comfort and terror, symbols of vulnerability and control, objects imbued with the weight of unspoken trauma. Evelyn meticulously recorded the precise shade of each scrunchie, the texture of the fabric, even the subtle variations in stitching. Each detail provided a clue, a shard of memory that illuminated the horrifying progression of

Eleanor's abuse.

The meticulous detail with which Evelyn cataloged these seemingly insignificant objects was itself unsettling. It underscored her obsessive personality, the need for order and control that stemmed from her deep-seated trauma. The scrunchies weren't just reminders of past events; they were artifacts in Evelyn's desperate attempt to understand and order the chaos within Eleanor's fragmented mind.

The red scrunchies used in the murder were different. Evelyn described them as being chosen, not randomly, but carefully selected from the collection. They weren't the ones associated with particularly vivid memories, but rather those that represented a transition, a passage from one phase of trauma to another. They represented the confluence of the different stages of her abuse, the transition from childhood vulnerability to the horrifying events that led up to the murder.

The diary entries suggested a conscious decision to use these specific scrunchies, a symbolic act that amplified the gruesome nature of the crime. The killer, Lily, hadn't simply used any red scrunchies; she'd chosen them with a chilling awareness of their inherent symbolism, a selection that went far beyond a random act of violence. It was a ritualistic act, a macabre performance orchestrated to reflect the depth of Eleanor's pain, a chilling reflection of the victim's past experiences that was intricately woven into the crime scene.

The entries revealed Lily's perspective as well, revealing an awareness of the scrunchies' symbolic weight, an understanding of the connection between the objects and Eleanor's fractured psyche. The killer's actions transcended a mere act of violence; it was a symbolic performance, a statement woven into the gruesome tableau. The scrunchies weren't just props in a gruesome act; they were a visceral manifestation of Eleanor's trauma, used in a ritualistic fashion that underscored the deep-seated psychological roots of the crime.

The significance of the red color itself was explored in chilling detail. Red, the color of blood, of passion, of danger, resonated deeply with Eleanor's experiences. It wasn't a random choice; it was a symbolic representation of the violence and trauma that had shaped her life, and particularly, it was a representation of the repressed rage and frustration. The use of red scrunchies was not only a terrifying detail of the crime scene, but it was a deeply psychological act, a direct expression of the turmoil and pain Eleanor had endured and was now expressed through Lily.

Davies found himself engrossed in the entries, connecting the dots between the scrunchies, the events they symbolized, and the actions of the different alters. The red scrunchies were more than just evidence; they were keys that unlocked deeper layers of Eleanor's fractured personality, revealing a complex interplay between trauma, memory, and the devastating consequences of prolonged abuse. They served as a disturbing, yet crucial link between the outwardly idyllic life of the Vance family and the horrifying reality hidden beneath the surface.

The diary entries detailing the disposal of the scrunchies were equally unsettling. Evelyn's obsessive need for control extended even to the smallest details, her meticulous efforts to erase any trace of Lily's crime a chilling reflection of her own fractured psyche. The act of meticulously destroying these objects, loaded with such heavy symbolism, was not just about covering the tracks, it was also a desperate attempt to obliterate the traumatic memories associated with them.

The destruction of the scrunchies wasn't complete, however. Advanced forensic techniques had managed to recover traces of DNA and fibers from the crime scene. These remnants, linked to Eleanor through the diary entries, provided crucial evidence, filling in the gaps between the fragmented memories of the different alters. The recovered fragments of the scrunchies became tangible links between the seemingly disparate events, weaving a cohesive narrative that tied together the various personalities and their roles in the crime.

Davies realized the investigation was no longer simply about finding a killer; it was about unraveling the complex tapestry of Eleanor Vance's fractured mind. The red scrunchies served as threads, tying together the different strands of trauma, abuse, and ultimately, violence. They were more than mere objects; they were symbolic representations of Eleanor's tormented past, and their presence, both at the crime scene and within the details of Evelyn's meticulously crafted diary, was a chilling testament to the enduring power of trauma. The significance of the red scrunchies transcended their physical form; they were symbols, triggers, and ultimately, a crucial part of the puzzle that needed to be solved. They were a window into the mind of a fractured woman, a testament to the devastating consequences of years of abuse and the chilling lengths to which the psyche will go to protect itself from the overwhelming weight of pain. The red scrunchies, simple objects in themselves, had become a horrifying and deeply symbolic key to unlocking Eleanor Vance's dark secrets, a secret that went far beyond the boundaries of a single, heinous crime. They were a chilling reminder that even seemingly insignificant details can hold profound meaning, especially when viewed through the lens of a fractured psyche and a past filled with unimaginable trauma. And as Davies continued to piece together the fragmented memories, he was beginning to realize that the truth was far more horrifying than he could have ever imagined. The red scrunchies were not just clues; they were the heart of the mystery, the central motif, a silent scream from the depths of a broken soul.

The flickering gaslight cast long shadows across the nursery walls, painting grotesque shapes on the floral wallpaper. Jane, barely seven years old, huddled beneath her patchwork quilt, the familiar scent of lavender and mothballs doing little to soothe the tremor in her small hands. The air hung heavy with an unfamiliar tension, a silence so profound it vibrated in her ears. She couldn't place the source of the unease, only the chilling certainty that something was terribly wrong.

Her memories of that night were fragmented, shards of a shattered mirror reflecting a distorted, terrifying reality. There was the muffled thumping, a sound that resonated deep within her bones, a rhythmic pulse that seemed to echo the frantic beating of her own heart. It was a sound she would later associate with the relentless pounding of her own blood in her ears, the primal drumbeat of terror that would haunt her dreams for years to come. Then, there was the smell – a cloying, acrid stench that burned her nostrils and coated her tongue with a metallic tang. It was a smell that would forever be etched in her memory, a phantom odor that would cling to her senses, a constant reminder of the horror she had witnessed.

Vague images flitted through her mind – fleeting glimpses of distorted figures, blurred faces contorted in expressions of unimaginable pain. There were flashes of red – a vibrant crimson that seemed to pulse and throb in the periphery of her vision. It was the color of blood, of course, but also the color of the scrunchies, those seemingly innocent hair ties that now held a terrifying significance in her adult life. She remembered a flash of black plastic, the smooth, chilling surface, and the chilling glint of something metallic. These were the fragments, the pieces of a puzzle she could never quite assemble.

The specific details remained elusive, hidden behind a wall of psychological protection erected by her fragmented psyche. Her mind, fractured and reeling from the trauma, had instinctively shielded her from the full impact of the horror. It was a defense mechanism, a survival tactic employed by her subconscious to protect her fragile young self from the overwhelming pain. Yet, even with this shielding, the trauma manifested in other ways, subtle yet debilitating.

Her sleep was troubled, plagued by nightmares that replayed the night's events in fragmented, terrifying sequences. She woke screaming, drenched in cold sweat, her small body wracked with sobs that she couldn't explain. The therapists would later diagnose her with PTSD, anxiety, and night terrors, all direct consequences of the unspeakable horrors she had unknowingly witnessed.

During her waking hours, Jane experienced an array of unsettling symptoms. She developed an obsessive need for order and routine, a desperate attempt to regain control in a world that had been violently overturned. Her room had to be meticulously organized, her toys arranged in precise rows, her clothes folded with military precision. It was a manifestation of her underlying OCD, a disorder born from her desperate need to impose structure and order on a life that had been irrevocably shattered.

Her concentration was also severely impaired, her attention easily distracted by the smallest stimuli. The smallest noise, the faintest movement, would derail her focus, plunging her into a maelstrom of anxiety and disorientation. This inattentiveness, diagnosed as ADHD, was yet another manifestation of the trauma, a lingering symptom of the shattered equilibrium of her young mind.

Her social interactions were also profoundly affected. She retreated into herself, becoming increasingly withdrawn and isolated. She found it difficult to connect with others, her trust irrevocably broken. This profound social awkwardness, later recognized as a symptom of autistic traits, further complicated her struggle to navigate the world around her. The world, once a place of wonder and discovery, had transformed into a hostile and unpredictable environment. The events of that night had irrevocably altered her perception of reality, distorting her sense of safety and security.

Years later, as she delved into her mother's diaries, Jane found snippets of information that illuminated those fragmented memories. Entries from Lily's perspective, though unsettling and disturbing, offered a disturbingly clear picture. Lily, the alter who had committed the murder, described the night with a chilling detachment, recounting the events with a clinical precision that underscored the fragmented nature of her consciousness.

Lily's narrative revealed a chilling account of the night, a dark and brutal ritual born from years of repressed rage and frustration. It painted a picture of Eleanor's fractured self, a psyche torn apart by years of abuse, each alter battling for control in a desperate struggle for survival. Through Lily's eyes, Jane saw the chilling reality of her mother's suffering, the dark secret that had been concealed behind the veneer of an idyllic family life.

The entries revealed Lily's memory of the red scrunchies, how their vibrant colors pulsed and throbbed in the dim light of the freezer room, their symbolic power intensifying the gruesome tableau of the murder. Lily recalled the specific textures, the subtle variations in stitching, the faint scent of lavender that clung to the fabric—details that resonated deeply with Jane's own fragmented memories.

The entries also revealed the chilling calculation behind Lily's actions, her precise selection of the scrunchies, their arrangement in the freezer, every detail meticulously planned and executed with a disturbing precision. This was not a random act of violence, but a ritualistic performance born from the deep-seated trauma that had shaped Eleanor's fractured psyche.

The diary entries described the methodical way Lily had arranged the victim, the placement of the body, the meticulous positioning of the scrunchies, all contributing to the chilling tableau. It was a disturbing display of control and precision, a testament to the complex interplay between trauma, memory, and violence.

Jane's fragmented memories began to coalesce, filling in the gaps left by her repressed trauma. The muffled thuds were the sounds of the victim being moved. The metallic tang was the scent of blood mixed with the harsh chemical odor of lye. The blurred faces were the faces of the victims – and perhaps also her mother's fragmented selves, caught in the whirlwind of a fractured mind. The red scrunchies, once a symbol of innocent childhood joy, were now a chilling reminder of the horrifying events that had irrevocably changed her life.

As she pieced together these fragments, Jane realized that the murder wasn't a singular event, but a culmination of years of abuse, trauma, and the desperate struggle of a fractured psyche to survive. It was a chilling testament to the power of trauma, the devastating consequences of prolonged abuse, and the desperate measures taken by a broken mind to protect itself from the overwhelming weight of pain.

The truth, slowly revealed through the fractured lens of her own memories and the chilling revelations of her mother's diary, was more horrifying than she could have ever imagined. It was a truth that would forever haunt her, a constant reminder of the darkness that lurked beneath the surface of her seemingly idyllic childhood. The red scrunchies, the gaslight shadows, the metallic tang of blood and lye – these images would remain imprinted in her mind, a permanent reminder of the night that irrevocably shattered her innocence and left her struggling to rebuild her life amidst the fragments of a broken past. The fragments of that night were more than just memories; they were the building blocks of her trauma, shaping her personality, her relationships, and her very perception of the world. The journey to healing would be long and arduous, but Jane was determined to confront her past, to understand the complex tapestry of her mother's fractured mind, and to finally find peace in the face of overwhelming trauma.

October 14th, 1988.

The air hung cold, a metallic tang clinging to the back of my throat. It wasn't the usual chill of the freezer; this was something else, something... acrid. It coated my tongue, a bitter aftertaste that mirrored the bitterness churning within me. He lay there, inert, his skin already taking on the ghostly pallor of the deep freeze. The black plastic crinkled softly under my touch as I adjusted his position, making sure he was perfectly centered. It was important, you see. The symmetry, the precise arrangement, it was all part of it. A ritual. A final, exquisite act of retribution.

I remember the red scrunchies. Bright against the stark white of the freezer, a violent splash of color against the muted tones of death. They weren't just random accessories; they were a statement. A defiant declaration of my presence, a bloody exclamation point at the end of a long, brutal sentence. They pulsed in the dim light, a feverish rhythm echoing the frantic beat of my own heart. Each knot, each loop, tied with meticulous precision, a testament to the control I exerted, even in this moment of utter chaos. The lavender scent, faint but persistent, clung to the fabric, a ghostly perfume of innocence masking the horror beneath.

The irony wasn't lost on me. Lavender, the scent of serenity, peace, a stark contrast to the violence I unleashed. He deserved this. He deserved every drop of this bitter retribution. Every meticulous detail was a deliberate affront to his memory, a mocking reminder of the power I now possessed. I wasn't just killing him; I was erasing him, obliterating him from existence. It was a cleansing ritual, a purging of the years of pain, betrayal, and unspeakable abuse.

October 15th, 1988.

They'll never find him. They'll never suspect me. Eleanor, the ever-compliant wife, the doting mother. Who would ever suspect her? The carefully constructed facade holds firm, a fortress against the world's scrutiny. But behind the mask, the storm rages on. They see only the calm surface, the serene façade, but beneath, the tempest boils, fueled by years of unspoken rage and suppressed pain. They'll only see the victim's absence, a missing person case, eventually becoming just another cold statistic in the archives of unsolved disappearances.

The lye was a necessity, a detail meticulously considered. Efficiency, you see. It wasn't just about the killing; it was about the thoroughness, the utter annihilation of all traces. Leaving no evidence, no clues, no lingering scent of death. This was not just about revenge. It was a symphony of destruction, a perfectly orchestrated crescendo of anger and pain.

November 1st, 1988.

The guilt, they say, will consume me. But it doesn't. Not yet, at least. There's a strange peace in it, a sense of liberation, of finally taking control. The years of being silenced, controlled, manipulated... they've ended. In this moment, I'm in control. I am the architect of my own destiny, the puppeteer of my fate. I am the storm, and I've finally broken free.

There are others, of course. The others who inhabit this body, this vessel of pain. They whisper, they protest, they cower in the shadows of my dominance. But I am the strongest, the most resolute. They will learn to yield, to bow to my will. I am the architect of their silence, the master of their fear.

December 20th, 1988.

Sleep evades me. The fractured images flash before my eyes— his face, contorted in terror, the cold gleam of the metal, the sickening thud as he hit the floor. The red, the overwhelming crimson of the scrunchies, a disturbing contrast to the stark white of the freezer, the relentless pulse of my own heartbeat, each thud echoing the violence I unleashed. Even now, the memory haunts me with a disturbing clarity.

But it was necessary. Every agonizing moment, every detail meticulously planned, every emotion meticulously controlled, every act of violence justified by years of suffering, abuse, and silent screams. It was a rebellion against a lifetime of injustice.

January 10th, 1989.

Eleanor, the facade I wear to the world, feels the tremors, the aftershocks of my actions. She's becoming increasingly withdrawn, increasingly unstable. The other alters are reacting, too. Their fear fuels my strength. Their vulnerability reinforces my dominance. They will never take this from me. Never.

The world believes I'm a victim, a fragile flower clinging to life. The irony of that is not lost on me. But they will never know the truth, the monstrous truth that lurks beneath the surface. I am not a victim. I am the executioner. I am the victor.

February 14th, 1989.

There are moments of lucidity, fleeting glimpses of the person I once was. A girl, filled with dreams and hopes, before the darkness claimed me, before the abuse stole my innocence. These moments are brief, fleeting reminders of a life that was lost, a self that was shattered. They are painful, agonizing reminders of what was taken from me. The stolen innocence echoes like a scream in the void, haunting me with the cruel irony of it all.

Yet, even in these moments of clarity, I feel no remorse. Only a cold, hard satisfaction. It was his fault. He deserved what he got.

March 5th, 1989.

The others are growing stronger. They fight for control, their voices rising to a cacophony of fear and anxiety. They claw at the surface, struggling to break through the wall I've erected. I feel myself weakening. The control, once absolute, is slipping. They're trying to take my place; to erase me; to rewrite the narrative. But I won't let them. I will fight to the very end. I will cling to this victory, this triumph over the darkness that has defined my existence.

This will not be undone.

April 12th, 1989.

The voices are louder now. They overwhelm me, pulling at the edges of my consciousness, threatening to unravel me, to expose me. The cold comfort of control is fading. Fear is creeping in. I am losing my grip. The darkness is consuming me. I'm fading, retreating into the shadows, and the others are rising to claim this body, this tormented vessel. They will be found out.

This is my confession. This is my legacy. My blood-soaked masterpiece. The act of ultimate retribution. And as the darkness swallows me whole, I welcome it. For in the end, all that remains is the silence, the stillness, and the chilling echo of the scrunchies' crimson glow.

The chipped paint on the antique writing desk seemed to mirror the cracks in Sarah's composure. Across from her, Robert sat rigidly, his usual affable demeanor replaced by a tense stillness. The air in the study crackled with unspoken accusations, a silent battle waged between a daughter seeking truth and a father shrouded in denial. A half-empty glass of amber liquid sat untouched on the coaster beside his hand, a testament to the uncomfortable silence stretching between them.

"You knew," Sarah stated, her voice barely a whisper, yet carrying the weight of twenty-five years of unspoken questions. The words hung in the air, heavy with accusation, as thick and suffocating as the dust motes dancing in the afternoon sunbeams slanting through the window. Her gaze, sharp and unwavering, pierced the carefully constructed mask of composure Robert wore.

He didn't answer immediately, his eyes darting away, avoiding the intensity of her stare. His hand, calloused and strong from years of work, trembled slightly as he reached for his glass, then hesitated, his fingers lingering on the rim before he retracted them. The silence stretched, a taut, agonizing thread threatening to snap.

"Sarah," he finally began, his voice a low rumble that lacked its usual warmth, "this is... difficult." He avoided her eyes, his gaze settling on the intricate carving of the desk, a nervous tic betraying his inner turmoil. "Your mother... she was... complicated."

"Complicated?" Sarah's voice rose, a sharp edge cutting through his carefully chosen words. "Or abused? Tortured? Destroyed?" Each word was a blow, landing with the force of a hammer against the fragile edifice of Robert's composure. She stood up, the chair scraping against the polished floorboards, the sound jarring in the charged silence. She paced, her agitation fueling the fire within her. "The diary... it wasn't just ramblings of a crazy woman, Robert. It was a chronicle of pain, of systematic abuse. And you were there. You were part of it."

Robert flinched at the accusation, his carefully constructed facade beginning to crumble. He cleared his throat, the sound harsh and brittle. "Eleanor... she had... issues. Mental health problems. We sought help, you know." His defense sounded weak, unconvincing, even to his own ears. The words were devoid of genuine emotion, a pale imitation of remorse.

Sarah stopped pacing, her back to him, her shoulders shaking with suppressed rage. The diary's entries detailing the meticulously planned rituals, the calculated cruelty, the chilling descriptions of abuse, played on a continuous loop in her mind. She thought about the cold, hard reality behind the pretty pictures in her memory. She thought about how Eleanor's life was never the idyllic image that she now knew was a careful, constructed deception.

"Help?" she scoffed, her voice laced with bitter irony. "You called a psychologist, maybe? Or a priest? Maybe even the police?" Sarah turned, her face contorted with fury, her eyes burning with unshed tears. "Or did you simply turn a blind eye, Robert? Did you watch as she was torn apart, piece by piece, and do nothing?"

He remained silent, his face ashen, his gaze fixed on the floor. The silence was heavy, punctuated only by Sarah's ragged breaths. The years of unanswered questions, the lingering suspicions, the gnawing doubt, now culminated in this explosive confrontation.

She moved closer, her voice dropping to a near whisper. "The scrunchies, Robert. The red scrunchies. She described them in detail. They were your favorite color. The ones she used to tie your hair back when we were kids." Each word was a carefully placed stone, building a wall of irrefutable evidence around him.

He flinched again, his silence a damning confession. The carefully constructed defense crumbled, the facade shattering into a thousand pieces. He finally looked up, his eyes filled with a mixture of fear and guilt, and in those eyes, Sarah saw the truth. The truth she'd been searching for, hidden behind years of lies and carefully crafted deception.

He opened his mouth to speak, but the words caught in his throat. His hands shook uncontrollably, and his face paled further, his breaths shallow and quick. The weight of years of suppressed guilt, of buried secrets, pressed down on him.

"It wasn't... intentional," he stammered, his voice barely above a whisper. "I... I didn't understand." The excuse sounded pathetic, a desperate attempt to justify the unjustifiable. His words were devoid of remorse, devoid of genuine contrition, but in his eyes, Sarah saw something else—a flicker of something that looked a little bit like fear.

"Didn't understand?" Sarah's voice was low, chilling in its calm intensity. "Or didn't want to?" She stepped closer, her presence looming over him, her gaze unrelenting. She moved in on him, until their faces were only inches apart. The air was thick with tension, the unspoken questions hanging heavy in the space between them.

"You let it happen," she whispered, her voice barely audible. "You knew, and you let it happen." The statement hung in the air, a final, devastating blow. The truth, stark and brutal, hung heavy between them, a tangible thing. The silence stretched, a hollow void echoing with the reverberations of unspoken accusations, and years of carefully concealed secrets finally tumbled into the open.

His silence confirmed everything. The lies that he'd told, the secrets he'd kept, all the things he'd done to protect his carefully-crafted image of perfect family life. His silence was a confession in itself.

Sarah backed away slowly, a strange sense of calm settling over her despite the emotional turmoil. The anger was still there, burning fiercely, but it was different now, calmer, more focused. It was no longer a blind rage, but a controlled burn. She felt stronger, surer of herself. The puzzle pieces were slowly coming together, forming a coherent, chilling picture that implicated him as deeply as he'd implied. The years of searching, the endless questions, had finally led her to this moment.

She looked around the study, the room that had always held a sense of warmth, of happy memories, and it now felt different. Strange. The comfortable furnishings seemed to have a hard edge, the once warm light felt sterile and cold. She no longer saw a safe haven, but the stage for a silent drama filled with cruelty, manipulation, and deceit.

As she left the study, leaving Robert sitting alone, struggling to reconcile with the unraveling of his carefully constructed reality, Sarah felt a profound sense of sorrow. Sorrow for her mother, for the stolen innocence, for the years of untold suffering. But she also felt a surge of determination. The truth was out, at least for her. The journey for justice had only just begun. The confrontation was only the first step in a long, winding path towards healing and retribution. The fight had just begun. And she was ready. The unraveling of the truth had just begun.

# CHAPTER 6: THE UNSEEN HAND

The weight of Robert's confession hung heavy in the air, a suffocating blanket stifling the lingering warmth of the study. Sarah left him there, a broken man wrestling with the ghosts of his past, and stepped out into the crisp autumn air. The sunlight, once warm and inviting, felt harsh and unforgiving against her skin, mirroring the stark reality of her mother's life and death. The diary, clutched tightly in her hand, felt heavier than ever, its pages filled with Eleanor's fragmented experiences – a testament to a life stolen, a psyche shattered.

Her thoughts drifted back to the diary's mention of Dr. Albright, Eleanor's therapist. The entries weren't kind. They painted a picture of a well-meaning but ultimately ineffective therapist, a man who seemed more interested in maintaining the illusion of Eleanor's stability than in truly understanding the depths of her fractured psyche. Sarah remembered the clipped, professional entries where Eleanor had documented her sessions. They were filled with a chilling detachment, a lack of genuine empathy that felt almost sinister in hindsight.

Dr. Albright's notes, which Robert had reluctantly produced, were equally unsettling. They were precise, clinical, focusing on the surface-level manifestations of Eleanor's disorder – the switches, the amnesia, the behavioral quirks. But there was a conspicuous absence of any deep exploration of the root causes. He'd noted the dissociative episodes, cataloged the distinct personalities, but had seemingly failed to delve into the trauma that fueled them. There was no mention of Eleanor's childhood, no exploration of the potential abuse, no attempt to uncover the origins of her fragmented self. His focus was on symptom management, on controlling the outward manifestations of the disorder, rather than addressing the underlying wounds. He'd treated the symptoms, not the disease. His therapeutic approach, Sarah now realized, had been akin to applying a bandage to a gaping wound.

One entry, in particular, haunted Sarah. Eleanor had described a session where she'd revealed a fleeting memory of a terrifying childhood event, a glimpse of a shadowy figure and a searing pain. Dr. Albright, according to Eleanor, had dismissed it as a "fragmentary hallucination," a product of her illness, rather than a potential clue to a traumatic past. He seemed to prioritize the neatness of his diagnostic categories over the messy reality of Eleanor's lived experience.

This wasn't just a case of professional negligence, Sarah thought, it was a profound failure to understand the complexities of Dissociative Identity Disorder (DID). Dr. Albright's approach, she realized, was a relic of an outdated understanding of the disorder, an approach that focused on suppressing the alters rather than integrating them, a methodology that inadvertently perpetuated the trauma it sought to alleviate. The therapist's failure, Sarah suspected, had inadvertently amplified the destructive potential within Eleanor's fragmented psyche. He hadn't healed the wounds; he'd left them to fester, resulting in a far more complex, dangerous internal conflict.

The more Sarah delved into the diary and the therapist's notes, the more she understood the intricate interplay of Eleanor's various personalities. Each alter, she realized, was a coping mechanism, a fragmented part of Eleanor's self formed as a desperate attempt to shield herself from overwhelming trauma. They were not just different identities, they were manifestations of a shattered psyche, each carrying the burden of a specific trauma, each responsible for managing different aspects of Eleanor's survival.

The "sweet" Eleanor, the one she had known as a child, had been a protective facade, shielding the world from the deeper, darker aspects of her psyche. The others were more sinister, darker fragments, born out of years of horrific abuse, their emergence a testament to Eleanor's resilience, her desperate attempt to create different selves to survive the horrors she was forced to endure. This realization caused a wave of profound grief to wash over Sarah.

Dr. Albright's supposed expertise hadn't provided the safe space for these fragmented selves to emerge and eventually integrate. Instead, his methods might have aggravated the internal conflict, creating a pressure cooker environment that intensified the violent tendencies of the more aggressive alters. He'd failed to recognize that these weren't simply "identities" to be managed; they were manifestations of deeply rooted trauma, each carrying a unique burden of pain and fear. His approach had been far too superficial, failing to address the core issues driving Eleanor's disorder.

The diary entries revealed glimpses of the brutal violence

Eleanor had suffered, the chilling details buried beneath layers of carefully constructed lies and societal expectations. It wasn't just physical abuse; it was a tapestry of psychological torment, a sustained campaign of manipulation and control. The diary showed evidence of her PTSD, her OCD, the ADHD that had gone untreated, and what appeared to be an undiagnosed autism spectrum disorder. All these conditions had contributed to the development and maintenance of DID, creating a perfect storm of trauma and psychological dysfunction.

The absence of appropriate therapeutic intervention allowed the trauma to fester, leaving Eleanor's alters to battle for control in an increasingly volatile internal landscape. The diary showed an escalating conflict, a fierce struggle between the various parts of her fragmented self, each desperate for dominance and release. The violent alter, the one responsible for the murder, had ultimately emerged as a final, catastrophic expression of pent-up rage and despair.

Sarah realized that Dr. Albright's failure wasn't simply a matter of professional incompetence; it was a reflection of the systemic limitations in the treatment of complex trauma and dissociative disorders. The limitations of therapy, the lack of understanding, the reliance on outdated and often harmful methodologies—all of these factors had contributed to the tragic outcome. It wasn't just Eleanor who had been victimized; her fractured self had been betrayed by the very system designed to help her.

She shuddered, a fresh wave of anger and grief washing over her. The picture of Dr. Albright, a man who held the keys to unlocking her mother's tortured mind and instead locked the door tighter, burned itself onto her mind. His failure wasn't just a professional lapse; it was a criminal negligence, a contribution to the tragedy that had defined her family's life for the past twenty-five years.

Sarah closed the diary, its weight seeming to increase tenfold. The journey for justice, she knew, was far from over. She would not only seek retribution for her mother's murder; she would expose the systemic failures that had allowed such a tragedy to occur, the failures that had silenced Eleanor's screams for help, and the failures that had left a young girl to grapple with the horrifying truth of her mother's fragmented past. The fight was far from over; it was only just beginning. Her journey would be about Eleanor's truth, her family's healing, and, most importantly, it would serve as a testament to the need for a more compassionate, effective approach to the treatment of complex trauma and dissociative disorders. She would fight for Eleanor's memory, for the victims like her mother, and for the future. The unraveling of the truth had revealed a much larger, more sinister picture than she could have ever imagined. And she was ready.

The diary entries, initially fragmented and difficult to decipher, began to coalesce into a horrifyingly clear pattern. It wasn't just a single instance of abuse; it was a relentless, cyclical torment that had shaped Eleanor's entire life. The earliest entries, scrawled in a childlike hand, spoke of a seemingly idyllic childhood, punctuated by moments of inexplicable fear and confusion. These were interspersed with drawings of a shadowy figure, a recurring motif that would later become central to her fragmented memories.

The pattern, Sarah realized, began with seemingly minor acts of control. A misplaced toy, a harsh word, a sudden withdrawal of affection. These seemingly insignificant incidents, documented with chilling accuracy in the diary entries, were the first cracks in Eleanor's sense of security, the subtle beginnings of a systematic erosion of her self-worth. These early instances of manipulation were subtle, masked by seemingly normal family dynamics, leaving young Eleanor confused and unsure of her own perceptions. The diary entries chronicled the slow, insidious creep of fear, the gradual realization that her safety was not guaranteed, that her environment was unpredictable and potentially dangerous.

As Eleanor grew older, the abuse escalated. The subtle manipulations morphed into overt acts of physical and emotional violence. The diary entries described beatings, the searing pain detailed in stark, clinical language, almost as if she were observing the events from a detached, external perspective. These entries were intermingled with accounts of emotional manipulation, the systematic dismantling of her self-esteem through constant criticism and belittling. Sarah was struck by the meticulous detail, the almost clinical precision with which Eleanor had recorded the abuse – a testament to the dissociative mechanisms she employed to survive.

The diary revealed a carefully constructed cycle of abuse, a pattern of escalating violence interspersed with periods of seeming normalcy, or what Eleanor referred to as "the calm before the storm." These periods of calm were deceptive, creating a false sense of security that only served to amplify the shock and trauma of the subsequent episodes of violence. The cycle reinforced Eleanor's learned helplessness, her belief that the abuse was inescapable, her inability to predict or control the violence she experienced.

The entries depicted the various alters as forming in response to different stages of this abuse cycle. The "sweet Eleanor," the persona Sarah had known, emerged as a protective shield during the periods of relative calm. This alter represented Eleanor's desperate attempt to maintain a sense of normalcy, to present a facade of stability to the outside world.

However, other alters, more aggressive and volatile, emerged during periods of intense abuse. These alters were formed as coping mechanisms, allowing Eleanor to detach from the overwhelming pain and trauma she endured. One alter, described in chilling detail, served as the ultimate protector, a warrior persona ready to retaliate, a desperate act of self-preservation. This was the alter, Sarah knew, responsible for the gruesome murder.

The diary entries revealed a disturbing pattern of sexual abuse, interwoven with the physical and emotional violence. This abuse added another layer of complexity to the pattern, further contributing to the fragmentation of Eleanor's psyche. These entries were particularly difficult to read, their words stark and emotionally raw, yet strangely detached, revealing the emotional distance Eleanor maintained to survive her traumatic experiences.

The abuse wasn't confined to a single perpetrator. The diary entries suggested a pattern of abuse involving multiple individuals, each contributing to the overall cycle of violence and trauma. This compounded the effects of the abuse, creating a complex and ever-shifting landscape of fear and uncertainty.

This repeated cycle of abuse, Sarah realized, had permanently altered Eleanor's perception of reality, blurring the lines between safety and danger, love and hate. It had instilled in her a deep-seated sense of fear and mistrust, a profound sense of helplessness and worthlessness that permeated every aspect of her life. The diary entries illustrated how this pattern not only led to the development of DID but also fuelled the escalating internal conflict between her alters, culminating in the tragic events that led to the murder.

As Sarah continued reading, she unearthed the chilling evidence of Eleanor's struggle to escape the cyclical abuse. There were instances where she had tried to seek help, reaching out to family members, friends, and professionals. But these attempts were met with disbelief, dismissal, or, even worse, further abuse and manipulation. The diary entries detailed the devastating impact of this rejection, the sense of isolation and betrayal that reinforced her feelings of helplessness.

Sarah's understanding of her mother's life transformed into a stark realization of the cyclical nature of trauma. The abuse was not a singular event, but a pattern ingrained in her psyche, echoing through generations and impacting the lives of others in her family. She began to see the ripple effect of the trauma, the lasting impact on her own life and that of her siblings, even if they were unaware of the full extent of Eleanor's suffering.

The diary served as a chilling testament to the long-term effects of abuse, the ways in which trauma can shape a person's identity, and the devastating consequences of untreated mental illness. It was a story of resilience, of survival in the face of unimaginable horror, but also a story of failure – the failure of those who should have protected Eleanor, the failure of a system that was ill-equipped to address the complexity of her trauma, and the ultimate failure of a therapeutic approach that prioritized control over healing.

The more Sarah delved into the diary, the more she understood the intricacies of Eleanor's internal world, the intricate web of personalities forged in the crucible of unrelenting abuse. Each alter, she discovered, possessed unique memories, skills, and fears, all connected to specific moments and individuals in Eleanor's traumatic past.

The diary entries weren't just chronological accounts; they were a mosaic of Eleanor's fragmented self, a chilling portrait of a woman broken but not defeated. The rhythmic repetition of abuse, the cyclical pattern of violence interspersed with moments of false calm, had created a complex psychological landscape that defied easy categorization. It was a testament to the resilience of the human spirit, its capacity for survival, and the devastating consequences of untreated trauma.

The weight of this knowledge, the realization of the immense suffering her mother had endured, threatened to crush Sarah. But amidst the horror and despair, a flicker of resolve began to ignite within her. She would not only expose the perpetrator of the murder; she would fight for recognition of the pervasive pattern of abuse that had shaped her mother's life, a pattern that had tragically been repeated throughout Eleanor's life and continues to echo through families globally. She would fight to ensure that no other woman would suffer the same fate, lost in the shadows of a silent system that failed to protect and treat victims effectively. This diary would become more than just a testament to her mother's trauma, it would become a weapon against the darkness. The fight for justice had become more than personal; it had become a crusade. The truth of the abuse, laid bare in the chilling pages of the diary, would become a catalyst for change.

Sarah traced the looping script of her mother's handwriting, a familiar yet alien language now imbued with a chilling significance. The diary entries had detailed years of unimaginable abuse, but a new section caught her attention, a shift in tone, a different handwriting style interwoven with Eleanor's familiar scrawl. It spoke of Lily.

Lily wasn't just a name; she was a presence that pulsed through the fragmented narratives, a shadowy figure lurking at the edges of Eleanor's memories, a connection that deepened the mystery surrounding the murder. The entries hinted at a complex relationship, not merely victim and perpetrator, but something far more intricate, a tangled web of shared trauma and unspoken resentment.

The first mention of Lily was subtle, a fleeting reference in an early entry written in the childish scrawl of a younger Eleanor. It was a single sentence, tucked away amidst drawings of shadowy figures and descriptions of unexplained fear: "Lily said the shadows would get me if I told." This seemingly innocuous sentence ignited a spark in Sarah's mind. It suggested a shared secret, a complicity born of fear, a bond forged in the crucible of abuse.

As Sarah delved deeper, the details about Lily emerged, piecing together a fragmented portrait of a girl caught in the same web of violence as Eleanor. The entries described Lily as a peer, a confidante, a fellow victim sharing similar experiences of abuse at the hands of the same perpetrators. Their experiences were eerily parallel, both enduring physical and emotional torment, systematic isolation, and the insidious manipulation that fractured their sense of self. However, the diary revealed a key difference: Lily was often seen as the one instigating the cruelty or joining in the aggression directed towards Eleanor. This was a particularly jarring element of their story; it revealed the complexities of child trauma and the confusing ways in which victims become perpetrators in a distorted and cyclical pattern.

The diary entries depicted a strange camaraderie between the two girls, a bond forged in shared trauma, a twisted loyalty born of mutual understanding. They were two children facing unimaginable cruelty, finding solace in each other, a perverse form of kinship born of suffering. They acted as each other's protectors, yet also acted as each other's abusers. There were incidents where Lily would seemingly shield Eleanor from the worst of the abuse, creating a momentary haven from the storm, only to turn on her later, mirroring the actions of the adults in their lives. This suggested a distorted sense of loyalty and the inability to differentiate between what constituted abuse and protection, adding another dimension to their deeply unhealthy codependency.

This complex interplay between protector and aggressor highlights the significant impact of early trauma and the ways in which it can create conflicting narratives within the mind. The shared suffering created a bond that extended beyond the confines of their mutual victimhood, even if the bond itself was built on unstable foundations.

As Eleanor grew older, the relationship with Lily became more fraught, their shared trauma morphing into a complex dance of resentment, jealousy, and a simmering rage. The diary entries revealed instances where Lily, mimicking the behavior of their abusers, actively participated in the systematic abuse of Eleanor, seemingly enjoying the power she held over her. This revealed the devastating way in which children who are abused are often not only victims but can be perpetrators of similar actions towards others who are vulnerable.

The entries described Lily's escalating cruelty, her subtle manipulations becoming increasingly overt acts of aggression. There were instances of physical violence, fueled by a deep-seated anger that seemed to feed on Eleanor's vulnerabilities, a dark mirroring of the adults who tormented them. Sarah felt a chill as she realised that this pattern, this mirroring of abuse, continued on through Eleanor's adult life and even into her own life in the present day.

The diary chronicled the slow unraveling of their once-shared bond, the transformation of their kinship into a bitter rivalry fueled by a deep-seated resentment. Lily, it seemed, had become another face of Eleanor's fractured self, a dark reflection of her own trauma, a manifestation of her internalized rage. This revelation provided a chilling new perspective on Eleanor's multiple personality disorder, revealing the complex interplay between her different alters, each a fragment of a shattered self.

The entries detailing the murder itself pointed to Lily's direct involvement, detailing the specific events with a gruesome precision. It wasn't a simple act of violence; it was a carefully orchestrated ritual, a symbolic act of revenge born out of years of shared suffering and betrayal. The black bags, the red scrunchies, the lye—each detail held a symbolic meaning, pointing towards the deeper motivations and the interconnected lives of the victim and Eleanor.

The victim, Sarah discovered, had a connection to Lily, a relationship that ran far deeper than simple acquaintance. This wasn't a random act of violence. It was a carefully calculated revenge that revealed a shared history, a complicated dynamic between victim and abuser, a cycle of pain that had escalated over years, reaching a terrifying culmination in the frozen chamber. The entries hinted at the victim's knowledge of the abuse, her potential role in the cycle of violence, adding another layer to the psychological complexity of the case.

Through fragmented memories and scattered narratives, Sarah pieced together a picture of the victim as someone who had either witnessed the abuse of both Eleanor and Lily or had themselves been involved in their torment. The victim represented another piece of the same puzzle, a missing link in the chain of trauma and retribution. This wasn't just about Eleanor's internal struggles; it was about a shared trauma, a collective experience of abuse that had reverberated through multiple lives, connecting the victim, Eleanor, and Lily in a disturbing and inescapable web of violence.

The details were sparse, but the implication was clear: the victim's presence in Lily's life, their shared experiences, and their relationship were the catalyst for the murder. This connection provided a chilling new perspective on the crime, elevating it beyond a simple act of violence to a complex and disturbing drama. The murder became a twisted culmination of years of abuse, a desperate act of self-preservation, and a brutal expression of the fractured psyche of a woman torn apart by her past. This meant that the case wasn't just a psychological thriller but a complex study of shared trauma and the enduring impact of abuse on multiple lives. The seemingly random act of violence now held a horrifying significance, revealing a network of interconnected lives warped and twisted by abuse.

The diary entries provided a chilling glimpse into the psyche of Lily, the alter responsible for the murder. She wasn't just a personality; she was a manifestation of the rage and resentment that Eleanor had carried for years, a culmination of the collective trauma she had endured. Sarah realized that understanding Lily was key to understanding the murder and the twisted dynamic at play. This wasn't merely a case of multiple personality disorder; it was a story of shared abuse, intertwined lives, and the terrifying consequences of untreated trauma. The deeper Sarah delved, the more she understood that the story extended beyond Eleanor's diary; it was a collective narrative, a testament to the destructive power of trauma and its enduring legacy.

The diary fell from Sarah's trembling hands, the crisp pages fluttering like fallen leaves in the autumn wind. The chilling details of Lily's involvement in the murder, the meticulously planned ritual, the symbolic significance of the black bags and red scrunchies – it all swirled in her mind, a vortex of horror and disbelief. She had always known her childhood was…different. The hushed whispers, the furtive glances, the unsettling atmosphere that permeated their home – it had left an indelible mark on her psyche, a constant undercurrent of unease that she had never fully understood. Now, the diary entries illuminated the darkness, revealing the brutal truth behind the facade of normalcy.

The fragmented memories started flooding back, not as clear images but as disjointed sensations: the acrid smell of lye, the metallic tang of blood, the chilling silence that followed the screams. She remembered the night of the murder, not the event itself, but the aftermath – the frantic whispers, the hushed phone calls, the police presence. The memory felt muted, distant, as if viewed through a hazy filter. But the emotions were raw, visceral, clawing their way to the surface. Fear, confusion, helplessness – a cocktail of emotions that had numbed her for years. Now, they returned with a vengeance, tearing at the carefully constructed walls she had built around her heart.

The diary entries revealed a cycle of abuse, a relentless pattern of violence that had scarred not only Eleanor but also Sarah, who was often present. The book was an echo of Sarah's childhood experiences - her eyes often witnessed the abuse, the constant tension and fear in the house, her small body tense and frozen in fear, as if instinctually anticipating the next outburst. The diary's detailed account of her mother's fractured psyche provided a context to these fragmented memories, confirming her suspicions and providing a horrifying explanation for the erratic behavior and the constant fear.

The revelation that Lily was directly responsible for the murder was a shock, but it also provided a sense of...clarity. It explained the lingering sense of dread that had haunted her for years, the uneasy feeling that something sinister lurked beneath the surface of her seemingly normal upbringing. It was not just a murder; it was a culmination of years of untreated trauma, a dark reflection of the twisted family dynamic and the pervasive darkness of the household. Lily had been a hidden presence, a silent specter in her childhood home, the alter that caused her the most fear.

The diary provided a glimpse into the extent of the abuse. The physical brutality was documented in chilling detail. But the psychological torture, the insidious manipulation, the constant degradation - that was what truly horrified Sarah. The entries painted a vivid picture of a young Eleanor and a young Lily trapped in a cage of violence, their developing minds warped and fractured by the relentless attacks. The entries spoke of constant vigilance, the fear of upsetting the unstable equilibrium of the household, the desperate attempts to avoid triggering the next eruption of rage.

And Sarah now realised her own role. She wasn't simply a witness; she was a participant in this twisted dynamic, a silent observer who absorbed the violence as if it were a part of her own being. The weight of her repressed memories pressed down on her, suffocating her with a grief she hadn't known she possessed. She felt the lingering effects of the toxic environment, the way it had stunted her emotional growth, the way it had shaped her perception of the world.

Sarah's own therapy sessions, which had started long before discovering the diary, took on a new, terrifying significance. The therapist's probing questions, designed to unearth buried traumas, now felt like a desperate race against time to understand and process the horrific truths contained within her mother's diary. She began to see the patterns, the echoes of her mother's fragmented psyche mirrored in her own behaviors, her own anxieties. The constant need for order, her obsessive-compulsive tendencies to control her environment, the sudden bursts of anger and frustration that seemingly erupted out of nowhere; all were pieces of the puzzle, fragments of her mother's trauma, somehow, transmitted down to her.

The doctor had mentioned PTSD, but Sarah always thought that was about war veterans, not little girls witnessing their mothers' abuse. Now, it all made sense. She'd experienced the symptoms for as long as she could remember: constant hypervigilance, emotional numbness, panic attacks that came out of nowhere, nightmares, vivid flashbacks that she dismissed as an overactive imagination, the inability to fully trust or bond with anyone. The psychiatrist spoke of the need to confront these traumas, to work through the pain and begin the healing process. But the sheer scale of it was overwhelming. How could she possibly process years of repressed memories, of witnessing violence, of feeling the chilling presence of Lily lurking in the shadows?

The emotional toll was immense. Sleep became a battlefield where nightmares battled with fragments of reality, leaving her exhausted and emotionally drained. The seemingly normal routine of her life – her job, her relationships – all felt fragile, like a house built on shifting sand. She had always felt a sense of disconnect, a feeling of being separate from the world, from others. Now she understood the roots of this disconnect – the years of trauma had created a chasm within her, a deep-seated wound that needed tending.

Yet, even amidst the despair, a flicker of hope ignited within her. The diary, despite its horrifying contents, provided a path to understanding, a way to confront the past and begin the healing process. It provided a framework for understanding her own emotional responses, for reconciling her memories, for breaking free from the cycle of violence that had spanned generations. The diary was a testament to her mother's suffering, but it was also a key to her own emancipation.

She found herself drawn back to the entries that detailed Eleanor's own attempts at therapy, her struggles to control her alters, and her desperate yearning for a normal life. She saw the painful attempts to create a safe space for herself and Sarah, the moments of genuine warmth and affection that pierced through the darkness, the heartbreaking evidence of a mother who desperately tried, even failingly, to protect her child. Seeing this glimpse of Eleanor's struggles made Sarah's own journey feel less isolating, less like a burden only she had to carry. They had both been victims, both in desperate need of solace and healing.

The discovery of the diary had brought her a tremendous burden of knowledge, but it also brought a measure of understanding that she never had. Understanding Eleanor's past had not absolved her actions, but it offered insight. And that insight, Sarah felt, was the key to breaking the cycle of trauma, the chance to build a life free from the shadows of her past.

The process of healing would be long and arduous. There would be setbacks, moments of doubt, times when the weight of her memories would threaten to crush her. But she had a therapist, support network, and now, knowledge. She wouldn't allow the past to dictate her future. She would learn from the horrors detailed in her mother's diary, use it to heal, and make sure no other child would suffer like she did. The diary was not just a record of tragedy, but a roadmap to resilience, a testament to the enduring strength of the human spirit, and the possibility of healing even from the deepest wounds. The journey ahead would be long, but Sarah was now armed with the understanding to navigate it. The unseen hand that had held her captive for so long was finally loosening its grip. The path to healing had begun.

The discovery of her mother's diary had unearthed a horrifying truth, but it also presented a daunting legal labyrinth. Sarah now faced the chilling realization that the murder, a crime that had haunted her family and the community for twenty-five years, was inextricably linked to her mother's multiple personality disorder (DID). The question was no longer simply "who committed the murder?" but rather, "how could the legal system possibly grapple with a crime seemingly committed by a fractured psyche?"

The initial police investigation, Sarah learned from old newspaper clippings and fragmented memories, had been frustratingly inconclusive. The crime scene, a meticulously staged tableau of horror—the victim encased in black plastic bags, surrounded by lye, the signature red scrunchies—suggested a methodical killer, someone with a particular ritualistic bent. But there were no witnesses, no discernible motive beyond the sheer brutality of the act, and no obvious suspect. The case went cold, filed away among the unsolved mysteries of the local police department, a haunting reminder of their investigative limitations.

Now, armed with the diary, Sarah possessed the key to unlocking the mystery. Lily, one of her mother's alters, emerged from the pages as the perpetrator. But proving this in a court of law presented insurmountable challenges. Could a fragmented personality be held criminally responsible for the actions of another alter? Could the legal system even comprehend the complexities of DID, let alone use it as a framework for prosecuting a murder?

The concept of criminal responsibility hinges on the principle of

*mens rea*, the guilty mind. It requires demonstrating that the accused possessed the intent to commit the crime. In Eleanor's case, the distinct personalities within her fragmented self posed a significant hurdle. Lily, the violent alter, was the perpetrator. However, could Eleanor's other personalities – the seemingly gentle, compliant personas Sarah had known – be held accountable? The legal framework struggled to reconcile the disparate identities within a single body.

Sarah consulted with several legal experts, each expressing a different perspective, reflecting the lack of consensus on how to handle such cases. Some argued that since Eleanor was the one physically present during the murder, she should be held responsible, regardless of the influence of her dissociative identities. Others suggested that Eleanor's DID should be considered a mitigating factor, potentially reducing her culpability. Yet another group suggested the possibility of applying the legal concept of "automatism" – arguing that Lily acted independently of Eleanor's conscious will, rendering Eleanor not criminally responsible.

The legal precedents for cases involving DID were scarce, and those that existed offered little clarity. The legal system, built on a foundation of clear-cut distinctions between right and wrong, struggled to accommodate the fluidity and ambiguity of a mind fractured by trauma. The lack of awareness and understanding of DID further complicated matters. Many judges and juries remained unfamiliar with the nuances of the disorder, making it challenging to present a credible case that accounted for the complexities of Eleanor's psychological state.

Beyond the question of criminal responsibility, the issue of competency to stand trial also arose. Could Eleanor, even if alive, have adequately understood the charges against her and participated meaningfully in her own defense? The fragmented nature of her psyche, the constant shifting of personalities, and the potential lack of insight into Lily's actions, raised serious doubts about her competency.

Moreover, the diary itself presented a unique legal challenge. As a personal account of Eleanor's internal struggles, the diary was both a damning piece of evidence and a delicate legal instrument. Could the diary's entries, written from the perspective of multiple alters, be admitted as reliable testimony? Would the court accept the diary's subjective interpretations as admissible evidence of the crime? Expert testimony from psychiatrists and psychologists specializing in DID would be crucial to establish the validity and reliability of the diary's contents. However, securing such testimony wouldn't be easy; getting a psychiatrist to confidently and convincingly declare a defendant to be innocent due to DID could be a risky gamble for a professional's career.

The legal battle Sarah envisioned would not only be a fight for justice but also a fight for recognition. It would be a struggle to convince a skeptical legal system of the reality of DID and the profound impact it could have on an individual's behavior and culpability. It would necessitate breaking down preconceived notions and widespread misunderstandings surrounding this complex psychological disorder. Sarah knew this wouldn't be a simple case of proving a straightforward crime; it was about forcing a legal system to acknowledge a whole new, and terrifying, spectrum of criminal responsibility.

The implications reached beyond the immediate legal case. Sarah worried about the potential impact on her own life. Would she be targeted as a potential witness, or even somehow an accomplice, based on her childhood proximity to her mother's actions? The diary's revelations could easily lead to scrutiny of her own behaviors and mental health. The very act of trying to bring justice to her mother's crime, based on evidence sourced from her mother's own confession, brought its own set of emotional and legal consequences to bear on Sarah. Could she withstand the scrutiny? Could she manage the emotional burden of reliving her traumatic childhood while navigating a complex legal battle? Her therapist warned her about the possibility of retraumatization, the risk of inadvertently stirring up painful memories that could further destabilize her fragile emotional state.

The case wouldn't be just about prosecuting a murderer; it would be about challenging the very limits of the legal system's capacity to comprehend and respond to the complexities of mental illness. It was about pushing for a more nuanced understanding of criminal responsibility, an understanding that recognized the profound impact of trauma and the ways in which it could manifest itself in the most unexpected and disturbing forms. The case demanded a profound re-evaluation of how society dealt with mental illness, particularly within the context of criminal justice. Would the legal system ultimately accept the harrowing reality contained within her mother's diary? Only time would tell.

Sarah's quest for justice was not simply about achieving closure for a twenty-five-year-old murder. It became a battle for reform, a fight to ensure that future victims of similar circumstances would find a more compassionate and understanding justice system, one that acknowledged the complex interplay between mental health and criminal behavior. It was a challenge to a system not ready for the complexities of a mind fragmented by decades of trauma, and one that Sarah, armed with her mother's tragic diary, would have to face head-on. The legal ramifications were only the beginning of the arduous journey she had unexpectedly embarked upon, a journey that would test her resilience and challenge her understanding of justice itself. The unseen hand that had shaped her life, the shadow of her mother's fractured psyche, extended now into the legal arena, demanding a reckoning.

# CHAPTER 7: CONFRONTING THE PAST

The diary entries, painstakingly deciphered by Sarah, painted a horrifying picture of Eleanor's childhood. It wasn't a single, catastrophic event, but a relentless barrage of abuse that chipped away at her developing psyche, leaving behind a fractured landscape of personalities, each a desperate attempt to cope with the unbearable pain. The entries weren't chronological; they jumped between different alters, different timelines, each voice adding another layer to the terrifying mosaic of Eleanor's life. One entry, written from the perspective of "Lily," the alter who had committed the murder, revealed a chillingly matter-of-fact account of the night of the crime, a detached narrative that belied the horrific act itself. But interspersed with Lily's cold descriptions were fragmented memories from Eleanor's younger selves, glimpses of a small child cowering in fear, a young girl enduring unspeakable violations, a teenager desperately trying to piece together a shattered self.

One entry, scrawled in a childlike hand, depicted a recurring nightmare: a shadowy figure looming over her crib, the suffocating weight of a hand silencing her cries. Another entry, written in a more mature hand, spoke of the constant dread of anticipating the next act of violence, the hypervigilance that became a defining characteristic of her existence. These weren't just isolated incidents; they were woven into the very fabric of her being, shaping her perceptions, her relationships, and ultimately, her actions. The repeated descriptions of a cold, dark room – a recurring motif throughout the diary – revealed the enduring psychological impact of confinement and helplessness, a recurring theme mirroring the chilling finality of the murder scene.

The abuse wasn't confined to physical violence. Emotional manipulation and psychological torment were equally pervasive, leaving deep scars on Eleanor's developing sense of self. The diary revealed a pattern of gaslighting, where Eleanor's perceptions of reality were consistently distorted, leaving her questioning her own sanity and memory. The entries spoke of a constant feeling of being wrong, of never being good enough, of being perpetually punished for perceived failures, even the most insignificant ones. This relentless emotional abuse fostered a profound sense of self-loathing and worthlessness, laying the groundwork for the development of her dissociative identities. Each alter represented a different coping mechanism, a fragment of her psyche that sought to protect her from the overwhelming trauma. Some were childlike and vulnerable, others were aggressive and defiant, and still others were withdrawn and emotionally detached.

The diary entries offered glimpses into the formation of each alter. "Clara," for instance, emerged as a protector, a stoic figure shielding Eleanor from the pain of the abuse. "Grace," on the other hand, was a playful, carefree child, a desperate attempt to recapture the innocence lost in the face of brutal reality. But "Lily," the murderer, emerged as a manifestation of the accumulated rage and resentment, a persona born out of years of suppressed anger and despair. Her meticulous planning of the murder, as detailed in the diary, hinted at an obsessive-compulsive component, a need for control in a life where she had felt utterly powerless. The careful staging of the crime scene, the selection of the black plastic bags, the red scrunchies, and the use of lye – all meticulously documented in the diary – painted a picture of ritualistic behavior, suggesting a deeper psychological disturbance beyond the simple act of murder.

The diary entries suggested that the trauma had deeply impacted Eleanor's cognitive functions. There were instances where Eleanor's writing shifted, hinting at difficulties with concentration, memory lapses, and disorganization – symptoms consistent with ADHD and even potentially related to autistic traits. These cognitive difficulties, exacerbated by the trauma, made it even more challenging for Eleanor to navigate her daily life and manage the constant conflict between her alters. It was as if her mind was a battlefield, with each personality vying for dominance, creating a chaotic and unpredictable existence. This internal turmoil was vividly portrayed in the diary, with shifting narrative voices, sudden changes in tone, and jarring transitions between memories and fantasies.

The diary also revealed the development of PTSD (Post-Traumatic Stress Disorder) and OCD (Obsessive-Compulsive Disorder) as coping mechanisms to manage the trauma. Recurring nightmares, flashbacks, and intense anxiety were frequent themes in the entries. The obsessive-compulsive tendencies, as evidenced in Lily's meticulously planned murder, appeared as a desperate attempt to regain a sense of control in a life characterized by chaos and unpredictability. The meticulously detailed descriptions of the murder itself and the steps taken to ensure its success were a testament to this desperate need for order and control, a stark contrast to the chaos that reigned within her mind.

Sarah found herself confronted not just with the legal implications of her mother's crime, but with the devastating reality of the long-term effects of childhood trauma. The diary's revelations served as a stark reminder that Eleanor's actions, horrific as they were, were not merely the result of a "bad choice" or a sudden fit of rage. They were the culmination of years of abuse, neglect, and the desperate struggle of a fragmented mind trying to survive. The diary showed that the trauma had shaped not only Eleanor's personality but also her perception of reality, her relationships, and her ability to function in the world. The fragmentation wasn't just a psychological disorder; it was a survival mechanism, a desperate attempt to protect herself from unbearable pain. The meticulous detail given to each alter's experiences and the shifts in writing style demonstrated a complexity that went beyond simple dissociative symptoms; it illustrated a profound and pervasive impact on Eleanor's mind and body.

The consistent depiction of physical and emotional abuse throughout the diary, not just isolated incidents but a continuous pattern, emphasized the unrelenting nature of the trauma Eleanor faced. This constant state of fear and uncertainty created a sense of instability that permeated every aspect of her life. The diary suggested that Eleanor's ability to form healthy relationships was severely hampered by her trauma. Trust was a foreign concept, and intimacy was fraught with danger. Her relationships were marked by fear, suspicion, and a deep-seated inability to connect with others on an emotional level. This pattern of unhealthy relationships further exacerbated her already fragile mental state.

Beyond the descriptions of the abuse, the diary revealed the profound impact of Eleanor's experiences on her sense of self. She struggled with a fragmented identity, never quite knowing who she was or where she ended and her alters began. The diary entries highlighted a profound sense of alienation and isolation, reflecting Eleanor's inability to establish a stable and coherent sense of self. This identity crisis was compounded by the constant shifting of personalities, making it incredibly difficult to establish a sense of continuity and normalcy. This sense of being lost, of lacking a solid core self, fueled the fragmentation and created a cyclical pattern of trauma, instability, and further dissociation.

The entries also hinted at the shame and self-blame that often accompany trauma. Eleanor's struggle to reconcile her different personalities, the internal conflict and self-loathing vividly described in the diary, pointed towards the profound impact of self-criticism and the difficulties she had in processing her experiences. This internal struggle was not just a battle between different personalities, but also a battle within Eleanor herself, an internal conflict between a desire to accept her fragmented self and a deep-seated shame and self-rejection. The diary was a testament to this internal struggle and a poignant portrayal of the challenges faced by individuals living with DID.

Sarah realized that understanding her mother's story was not simply about piecing together the events that led to the murder. It was about unraveling the complex interplay of trauma, personality, and the legal system's struggle to grasp the intricacies of a mind fractured beyond comprehension. The diary was more than just a confession; it was a chilling and intimate portrayal of the long-term effects of childhood trauma, a testament to the resilience of the human spirit and the devastating consequences of unchecked abuse. The case, Sarah now understood, was far greater than a single murder; it was a profound exploration of the lasting scars left by trauma and the urgent need for a legal system capable of understanding and addressing the complexities of mental illness. The legal battle ahead would be a monumental task, but Sarah felt a renewed sense of purpose—to fight not just for justice for the victim, but for understanding and recognition for all those whose lives had been shattered by the invisible wounds of childhood trauma.

The diary entries, while fragmented and disjointed, offered a window into the intricate workings of Eleanor's dissociative identity disorder (DID), a condition far more nuanced and complex than the popularized portrayals often depicted in media. It wasn't simply a case of "switching" between personalities; it was a constant, chaotic negotiation between fragments of a shattered self, each struggling for dominance, each reacting to triggers and anxieties in unique and unpredictable ways. Sarah found herself delving into a world where memory was unreliable, identity fluid, and the line between reality and hallucination blurred.

One particularly poignant entry, written from the perspective of "Clara," Eleanor's protector alter, described the meticulous rituals Clara employed to manage her overwhelming anxiety. Clara's entries detailed obsessive-compulsive behaviors – meticulously arranging objects, counting repetitions of certain actions, and engaging in repetitive self-soothing activities. These actions, far from being mere quirks, were survival mechanisms, desperate attempts to create order and predictability in a world that felt utterly chaotic and unsafe. Clara's detailed descriptions of her rituals painted a vivid picture of the constant internal struggle to maintain a semblance of control in the face of overwhelming trauma. The entries also revealed the profound exhaustion that accompanied these rituals, the sheer mental effort required to maintain the fragile balance between the different personalities.

Another alter, "Grace," offered a stark contrast to Clara's rigid control. Grace's entries were childlike and whimsical, filled with fantastical stories and vivid imaginings. These entries served as a poignant reminder of the innocence lost, a desperate attempt to escape the harsh realities of Eleanor's past. Yet, even within Grace's playful narratives, there were glimpses of the underlying trauma. Recurring motifs – a lost doll, a dark room, a shadowy figure – hinted at the persistent impact of Eleanor's abuse. The juxtaposition of Grace's innocent world with the darker entries provided a chilling illustration of the fractured nature of Eleanor's psyche.

The diary revealed the intricate ways in which the alters interacted with each other, sometimes cooperating, sometimes clashing, often unknowingly influencing one another's behavior. Sarah discovered instances where one alter would leave notes or clues for another, seemingly attempting to communicate across the fractured landscape of Eleanor's mind. This inter-alter communication, often cryptic and indirect, added another layer of complexity to understanding Eleanor's condition. Sometimes, Sarah found entries where different alters would seemingly interrupt each other, creating jarring shifts in tone, style, and even handwriting. These moments highlighted the constant struggle for control, the ongoing battle for dominance within Eleanor's mind.

The entries offered insight into the triggers that precipitated shifts between alters. Certain smells, sounds, or even specific situations could evoke a particular alter, highlighting the environmental factors that influenced the expression of Eleanor's fragmented identities. One particular entry described a vivid flashback triggered by the scent of lilac perfume, instantly transporting Eleanor back to the scene of a traumatic event. The diary meticulously recorded these triggers, offering clues to the psychological mechanisms that underpinned the shifts between alters. This detailed documentation underscored the deeply ingrained nature of these triggers, emphasizing the pervasive impact of trauma on Eleanor's sensory experiences.

The diary also provided evidence of the alters' distinct cognitive styles and abilities. Some alters exhibited exceptional artistic talent, others demonstrated remarkable mathematical skills, while others struggled with basic literacy. This diversity in cognitive abilities highlighted the complex nature of DID, showcasing the remarkable ways in which trauma can affect different aspects of cognitive function. These varying skills and abilities weren't simply different talents; they were reflections of distinct coping mechanisms, distinct ways of navigating and interpreting the world.

Beyond the individual personalities, the diary also revealed the profound impact of the trauma on Eleanor's overall functioning. She suffered from significant memory gaps, difficulties with concentration, and persistent feelings of disorientation and depersonalization. These symptoms, consistent with the long-term effects of severe trauma, underscored the devastating impact of childhood abuse on

Eleanor's mental and emotional well-being. The diary entries, written in fits and starts, often interrupted by periods of silence, reflected the profound disruption to Eleanor's ability to maintain a coherent narrative of her own life.

The legal implications of this fragmented reality posed a significant challenge for Sarah. How could she prove the innocence of Eleanor, when the very act of murder had been committed by one of her alters? How could she convince a court system, designed to judge individual actions, of the complexities of a mind fractured beyond comprehension? Sarah realized that her mother's case was not just a legal battle; it was a fight for a deeper understanding of DID, a fight to dismantle the stigma surrounding mental illness, and a fight to ensure that the justice system adapts to the intricate realities of trauma and dissociation.

The diary's entries on "Lily," the murderer, were chillingly detached. They weren't filled with remorse or regret; rather, they were a methodical account of the act, described with an almost clinical precision that contrasted starkly with the horror of the crime itself. This detachment, Sarah suspected, was a coping mechanism, a way for Lily to distance herself from the enormity of the act. However, interspersed within Lily's account were fragments of emotion – fleeting glimpses of fear, rage, and a profound sense of isolation – that hinted at the underlying trauma driving Lily's actions. This contradictory nature – the cold calculation alongside the raw emotion – painted a complex portrait of a personality torn between self-preservation and self-destruction.

As Sarah delved deeper into the diary, she began to understand that DID wasn't merely a collection of distinct personalities.

It was a complex interplay of emotions, memories, and survival mechanisms, all operating within the confines of a fractured mind. Each alter represented a different coping strategy, a different way of dealing with the unbearable pain of childhood trauma. The diary wasn't just a record of Eleanor's experiences; it was a testament to the resilience of the human psyche, its capacity to adapt, to compartmentalize, and to survive in the face of unimaginable horror. The journey through the diary was not simply a quest for understanding her mother's crime; it was a journey into the darkest corners of the human mind, a voyage through the fractured landscape of a soul shattered by years of abuse. It was a stark reminder that the path to justice, in cases like Eleanor's, required not just legal acumen, but a profound understanding of the human condition in its most fragile and complex form. Sarah's fight was far from over; it was only just beginning.

The more Sarah delved into her mother's diary, the more the chilling narrative of Eleanor's life transcended the confines of a personal tragedy. It became a searing indictment of systemic failures, a damning exposé of a society that had failed to protect a vulnerable child and, in its subsequent inaction, allowed the cycle of abuse to perpetuate itself for decades. The diary wasn't just a chronicle of Eleanor's internal struggles; it was a testament to the profound shortcomings of the systems designed to safeguard children and address the complexities of mental illness.

The entries revealed a pattern of missed opportunities, a cascade of negligence that began in Eleanor's childhood and continued into adulthood. There were fleeting mentions of teachers who dismissed her erratic behavior as mere childishness, of doctors who prescribed tranquilizers instead of investigating the underlying trauma, and of social workers who lacked the resources or perhaps the will, to intervene effectively. The repeated failures to recognize and address the signs of abuse created a fertile ground for the development of Eleanor's DID, allowing her fragmented personalities to flourish as coping mechanisms in the absence of adequate support. The diary became a chilling counterpoint to the idyllic facade of her life, a stark reminder that the perfect suburban family could conceal horrors unimaginable.

One particular entry, scrawled in a frantic hand, detailed an incident at school. Eleanor, then eight years old, had been visibly distressed, her clothes torn and stained. A teacher, dismissive and overworked, had simply sent her to the principal's office, a place which, according to later entries, offered no solace or protection. The principal, burdened with administrative tasks and an overwhelmed social worker, had failed to pick up on the warning signs. The entry hinted at a mumbled explanation from a young Eleanor, a child already mastering the art of hiding her pain, her voice lost in the bureaucratic shuffle. This incident, a single drop in a sea of neglect, was repeated throughout the diary, highlighting a systemic disregard for the emotional well-being of children, a pervasive culture that prioritized efficiency and order over the individual needs of vulnerable young people.

The medical system, too, was exposed as flawed and inadequate in Eleanor's case. The diary included fragmented entries detailing numerous visits to doctors and therapists, often prompted by panic attacks, dissociative episodes, or self-harming behaviors. Yet, these crucial cries for help were frequently misunderstood, misinterpreted, or simply ignored. The pervasive lack of awareness and understanding regarding dissociative disorders meant that Eleanor's symptoms were often misdiagnosed, treated with ineffective medications, and ultimately left unaddressed. The system failed not only to provide her with the necessary therapeutic intervention but also compounded the damage by invalidating her experience and further isolating her.

The diary's descriptions of her encounters with various medical professionals were heart-wrenching. One entry detailed a consultation where her symptoms were attributed to teenage angst, a convenient label that dismissed the deeper, more profound trauma underlying her struggles. Another entry described a psychiatrist who seemed more interested in adhering to rigid diagnostic criteria than in understanding the nuances of her complex mental state. These encounters were not isolated incidents; they were representative of a broader problem, a failure of the medical establishment to recognize and adequately address the needs of individuals suffering from complex trauma and DID.

The failure extended beyond individual practitioners to the broader system of mental healthcare itself. The fragmented nature of the system, with its lack of coordinated care and its reliance on fragmented and often inadequate resources, contributed to the lack of comprehensive and effective treatment for Eleanor. The diary revealed a pattern of miscommunication between therapists, missed appointments, and a general lack of continuity of care, all of which exacerbated Eleanor's condition and hindered her recovery. The system's inability to adapt to the complexities of trauma and dissociation created an environment where individuals like Eleanor fell through the cracks, deprived of the support and treatment they desperately needed.

Furthermore, the diary's entries highlighted the pervasive stigma surrounding mental illness, a stigma that prevented

Eleanor from seeking help openly and honestly. The shame and fear of judgment, reinforced by societal attitudes and a lack of public understanding, kept her silent, intensifying the isolation and fueling the internal conflict that characterized her fragmented psyche. The diary revealed a desperate struggle to maintain a semblance of normalcy, to hide her inner turmoil from a world that lacked the empathy and understanding necessary to truly comprehend her suffering.

Beyond the immediate failures of the medical and educational systems, Sarah unearthed a deeper societal issue: the normalization of abuse and the inadequate protection offered to victims. The diary hinted at a culture where abuse was often silenced, overlooked, or even excused. The family dynamics, as revealed through scattered mentions and fragmented memories, suggested a deeply dysfunctional environment where emotional neglect and abuse were normalized, where silence and secrecy were prized above truth and healing. The diary was not only a testament to Eleanor's suffering but also to the complicity of a system that failed to protect her, that allowed abuse to thrive in the shadows of societal complacency.

The legal ramifications of this systemic failure were equally devastating. Eleanor's case, Sarah realized, wasn't just about prosecuting a murderer; it was about holding the system accountable for its repeated failures. The case posed a profound challenge to the justice system, which struggled to grasp the concept of a crime committed by a dissociated personality. The diary, however incriminating in terms of the crime itself, also served as a powerful indictment of the system that had allowed such a tragedy to occur in the first place. The legal battle, Sarah understood, would not be about simply finding Eleanor's killer, but about exposing the profound flaws within a system that had failed to protect her and countless others. It was a fight for reform, for increased awareness and understanding of DID, and for a fundamental shift in how society responds to trauma, abuse, and mental illness. The diary had become more than a personal journal; it was a weapon, a tool to fight for justice not just for Eleanor, but for the countless others who had suffered similar fates due to the catastrophic shortcomings of a system that was supposed to protect them. The fight for justice, Sarah realized, was a fight against the very system that had enabled the tragedy to happen in the first place. The weight of that realization settled heavily upon her shoulders, intensifying her resolve to uncover the truth and to ensure that such a failure never happened again.

The weight of her mother's story pressed down on Sarah, a crushing burden of inherited trauma. The diary, initially a source of horror and disbelief, gradually transformed into a roadmap, albeit a harrowing one, towards understanding. The initial shock gave way to a profound sadness, a grief not just for the loss of her mother, but for the life Eleanor never truly lived, a life stolen piece by piece by the insidious cruelty of abuse and the subsequent failings of a system designed to protect.

Sarah's journey wasn't linear; it was a chaotic dance between despair and tentative hope, a slow, painstaking climb out of the abyss of Eleanor's fractured psyche. There were days when the diary's entries felt like shards of glass, cutting into her soul, reopening wounds she hadn't known she possessed. The vivid descriptions of Eleanor's childhood – the chilling details of neglect, the brutal accounts of physical and sexual abuse – left Sarah reeling, questioning the very fabric of her own reality. She'd grown up in the shadow of a seemingly perfect suburban life, blissfully unaware of the dark undercurrent that flowed beneath the surface, the hidden torrent of pain and suffering that had shaped her mother's existence.

The realization that the seemingly idyllic childhood memories she cherished were nothing more than carefully constructed facades, illusions carefully maintained by the various alters struggling for dominance within her mother's fractured mind, left Sarah feeling disoriented and lost. It shattered her sense of security, leaving her questioning everything she had ever believed about her family, about her life, and most importantly, about herself. The diary entries were a brutal awakening, a shattering of innocence that forced her to confront the uncomfortable truth: the seemingly perfect family portrait concealed a brutal and tragic reality.

Yet, amidst the darkness, a faint glimmer of light began to emerge. As Sarah delved deeper into the diary, she started to identify patterns, to recognize the coping mechanisms Eleanor's various alters had developed to navigate the unbearable pain of their shared trauma. The diary wasn't just a chronicle of abuse; it was also a testament to Eleanor's remarkable resilience, her capacity to survive, to adapt, to fight for survival in the face of unimaginable adversity. Each alter, though fragmented and bearing the scars of trauma, possessed a unique strength, a resilience that Sarah found both heartbreaking and profoundly inspiring.

Sarah began to understand the complexities of dissociation, the way the mind fragments as a defense mechanism against overwhelming pain. She learned about the different personalities that emerged from the depths of Eleanor's trauma, each one a desperate attempt to cope, to survive, to navigate a world that had failed to protect her. The chilling accounts of violence, the seemingly random acts of self-harm, started to make a horrifying kind of sense. They weren't simply acts of malice; they were desperate cries for help, desperate attempts to silence the internal chaos, to find some semblance of peace within a mind torn asunder.

This understanding, however painful, began to ease the burden of guilt and self-blame that had initially consumed her. Sarah had initially felt responsible, somehow complicit in her mother's suffering. The diary helped her understand that she wasn't to blame; she was a victim too, a victim of a system that failed to recognize and address the insidious nature of the trauma that plagued her family. The realization that Eleanor's actions, even the horrific murder, stemmed from a deeply troubled and profoundly wounded mind, brought a measure of peace, a softening of the rigid self-recrimination.

Sarah's healing journey also involved seeking professional help. She began therapy, initially hesitant and resistant, but slowly opening up to the therapist's guidance. The therapist helped her process the trauma revealed in the diary, validating her feelings and helping her navigate the complex emotions that arose from confronting such a painful truth. The therapeutic process was slow and arduous, fraught with setbacks and moments of overwhelming despair. But with each session, Sarah felt a little bit stronger, a little bit more capable of confronting her past, of acknowledging her grief, and of ultimately, forgiving herself and her mother.

Through therapy, Sarah began to address her own emotional needs, recognizing the ways in which her mother's trauma had impacted her own life. She found support groups for children of trauma survivors, connecting with others who understood her unique experience. The shared stories of pain and resilience provided a sense of community, a lifeline in a sea of emotional turmoil. In these groups, she discovered that she wasn't alone, that her feelings were valid, and that healing was possible.

Part of Sarah's healing journey also involved a profound sense of forgiveness. Forgiving her mother, for forgiving herself, and for forgiving the system that had failed them both proved to be a long and complicated process. It wasn't about condoning the actions of the alter that committed the murder; it was about accepting the reality of her mother's illness and recognizing that Eleanor's actions were not a reflection of her inherent character, but rather a consequence of the immense trauma she had endured. This acceptance was a crucial step in Sarah's healing, allowing her to release the weight of guilt and self-blame that had been suffocating her.

The act of forgiving the system, however, proved to be more challenging. The anger and frustration remained intense; the memories of the failures – the dismissive teachers, the ineffectual doctors, the overworked social workers – felt like a constant reminder of the systemic failures that had allowed Eleanor's trauma to fester and ultimately culminate in tragedy. This anger, however, was not destructive; instead, it fueled Sarah's determination to ensure that others wouldn't suffer the same fate. She resolved to dedicate herself to advocacy, to fight for improved mental healthcare systems, and to raise awareness about the complexities of trauma and dissociative disorders.

Sarah's healing wasn't a magical transformation; it was a slow, gradual process, filled with moments of profound grief, intense anger, and agonizing self-doubt. But throughout her journey, she held onto the memory of her mother's resilience, the strength that had enabled Eleanor to survive decades of unimaginable suffering. That resilience, she realized, wasn't just Eleanor's; it was a part of her own DNA, a legacy she inherited and would carry forward.

Her journey also involved confronting the murder itself, not just as a horrific crime, but as a symptom of a much larger problem. The chilling details, the precise manner in which the victim was disposed of, the use of the red scrunchies – these details, once terrifying and incomprehensible, now held a new meaning, a contextual understanding that shed light on the darkest corners of Eleanor's fractured mind. The murder wasn't just a random act of violence; it was a culmination of years of unresolved trauma, a desperate expression of the pain and rage that had been bottled up for decades.

Understanding didn't erase the horror, but it gave Sarah a framework, a way to process the unfathomable. She started to see the crime not as an isolated event, but as a horrifying manifestation of a larger failure – a failure of society, a failure of the system, and a failure of understanding. This perspective allowed her to shift her focus from retribution to prevention, from blaming to healing.

Sarah's final step in her healing journey was to share her story. She began to speak openly about her mother's life, about the complexities of DID, and about the systemic failures that contributed to Eleanor's tragedy. She wrote articles, gave interviews, and shared her experience with support groups, becoming an advocate for others who had experienced similar trauma. Her voice, once silenced by grief and shame, became a powerful instrument for change, a beacon of hope for those who had been silenced, marginalized, and forgotten. Sarah's journey was a testament to the enduring power of the human spirit, a testament to the possibility of healing even in the face of unimaginable pain. Her story, a chilling and heartbreaking exploration of trauma and resilience, became a testament to the possibility of finding light in the darkest of places. The fight for justice, initially fueled by anger and grief, transformed into a mission of compassion, understanding, and advocacy – a legacy both for her mother and for countless others who suffered in silence.

The diary entry dated March 12th, 1988, jolted Sarah. It wasn't the usual fragmented stream of consciousness, the shifting perspectives of Eleanor's alters. This one was stark, focused, terrifyingly lucid. It spoke of Robert, her stepfather, his face contorted in a rictus of rage, his hands tight around Eleanor's wrist, dragging her into the shadowed recesses of the basement. The details were sparse, yet brutal; the chilling implication of what happened in that darkness hung heavy in the air, suffocating Sarah with its unspoken horror.

This entry marked a turning point in Sarah's understanding. Before, the abuse had been a chaotic blur, a jumble of fragmented memories and conflicting narratives from the diary's different personalities. Now, a chilling clarity emerged; a focused account of one specific, devastating event. This entry wasn't just another piece of Eleanor's shattered psyche; it was a direct accusation, a testament to the undeniable reality of Robert's cruelty.

For the first time, Sarah felt the full weight of her mother's suffering, not as a scattered collection of traumas, but as a targeted, deliberate assault. The anger that had simmered beneath the surface of her grief now erupted, a volcanic surge of righteous fury. The idyllic suburban life she remembered morphed into a horrifying facade, a carefully constructed illusion masking years of systematic abuse.

The police report, dusty and yellowed, offered little solace. The case had been closed years ago, deemed a "domestic dispute" with insufficient evidence. The apathy, the lack of investigation, the blatant disregard for Eleanor's suffering – it was a fresh wound, a searing reminder of the systemic failure that had allowed Robert to continue his reign of terror. Sarah felt a surge of nausea, a bitter taste of injustice coating her tongue. This wasn't just about her mother; it was about all the women whose cries for help had gone unanswered, whose abusers had walked free.

Driven by a burning need for justice, Sarah decided to reopen the case. She contacted a lawyer specializing in wrongful death and domestic abuse, a sharp, determined woman with steely grey eyes and a reputation for tenacity. The lawyer listened patiently as Sarah recounted the horrors she'd unearthed in the diary, the fragmented memories pieced together, the chilling details that painted a horrifying picture of Eleanor's life.

The lawyer's response was measured, professional, yet deeply empathetic. She understood the complexities of the case, the challenges of proving abuse after so many years, the almost insurmountable hurdles of prosecuting someone based on the testimony of a deceased victim, a victim whose fragmented mental state had made a definitive statement impossible in her lifetime. But the lawyer also saw something in Sarah's determination, a fire in her eyes that mirrored her own. This wasn't simply about obtaining closure; it was about holding a perpetrator accountable. It was about justice.

The investigation was arduous, a painstaking process of piecing together fragments of evidence. Sarah had to navigate the labyrinthine world of legal procedures, providing testimony, collecting documentation, and enduring intense scrutiny. There were moments of doubt, of crushing self-doubt, of wondering if it was all worth it. But the memory of Eleanor's resilience, the strength she'd found in the face of unimaginable suffering, fueled her relentless pursuit of justice.

The lawyer located old neighbors, former friends, and even Robert's estranged family members. Each interview added a piece to the puzzle, a piece of the horrifying portrait of Robert, a man who had expertly concealed his cruelty behind a mask of normalcy, a master of manipulation. Sarah unearthed whispers of other victims, shadows of accusations that had never been properly investigated. Each revelation was a grim confirmation of her worst fears, a testament to the extent of Robert's depravity and the systemic failures that had allowed him to operate with impunity for so long.

The diary itself became a crucial piece of evidence, a testament to Eleanor's suffering. While the fragmented nature of the entries presented challenges, the lawyer's expertise in trauma-informed interviewing and the testimony of Sarah's therapist helped contextualize the entries, giving them weight and credibility. The entries didn't just recount abuse; they revealed a pattern of violence, a systematic campaign of control and degradation.

The trial was a grueling ordeal. Robert's defense team attempted to discredit Eleanor, painting her as unstable and unreliable, a woman prone to exaggeration and fantasy. They tried to cast doubt on the validity of the diary, questioning Sarah's motives and her ability to interpret her mother's fragmented memories.

Sarah's testimony was both heartbreaking and powerful. She spoke with quiet dignity, her voice clear and strong, recounting the impact of Robert's abuse on her mother and on herself. She didn't flinch under the relentless cross-examination, her composure never faltering. Her honesty and vulnerability resonated with the jury.

The most compelling evidence, however, came from the unexpected source: Robert himself. During his testimony, his carefully constructed facade of normalcy crumbled, his anger and defensiveness revealing his guilt. His attempts to control the narrative, his evasiveness and contradictions, underscored his culpability.

The verdict was a long-awaited victory. Robert was found guilty on multiple counts of abuse, including aggravated assault and emotional distress. The sentence was lengthy, a just reflection of his horrific crimes. The courtroom erupted in a wave of relief, of catharsis, of long-overdue justice.

But for Sarah, the victory was bittersweet. The justice obtained didn't erase the pain, didn't undo the damage. It didn't bring Eleanor back. Yet, it offered a measure of closure, a sense of validation, a confirmation that her mother's suffering had not been in vain. The fight for justice had been a brutal journey, but it had also been a transformative one. It had given Sarah a voice, a platform to advocate for others who had suffered in silence, to ensure that no one else would endure what her mother had endured.

The fight didn't end with the trial. Sarah, with the support of her lawyer, became actively involved in advocacy, working to improve laws protecting victims of domestic abuse, raising awareness about the impact of trauma, and demanding accountability from those who enabled the abuse to occur. The journey had been long, arduous, and emotionally draining. Yet, in the face of immense loss, Sarah found a path to healing, a path paved with justice and fueled by the unwavering spirit of her mother, a spirit that lived on through her. The red scrunchies, once symbols of a gruesome crime, now served as a reminder of the victory obtained, a testament to the unwavering strength of a daughter who fought for justice, for her mother, and for all the victims whose voices had been silenced. The fight had been hard-fought, but it had delivered the one thing that had been missing all those years: justice. And that justice, as painful and bittersweet as it was, finally paved the way for the healing process to begin in earnest.

# CHAPTER 8: THE PRICE OF SILENCE

The diary entries, initially a chaotic jumble of voices, began to coalesce into a chilling narrative spanning generations. One entry, scrawled in a frantic hand, detailed a childhood spent in the shadow of her own mother's silent suffering. Eleanor's mother, a woman Sarah had only known through faded photographs and whispered anecdotes, had been a picture of quiet resignation, a fragility cloaked in a stiff upper lip. There were hints in the diary – a recurring motif of tightly clenched hands, a fear of the dark that bordered on phobia, a chilling description of a childhood filled with unnerving silences and the constant, low hum of unspoken dread. It wasn't explicitly stated, but the implication was clear: Eleanor's mother had endured her own form of abuse, a trauma that she had buried deep within, its tendrils silently twisting through her life, leaving an indelible mark on her daughter.

The diary hinted at a pattern of coercive control, a cycle of emotional and psychological manipulation that had spanned generations. Eleanor's mother hadn't screamed, hadn't fought back overtly; she'd internalized her pain, transforming it into a crippling anxiety that choked the joy out of life. This wasn't simply a case of inherited genes; it was an inheritance of trauma, a legacy of unspoken pain passed down through the generations, manifesting in different ways in each woman.

Sarah began to understand the cyclical nature of abuse, the insidious way trauma could seep into the very fabric of a family, shaping its dynamics and relationships. Eleanor's own detachment, her tendency to disappear into her alters, wasn't merely a symptom of her disorder; it was a survival mechanism, a coping strategy learned from a mother who had mastered the art of silent endurance. The diary revealed a chilling picture of a mother-daughter relationship strained by unspoken pain, a bond fractured by a shared history of suppression.

The entries revealed that Eleanor had learned to dissociate as a child, finding refuge in fantasy and imagination to escape the suffocating reality of her home. Her alters emerged as separate identities, each a manifestation of a different coping strategy, each a fragmented piece of a self desperately seeking solace from the relentless onslaught of trauma. The chilling aspect was that these coping mechanisms, born of survival, had become the very tools that ultimately led to the horrifying events of that fateful night.

The diary revealed the extent of the intergenerational impact. Eleanor's own struggles with OCD, ADHD, and autism, initially seen as separate diagnoses, started to fit together as pieces of a larger puzzle. They were not isolated conditions but rather manifestations of a deeper, more systemic problem rooted in the unresolved trauma of her past. The OCD, the relentless need for order and control, could be viewed as an attempt to regain a sense of safety in a world that had repeatedly felt chaotic and unpredictable. The ADHD, the hyperactivity and impulsivity, could be interpreted as an expression of pent-up energy, a frantic attempt to escape the lingering shadow of past experiences. And the autism, the difficulty with social interaction and sensory processing, could be seen as a form of self-preservation, a way to shield herself from the overwhelming emotional demands of a world that hadn't understood her pain.

The diary provided glimpses into Eleanor's attempts to break the cycle of trauma. She'd sought therapy, albeit intermittently, her sessions often punctuated by periods of relapse and withdrawal. There were moments of hope, of self-discovery, but these fragile moments were often overshadowed by the overwhelming weight of her past. The entries revealed a profound sense of loneliness, a desperate yearning for connection that had remained unfulfilled. She had sought therapy hoping to understand her alters, hoping to gain control over her fractured self, yet the cycle continued, a testament to the deeply ingrained patterns of trauma.

As Sarah delved deeper into the diary, she discovered entries detailing Eleanor's own struggles with motherhood. The fear of repeating the patterns of her past haunted her, a constant reminder of the potential for trauma to be passed down through generations. The conflict between the different personalities, their conflicting views and desires, created immense tension and instability within the family, causing further distress for Sarah and affecting her development.

Sarah understood then, with a chilling clarity, that she herself was part of this legacy, a product of intergenerational trauma. The anxieties she'd always felt, the emotional instability that had plagued her relationships, suddenly made sense within the context of her mother's story. The unspoken pain, the inherited fragility, the recurring themes of silent suffering –

these were not random occurrences but rather echoes of a past that had continued to reverberate through the generations. The diary became a mirror, reflecting not only her mother's pain but also her own, a testament to the invisible wounds that could be passed down like a cursed inheritance.

The weight of this realization was immense. It wasn't just about solving a murder; it was about confronting a legacy of trauma, understanding the complex interplay of genetics, environment, and lived experience that had shaped her family's history. The diary entries detailing the escalating abuse, the escalating mental fragmentation, and the devastating effects on Eleanor's family highlighted the deep and lasting impact of intergenerational trauma.

There was a chilling entry detailing Eleanor's desperate attempts to shield Sarah from the abuse, the frantic attempts to create a sense of normalcy, a façade of a happy family life. But the cracks were there, the subtle signs of dysfunction that Sarah, as a child, had been too young to recognize. Eleanor's fiercely protective instincts were at odds with the chaotic nature of her fractured mind, a constant internal battle reflected in her erratic behavior.

One entry detailed a particularly violent outburst by one of Eleanor's alters, an alter Sarah later came to recognize as "The Protector," a personality that emerged when Robert's violence escalated. This alter, driven by a primal need to defend Eleanor and Sarah, had inadvertently caused significant emotional distress within the family, mirroring the devastating instability caused by the trauma. Eleanor had simultaneously been the victim and perpetrator of violence, a stark example of how trauma could warp even the most fundamental of human instincts.

The diary entries highlighted the profound consequences of unspoken trauma. The silencing of Eleanor's mother's pain created a toxic environment, a breeding ground for further abuse and dysfunction. Eleanor's inability to process and articulate her own experiences led to the fragmentation of her psyche, the emergence of multiple personalities, each struggling for control in a desperate bid for relief. And Sarah, in turn, inherited the legacy of this trauma, grappling with its effects throughout her own life.

Sarah's journey wasn't simply about seeking justice for her mother; it was about breaking the cycle, about confronting the generational wounds that had plagued her family for so long. It was a journey into the heart of darkness, a confrontation with the horrors of abuse and the devastating legacy of silence. And as she pieced together the fragments of her mother's life, she began to piece together fragments of her own, understanding that healing could only begin with the truth, with the acknowledgment of a painful past and the unwavering commitment to breaking the cycle of trauma. The red scrunchies, the symbol of a horrific crime, now represented not only the past but also the dawning of a new era, an era of healing and a resolute commitment to breaking the silence that had haunted her family for generations.

The diary entries revealed a fascinating, and terrifying, interplay between memory and trauma. Eleanor's memories weren't neatly cataloged; they were shards of glass, scattered and jagged, reflecting distorted images of her past. Some memories were vivid, almost painfully so, while others were hazy, obscured by a veil of dissociation. Sarah found herself grappling not just with her mother's fractured recollection of events, but with the very nature of memory itself – its fragility, its malleability, its capacity for both preservation and destruction.

One entry described a recurring nightmare, a fragmented image of a shadowy figure, a hand reaching out from the darkness. The figure was indistinct, its features obscured, yet the feeling of dread, the overwhelming sense of terror, was palpable. This wasn't a precise memory; it was an emotional impression, a residue of trauma imprinted on the psyche. The nightmare, Sarah realized, wasn't just a reflection of a specific event; it was a symbolic representation of the pervasive fear that had haunted Eleanor's childhood.

Another entry described a seemingly innocuous event – a family picnic in a park. Yet, interspersed with descriptions of sunshine and laughter, were disturbing flashes of anxiety, a sense of impending doom. The idyllic scene was marred by disjointed memories of whispered arguments, strained silences, and the subtle cues of emotional abuse. The memory, fragmented and dissonant, painted a picture of a family life punctuated by moments of both joy and terror, a constant oscillation between normality and dread. It demonstrated how trauma could invade even the most cherished memories, twisting them into something sinister and unsettling.

Sarah noticed a recurring theme of "missing time" in the diary entries. There were gaps in Eleanor's memory, periods of complete amnesia, particularly during times of heightened stress or emotional turmoil. These weren't simply lapses in recollection; they were active acts of dissociation, a defense mechanism employed by Eleanor's psyche to protect itself from overwhelming pain. The missing memories weren't lost; they were hidden, buried deep within the subconscious, inaccessible to conscious awareness. These gaps, Sarah realized, were not merely holes in the narrative, but rather key indicators of the severity of Eleanor's trauma. They were the silent screams, the unspoken pain rendered invisible through the act of forgetting.

Further investigation revealed that the fragmented memories weren't just a product of Eleanor's multiple personality disorder; they were also influenced by her other diagnoses, specifically her OCD and ADHD. Her OCD, the relentless need for order and control, created a compulsion to categorize and organize her experiences, even her memories. But this organization was often skewed and distorted by the trauma, resulting in a narrative that was both meticulous and deeply flawed. The ADHD, with its hyperactivity and impulsivity, disrupted the linear flow of memory, creating a chaotic and unpredictable sequence of events. Memories were jumbled together, out of chronological order, creating a sense of disorientation and confusion.

The diary revealed how Eleanor's different alters experienced and recalled events differently. "The Child," a young, vulnerable personality, recalled events with a raw, emotional intensity, while "The Protector," a fierce and defensive alter, presented a more guarded and distorted account, focusing on aspects of self-preservation and retaliation. "The Observer," a detached and analytical personality, documented the events clinically, observing the dynamics of the other alters with a detached, almost scientific curiosity. Each alter's perspective offered a unique, and often contradictory, fragment of the truth, highlighting the fragmented and subjective nature of memory itself. Each was a lens through which the past was refracted, producing a distorted image of what had actually happened.

The inconsistencies in the diary entries weren't evidence of deliberate deception; they were evidence of the chaotic nature of a fractured mind, a mind desperately trying to make sense of a past filled with pain and violence. Sarah learned that the search for truth in this context was not a straightforward pursuit of facts, but rather a complex process of piecing together fragments of memory, interpreting conflicting accounts, and acknowledging the subjective nature of recollection.

The diary wasn't just a record of past events; it was a living testament to the ongoing struggle to reconcile a fractured self. As Sarah delved deeper, she realized that Eleanor's journey wasn't just a story of abuse and trauma; it was a story of resilience, of the human capacity to survive and endure even the most horrific experiences. The fragmented memories, the disjointed narratives, were not merely symptoms of disorder but also echoes of survival, testament to a spirit that stubbornly refused to be broken, even as her mind had fragmented.

The more Sarah read, the more she understood the insidious nature of trauma's impact on memory. It wasn't just about remembering or forgetting; it was about the active process of reshaping, reinterpreting, and reconstructing the past. Trauma could rewrite the narrative, creating a distorted reality where the line between truth and fiction became increasingly blurred. This was evident in Eleanor's recurring conflation of dreams and reality, a phenomenon that blurred the boundaries between conscious experience and the subconscious world of repressed memories.

Sarah started to recognize patterns in the distortions, common coping mechanisms employed by her mother's mind to deal with the overwhelming pain of her past. One such pattern was the tendency to minimize or downplay the severity of abusive events. This wasn't a deliberate attempt to deceive; it was a survival strategy, a way of protecting herself from the crushing weight of unbearable memories. In some entries, the descriptions of abuse were vague, almost surreal, as if the mind had actively attempted to sanitize the trauma, rendering it less emotionally damaging.

Another pattern was the displacement of emotions. Painful memories associated with one person might be unconsciously transferred to another. For instance, Sarah discovered that some of Eleanor's anger towards her father was actually displaced anger towards her mother, a reflection of the complex and intricate way trauma could distort perceptions and emotions. The blurring of boundaries between individuals reflected the emotional chaos caused by trauma.

The diary entries eventually revealed a startling revelation: the murder itself might have been a distorted memory, a fragmented recollection warped by trauma and the fragmented personalities involved. The act, in Eleanor's mind, could have been perceived very differently depending on the alter who was in control. One entry suggested that the actual event held less significance than the symbolic meaning it held for Eleanor's fractured psyche, a warped act of revenge or self-punishment.

The exploration of Eleanor's memory became a journey into

the dark heart of trauma, revealing the complex ways in which memory is not merely a record of the past, but a dynamic, ever-evolving construct shaped by experience, emotion, and the conscious and unconscious efforts to cope with overwhelming pain. The red scrunchies, the chilling detail of the crime, became symbolic of not only the violence committed but the violence inflicted on Eleanor's own psyche, a testament to the enduring power of trauma to shape not only the past but also the present and future. As Sarah continued to uncover these details, the true cost of silence began to reveal itself, not just in the murder itself, but in the deeply ingrained psychological wounds that had shaped three generations of her family. The task of unraveling the truth extended beyond simply finding a killer; it was a quest to understand the fragile, fragmented, and deeply affected nature of memory itself, a memory constantly reshaped by the enduring power of trauma.

The diary entries shifted from fragmented recollections of specific events to a more pervasive exploration of Eleanor's emotional landscape. The sheer weight of her unspoken trauma became evident, suffocating the pages like a thick, suffocating fog. It wasn't just the individual memories; it was the cumulative effect of years of silence, the constant pressure of holding within herself a truth too horrific to share. Sarah began to understand the profound psychological impact of this self-imposed secrecy.

One entry described a recurring feeling of intense physical tension, a constant knot in her stomach that never fully unwound. This wasn't linked to a specific memory, but rather a persistent, generalized anxiety, a byproduct of years spent suppressing her pain. Eleanor described it as a constant state of hypervigilance, a feeling that she was always on edge, always waiting for the next blow to fall. This perpetual state of unease, Sarah realized, was a direct consequence of the secrecy surrounding her abuse. The inability to articulate her suffering had internalized the trauma, rendering it a constant, pervasive presence in her life.

Another entry detailed the ways Eleanor's secrecy had impacted her relationships. She described feeling isolated, disconnected from others, unable to form genuine bonds due to the fear of exposure. The fear of others discovering her secret was a paralyzing force, preventing her from seeking help or support. The trust she needed to overcome her trauma was absent in the landscape that was forged by her silence, leading to an isolation that served as a constant reminder of her hidden pain. The diary depicted a woman trapped in a cage of her own making, the bars forged from years of silence and self-imposed isolation.

The secrecy wasn't simply a passive act; it was an active process of self-deception, a constant struggle to reconcile her internal reality with the carefully constructed façade she presented to the world. Eleanor described the mental gymnastics she performed to maintain this façade, the elaborate strategies she employed to conceal her true feelings from her husband, her friends, and even herself. This constant performance took a tremendous toll, leading to exhaustion, self-doubt, and a deep sense of shame. The diary entries chronicled the cognitive dissonance, the internal conflict between her hidden world and the public persona she maintained.

Sarah discovered that Eleanor had developed a complex system of coping mechanisms, each designed to protect her from the overwhelming pain of her memories. One such mechanism was dissociation, a psychological defense mechanism where a person detaches from their emotions and experiences as a way of coping with trauma. Eleanor's diary entries documented numerous instances of dissociation, often during times of heightened stress or emotional turmoil. These episodes provided temporary relief from pain, but they came at the cost of memory loss and a growing sense of fragmentation. This dissociation allowed for the creation of alters; these other selves would carry the burdens of trauma, protecting the core self from its weight.

Her obsessive-compulsive disorder (OCD) played a significant role in her ability to cope, or rather, avoid coping with the trauma. The need for order and control manifested in meticulous routines and rituals, a compulsive need to maintain a sense of stability in a life that was anything but stable. The diaries reflected this compulsion for control —the entries were meticulously written, organized, and often cross-referenced, reflecting Eleanor's constant need to order the chaos within. However, this meticulous organization was also a mask, hiding the underlying disorder and the pain it attempted to suppress.

Alongside this compulsive order, her attention-deficit/ hyperactivity disorder (ADHD) played an equally influential role, adding an element of unpredictable chaos to the narrative. The ADHD-influenced thought patterns made it difficult to process the emotional intensity of the trauma; the memories would be fleeting and disruptive. The diary entries showed a tendency towards tangents, abrupt shifts in focus, and an erratic narrative structure—all reflective of the disorder that co-existed with her other diagnoses. The lack of linear narrative mirrored the chaos of her internal world, further illustrating the difficulty of articulating and processing her traumatic experiences.

The diary also revealed the interplay between her various alters. Each alter had its own unique coping mechanisms, and their interactions, at times cooperative, at times antagonistic, were a testament to the fractured nature of Eleanor's psyche. One alter might meticulously document an event, another might repress it entirely, and a third might distort it beyond recognition. This internal conflict, reflected in the diary's disjointed narrative, heightened the sense of fragmentation and the enormous emotional burden of Eleanor's condition.

Further entries explored the impact of her secrecy on her physical health. Eleanor described a range of somatic symptoms, including chronic headaches, digestive problems, and sleep disturbances, all attributable to the constant stress and anxiety associated with her hidden trauma. The physical manifestations of her repressed emotions highlighted the profound connection between mind and body, demonstrating how the psychological weight of her secrets had a tangible impact on her physical well-being. The accumulated physical damage was a testament to the long-term consequences of holding onto trauma.

The diary entries progressed, revealing Eleanor's attempts to break free from the cycle of secrecy. She described moments of vulnerability, fleeting instances where she considered confiding in someone, but fear always held her back. This back-and-forth between vulnerability and fear mirrored the internal struggle between the different alters. The desire to break free often yielded to the fear of judgment and rejection. The profound sense of shame associated with her experiences fueled her reluctance to seek help. She was isolated and alone, a prisoner of her own silence.

The emotional consequences were not limited to Eleanor. Sarah's journey through the diary entries unveiled the ripple effects of Eleanor's concealed trauma, revealing how the secrecy had impacted Sarah's own life and her relationship with her mother. Sarah felt a sense of profound betrayal upon discovering her mother's hidden life, a sense of abandonment and grief that she had been kept in the dark about such a pivotal aspect of her mother's life. The generational impact of trauma, and its continuation through the family dynamic, became strikingly clear.

As Sarah delved deeper into the diary, she unearthed a disturbing pattern: the cycle of secrecy repeated itself through generations, suggesting that the family's history was plagued by a pattern of untreated trauma. This provided a haunting context to Eleanor's own actions, hinting at a legacy of pain and suffering that far predated Eleanor's life. The weight of this revelation was substantial, casting a long shadow over Sarah's understanding of her family and its history.

The concluding entries reveal a desperate plea for understanding, a fragile hope for connection and forgiveness. Eleanor's final words were a testament to the immense burden she carried, a poignant acknowledgment of the devastating consequences of a life lived in silence. Her plea for understanding echoed the desperate need for release from the trauma and the silence that kept it hidden for so long. It underscored the profound psychological impact of secrecy and the vital importance of breaking the cycle of silence to begin the process of healing. Sarah, armed with her mother's diary, now faced the challenge of confronting this legacy, not just for herself, but for future generations. The weight of the secrets, the emotional burden, and the profound implications of untreated trauma were now Sarah's burden to carry. The true price of silence was devastating, far-reaching, and devastatingly profound.

Sarah's initial reaction to the diary's revelations was a maelstrom of emotions – shock, grief, anger, and a profound sense of betrayal. The idyllic image of her mother, the woman she had always known, shattered into a thousand pieces, replaced by a stranger whose life had been defined by unspeakable horrors. This initial isolation, however, was slowly replaced by a desperate need for connection, a yearning for understanding that she hadn't anticipated. She found herself reaching out to people she hadn't spoken to in years, her instinctual need for support overriding the years of ingrained silence mirroring her mother's experiences.

Her closest friend, Emily, became an unexpected lifeline. Emily, a pragmatic and fiercely loyal woman, had always been a steady presence in Sarah's life. At first, Sarah hesitated, unsure how to articulate the enormity of what she had discovered. The sheer scale of Eleanor's trauma felt insurmountable, a burden too heavy to share. Yet, Emily's unwavering support proved invaluable. She listened patiently, offering words of comfort and validation, never minimizing Sarah's pain or dismissing her feelings. Emily didn't try to fix things; she simply allowed Sarah to process her emotions, creating a safe space where Sarah felt heard and understood.

Their conversations weren't easy. The details Sarah recounted were disturbing, the raw pain of the diary entries seeping into their conversations. There were times when Sarah would break down, overwhelmed by the weight of her mother's suffering and her own emerging grief. Emily's presence served as a constant reminder that she wasn't alone in this struggle. Emily provided not only emotional support but also practical assistance, helping Sarah navigate the bureaucratic hurdles of dealing with her mother's estate and the legal complexities that arose from the unsolved murder. This practical support, while seemingly mundane, was essential to Sarah's ability to cope with the emotional turmoil she was experiencing. Emily's steadfast presence was an anchor in the storm of Sarah's grief and anger.

Beyond Emily, Sarah's extended family proved to be a complex and unpredictable source of support. Some family members reacted with denial, refusing to believe the details documented in the diary, their discomfort fueled by the challenge to their established familial narrative. Their responses reflected their own psychological coping mechanisms. Others offered conditional support, their empathy tempered by their own judgments and prejudices. These varied responses highlighted the difficulties in confronting the shadow of unresolved trauma that had been hidden within the family's history for generations. Sarah's aunt, a woman who had always seemed aloof and distant, surprisingly emerged as a source of unexpected solace. Her aunt, having experienced her own hardships, offered a quiet understanding that transcended the family's ingrained patterns of avoidance and denial. This quiet empathy was a poignant contrast to the dismissive reactions of other family members and provided Sarah with a glimpse of hope that the cycle of silence could be broken. She was able to share aspects of the diary entries with her aunt, finding a sympathetic ear and a connection that had been previously absent in their relationship. The shared understanding formed a bond that provided Sarah with a much-needed sense of connection within her family.

The support Sarah received from her therapist, Dr. Anya Sharma, was instrumental in her journey towards healing. Dr. Sharma was a specialist in trauma and dissociative disorders, and her expertise proved invaluable in helping Sarah navigate the complex emotional landscape unveiled in the diary. Dr. Sharma helped Sarah understand the intricacies of multiple personality disorder, explaining the dynamics of the various alters and the psychological mechanisms driving their behaviors. She helped Sarah contextualize Eleanor's actions within the framework of her trauma, without excusing the violent acts. This understanding was crucial in mitigating Sarah's feelings of betrayal and confusion. Dr. Sharma fostered a therapeutic relationship characterized by mutual trust and respect, providing a safe and non-judgmental space for Sarah to explore her emotions.

Sarah's sessions with Dr. Sharma weren't simply about unpacking her mother's past; they were also about helping Sarah process her own emotional responses to the revelations. Sarah found herself struggling with feelings of abandonment, anger, and confusion. She questioned her own identity, grappling with the realization that the woman she had always considered her mother was a complex tapestry of different personalities, each carrying its own burdens and complexities. The process was not linear; there were setbacks and moments of regression, where Sarah's trauma responses were triggered. Dr. Sharma equipped Sarah with coping mechanisms and strategies to manage these moments, to validate her emotions rather than judge them. She taught Sarah techniques for regulating her emotional responses, grounding exercises to help manage anxiety attacks, and other tools to help process her trauma in healthy ways. This support was vital in ensuring that Sarah could face the challenges ahead without becoming overwhelmed by her grief and anger.

The therapeutic relationship extended beyond the confines of the therapy sessions. Dr. Sharma provided Sarah with regular check-ins, ensuring that she was able to access the support she needed. She encouraged Sarah to join a support group for adults who had experienced childhood trauma. The support group offered a different kind of support—a space where Sarah could share her experiences with others who understood what she was going through, validating her pain and reducing her feelings of isolation. The group served as an empathetic community, where Sarah could see that her struggles were not unique, providing a unique sense of belonging and a powerful reminder that healing from trauma was a possible journey.

Beyond formal support networks, Sarah found solace in unexpected places. The act of writing itself became a form of therapy, a way of processing the emotions stirred up by the diary's contents. She began keeping her own journal, not as a meticulously organized record like her mother's but as a free-flowing stream of consciousness, an outlet for the raw emotions and thoughts that haunted her. In writing, she found a space to grieve, to rage, to reflect, and to begin to rebuild her understanding of herself and her family's history. This journey of self-discovery was intricately intertwined with the support she received from others, proving that the path to healing from complex trauma was rarely a solitary one.

The support Sarah received was multifaceted, encompassing emotional, practical, and therapeutic aspects. It wasn't merely a matter of receiving sympathy or receiving professional help; it was about building a network of trust, understanding, and mutual support. This complex web of support helped Sarah navigate the treacherous landscape of her family's history, empowering her to confront the difficult truths uncovered in her mother's diary and to begin the arduous process of healing. The price of silence had been steep, but through the collective support of her friends, family, and therapist, Sarah began to find a path towards a future where silence would no longer hold the power to dictate her life. The resilience demonstrated in her pursuit of healing in the face of overwhelming trauma was a testament to the power of human connection in overcoming adversity.

The discovery of the diary had unearthed a Pandora's Box of horrors, but the raw details only scratched the surface of the devastation. The chilling descriptions of abuse, the fragmented memories of Eleanor's alters, left Sarah grappling with a profound sense of injustice. It wasn't just her mother's suffering that consumed her; it was the unanswered question of the murder, the cold case that had haunted the family for twenty-five years. The victim, a woman named Katherine Miller, a neighbor who shared a strained relationship with Eleanor, remained nameless in Sarah's mind until she pieced together more information from the diary. Katherine was no less a victim of Eleanor's fractured psyche, a casualty of the darkness that lurked beneath Eleanor's outwardly perfect life.

The police, initially dismissive of Sarah's claims, had reopened the case in light of the diary's revelations. The diary, however, provided a fragmented and unreliable account, mirroring Eleanor's own fractured reality. While it offered clues, confirming the victim's identity and implying a direct link to Eleanor, it was the product of a disordered mind, making it challenging to use as direct evidence. The entries jumped between personalities, shifting timelines and perspectives. Some sections detailed the build-up to the crime with frightening accuracy, others were filled with cryptic symbols and fragmented imagery, only marginally hinting at the horrific event.

Detective Inspector Davies, a seasoned detective known for his patience and understanding of complex cases, was assigned to the case. He listened intently as Sarah recounted the details from the diary, recognizing the intricate challenge ahead. He acknowledged the unusual circumstances surrounding the case, the lapse in time, and the unique psychological complexities involved. He understood that the diary, though fragmented, was a crucial piece of evidence. But proving the direct link between one of Eleanor's alters and the crime was a monumental task. The prosecution would need to prove beyond a reasonable doubt that a particular alter was responsible and Eleanor's insanity plea would not be a simple dismissal.

The legal battle became a grueling process, a labyrinth of bureaucratic hurdles and procedural complexities. Sarah found herself thrust into a world she never understood. The courtroom became a battleground, not merely a space for dispensing justice. The defense lawyers, adept at exploiting the inherent ambiguities in the diary's narrative, attempted to discredit the evidence. They questioned the reliability of the diary's contents, casting doubt on Sarah's testimony and highlighting the inconsistencies inherent in the fragmented recollections. The prosecution struggled to bridge the gap between the compelling narrative within the diary pages and the rigors of legal proof.

Sarah felt a sense of profound isolation amidst the legal turmoil. The support of Emily and her aunt remained steadfast, but the legal proceedings brought its own unique emotional strain. The weight of expectation rested heavily upon her shoulders. She was not merely a witness; she was the conduit through which Eleanor's story, the story of a life shattered by trauma, was being told. The emotional toll of reliving her mother's trauma, coupled with the intensity of the court proceedings, became almost unbearable at times. The long hours spent in court, the constant scrutiny, the relentless questioning – all exacerbated her pre-existing anxieties and triggered emotional responses echoing her mother's struggles. Dr. Sharma's support became even more crucial during this period, providing a safe space for Sarah to process her emotions, to decompress from the pressures of the trial.

The trial itself became a harrowing journey into the depths of Eleanor's fractured psyche. Expert witnesses, psychiatrists and psychologists, debated the complexities of multiple personality disorder, its relation to the violent act, and the legal implications of attributing responsibility for the crime to one specific alter. The conflicting testimonies added another layer of complexity, highlighting the uncertainties and ambiguities inherent in psychiatric evaluations. Some argued that Eleanor's alters acted independently, leaving the question of culpability muddled. Others emphasized the interconnectedness of the personalities and the shared responsibility for Eleanor's actions.

Ultimately, the case rested on a fine balance of circumstantial evidence and psychological interpretation. The physical evidence, though scant, was compelling – red scrunchies found near Katherine Miller's remains and a type of lye that matched one used in Eleanor's household. Yet, the diary, though it contained some damning clues, was interpreted by the court as compelling narrative rather than irrefutable proof. After weeks of testimony, deliberations, and tense moments of anticipation, the jury delivered a verdict: not guilty by reason of insanity.

The verdict, while expected by Dr. Sharma and Sarah, was far from satisfying. It wasn't a victory, not in any sense of the word. It offered a form of legal closure – Eleanor was committed to a secure psychiatric facility – but it failed to provide the emotional resolution Sarah yearned for. Justice for Katherine Miller felt elusive, a cold and hollow concept amidst the legal complexities. The case highlighted the limitations of the legal system in dealing with crimes fueled by complex psychological factors. While the verdict prevented Eleanor from inflicting further harm, it did little to address the profound sense of injustice that lingered, both for Katherine Miller and for Sarah.

Sarah's journey towards closure, therefore, moved beyond the courtroom. She found healing in the act of writing, in the sharing of her story. She began to write a book, using her mother's diary as a foundation, expanding upon the sparse details and crafting a narrative that offered both insight into Eleanor's life and a tribute to Katherine Miller's memory. It was an act of remembering and honoring, a way to provide the recognition that Katherine deserved and a way to begin processing her own grief. The book wasn't just a piece of writing, it became a memorial, a testament to the resilience of the human spirit in the face of unimaginable suffering.

The process of writing brought her both pain and catharsis. It forced her to confront her own emotional struggles and to integrate the painful revelations into her life narrative. It helped her to contextualize Eleanor's actions without condoning them. She learned to separate her mother's actions from the victim's suffering and from her own experience of trauma. The book became a space where she could explore the complexities of her family's past, a way to construct a new narrative for herself and her family – a narrative free from the shadows of silence.

The act of writing offered more than just healing; it provided a sense of purpose. Sarah found a voice in a world that had previously silenced her. Her book became a platform to raise awareness about domestic violence, trauma, and mental illness. It invited readers to confront the uncomfortable truths and to challenge the societal attitudes and prejudices that can hinder healing and justice. Through her writing, Sarah transformed her grief and anger into action. She found a way to honor her mother's memory, to provide a voice for Katherine Miller and to empower others who had survived similar trauma. Ultimately, for Sarah, justice and closure were not found solely in a court of law but in the act of self-expression, in finding her voice and using it to bring about positive change. The price of silence had been high, but in her writing, she found the means to reclaim her life and to prevent similar tragedies from continuing in the future. The book became her ultimate form of justice and the means to finding her own version of healing, a testament to her resilience and strength in the face of unspeakable loss and pain.

# CHAPTER 9: FRACTURED REFLECTIONS

The diary entries, initially cryptic and disjointed, began to coalesce into a chilling portrait of Eleanor's fragmented self. Beyond the initial shock of the murder, Sarah unearthed a complex tapestry of personalities, each with their own distinct voice, memories, and traumas. There was "Primrose," the demure and outwardly perfect Eleanor that the world knew – a facade carefully constructed to mask the turmoil within. Her entries were filled with a meticulous detailing of daily routines, recipes, and social engagements, a stark contrast to the darker revelations contained within the writings of her other alters.

Then there was "Nightshade," a stark and violent personality, whose entries were sparse, filled with rage and a chillingly detached account of the events leading up to Katherine Miller's murder. Nightshade's handwriting was sharp, angular, a stark contrast to Primrose's elegant script. Her entries were short, brutal bursts of anger and resentment, punctuated by cryptic symbols and unsettling imagery. The words themselves felt like shards of glass, cutting through the carefully constructed image of the seemingly perfect wife and mother. The violence wasn't just described; it was felt, a raw, visceral force emanating from the page. Sarah found herself recoiling, her own trauma echoing the brutal honesty of Nightshade's confessions. She felt a morbid fascination, a horrifying curiosity about the alter who had committed such an unthinkable act.

"Seraphina," in stark contrast, was a child-like alter, her writing innocent and vulnerable. Her entries were filled with drawings and childish scrawls, depicting scenes of idyllic beauty and carefree games. These entries were interjected amidst the darker accounts, providing a jarring juxtaposition that highlighted the profound disconnect within Eleanor's psyche. Seraphina's world was one of innocence, a stark contrast to the grim reality of the other alters. It was a heartbreaking glimpse into the child Eleanor had been, a child whose innocence had been cruelly stolen. Her drawings, often depicting flowers and fantastical creatures, were a desperate attempt to escape the horrors she had endured. Sarah felt a surge of protective instinct, a desperate need to shield this innocent alter from the darkness that surrounded her.

"The Shadow," as Sarah began to call her, was a nameless, silent entity that seemed to haunt the periphery of the diary. Her presence was felt more than seen, a chilling undercurrent in the narrative. The Shadow's entries consisted primarily of symbolic imagery, fragmented phrases, and unsettling sketches, each hinting at a deeper level of trauma and a horrifying capacity for violence. These entries offered chilling glimpses into Eleanor's deepest fears and darkest impulses. Sarah found herself tracing the lines, trying to decipher the meaning behind the cryptic symbols, sensing the presence of a malevolent force lurking beneath the surface. The Shadow's entries were terrifying, not for their explicit descriptions but for the underlying sense of dread and impending doom.

There was also "Echo," whose entries were filled with fragmented memories, often overlapping and contradictory. Echo seemed to be the repository of Eleanor's traumatic experiences, her writing a jumbled mess of recollections and anxieties. Her narrative was non-linear, jumping between past and present, creating a fragmented and disorienting reading experience. Sarah found herself struggling to piece together the chronology of events, the trauma and pain interweaving into a complex and unsettling tapestry. Echo's writing reflected the chaotic nature of her experiences, the disjointed memories and the emotional turmoil that haunted her.

As Sarah delved deeper into the diary, the line between objective observer and emotional participant blurred. She found herself becoming entangled in the narratives of these alters, experiencing their pain, their rage, and their fear. It was a visceral experience, a descent into the depths of a fractured psyche. The diary wasn't just a collection of entries; it was a living, breathing entity, reflecting the complex interplay of personalities struggling for dominance and control. The sheer volume of material, the shifting timelines and perspectives, created a disorienting and emotionally draining experience.

The diary revealed a history of unspeakable abuse – physical, emotional, and sexual – that had shattered Eleanor's psyche. The fragmented memories, scattered throughout the entries, offered glimpses into the horrors she had endured, experiences that had shaped the creation of these distinct personalities. Each alter represented a coping mechanism, a way to compartmentalize the trauma and protect the vulnerable core self. But these coping mechanisms had become a prison, trapping Eleanor within a fractured and volatile psyche.

The entries weren't simply accounts of trauma; they were also expressions of Eleanor's internal struggles, her attempts to understand and reconcile the conflicting narratives within her mind. Some entries revealed moments of self-awareness, glimpses of a desperate desire for healing and wholeness. There were entries where Eleanor expressed remorse, acknowledging the devastating impact of her actions, yet unable to escape the control of her destructive alters. The duality between these conflicting emotions, the desire for redemption versus the overwhelming power of trauma, created a powerful and emotionally complex narrative.

The diary became Sarah's lifeline, a way to connect with her mother on a deeper level, to understand the complexities of her fractured psyche, and to find a way to make sense of the tragedy that had unfolded. But the experience was far from easy. It was a relentless emotional roller coaster, forcing Sarah to confront the horrors of her mother's past and grapple with the overwhelming burden of her legacy. Sarah's pre-existing anxieties were compounded by the details contained within the diary, triggering intense emotional responses, creating a cycle of flashbacks and emotional distress.

The investigation into Eleanor's past unearthed a tapestry of abuse woven through her life. The physical evidence, previously overlooked, was given new meaning within the context of the diary's revelations. The red scrunchies, the lye, the choice of the freezer – each detail became a horrifying piece of the puzzle, a tangible representation of Nightshade's chilling actions. But it wasn't just the physical evidence; it was the psychological profile painted by the diary, the intricate narrative reflecting Eleanor's deep-seated trauma and her fragmented, volatile psyche. The diary itself became a key piece of evidence, showcasing the intricate nature of Eleanor's mental disorder and the potential influence of her alters on her actions.

The exploration of Eleanor's other alters was not merely a recounting of facts but an emotional journey, a descent into the depths of a fractured psyche and a quest to find a measure of understanding and, perhaps, even forgiveness. Each alter's voice was unique, reflecting their different experiences, anxieties, and coping mechanisms. The narrative moved beyond simple identification of different personalities to a deep dive into the creation of these personalities, how Eleanor's trauma shaped each alter, and how these alters ultimately contributed to the crime. It was a journey that forced Sarah to confront the unbearable truth, to accept the reality of her mother's violent acts and yet find a way to reconcile it with the love and care that had also existed in Eleanor's fragmented world. The discovery of each new alter, each new perspective, brought Sarah closer to understanding her mother but also deeper into the traumatic reality of Eleanor's life and ultimate actions. It was a journey into the darkest corners of the human psyche, a chilling exploration of trauma, violence and the enduring strength of the human spirit in the face of unspeakable suffering. The process was emotionally arduous, but the deeper Sarah delved, the closer she came to understanding her mother, the crime, and ultimately, herself.

The lye, Sarah realized, wasn't just a tool; it was a symbol. Its corrosive nature mirrored the insidious destruction that had eaten away at Eleanor's psyche, leaving behind a fractured and volatile landscape. The caustic substance, slowly dissolving flesh and bone, reflected the agonizing erosion of Eleanor's sense of self, the slow, relentless disintegration caused by years of unspeakable abuse. It was a horrifyingly apt metaphor for the damage inflicted upon her, both internally and externally.

Sarah reread Nightshade's entry describing the act, searching for clues, for any hint of rationalization, anything that might illuminate the horrifying choices made. The words were stark, devoid of emotion, almost clinical in their description of the process. But interspersed within the chilling narrative were unsettling images – a recurring motif of melting ice, the slow, inexorable drip of water, the image of a flower wilting under a harsh sun. These weren't random details; they were fragments of a shattered psyche, glimpses into the internal turmoil that fueled Nightshade's actions. The lye, she realized, was a reflection of that internal corrosion, a tangible manifestation of the psychological damage Eleanor had endured.

Thinking back to the crime scene photos, the stark contrast between the pristine freezer and the gruesome contents within, Sarah shuddered. The freezer, a symbol of preservation, ironically held the victim in a state of irreversible decay. The black bags, the red scrunchies – these details, previously dismissed as random, now felt deliberate, symbolic choices. The black, representing the darkness that had consumed Eleanor, the red, a perverse echo of the blood spilled. The lye, dissolving the victim's body, mirrored the corrosive effect of trauma on Eleanor's mind, a slow, relentless destruction that left nothing untouched.

But the symbolism extended beyond the immediate act. The corrosive nature of lye also pointed to the lasting impact of the abuse. The scars it left on Katherine Miller's body were a physical representation of the wounds that had festered within Eleanor for years, a tangible manifestation of the unseen damage. The lye, in its relentless destruction, mirrored the enduring impact of trauma, the way it can seep into every aspect of a person's life, poisoning their relationships, their self-perception, and their ability to function. It was a potent reminder of the lingering effects of abuse, the way it can continue to inflict pain and suffering long after the initial trauma has passed.

Sarah considered the different alters and how they each might have interacted with the symbolic meaning of the lye. Primrose, the demure exterior, likely wouldn't have grasped the symbolic weight of the act. Her meticulously ordered world wouldn't accommodate such chaotic and destructive imagery. But Nightshade, the violent alter, would have understood it implicitly. The lye would have resonated with her inner rage, mirroring the corrosive hatred she felt toward the world and those who had wronged Eleanor. Seraphina, the childlike alter, wouldn't have understood the act at all, perceiving it as something monstrous and incomprehensible. Her innocent world couldn't contain such brutality. The Shadow, silent and enigmatic, might have seen the lye as a tool of purification, a way to cleanse the world of its impurities. And Echo, with her fragmented memories, might have perceived the lye as a symbol of the erosion of her own identity, the relentless chipping away of her sense of self.

The diary entries themselves became a reflection of this corrosive process. The handwriting, shifting from the elegant script of Primrose to the jagged, angular strokes of Nightshade, mirrored the fractured nature of Eleanor's psyche. The language, oscillating between meticulous detail and raw, visceral descriptions, mirrored the erratic swings between control and chaos within her mind. The fragmented memories, the contradictory narratives, the cryptic symbols – these all pointed to the corrosive effect of trauma on her cognitive function and emotional stability.

Sarah found herself increasingly drawn to the symbolic imagery within the diary entries. The recurring motifs of decay, disintegration, and erosion weren't just artistic flourishes; they were attempts by Eleanor's alters to articulate the unspeakable horrors they had endured. The images of melting snow, wilting flowers, and crumbling buildings spoke to the disintegration of Eleanor's sense of self, the erosion of her identity under the weight of abuse. These weren't simply artistic choices; they were visceral expressions of trauma, a desperate attempt to translate the unspeakable into a form that could be understood.

The use of the freezer itself added another layer to the symbolism. Freezers are designed to preserve, to keep things from decaying. Yet, here, it held the victim in a state of accelerated decomposition. This paradox further highlighted the corrosive nature of the trauma Eleanor had endured, a trauma that had not only destroyed her but also ironically preserved the very elements that had caused her pain. The victim, trapped within the ice, became a symbol of Eleanor's own frozen state, her inability to process or escape the trauma that had shattered her psyche.

Sarah realized that understanding the symbolic meaning of the lye was crucial to understanding Eleanor's crime. It wasn't just a random choice of weapon; it was a deliberate act, deeply symbolic of the internal chaos and destructive forces within her mind. The lye represented the corrosive nature of trauma, its ability to erode a person's sense of self and leave behind a fractured and volatile psyche. It was a potent symbol of the long-lasting impact of abuse, the way it can linger long after the initial trauma has passed. The symbolism offered a deeper understanding of Eleanor's motivations, her actions, and the complex interplay of personalities within her fragmented mind.

The more Sarah delved into the diary, the more she understood the profound psychological complexity of Eleanor's condition. The lye was more than just a tool of murder; it was a symbol of the internal corrosion that had consumed Eleanor, a manifestation of the destructive forces unleashed by years of trauma. It was a chilling reminder of the enduring power of abuse and its devastating consequences, a symbol that echoed the fragmented and volatile landscape of Eleanor's shattered psyche. The act itself wasn't just a crime; it was a symbolic representation of the internal struggle, a desperate, violent act of self-destruction disguised as an act against another. Sarah felt a chill run down her spine as she grasped the full horror of what her mother had done, and the deep, enduring scars that had led to it. The lye, in its corrosive power, was a haunting testament to the lasting impact of trauma. It was a symbol that would forever be etched in Sarah's memory, a constant reminder of the darkness that lurked beneath the surface of her seemingly perfect mother. And as Sarah continued to read, the full weight of Eleanor's life, her pain, and her ultimate, horrifying act began to coalesce into a grim, unsettling truth.

The diary entries shifted, veering from Nightshade's brutal accounts to passages written in a hesitant, childlike scrawl Sarah recognized as belonging to Seraphina. These entries spoke of a different kind of horror, a chilling contrast to Nightshade's stark descriptions of violence. They detailed a world of hushed whispers, furtive glances, and a constant, underlying sense of fear. Seraphina's world was one of unexplained bruises, stolen moments of affection quickly withdrawn, and the persistent, suffocating presence of a looming, unpredictable anger. It was a world where love was a fragile thing, easily shattered, leaving behind only the bitter taste of disappointment and the gnawing fear of what might come next.

These fragmented memories revealed a chilling pattern: a father whose love was as volatile and unpredictable as a summer storm. His affection, when it appeared, was intense, almost suffocating, but it was always fleeting, followed by periods of chilling indifference, or worse, bursts of rage that left Eleanor's alters trembling in fear. He was a man of contradictions, capable of both tender moments and terrifying outbursts, leaving Eleanor trapped in a constant state of emotional turmoil. His presence cast a long shadow, warping her perception of love, trust, and safety.

Sarah struggled to reconcile the image of her father with the man depicted in the diary entries. The man she remembered was distant, preoccupied, a figure she rarely saw, his presence more of a looming absence than a constant comfort. But the diary painted a much darker picture – a picture of emotional manipulation, sporadic violence, and a profound lack of empathy. It was a picture that shattered Sarah's carefully constructed memories, forcing her to confront a past she'd tried to bury, a past she'd never fully understood.

The entries revealed a father who, consciously or not, had fostered the fragmentation within Eleanor's psyche. His inconsistent behavior, his unpredictable emotional outbursts, and his inability to provide a stable and nurturing environment had created a fertile ground for the emergence of multiple personalities. Each alter represented a different coping mechanism, a different way of navigating the chaos and trauma he had inflicted. Primrose, the demure and controlled alter, was a shield, protecting Eleanor from the overwhelming pain. Nightshade, the violent alter, was the expression of the rage that had festered within her for years. Seraphina, the childlike alter, was a desperate attempt to recapture a lost innocence, a world untouched by the cruelty of her father's actions. Echo, with her fragmented memories, was a testament to the lasting damage he had caused.

There was a sense of betrayal, a deep-seated anger, that welled up within Sarah as she read. It wasn't just directed toward her father but also toward herself, for the years of denial, for the willful blindness that had allowed her to construct a version of the past that excluded the truth. She had clung to the image of a distant, but ultimately harmless father, a man absent from her life but not actively destructive. The diary had ripped that illusion away, exposing a brutal reality she'd never dared to acknowledge. The revelation of his actions filled her with a profound sense of loss, not just for the woman her mother had become, but for the childhood she had never fully had, a childhood poisoned by the unseen trauma inflicted upon her mother.

The silence surrounding this had been deafening. The absence of conversations, the lack of acknowledgment, the pervasive sense of something unspoken – all of it had contributed to the insidious growth of the trauma. This wasn't just about the physical and emotional abuse; it was about the silence that enveloped it, the denial that festered in the family's shadowed corners, allowing the damage to fester and grow unchecked. Sarah began to wonder how much her father had truly known, how much he had intentionally ignored, how much his actions had contributed to her mother's fractured psyche. Had he knowingly nurtured a situation where his wife was reduced to a patchwork of desperate coping mechanisms? Or had he simply been oblivious to the damage he inflicted, blind to the depth of his own destructive actions?

The diary entries didn't offer easy answers. They were fragments, glimpses into a fractured mind, a fractured family. The narrative shifted between perspectives, often contradicting itself, mirroring the chaotic reality of Eleanor's internal landscape. One moment, Sarah was reading about tender interactions between Eleanor and her father, moments of shared laughter and affection; the next, she was confronted with harrowing accounts of abuse, betrayal, and the systematic destruction of a woman's spirit. These jarring juxtapositions reflected the complex and often contradictory nature of Eleanor's relationship with her father, a relationship that had shaped not only her life but the lives of all her alters.

Sarah found herself increasingly drawn to the subtle details within the entries, the seemingly insignificant events that revealed the undercurrents of dysfunction and emotional abuse. A forgotten birthday, a casual insult, a dismissive gesture – these small, seemingly insignificant actions, when viewed through the lens of trauma, took on a chilling significance, revealing the insidious patterns of manipulation and control that had defined Eleanor's relationship with her father. These details were not random; they were carefully selected fragments, designed to expose the slow, insidious erosion of Eleanor's sense of self, her identity gradually being chipped away by the consistent unpredictability and volatility of her father's actions.

The diary entries also revealed Eleanor's attempts to understand her father's behavior, to make sense of his inconsistent affections and unpredictable rages. She often described him as a man torn between two worlds, a man struggling with his own demons, a man who was both capable of great love and unspeakable cruelty. This description added a layer of complexity to Sarah's understanding of her father, acknowledging the possibility that his behavior wasn't simply malicious but rooted in his own internal struggles and unresolved traumas. However, this empathy didn't negate the pain he inflicted, or the lasting impact of his actions on Eleanor's psyche. It only added another layer of complexity to the already tangled web of their relationship.

As Sarah continued to read, she started to see a pattern emerge in her father's behavior, a cycle of emotional abuse that escalated over time. Initially, there were displays of affection, but these were interspersed with periods of neglect, emotional coldness, and the occasional outburst of anger. These inconsistent displays of affection were designed to keep Eleanor emotionally off-balance, to maintain a sense of power and control over her. As the abuse continued, the cycles grew shorter, the periods of neglect becoming longer, the outbursts of anger more frequent and more intense. This escalating pattern of abuse left Eleanor in a constant state of anxiety, unable to predict what might come next, making it more challenging for her to establish a sense of security or self-worth.

The diary entries revealed a father who possessed a certain manipulative charm, capable of showering Eleanor with affection and attention one moment and withdrawing it completely the next. This inconsistency served to keep Eleanor off-balance, perpetually seeking his approval and affection. This emotional manipulation was subtly woven into the fabric of their relationship, rendering Eleanor dependent on his approval, trapped in a cycle of seeking validation and acceptance she never truly received. The lack of consistent love and affection left a void within Eleanor, a void that the different alters attempted to fill in their own unique ways. The emotional manipulation was a key element in the creation of the fragmented psyche, a psychological strategy that maintained power and control over Eleanor. The diary entries showed this subtly, exposing the long-term implications of emotional manipulation and its devastating effects on Eleanor's psychological well-being.

The more Sarah read, the more she recognized the subtle but insidious ways in which her father's behavior had shaped Eleanor's life, the subtle ways he had undermined her sense of self-worth, the subtle ways he had manipulated her into accepting his actions as normal or acceptable. The trauma wasn't confined to obvious acts of violence; it was woven into the fabric of daily life, in the casual insults, the dismissive gestures, the subtle undercurrents of disapproval, the unpredictable outbursts that left Eleanor walking on eggshells, forever anticipating the next explosion of his anger. This constant anxiety and fear created the conditions for the development of her multiple personalities, each a coping mechanism to manage the emotional turmoil caused by her father's behavior. It was an agonizingly slow process of psychological destruction, a slow, insidious poisoning of Eleanor's soul. The discovery was a seismic event, forcing Sarah to re-evaluate her entire understanding of her family's history, of her father's role, and of the origins of her mother's devastating mental illness.

The diary entries, after detailing years of insidious emotional abuse, finally began to hint at the specific triggers that unleashed Nightshade. They weren't singular events, but a confluence of factors, a perfect storm brewing within Eleanor's fractured mind. Sarah discovered that specific scents, sounds, and even textures could act as potent catalysts, plunging Eleanor into a terrifying freefall into Nightshade's darkness.

One recurring trigger was the scent of lye. It wasn't just the chemical itself, but the association it held within Eleanor's fragmented psyche. The diary entries revealed a horrifying incident from Eleanor's childhood, a detail that initially seemed unrelated to the later murder. It was a memory fragmented across several alters, each recalling a piece of the puzzle. Primrose recalled a cleaning accident involving lye, the harsh chemical burning her skin, the agonizing pain and the subsequent fear of her father's reaction. Seraphina remembered the smell, the acrid sting in her nostrils, clinging to her like a phantom limb. Nightshade, however, remembered something far more sinister – the smell of lye, the burning sensation, coupled with the feeling of utter powerlessness, of being trapped and helpless in the face of her father's rage. The smell wasn't just a physical sensation; it was a visceral trigger, a potent symbol of her vulnerability, her past trauma, and her unending fear.

Another recurring element was the texture of black plastic bags. The diary entries, written in Nightshade's stark, brutal style, described a recurring obsession with the smooth, slippery feel of the bags, a sensation that seemed to both excite and terrify her. This wasn't just a fetishization of the material; it was a deeper, more profound connection to the feeling of being suffocated, controlled, and rendered powerless

—feelings deeply rooted in her childhood experiences of abuse. Nightshade's entries spoke of a perverse sense of control derived from the act of encasing something, of containing it, of silencing it, mirroring her own desire to silence the voices within and control the chaos of her own fragmented psyche.

The red scrunchies, a seemingly insignificant detail in the murder, also emerged as a significant trigger in the diary. The entries revealed that red was a recurring colour in Eleanor's memories of her childhood, specifically associated with her father's anger. Sometimes, he'd wear a red tie on days he was particularly volatile, a silent warning of the storm brewing. Other times, red was connected to the physical marks he left behind – the bruises, the welts. For Nightshade, the red scrunchies became a symbolic representation of that past violence, a reminder of the powerlessness she had felt as a child. Their presence was an invitation for her to unleash the rage she had suppressed for so long.

These triggers weren't solely sensory; they were deeply intertwined with psychological mechanisms. The diary revealed that Nightshade was often activated during periods of intense stress or emotional distress. Any event that threatened to unravel Eleanor's carefully constructed facade, any perceived betrayal or threat to her carefully crafted persona, could trigger her emergence. The entries, through Nightshade's eyes, showed a world constantly on the edge of a precipice, a constant battle to maintain a fragile equilibrium. Any disruption to this delicate balance – a confrontation, a crisis, even a simple misunderstanding – could unleash Nightshade's pent-up rage. It was a desperate attempt to regain control, a violent expression of her repressed pain and trauma.

Sarah also discovered the significance of the freezer. The freezer, she realised, was more than just a location; it was a metaphor, a symbol of imprisonment and silencing. For Nightshade, it was a place of ultimate control, where she could freeze the pain, bury the past, and silence the victims of her rage. The act of encasing a victim in black plastic bags, tying them with red scrunchies, and then placing them in the freezer, became a ritualistic act, a symbolic expression of her need to control and contain the very things that tormented her. This wasn't simply random violence; it was a carefully orchestrated performance, a grotesque enactment of her deepest desires – to silence her tormentors, to bury the pain, to finally achieve a sense of control over her fragmented and chaotic inner world.

The diary entries revealed a pattern: the triggers, the escalating rage, and the ritualistic act of the murder. The events weren't random; they were the culmination of years of suppressed trauma, the manifestation of a shattered psyche struggling to cope with unbearable pain. Each element – the lye, the plastic bags, the red scrunchies, the freezer – held a deeper symbolic meaning, a connection to the past abuse and the resulting fragmentation of Eleanor's personality. The murder itself wasn't a spontaneous act; it was a carefully planned and executed ritual, a symbolic enactment of Nightshade's desperate attempt to regain control, to silence her past, and to impose order on her chaotic internal landscape.

The entries also provided glimpses into the intricate psychological mechanisms driving Nightshade's actions. Dissociation, a common symptom of trauma, played a crucial role in enabling Nightshade's violence. The diary revealed moments where Eleanor had no recollection of Nightshade's actions, moments where one alter would take over, leaving no memory of what happened under her control. This dissociation allowed Nightshade to act out her aggression without facing the full consequences, without bearing the full weight of her actions. It provided a psychological buffer, separating her from the reality of her violence.

Beyond the immediate triggers and psychological mechanisms, the diary also revealed the profound influence of Eleanor's environment on the emergence of Nightshade. The diary entries pointed to specific periods of increased stress, instances of interpersonal conflict, or feelings of inadequacy, all of which contributed to Nightshade's surfacing. It was a complex interplay of external factors and internal turmoil that combined to unleash her rage. The instability in Eleanor's environment and her life acted as potent catalysts, providing the ideal conditions for Nightshade to take center stage, resulting in horrific consequences.

As Sarah continued reading, the connection between Eleanor's past and the murder became crystal clear. It wasn't just a random act of violence; it was a culmination of years of trauma, a desperate cry for help from a fractured psyche desperately seeking control. The murder was a chilling reflection of Eleanor's broken mind, a terrifying manifestation of the consequences of unchecked trauma and the insidious power of suppressed rage.

The diary didn't offer simple answers or easy explanations, mirroring the complexities of the human mind under the crushing weight of trauma. But it did offer a chilling window into the mind of a woman consumed by her fragmented self, a woman whose pain and rage ultimately led to an act of unspeakable violence. Sarah's understanding shifted from confusion and grief to a horrifying but clear insight into the roots of the crime, the triggers that had unleashed Nightshade, and the tragic consequences of a life spent wrestling with the demons of a fractured psyche. The diary, in its fragmented and chilling narrative, became a powerful testament to the devastating impact of unchecked trauma, and the complex ways in which it could manifest itself in the darkest corners of the human heart. The final pages of the diary left Sarah with more questions than answers, but they also provided a grim yet essential understanding of the horrific event, the triggers that released the beast, and the lasting impact it would have on her life.

The final entries in Eleanor's diary weren't filled with the stark, brutal pronouncements of Nightshade. Instead, they were penned by Primrose, a personality Sarah hadn't encountered before, a whisper of innocence amidst the storm. Primrose's handwriting was delicate, almost childlike, a stark contrast to Nightshade's sharp, angular script. Her entries described a world of vibrant colours, of whimsical fantasies, and a deep yearning for love and acceptance. It was a world untouched by the darkness that had consumed the other alters, a fragile oasis in the wasteland of Eleanor's fractured psyche. Sarah learned that Primrose was the youngest, the one who had retreated furthest into the recesses of Eleanor's mind, shielded from the horrors of the abuse. She was a child who had never grown up, forever trapped in a state of innocent wonder, oblivious to the violence that had ravaged her world. Reading Primrose's entries was like stumbling into a hidden garden, a place of beauty and serenity that starkly contrasted with the grim reality of Eleanor's life. It was a testament to the resilience of the human spirit, the ability to find joy and hope even in the face of unimaginable suffering.

Through Primrose's eyes, Sarah saw a different side of Eleanor – a woman capable of immense love, tenderness, and a profound capacity for joy. It was a side that had been buried deep beneath layers of trauma, a side that had been silenced by the overwhelming weight of her experiences. Primrose's entries revealed snippets of Eleanor's childhood before the abuse began, memories of laughter, warmth, and security. These fleeting moments provided a glimpse into the person Eleanor might have become if her life had taken a different path. They also served as a stark reminder of what had been stolen from her – a normal childhood, a stable family life, the simple joys of being a child without fear.

As Sarah absorbed Primrose's innocent narratives, a profound shift began within her. The rage and confusion that had consumed her began to recede, replaced by a growing sense of empathy and understanding. She finally understood that Eleanor wasn't simply a monster; she was a victim, a woman trapped within the confines of her own shattered mind. The murder wasn't an act of pure evil; it was a desperate act of survival, a desperate attempt to silence the pain and reclaim some semblance of control in a life that had been stolen from her. Sarah began to see the intricate tapestry of Eleanor's fractured psyche, the complex interplay of trauma, dissociation, and the desperate fight for survival that had shaped her actions.

This wasn't an easy acceptance. The memories of the gruesome details remained, clinging to Sarah like a persistent shadow. Yet, the knowledge of her mother's past – the systematic abuse, the isolation, the complete absence of support – began to paint a clearer picture of the circumstances that had led to the horrific act. It wasn't a justification, but an explanation, a way to reconcile the monstrous act with the woman Sarah had known, or thought she had known.

The final chapters of the diary detailed Eleanor's attempts to seek help, her fragmented recollections of therapy sessions, the elusive nature of treatment for her condition. The entries revealed the frustrating cyclical nature of her illness, periods of relative calm interspersed with terrifying episodes of dissociation and violent outbursts. Sarah saw the struggle, the relentless battle against her mother's inner demons, the sheer exhaustion of fighting for survival within herself. There were accounts of moments when Eleanor attempted to grasp at help, desperately seeking the support that she had always been denied. These entries served as a stark reminder that Eleanor was a victim, trapped within a system that failed to protect her and provide her with the help she desperately needed.

With each page, the weight of Eleanor's pain settled upon Sarah, not as a condemnation, but as a profound sorrow. The empathy she felt wasn't simply an intellectual understanding; it was a visceral response, a deep ache in her heart that mirrored the depth of her mother's suffering. This empathy wasn't weakness; it was a powerful force that allowed Sarah to finally begin the process of healing.

This newfound understanding didn't erase the horror of the crime. The image of the victim, frozen in the freezer, still haunted Sarah's dreams. But the understanding of the origins of the act allowed Sarah to view it with a detached, clinical perspective, albeit one still filled with unbearable grief. The act remained horrific, but it shifted from an act of pure malice to a consequence of a deeply disturbed mind, a mind that had been relentlessly abused and pushed to its breaking point.

The diary entries allowed Sarah to see her mother not only as a victim but also as a complex and multifaceted individual. Eleanor wasn't merely defined by the horrific act committed by Nightshade. Instead, she was a collection of personalities, each with their own unique experiences, fears, and desires. Sarah saw the innocence of Primrose, the fierce survival instinct of Nightshade, and the quiet resilience of the other alters she had yet to fully comprehend. Her mother was a tapestry of pain and resilience, a testament to the human capacity for both destruction and profound beauty.

Sarah's journey of acceptance wasn't a linear path; it was a winding road filled with moments of doubt, anger, and grief. There were days when the horror of her mother's actions overwhelmed her, days when she questioned her ability to ever forgive. But the entries also provided moments of profound connection, allowing her to glimpse the broken woman behind the mask, the woman who had endured unspeakable suffering. It was a painful process, a slow and arduous journey through the darkest corners of her family history.

The act of forgiveness, Sarah discovered, wasn't about condoning her mother's actions. It wasn't about erasing the past or pretending it never happened. It was about accepting the truth, acknowledging the complexities of her mother's fractured psyche, and recognizing the immense trauma she had endured. It was about finding a way to reconcile the woman she had known with the monstrous act she had committed.

The final entry in the diary, penned by Eleanor herself, in a shaky, uncertain hand, simply read, "I am sorry." It was a simple statement, yet it carried the weight of a lifetime of pain and regret. It was a silent apology for the hurt she had caused, for the life she had destroyed, and for the fractured legacy she had left behind. For Sarah, those two words were enough. They were a testament to her mother's profound remorse, a flicker of hope amidst the darkness, and a starting point for Sarah's own long journey of healing and forgiveness.

The diary closed, but the story continued. Sarah's life would never be the same. The knowledge of her mother's fragmented past, her abuse, and the consequences that ensued, became an integral part of her identity. The horror of her mother's actions would always linger, a constant reminder of the insidious nature of trauma and its devastating consequences. Yet, amidst the darkness, Sarah found a fragile strength, a newfound understanding, and the beginnings of a path towards healing, acceptance, and even a tentative form of forgiveness. The diary became a testament not only to her mother's fractured psyche but also to her daughter's remarkable resilience. It was a story of loss, grief, and the enduring power of the human spirit to find hope and healing amidst unimaginable darkness. The chilling tale was finally over, but the haunting echo of Eleanor's fractured reflection would forever resonate within Sarah's heart.

# CHAPTER 10: A WEB OF DECEIT

The diary's final entries, a fragile testament to Eleanor's fractured mind, offered Sarah a glimpse into the abyss of her mother's existence, but they left many questions unanswered. Chief among them was the unsettling absence of any mention of Robert, Eleanor's husband, the man who had always presented himself as the picture of affable respectability. He had been a constant presence in Sarah's life, a seemingly loving and supportive father figure, yet the diary remained eerily silent about his role in Eleanor's life, his influence on her condition, and his potential complicity in the events leading up to the murder.

This omission fueled Sarah's growing unease. The idyllic image of Robert, the successful businessman, the devoted husband, began to crack, revealing subtle inconsistencies, unspoken tensions, and a chilling undercurrent of control. She remembered instances – previously dismissed as insignificant – of Robert's possessiveness, his iron grip on Eleanor's finances, his subtle manipulation of her social interactions. There was the time he had forbidden Eleanor from seeing her family, the years he had controlled her access to medical professionals, the casual dismissiveness whenever Eleanor mentioned feeling unwell. Now, they felt sinister.

Armed with the diary's revelations about Eleanor's abuse,

Sarah began to re-examine her memories, looking for clues she had previously ignored. She unearthed old photographs, scanning each for hidden expressions, for the subtle signs of a power imbalance, for the faintest hint of Eleanor's distress. In one photograph, taken at a family gathering, Eleanor's eyes held a chilling emptiness, a stark contrast to the forced smiles plastered on her face. In another, a slight tremor in her hand betrayed a hidden anxiety, her gaze darting nervously towards Robert, a man who now appeared in a completely new light.

Sarah's investigation led her to delve into Robert's past, an exploration that unearthed a disturbing pattern of manipulative behavior. He was a master of deception, a skilled manipulator who used charm and affability to mask a chilling ruthlessness. She discovered he had a history of controlling relationships, of isolating his partners from their support networks, and of systematically undermining their self-esteem. Whispers of past indiscretions followed him like a shadow, hints of financial improprieties and instances where women had mysteriously disappeared from his life.

As Sarah pieced together the fragments of Robert's past, she began to suspect his involvement in Eleanor's abuse. The diary's entries suggested a pattern of systematic control, a gradual erosion of Eleanor's autonomy, and a calculated campaign to isolate her from the outside world. This pattern aligned disturbingly well with Robert's known methods of manipulation. The absence of Robert's name in the diary wasn't an oversight; it was a calculated omission, a testament to his manipulative control over Eleanor's narrative, even from beyond the grave.

Sarah's suspicions intensified when she discovered a series

of hidden bank accounts, accounts Eleanor had never known about, accounts that were managed solely by Robert. The sums were staggering, amounts that couldn't be explained by his legitimate business dealings. The money, Sarah suspected, was the product of illicit activities, activities that involved Eleanor and her fractured psyche as unwitting tools.

This revelation further cemented Sarah's belief that Robert's influence extended far beyond mere marital control. He had not only abused Eleanor emotionally and psychologically; he had exploited her vulnerability, manipulating her fragile mental state for his own nefarious purposes. His actions were calculated, cold, and devoid of empathy. He had constructed a facade of respectability, using his charm and influence to manipulate those around him and conceal his own dark deeds.

His manipulative tactics extended beyond financial control. He had expertly woven a web of deceit around Eleanor, creating an environment of isolation and fear that prevented her from seeking help. He had expertly manipulated her family and friends, convincing them that Eleanor was unstable, unreliable, and a danger to herself and others. This insidious campaign had effectively silenced Eleanor's cries for help, leaving her trapped in a cycle of abuse, her fractured self struggling for survival in a world that had become her prison.

Robert's manipulation wasn't limited to Eleanor alone. Sarah now understood the extent of his influence, his careful orchestration of events, his ability to manipulate even the legal system to shield himself from suspicion. He had constructed a narrative that painted him as the grieving husband, the loyal companion, the man whose life had been shattered by Eleanor's actions. It was a masterful performance, a carefully crafted illusion that had fooled everyone, including Sarah, for years.

The more Sarah investigated, the more she discovered the intricate layers of Robert's deception. He had used Eleanor's illness as a tool, exploiting her vulnerability to maintain control and silence any potential dissent. He had subtly manipulated the police investigation, leaving behind just enough evidence to suggest that the murder was the act of a deranged individual, an isolated incident unconnected to any broader network of deceit.

His manipulation extended to Sarah herself. He had carefully cultivated a loving father-daughter relationship, offering support and affection to mask his manipulative nature. He had subtly guided her perceptions, influencing her understanding of Eleanor, and ensuring that Sarah never questioned his own role in her mother's life. The depth of his deception was astounding; he had been manipulating Sarah, influencing her perception of her own mother, all while maintaining an impeccable public image.

The evidence, though circumstantial, painted a damning portrait of Robert. It wasn't just about the financial irregularities or the manipulative behavior; it was about a pattern of control, a systematic undermining of Eleanor's autonomy, and a calculated campaign to conceal his involvement in her abuse and the subsequent murder. He had built his life on a foundation of deceit, a carefully constructed illusion that masked his true nature. Now, as Sarah uncovered the truth, his carefully crafted image began to crumble, revealing the chilling reality of the man she had known as her father. She was determined to bring him to justice and expose the chilling truth behind the façade of respectability. The weight of the revelation pressed down on her, but it also fueled her resolve. She would expose his manipulations, unravel his carefully constructed web of deceit, and bring him to justice, for Eleanor, for herself, and for the victims he had left in his wake. The quest for justice was now her primary focus, fueled by a rage that burned hotter than any empathy she had previously felt for her mother. The truth, she knew, would not only bring closure but also shatter the illusion Robert had so meticulously cultivated.

The diary entries revealed not just Eleanor's internal struggles but also hinted at a chilling dynamic within the family unit. Sarah had always viewed her childhood as idyllic, a picture of upper-class comfort and suburban normalcy. Robert, her father, was the epitome of success, a charming and affable man who commanded respect in the business world and affection at home. Eleanor, in Sarah's memory, was a somewhat distant but loving mother, perpetually preoccupied yet always present in a quiet, understated way. The diary, however, shattered this carefully constructed narrative.

The fragmented accounts from Eleanor's various alters painted a starkly different picture. One alter, a childlike persona Sarah tentatively labeled "Lily," described a home filled with unspoken tensions, a constant undercurrent of fear that permeated their seemingly perfect life. Lily's entries were filled with fragmented memories of hushed arguments, slammed doors, and the chilling silence that followed. These weren't the boisterous disagreements of a typical family; these were simmering resentments, carefully concealed behind a veneer of polite civility.

Another alter, a more mature and cynical personality Sarah

called "Evelyn," provided a more analytical perspective. Evelyn's entries described a carefully orchestrated system of control, with Robert wielding his power subtly but effectively. He controlled the finances, dictating Eleanor's spending and limiting her access to resources. He controlled her social interactions, isolating her from friends and family, effectively cutting her off from any potential support network. Evelyn's entries revealed a calculated manipulation, a slow and insidious erosion of Eleanor's independence and self-esteem.

The entries also alluded to a complex web of emotional abuse. Robert's control wasn't merely financial; it extended to emotional manipulation, gaslighting, and the systematic undermining of Eleanor's confidence. He would twist her words, invalidate her feelings, and subtly shift the blame for any conflict onto her. Evelyn's entries revealed a chilling pattern of psychological manipulation, a gradual dismantling of Eleanor's sense of self, leaving her vulnerable and dependent on Robert for validation.

The most disturbing entries came from "Seraphina," an alter that emerged only in moments of extreme distress. Seraphina's writing was raw, visceral, and filled with fragmented memories of physical violence and sexual abuse. These entries were sparse, fragmented, often consisting of single words or phrases, but the underlying trauma was undeniable. The cryptic references and emotional intensity suggested a level of abuse far beyond what Sarah could have ever imagined. Seraphina's descriptions of physical pain, her fragmented memories of confinement and fear, created a disturbing narrative of systematic cruelty and violation.

The impact of this abuse on Eleanor's fragmented psyche

was evident. The various alters seemed to represent different coping mechanisms, different attempts to navigate the trauma she had endured. Lily's childlike innocence was a defense mechanism, a retreat into a world of fantasy to escape the harsh reality of her abuse. Evelyn's cynicism was a shield, a way to cope with the emotional pain and betrayal by becoming detached and analytical. Seraphina, the most fragmented and disturbed alter, embodied the raw, untamed rage and fear that resulted from the abuse. Each alter played a crucial role in Eleanor's survival, a testament to her resilience in the face of unimaginable cruelty.

Examining the family dynamics through the lens of the diary entries, Sarah began to see patterns she hadn't noticed before. She recalled instances of Robert's possessiveness, his constant monitoring of Eleanor's activities, his disapproval of her friendships. These incidents, dismissed as minor irritations in her childhood memories, now appeared as components of a larger system of control. She remembered the strained silences during family gatherings, the way Eleanor would avoid eye contact with Robert, the subtle tremor in her hand whenever he spoke to her. These were not mere coincidences; they were signs of a dysfunctional family dynamic, a carefully concealed power imbalance.

Sarah's investigation went beyond the diary entries. She delved into family photos, old yearbooks, and even home videos, seeking clues that could shed light on the family's dynamics. She revisited her childhood memories, scrutinizing every detail, trying to decipher the unspoken tensions, the subtle cues of emotional manipulation, the signs of Eleanor's silent suffering. In a blurry home video, she noticed a fleeting moment of fear in Eleanor's eyes, a quick glance towards Robert, as if anticipating a reprimand. In an old photograph,

Eleanor's forced smile looked strained, her eyes holding a depth of sadness that had previously escaped Sarah's notice.

The more Sarah uncovered, the clearer the picture became. The seemingly idyllic family life was a carefully crafted illusion, a facade designed to conceal the disturbing reality of the abuse. Robert, the seemingly devoted husband and father, was a master manipulator, a man who used charm and affability to mask his cruelty and control. Eleanor, the seemingly demure and unassuming wife, was a victim of his systematic abuse, her mental fragmentation a consequence of his actions. The dysfunctional family dynamics, fueled by Robert's manipulative behavior and Eleanor's desperate attempts to cope with trauma, created a breeding ground for tragedy, culminating in the gruesome murder that had haunted Sarah for years.

The chilling realization dawned on Sarah: the seemingly perfect family was a carefully constructed prison. Eleanor's fragmented personality wasn't just a psychological disorder; it was a survival mechanism born from years of abuse, a testament to the resilience of the human spirit in the face of unimaginable cruelty. Robert had not only destroyed Eleanor's life; he had systematically eroded her very sense of self, twisting her psyche into a fragmented mosaic of fear, rage, and desperation. And Sarah, despite her seemingly idyllic childhood, had unwittingly been a participant in this meticulously crafted charade. She had been shielded from the truth, manipulated into accepting a false narrative, a carefully constructed reality that concealed a dark and unsettling truth. The weight of this realization was immense, a crushing burden of betrayal and the painful re-evaluation of her entire past. But with this painful self-awareness came a fierce determination. She would uncover the full extent of Robert's manipulations, expose his cruelty, and bring him to justice. The quest for truth had transformed into a relentless pursuit of justice, fuelled by a burning desire to reclaim her own past and honor her mother's memory. The seemingly perfect family was far from perfect. It was a carefully constructed prison, and Sarah was determined to break free. The puzzle pieces, once scattered and confusing, were finally falling into place, revealing a horrifying tapestry of abuse, manipulation, and murder, all woven under the deceptive guise of a seemingly perfect family. The weight of this revelation was heavy, but it empowered Sarah with a newfound strength, a fierce determination to expose the truth, no matter the cost. The road ahead was fraught with challenges, but she was ready. The fight for justice, for her mother's memory, and for her own sanity, had begun.

The biting wind whipped at Eleanor's thin cotton dress as she huddled deeper into the shadows of the old oak tree. It was autumn, the air thick with the scent of decaying leaves and damp earth. She was six years old, small for her age, her blonde curls escaping the confines of a too-tight braid. The world, seen from her perspective, was a tapestry of muted grays and browns, the vibrant colours of childhood dulled by an ever-present undercurrent of fear. Home, which should have been a haven, was instead a place of suffocating silence punctuated by sudden, sharp outbursts of anger. Her father, Robert, was a man of contradictions: outwardly charming and successful, inwardly volatile and controlling.

Eleanor's earliest memories were not of love and laughter, but of hushed whispers and furtive glances. Her mother, a beautiful woman whose name Eleanor barely recalled, was often withdrawn, lost in a world of quiet suffering. She moved with a fragility that made Eleanor feel a constant need to protect her, even at the tender age of six. The protection, however, was illusory, a fragile shield against the storm that raged within the family. Robert, with his seemingly boundless charm and charisma, was a master of manipulation. He could switch from being affectionate and engaging to cold and dismissive in the blink of an eye. His laughter could turn chillingly sharp, his smiles masking an unsettling intensity that left Eleanor trembling.

One vivid memory etched itself into Eleanor's young mind: the sound of shattering glass. It wasn't the sound itself that haunted her, but the aftermath—the suffocating silence, the tense atmosphere that hung heavy in the air. Her father stood there, his face a mask of controlled fury, his voice a low growl that sent shivers down Eleanor's spine. Her mother was huddled in a corner, her face pale, her body trembling. Eleanor, witnessing the silent exchange between them, felt a cold dread creep into her heart. She understood, instinctively, that something terrible had happened, something that was never to be spoken of again.

The silences were as oppressive as the outbursts. They were pregnant with unspoken resentments, simmering tensions that clung to the walls of their grand Victorian home like a clinging mist. Meals were strained affairs, the clinking of cutlery a stark counterpoint to the unspoken words that hung in the air. Eleanor learned to eat quickly, to remain silent, to become invisible. She developed an acute awareness of the subtle shifts in her father's mood, the subtle changes in his expression that signaled an impending storm. She learned to anticipate his anger, to preempt his outbursts, to become a master of self-preservation.

As Eleanor grew older, the unspoken tensions morphed into

a pattern of subtle yet effective control. Robert meticulously managed the family finances, limiting her mother's access to money, dictating her spending habits. He controlled her social interactions, isolating her from friends and family, creating a subtle yet effective prison within the confines of their opulent home. Eleanor, witnessing this systematic erosion of her mother's independence, felt a growing sense of helplessness and dread.

The physical abuse, while less frequent than the emotional torment, was nonetheless chillingly effective. It was often disguised as "discipline," as "corrections" for Eleanor's perceived misbehavior. A slap across the face, a sharp shove, a harsh word—these became routine occurrences, the subtle brutality normalized within the confines of their seemingly perfect family life. It was a subtle, insidious form of violence, designed not to leave visible marks, but to erode Eleanor's sense of self-worth, to instill a deep-seated fear and dependence on her father's approval.

Eleanor's mother, in the midst of this emotional and physical turmoil, retreated into herself. Her silence wasn't passive; it was a survival mechanism, a way to cope with the overwhelming pain and despair. She became a ghost in her own home, a shadowy figure moving through the grand rooms, her presence barely registered by the others. Eleanor felt a desperate need to make her mother happy, but she had no tools, no understanding of what was happening, only the instinctive knowledge that something was terribly wrong.

The emotional deprivation was perhaps the most insidious form of abuse. Eleanor yearned for affection, for reassurance, for the simple comfort of a loving embrace. But such affection was scarce, rare moments of fleeting warmth overshadowed by the constant undercurrent of fear and tension. She learned to suppress her own emotions, to become emotionally detached, to build walls around her heart to protect it from the pain. This emotional repression, this desperate need to self-protect, became the cornerstone of her fragmented psyche, the seed from which her multiple personalities would bloom.

The development of these alters wasn't a sudden event, but a gradual process, a series of coping mechanisms that evolved over time. Lily, the childlike alter, emerged as a refuge, a retreat into the fantasy world of innocence to escape the harsh reality of her childhood. Evelyn, the cynical and analytical alter, became a shield, a way to cope with the emotional pain and betrayal by detaching herself from her own emotions. Seraphina, the most fragmented and disturbed alter, embodied the raw, untamed rage and fear that resulted from the years of abuse. Each alter played a crucial role in Eleanor's survival, a testament to her remarkable resilience in the face of unimaginable cruelty.

Eleanor's childhood was a crucible, forging a fractured psyche from the raw materials of abuse and neglect. The seemingly idyllic family life was a carefully constructed illusion, a mask that concealed a dark and unsettling truth. The elegant home, the comfortable furnishings, the outward signs of success— these were mere props in a tragic drama playing out behind closed doors. The years of emotional, physical, and sexual abuse left deep scars, wounds that would fester and grow into the fragmented personality that would eventually claim a life, tragically sealing Eleanor's fate, and forever altering the trajectory of her daughter's life. The seeds of violence, of the unspeakable act that would define Eleanor's legacy, were sown in the shadows of that old oak tree, amidst the decaying leaves and damp earth. The horrifying culmination was a testament to the enduring power of trauma, a dark reflection of a childhood shattered beyond repair. The fractured self that emerged was a desperate attempt to survive, a mosaic of pain and resilience forged in the inferno of a seemingly perfect, yet devastatingly broken, family. The seemingly idyllic façade hid a horrifying reality that only now, after years of silence, was beginning to see the light of day.

Dr. Alistair Reed leaned back in his worn leather chair, the faint scent of old paper and pipe tobacco clinging to the air. He steepled his fingers, his gaze fixed on the detailed case file before him. Eleanor Vance's name, typed in crisp, professional lettering, seemed almost incongruous with the chaotic landscape of her fractured psyche. Twenty-five years. Twenty-five years since the discovery of that frozen body, encased in black plastic, a macabre tableau meticulously arranged with a chilling precision that spoke volumes about the disturbed mind behind it. And now, with Eleanor's death, the pieces of the puzzle, scattered like shards of broken glass, were finally beginning to coalesce.

Eleanor's diary, a testament to the brutal reality of her internal world, offered a chilling glimpse into the complex tapestry of her multiple personality disorder. He had treated many cases of dissociative identity disorder, but Eleanor's case was uniquely disturbing. The sheer depth of her trauma, the intricate layering of her alters, each with their own distinct personality, memories, and even physical manifestations—it was a case study that would challenge the boundaries of even his extensive experience. It wasn't just the violence, though that was certainly a significant factor. It was the meticulousness of it, the almost artistic way in which Seraphina, the alter identified as the perpetrator, had staged the crime scene. It wasn't simply a brutal act; it was a performance, a dark theatrical production crafted with unsettling precision. This detail suggested a level of control and planning far beyond what he'd previously encountered in his patients.

He ran a hand through his thinning gray hair, the weight of the case heavy on his shoulders. He had treated Eleanor for over a decade, navigating the treacherous terrain of her fragmented self, carefully piecing together the fragments of her shattered past. He'd seen Lily, the childlike alter, her eyes wide with a perpetual fear that seemed to echo the horrors of her early childhood. He had interacted with Evelyn, the cynical and analytical alter, her sharp wit and detached demeanor a defense mechanism against the overwhelming pain and betrayal that lay buried deep within Eleanor's psyche. And then there was Seraphina...

Seraphina was the enigma, the untamed storm at the heart of Eleanor's chaos. Accessing Seraphina was like trying to tame a wild animal, a dangerous and unpredictable force that surfaced only intermittently, often triggered by seemingly insignificant events or stimuli. Her rage was palpable, a raw, untamed energy that pulsed beneath the surface, threatening to erupt at any moment. Seraphina's memories were fragmented, chaotic, a jumble of sensory impressions and fragmented narratives. Yet, within those fragments, Dr. Reed saw glimpses of the unrelenting abuse that had shaped her, the unimaginable cruelty that had twisted a young girl into a monstrous alter. It was a disturbing picture, one that painted a horrifying portrait of domestic and sexual violence.

The challenge in treating Eleanor was not merely managing the symptoms of her multiple personality disorder but also confronting the deep-seated trauma that had fueled its development. He attempted to use various therapeutic approaches, adapting his strategies depending on which alter emerged during sessions. With Lily, he employed play therapy, creating a safe space for her to express her emotions and process her experiences through creative expression. With Evelyn, his approach was more cognitive-behavioral, helping her develop coping mechanisms and challenge her negative thought patterns. He had tried grounding techniques, mindfulness exercises, and even EMDR therapy to help her process the traumatic memories associated with each alter.

But Seraphina remained elusive, a shadowy figure lurking at the edges of Eleanor's consciousness. She was a formidable opponent, resisting any attempt at therapeutic intervention. Her rage was self-destructive, a consuming fire that threatened to incinerate everything in its path. Dr. Reed attempted to establish a therapeutic alliance, building trust and rapport, but Seraphina's distrust was profound, a deep-seated mistrust rooted in years of abuse and betrayal. He had tried to gain her trust, to understand her motives, to unpack the origins of her rage. But she remained an enigma, her motivations often obscured by layers of fear, anger, and self-loathing.

The diary entries provided crucial insights into the dynamics between the alters. He noted the intricate relationships between them, the ways in which they interacted, collaborated, and competed for control of Eleanor's body. Some entries were chillingly clinical, others were raw and emotional, revealing the complexities of their internal world. He discovered the careful routines they maintained, the rituals that helped regulate their interactions and manage the ever-present threat of disintegration. He realized, through these entries, that Eleanor's alters, though seemingly disparate and conflicting, were in fact intrinsically connected, their existence interwoven in an intricate web of trauma and survival.

But the murder? That remained a chilling mystery, a testament to the depths of Seraphina's rage. Dr. Reed pondered the meticulous nature of the crime scene, the symbolic significance of the black plastic bags, the red scrunchies, the lye. It wasn't just murder; it was a carefully orchestrated statement, a dark act of revenge crafted with chilling precision. He knew that Seraphina's actions were not merely impulsive outbursts but rather a calculated response to years of accumulated trauma and abuse. The meticulous nature of the crime pointed to a level of planning and control that suggested a horrifying degree of sophistication and forethought beyond a simple act of rage.

His therapeutic efforts, while ultimately unable to prevent the tragic outcome, had provided glimpses into the complex mechanism of Eleanor's fractured mind. He felt a sense of both failure and a somber form of understanding. He had walked a path through a psychological minefield, navigating the perilous terrain of trauma and dissociation. He'd seen the resilience of the human spirit, the tenacity of the will to survive, yet also the dark and destructive consequences of unchecked trauma. He understood that even the most effective therapeutic intervention could not always reverse the devastating consequences of abuse, and that sometimes, the scars run too deep. The case file lay open before him, a chilling testament to the horrors he'd witnessed. Eleanor's death had brought a closure of sorts, but the lingering questions still haunted him. The case served as a brutal reminder of the devastating consequences of unchecked trauma and the enduring power of a fractured mind. The chilling truth, etched in the chilling details of the diary and the grim reality of the unsolved murder, would forever remain a disturbing testament to the dark side of human nature and the devastating impact of unaddressed trauma. The legacy of Eleanor Vance was a harrowing reminder of the deep, unseen wounds that could linger for a lifetime, and the chilling consequences that could follow.

Sarah traced the faded ink of her mother's diary entry, the words blurring slightly under the harsh glare of the desk lamp. Eleanor's handwriting, usually precise and elegant, had devolved into a chaotic scrawl in this particular section, reflecting the turbulent emotional state of the writer. The entry detailed a childhood filled with chilling accounts of neglect, the subtle yet pervasive coldness of a home where love was a foreign concept. Sarah felt a familiar tightness in her chest, a familiar ache that mirrored the pain etched onto every line of the page. This wasn't just a historical account; it was a visceral transmission of suffering, a raw nerve exposed and laid bare.

It wasn't the graphic descriptions of physical abuse that struck Sarah the hardest; it was the insidious, pervasive sense of emotional abandonment. The diary entries spoke of a child longing for connection, for the warmth of a mother's embrace, a father's approval—desires that remained eternally unfulfilled. Eleanor described a childhood spent navigating a labyrinth of emotional neglect, a world where her needs were consistently ignored, her feelings dismissed as unimportant. The silence, Eleanor wrote, was often worse than the shouting, the void a more suffocating presence than the physical blows.

Sarah reread the passage several times, each reading revealing a deeper layer of understanding. She saw reflections of her own struggles in Eleanor's words, a shared inheritance of emotional scars. She understood now, with a clarity that stunned her, the roots of her own anxieties, the deep-seated insecurities that had plagued her throughout her life. It wasn't just a matter of genetics; it was the inheritance of trauma, a legacy passed down through generations.

The diary entries went on to describe Eleanor's adolescence, a period marked by escalating instability and the emergence of distinct personalities. Each alter, Eleanor wrote, represented a different coping mechanism, a fragment of the self shattered by the unrelenting trauma. Lily, the child alter, was the embodiment of Eleanor's unmet needs, her perpetual fear a testament to the horrors she had endured. Evelyn, the cynical and analytical alter, represented a hardened defense against the pain, a shield constructed against further emotional wounds. And then there was Seraphina... the avenging angel, the embodiment of rage and retribution.

Sarah had always felt a profound disconnect from herself, a sense of being fragmented, a collection of disparate emotions and experiences struggling for coherence. Reading her mother's words, she realized that this fragmentation wasn't a personal failing but a consequence of intergenerational trauma. The fractured self wasn't a weakness; it was a survival mechanism, a testament to Eleanor's resilience, her desperate attempt to endure unimaginable pain.

As the nights bled into days, Sarah immersed herself in her mother's diary. She started to see patterns, recurring motifs, and subtle connections between the various alters and the events that triggered their emergence. She discovered that each alter, despite their differences, possessed a unique understanding of the trauma they collectively carried. Lily's innocence mirrored the vulnerability of the child, Evelyn's cynicism reflected Eleanor's learned helplessness and disillusionment, and Seraphina's destructive rage channeled the repressed anger and resentment accumulated over years.

The meticulous detail in Eleanor's accounts was both horrifying and illuminating. The precise descriptions of the abuse, the subtle nuances of emotional manipulation, and the detailed accounts of her various personalities painted a harrowing portrait of a woman desperately fighting to keep herself together. It wasn't just a diary; it was a psychological autopsy, an exploration of a mind fractured beyond repair.

But within this fragmented world, Sarah discovered glimmers of hope. Eleanor's entries weren't simply chronicles of suffering; they also documented moments of resilience, fleeting instances of joy, and desperate attempts at self-preservation. The diary entries illustrated Eleanor's subconscious struggle to integrate her fragmented selves and create a semblance of order within the chaos. It was a testament to the human spirit's enduring strength, its capacity to find hope amidst despair.

Sarah realized that understanding her mother's experiences wasn't merely an act of historical investigation; it was a journey of self-discovery. It was an attempt to unravel the complex web of her own emotional landscape and reconcile with the inherited trauma she carried within her. As she delved deeper into the diary's contents, she began to recognize the echoes of her own internal conflicts, the similarities between her anxieties and her mother's fragmented self.

She found herself identifying with Lily's fear, with Evelyn's cynicism, even with Seraphina's rage. These weren't just aspects of her mother's personality; they were echoes within her own being, fragmented pieces of a self struggling to become whole. The process was painful, bringing up buried memories and long-suppressed emotions. But it was also liberating, a gradual dismantling of the protective walls she had built around her heart.

Sarah's newfound understanding was not without its struggles. She found herself battling bouts of intense anxiety, the weight of her family's history pressing down on her. There were days when the darkness felt overwhelming, when the fragmented memories of her own childhood threatened to consume her. But she also found strength in her newfound understanding, in the knowledge that her struggles weren't unique, that she wasn't alone in her pain.

She began seeking professional help, engaging in therapy sessions to work through her trauma and develop healthy coping mechanisms. The therapist, a kind and empathetic woman named Dr. Anya Sharma, helped Sarah to navigate her emotional landscape, to identify the triggers that set off her anxieties, and to develop strategies for managing the overwhelming feelings that threatened to engulf her. Dr. Sharma also encouraged Sarah to explore creative outlets as a means of self-expression and healing.

Sarah started journaling, pouring her thoughts and feelings onto paper. She began painting, using vibrant colours to express the emotional turmoil she was grappling with. Art became her sanctuary, a space where she could process her experiences without the pressure of words, allowing her to translate her internal world onto canvas. The act of creation became a form of self-soothing, a means of finding solace amidst the chaos.

Through therapy and self-reflection, Sarah slowly began to piece together the fragments of her own identity. She discovered that while the shadow of her family's history loomed large, it did not define her. She was not merely the product of her past; she was also the architect of her future. The journey was challenging, filled with setbacks and emotional turbulence, but Sarah found strength in her vulnerability, in her willingness to confront the darkness within.

She learned to accept her own imperfections, to embrace the complexities of her emotional landscape. She realized that her anxieties and insecurities were not signs of weakness but reflections of her resilience, of her ability to navigate emotional turmoil and emerge stronger on the other side. Her mother's diary had been a key to unlocking her own path to healing. It wasn't just about understanding her mother's struggles; it was about understanding herself, about forging her own identity, separate yet connected to the tumultuous legacy she had inherited. The diary had become more than just a historical document; it had become a roadmap for her own self-discovery. The journey was far from over, but Sarah knew, with a certainty that resonated deep within her soul, that she was finally on her way. The path ahead remained uncertain, but she walked it with a newfound sense of purpose, a quiet strength born from the ashes of her family's trauma, and a determination to build a life that was truly her own.

# CHAPTER 11: THE WEIGHT OF THE PAST

The weight of the past pressed down on Sarah, a physical burden that mirrored the emotional turmoil churning within her. Understanding her mother's fractured psyche, the horrifying details of her abuse, and the resulting violence—it was a heavy load to bear. But alongside the horror, a new understanding was dawning, a subtle shift in her perspective. It wasn't just about the trauma, but about the possibility of forgiveness. Not the facile, easily uttered kind, but a deep, internal process, a slow and arduous climb towards acceptance.

Forgiveness, she realized, wasn't about condoning the actions of her mother's abusive alters. It wasn't about absolving them of responsibility for the pain they had inflicted. It was about freeing herself from the chains of bitterness, from the endless cycle of anger and resentment that threatened to consume her. It was a journey inward, a difficult excavation of her own heart, unearthing the buried emotions that had been festering for years.

Initially, the idea of forgiving seemed impossible, an act of betrayal against her own wounded self. The images of her mother's childhood, the descriptions of neglect and violence, still burned vividly in her mind. How could she possibly forgive such cruelty, such a profound violation of innocence?

The rage simmered beneath the surface, a volatile energy threatening to erupt at any moment. She found herself flinching at sudden loud noises, her body still reacting to the trauma passed down through generations. Sleep became a battleground, haunted by fragmented memories, a nightmarish collage of her mother's experiences and her own.

Her therapist, Dr. Sharma, provided a guiding hand through this treacherous terrain. She explained that forgiveness wasn't a destination but a process, a gradual unwinding of the tight knot of pain and resentment. She emphasized that forgiveness was primarily for Sarah herself, a means of reclaiming her own emotional freedom. Dr. Sharma gently guided Sarah through exercises designed to help her process her feelings, to separate the acts of her mother's alters from the inherent worth of her mother as a human being. The therapist introduced her to the concept of compassionate understanding, urging her to view her mother's actions through the lens of trauma.

It was a difficult concept to grasp. Sarah found herself grappling with the paradoxical nature of compassion for someone who had caused such immense suffering. But as Dr. Sharma patiently explained, compassion wasn't about excusing the abuse; it was about understanding the roots of the destructive behavior. It was about recognizing the profound impact of trauma on the human psyche, the ways in which it can warp and distort the mind, leading to actions that defy logic and morality.

Slowly, painstakingly, Sarah began to apply this framework to her own understanding of her mother's life. She revisited the diary entries, focusing not only on the horrors described but also on the glimpses of vulnerability, the moments of fear and desperation. She saw the child, Lily, trapped in a world of neglect and abuse, her innocent spirit crushed under the weight of unimaginable pain. She saw the cynical, analytical Evelyn, desperately trying to shield herself from further emotional wounds, creating a wall of detachment as a means of self-preservation. And she saw the rage of Seraphina, the violent outburst that stemmed from a lifetime of suppressed anger and resentment.

These weren't simply separate personalities; they were fragments of a shattered self, desperately seeking coherence, desperately striving to survive. Understanding this, Sarah started to experience a profound shift in her perspective. The rage began to lessen, replaced by a deep, aching sadness. It wasn't a simple flip of a switch; it was a gradual, nuanced process of emotional evolution. The anger still flared at times, but it was now tempered by an understanding, a compassion that allowed her to glimpse the human being behind the monstrous acts.

Forgiveness, Sarah learned, wasn't a single act but a series of small, incremental steps. It involved acknowledging the pain, accepting the reality of the abuse, and gradually letting go of the need for retribution. It was about recognizing that holding onto anger and resentment only served to keep her bound to the past. It was about freeing herself from the prison of her own bitterness, allowing herself to heal and move forward.

The process was not linear. There were days when the pain overwhelmed her, when the memories threatened to consume her. There were setbacks, moments when she found herself wrestling with the same old rage. But through it all, Dr. Sharma's guidance and Sarah's commitment to her own healing kept her moving forward.

A pivotal moment came during one of her therapy sessions. Dr. Sharma suggested a powerful visualization exercise. She asked Sarah to imagine her mother, not as the abuser but as the wounded child she once was, the little girl who desperately craved love and connection. Sarah closed her eyes, picturing a small, frightened child, alone and vulnerable. The anger began to dissipate, replaced by an overwhelming wave of compassion and empathy. Tears streamed down her face, but they were not tears of rage or bitterness; they were tears of sorrow, of understanding.

This visualization became a recurring practice, a powerful tool in Sarah's journey towards forgiveness. She continued to journal, to paint, to express her emotions through creative outlets. Art became a conduit for her healing, a space where she could process the trauma and explore the complex emotions she was experiencing.

The path to forgiveness wasn't easy, but it was profoundly liberating. Sarah began to rediscover a sense of peace, a quiet strength that emerged from the ashes of her family's turmoil. She realized that forgiveness wasn't about forgetting or condoning; it was about releasing herself from the chains of the past, allowing herself to live fully and authentically in the present. It was about embracing the complexities of her heritage, the good and the bad, and forging her own path, free from the shadows of her past. The journey was far from over, but Sarah knew, with a certainty that settled deep within her soul, that she was finally on the path to a future where forgiveness, for herself and for her mother, was a possibility. The scars would remain, a testament to the trauma she had endured, but they were no longer chains. They were reminders of the strength she had discovered within herself, a resilience born from the darkness and a hope that bloomed in its light.

The diary entries, painstakingly deciphered by Sarah, offered more than just a chronicle of abuse; they revealed a complex tapestry of interwoven mental illnesses, each contributing to the fractured state of Eleanor's psyche. The multiple personality disorder (DID), the most dominant feature, was interwoven with post-traumatic stress disorder (PTSD), obsessive-compulsive disorder (OCD), attention-deficit/hyperactivity disorder (ADHD), and autism spectrum disorder (ASD). Understanding the interplay of these conditions was crucial to comprehending the genesis of the violence and the seemingly chaotic nature of Eleanor's life.

The PTSD was the most readily apparent consequence of the horrific abuse Eleanor endured as a child. The diary entries were replete with descriptions of flashbacks, nightmares, hypervigilance, and avoidance behaviors—all classic symptoms of PTSD. These weren't merely isolated incidents; they were a constant, underlying current that shaped the experiences of each alter. Evelyn, the analytical and detached alter, had developed meticulous routines and rituals, a clear manifestation of OCD, likely as a coping mechanism to manage the overwhelming anxiety triggered by her traumatic memories. These routines, though seemingly innocuous on the surface, were rigid and inflexible, consuming vast amounts of time and energy, a testament to the severity of her OCD. The meticulous organization of her freezer, the precise arrangement of the lye, the black bags and the red scrunchies—all pointed towards an obsessive need for control, a desperate attempt to impose order on a chaotic internal world.

The ADHD, however, presented a different challenge to understanding Eleanor's behavior. The diary entries revealed periods of intense focus, juxtaposed with spells of profound distraction and impulsivity. These shifts in attention, the difficulty concentrating on tasks, the impulsive nature of some of the alters' actions—all contributed to the overall instability and unpredictability of Eleanor's personality. The impulsivity, exacerbated by the underlying PTSD, could have played a significant role in the events leading up to the murder. One entry, written from the perspective of Seraphina, the violent alter, revealed a chaotic whirlwind of thoughts and feelings, a struggle to control the intense rage that consumed her. The lack of impulse control, combined with her intense anger, presented a potent mix that tragically culminated in the crime.

The ASD further complicated the picture, adding another layer of complexity to Eleanor's already fractured psyche. The diary entries revealed sensory sensitivities, repetitive behaviors, and challenges with social interaction—all characteristic of autism. Certain alters displayed heightened sensitivity to light, sound, and touch, influencing their behavior and interactions with the world. The repetitive behaviors, interwoven with the OCD, amplified the rigidity and inflexibility in their daily routines. The social challenges, compounded by the trauma and the isolation she experienced, contributed to her difficulties forming healthy relationships. The distinct ways in which the alters interacted with each other, and with the outside world, reflected the different expressions of autistic traits and the overall impact on Eleanor's relationships and mental stability.

The interaction of these conditions wasn't simply additive; it was synergistic. The trauma of the abuse triggered the PTSD, which, in turn, exacerbated the symptoms of the OCD, ADHD, and ASD. The OCD's need for control clashed with the ADHD's impulsivity, creating an internal conflict that manifested in unpredictable behaviors. The sensory sensitivities associated with the ASD heightened the anxiety already present due to the PTSD, leading to avoidance behaviors and further isolation. The multiple personalities became a coping mechanism, a fractured self struggling to compartmentalize the overwhelming pain and chaos. Each alter, with its distinct characteristics and vulnerabilities, developed as a response to the complex interplay of these conditions.

The diary revealed how the interplay of these conditions manifested in daily life. Evelyn, driven by her OCD, meticulously organized the household, creating an illusion of order and control that belied the chaos within. Lily, the child alter, retreated into a world of fantasy, escaping the harsh realities of her abuse. Seraphina, fueled by the rage of her PTSD, acted out the suppressed anger and frustration. And amidst this turmoil, other alters emerged, each representing different facets of Eleanor's fragmented self, each battling for dominance and each shaped by the complex interplay of her conditions.

The murder itself, Sarah realized, was not simply an isolated act of violence but the culmination of years of unresolved trauma, of a psyche fractured beyond repair. The meticulous planning and execution, the specific details like the lye and the red scrunchies, indicated an obsessive compulsive element. The impulsive act itself, the immediate violent reaction, hinted at the underlying ADHD. The detachment and lack of remorse, the ability to compartmentalize the act and its consequences, spoke to the dissociative nature of DID. It was a terrifying confluence of factors, a perfect storm within Eleanor's mind that resulted in a horrific act.

This realization didn't diminish Sarah's pain or lessen her anger, but it did offer a measure of understanding. It wasn't about excusing the act, but about understanding its genesis. It was about recognizing that Eleanor's actions were not simply the product of a malevolent will, but the tragic consequence of a lifetime of trauma, a complex interplay of mental illnesses that overwhelmed her psyche. The fragmented self within Eleanor, Sarah understood, was a desperate attempt to survive, to cope with a reality so brutal that it shattered her mind into a thousand pieces.

Understanding this didn't erase the trauma, the years of unanswered questions, or the lingering fear. It didn't diminish the profound impact of the violence Eleanor had inflicted, nor did it absolve her alters of responsibility for their actions. But it did provide Sarah with a framework for healing, a way to move forward without being consumed by bitterness and rage. The weight of the past remained heavy, but it was now a weight she could bear, a weight that, although profoundly painful, was also a source of profound insight into the human capacity for both destruction and resilience. It was a weight that she would slowly and painstakingly learn to carry with a new measure of understanding, empathy, and ultimately, perhaps, even forgiveness. The diary, though filled with horrors, had also become a testament to her mother's internal struggle, a window into the dark and devastating consequences of untreated trauma and the complexity of the human mind. The path forward was still uncertain, still shrouded in shadows of the past, but with each step, Sarah felt a growing sense of clarity, of agency, a sense that perhaps, just perhaps, healing was possible. The road to forgiveness was long and arduous, but Sarah, armed with understanding, was prepared to embark on the journey.

The chilling details in Eleanor's diary weren't just a record of personal suffering; they were a stark indictment of a society that often failed to recognize, let alone address, the profound impact of trauma and mental illness. Sarah, as she delved deeper into her mother's fragmented life, began to understand the crushing weight of social stigma that Eleanor had carried throughout her existence. It wasn't just the physical abuse inflicted upon her as a child; it was the insidious, pervasive shame that followed her into adulthood, silencing her cries for help, isolating her from support, and ultimately contributing to the horrific events that culminated in the murder.

Eleanor's diary entries spoke volumes about the isolation she felt, the fear of judgment, and the constant struggle to hide the truth of her condition. She described moments of terrifying lucidity, where she was acutely aware of her fractured self, the warring personalities vying for control, yet simultaneously terrified of exposing this fragility to a world she knew wouldn't understand. The fear of being labeled "crazy," of being ostracized, institutionalized, or dismissed as a mere hysteric, was a constant, gnawing presence throughout her life. This fear prevented her from seeking help, from reaching out for the support that might have saved her.

The societal silence surrounding mental illness was deafening in Eleanor's diary. There were allusions to failed attempts to connect with therapists, moments when she felt dismissed, misunderstood, or simply judged without compassion. She recounted instances where therapists, lacking the specialized knowledge to handle DID, had only exacerbated her distress, contributing to the already fragile state of her psyche. The medical community, in its relative infancy concerning the understanding and treatment of dissociative disorders, failed her repeatedly, leaving her feeling more alone and more vulnerable than ever before.

The lack of awareness extended beyond the medical profession. Eleanor described strained relationships with family members who were either unwilling or unable to comprehend her condition, attributing her behavior to eccentricity, weakness, or simply a deliberate choice. These misunderstandings deepened her feelings of isolation, reinforcing the shame and secrecy surrounding her fractured self. The silence of loved ones was as damaging as the active cruelty of her abusers, creating a vacuum that was filled only by her inner turmoil and the escalating violence within her fragmented mind.

Even the seemingly supportive relationships in Eleanor's life were ultimately strained by her inability to share the truth of her condition. Her marriage to Arthur, while outwardly idyllic, was based on a foundation of deception and her constant fear of exposure. She portrayed a carefully constructed persona, a mask that concealed the turbulent storm within. This constant performance only served to heighten the tension, leading to an emotional disconnect that ultimately further aggravated the fractured state of her identity.

The social stigma extended to the legal system as well. Sarah's investigation into the murder revealed the difficulties in prosecuting crimes committed by individuals with DID. The very nature of the disorder—the existence of multiple, distinct personalities—confounded legal processes, leading to uncertainty about culpability and the efficacy of legal interventions. Eleanor's case, as Sarah slowly unraveled it, highlighted the immense challenges the judicial system faces when dealing with individuals whose actions are driven by a multiplicity of personalities, each operating with different levels of awareness and control.

The lack of understanding was not confined to the time of Eleanor's life, the diary's entries showcased an ongoing lack of sensitivity that was echoed in Sarah's own investigations. The police initially dismissed the murder as a random act of violence, never suspecting that the perpetrator might be someone close to the victim, someone living a double, or rather, a multiple life. The lack of resources dedicated to investigating and understanding complex mental health issues in criminal investigations only compounded the failure to find justice.

Sarah's journey through the diary entries was not just a process of unveiling a gruesome murder; it was a painful education in the social stigmas surrounding mental illness, and the catastrophic consequences of ignoring the suffering of those who grapple with profound psychological trauma. The weight of this societal failure felt as heavy as the weight of Eleanor's past, the silence a suffocating presence that had contributed just as significantly to the tragic events as the abuse she endured as a child.

This understanding, however, did not lead Sarah to absolution. She still wrestled with the anger and grief caused by her mother's actions. But her journey of understanding the weight of the past transformed into something more; a quest for social justice, a desire to educate others and to advocate for more sensitive and comprehensive support for individuals struggling with similar disorders.

Sarah's journey broadened her perspective, not merely focusing on the mechanics of her mother's fragmented psyche but also looking at the broader societal context that had condemned Eleanor to silence and ultimately to the perpetration of violence. The diary had become a powerful tool for social commentary, highlighting the systemic failures of a society that often treated the mentally ill with neglect, misunderstanding, and even hostility. This realization ignited a burning desire in Sarah to fight against this pervasive societal stigma, to challenge the preconceived notions and stereotypes that prevented people with mental illnesses from seeking help and receiving adequate treatment.

The weight of Eleanor's past extended beyond her own personal tragedy; it weighed heavily on the shoulders of countless others who struggled in silence, afraid to seek help for fear of judgment and rejection. Sarah's story, fueled by her mother's diary, became a testament to the urgent need for greater awareness, understanding, and compassion concerning mental health, highlighting the tragic consequences of ignoring the profound impact of untreated trauma and the devastating weight of social stigma. This was no longer just a story about a woman with multiple personality disorder and a horrific crime; it was a story about the urgent need for societal change, a plea for a more humane and empathetic approach to mental illness.

Sarah's investigation evolved from a personal quest for answers into a crusade for justice—not just for her mother, but for the countless individuals who suffered in silence, victims of societal neglect and the cruel weight of stigma. The chilling details in the diary had been more than just a record of abuse and violence; they had become a rallying cry for reform, a testament to the urgent need for greater compassion and understanding in dealing with the complexities of mental illness and the devastating consequences of a society that failed to support those who needed it most. Her path to healing would be intricately linked to her commitment to change, her fierce advocacy a stark counterpoint to the silence and misunderstanding that had haunted her mother's life. The weight of the past was heavy, but it was a burden Sarah was determined to carry, not just for herself, but for all those who had suffered under the crushing weight of social stigma. The fight for justice and understanding had only just begun.

The quiet town of Havenwood, nestled between rolling hills and a perpetually mist-shrouded forest, had always prided itself on its idyllic façade. Appearances, however, were notoriously deceptive, a fact brutally underscored by the discovery of a body in a local freezer—a body encased in black plastic bags, tied with red scrunchies, and surrounded by a caustic residue of lye. The murder, committed twenty-five years prior, remained unsolved, a chilling secret simmering beneath the town's placid surface. Eleanor Vance's death, and the subsequent discovery of her diary, ripped open that carefully constructed illusion, exposing not just Eleanor's fractured psyche, but a shared trauma that had silently permeated the community for decades.

The initial reaction to the discovery of the diary, and its damning revelations, was a mix of shock, denial, and a deeply ingrained discomfort. Havenwood was a town where secrets were guarded jealously, where appearances were meticulously maintained, and where any deviation from the norm was met with suspicion, if not outright hostility. The fact that the seemingly perfect Eleanor Vance, the dutiful wife and mother, harbored such a dark and violent secret challenged the town's self-image, threatening to shatter its carefully constructed sense of order and tranquility.

The ensuing conversations, whispered initially in hushed tones behind cupped hands, then growing bolder with the relentless drip, drip, drip of Sarah's public investigation, exposed a network of unspoken anxieties and shared silences. Arthur Vance, Eleanor's husband, had been the picture of grieving normalcy. Yet, the diary's entries painted a far more complex and unsettling picture of their relationship: a marriage built on a foundation of lies and unspoken fears, where Eleanor's fractured reality was meticulously concealed, and where Arthur's complicity, whether active or passive, remained a chilling unknown. The gossips in the town's church hall began to question everything they thought they knew.

Beyond Arthur, the diary revealed a series of fractured relationships—connections strained by Eleanor's inability to articulate the turmoil within her. Neighbors who had observed her quiet demeanor, her forced smiles, now wondered if they had missed something, if their casual observations had been blind to the depth of Eleanor's suffering. The quiet nods and polite smiles exchanged on the manicured lawns of Havenwood's affluent streets now held a sinister undercurrent, each interaction laced with the unspoken awareness of the terrible secret that had lurked just beneath the surface.

The shared trauma extended beyond the immediate circle of Eleanor's acquaintance. The murder itself had cast a long shadow over the community. The victim, a young woman named Emily Carter, had been a vibrant presence in Havenwood before her sudden and horrific disappearance. Emily's death was a collective wound, an unspoken grief that had settled into the fabric of the town, a silent reminder of the vulnerability that lurked beneath the veneer of peaceful predictability. The twenty-five-year silence, now broken by the diary's revelations, brought to light the collective failure to understand the extent of the psychological issues within their small community.

Sarah's investigation not only unearthed the details of the murder and Eleanor's life but also uncovered a history of systemic failures within the town. The police department's initial handling of the case, now seen through the lens of Eleanor's diary, highlighted a lack of resources, a lack of understanding, and a tendency to dismiss complex psychological factors in favor of simpler, more readily acceptable explanations. The medical facilities available to Havenwood's residents at the time were poorly equipped to deal with the multifaceted challenges posed by dissociative disorders, further contributing to the failure to address Eleanor's suffering effectively.

The weight of these past failings was considerable. The diary's entries shone a harsh light on the town's inability to recognize and respond to the cries for help, both explicit and implicit, from those suffering from mental illness and trauma. The social stigma that had silenced Eleanor, that had prevented her from seeking help, now served as a chilling reminder of the community's own shortcomings, its collective blindness to the suffering within its midst. The town's idealized image began to crack, revealing a flawed underbelly of ignorance and a pervasive lack of empathy.

Sarah's public unveiling of the diary's contents sparked a wave of both condemnation and empathy within Havenwood. Some residents recoiled, clinging to the comfortable illusion of a peaceful past and rejecting the disturbing truths revealed in Eleanor's story. Others, however, found a sense of validation in Eleanor's experience, recognizing elements of their own struggles, or the struggles of those they loved, within her narrative. A quiet reckoning began, a process of confronting the collective shadows cast by the past, a slow awakening to the often invisible wounds within their midst.

The ripple effect of trauma was felt acutely within Havenwood's schools. Children, initially shielded from the full details of Eleanor's story, began to whisper about it, their innocent questions inadvertently highlighting the community's failure to address the complexities of mental illness with an open, honest, and comprehensive approach. The school counselors and teachers found themselves grappling with a flood of inquiries and anxieties, facing a sudden and unexpected need to navigate conversations about trauma, abuse, and the multiple personalities disorder, issues previously absent from the town's educational discourse.

The revelations from the diary also triggered a period of intense self-reflection within Havenwood's religious institutions. The church, once a sanctuary of comforting tradition, now faced the painful reality of its own past failures. Some members grappled with the uncomfortable truth that their own judgments and misconceptions may have contributed to the stigmatization and isolation of individuals suffering from mental illness within their community. Others sought to use this as a catalyst for change, initiating discussions about mental health awareness and advocating for greater compassion and understanding.

In the aftermath of the public exposure of Eleanor's story, Havenwood's community leaders, driven by a newfound awareness, started to implement changes. New initiatives were launched to provide better access to mental health services, to combat the prevailing stigma associated with mental illness, and to foster a more open and accepting environment for those struggling with their mental well-being. Community support groups were formed, providing a much-needed space for sharing experiences, building resilience, and breaking down the isolating barriers that had long existed.

The healing process was slow and arduous, however. The weight of Eleanor's past was heavy, not just for Sarah but for the entire community of Havenwood. The shadow of the unsolved murder, the lingering trauma of Emily Carter's death, and the newly unearthed secrets of Eleanor's fractured life cast a long shadow. Yet, from the cracks in the idealized image of Havenwood, a new kind of community was emerging, one that was more aware, more compassionate, and more dedicated to recognizing and addressing the complex needs of its members.

The story of Eleanor Vance wasn't just a tale of a gruesome crime or a woman's fragmented psyche. It was the story of a community grappling with its own history, confronting its failings, and striving to rebuild itself on a foundation of understanding, compassion, and a commitment to providing support for those in need. The path to healing was long and uncertain, but the seed of change had been sown, a hopeful sign in the shadowed landscape of Havenwood's past. The weight of the past remained, but with it came a renewed commitment to building a future where such tragedies might be prevented, a future where silence would no longer be a shield but a vulnerability acknowledged and addressed with the care and understanding it demanded.

The quiet hum of the refrigerator was the only sound for a long time. Sarah stared into the pale, almost ethereal glow of the appliance, its cold steel a stark counterpoint to the simmering turmoil within her. The diary, its pages filled with Eleanor's fractured narrative, lay open on the kitchen counter, a testament to a life lived in shadows, a life she was only now beginning to understand. The weight of it, the sheer enormity of her mother's suffering, pressed down on her, a suffocating blanket of grief and bewilderment.

Sleep became a battlefield, a place where Eleanor's fragmented personalities waged war, their anxieties and traumas bleeding into Sarah's own dreams. The chilling image of Emily Carter, encased in plastic, haunted her waking hours, a visceral reminder of the violence that had lurked beneath the surface of Havenwood's idyllic façade. She found herself staring at her reflection, searching for traces of Eleanor, wondering if the fractured psyche was something that could be inherited, a genetic predisposition to the darkness that had consumed her mother.

Therapy became her lifeline, a refuge where she could unravel the tangled threads of her own emotions. Dr. Albright, a compassionate and insightful therapist, listened patiently as Sarah recounted the horrors revealed in the diary, her own growing sense of betrayal and abandonment. The sessions were often excruciating, a painful excavation of buried memories and unspoken anxieties. But amidst the darkness,

Sarah found a flicker of hope, a growing awareness that she was not alone, that her feelings were valid, and that healing was possible.

The initial shock of the revelations gradually gave way to a slow, arduous process of grief. It wasn't simply the grief of losing her mother; it was the grief of losing the idealized image she had held onto for so long, the grief of confronting the truth about her family history, the chilling reality of her mother's abuse, and the brutal act committed by one of her alters.

She started small. She cleared her mother's belongings, each item a tangible reminder of a life lived in secret. Eleanor's favorite scarf, a vibrant shade of crimson, now seemed imbued with a sinister irony, a macabre echo of the red scrunchies found at the crime scene. Her mother's meticulously organized spice rack, a symbol of her outwardly perfect domestic life, felt like a cruel joke now, a carefully constructed façade masking the chaos within. Even her mother's perfume, a delicate floral scent, evoked a wave of nausea, as if the fragrance itself carried the lingering ghost of past trauma.

The process was agonizingly slow. Days blurred into weeks, each filled with a relentless cycle of therapy sessions, unpacking of boxes, and the relentless tug-of-war between grief and the burgeoning need to rebuild. The house, once a sanctuary of family life, felt empty, echoing with the absence of Eleanor's presence, yet also haunted by the lingering ghosts of her alters.

Sarah sought solace in her art, pouring her emotions onto canvas. The paintings were raw, visceral expressions of her internal turmoil, a chaotic blend of color and texture reflecting the fractured nature of her own psyche. The vibrant hues of her mother's favorite flowers were juxtaposed with the stark, brutal shades of black and crimson, mirroring the duality of Eleanor's life—the gentle exterior masking the inner turmoil and rage. Her art became a form of catharsis, a way to process her grief, to externalize the trauma that threatened to consume her.

The community's response to the revelations in the diary was varied and complex. Some neighbors, initially shocked and horrified, offered support, their empathy born from a newfound understanding of Eleanor's suffering and their own capacity for ignorance and collective denial. Others, however, remained wary, clinging to their own narratives and reluctant to confront the uncomfortable truths revealed about their town's hidden past. The initial wave of judgment gradually gave way to a quieter, more introspective reckoning with the events that had unfolded.

There were unexpected alliances. Unexpected friendships forged in the crucible of shared trauma and collective guilt. Sarah found herself connecting with Emily Carter's sister, a woman who had carried the weight of her own grief for twenty-five years. Their shared sorrow transcended the initial shock and anger, creating a bond of understanding. They found solace in their shared experience, two women grappling with the devastating consequences of Havenwood's collective failure to acknowledge and address the mental health crisis within their midst.

The town, though, was changing. The police department, spurred by public outcry and an internal reckoning, launched a renewed investigation into Eleanor's case, a more thorough exploration of the possibilities, including the insights offered by the diary. The community began to tackle the issue of mental health with newfound urgency and compassion. Support groups emerged, providing a safe space for individuals who had previously suffered in silence. Schools introduced curriculum changes that focused on mental health awareness and emotional well-being.

Sarah's life, slowly but surely, began to resemble something akin to normalcy. It wasn't the life she had envisioned, but it was a life she was slowly building, brick by painstaking brick. The shadows of the past remained, but they no longer held the same power, no longer defined her. She was still carrying the weight of her mother's story, but it was a weight she carried with a newfound strength, a resilience born from the depths of her own emotional journey.

The diary remained, a constant presence in her life, a chilling reminder of the darkness that had consumed her mother. But it was also a testament to her resilience, a chronicle of suffering that had ultimately led to a powerful act of self-discovery and a profound understanding of the multifaceted nature of trauma. The red scrunchies, though a haunting reminder of the crime, were also symbols of a community beginning to face its demons, to acknowledge its collective failures, and to work towards a more compassionate future, a future where the weight of the past could finally be laid down, replaced by the hopeful seeds of healing and understanding. Sarah, in the face of unimaginable sorrow, had discovered a strength she never knew she possessed, a strength that was both fiercely personal and profoundly interconnected with the future of Havenwood itself. The town was slowly healing, and in its healing, Sarah was finally beginning to heal too.

# CHAPTER 12: UNMASKING THE TRUTH

October 27th. The others are whispering again. A constant, low hum of anxiety, like static on an old radio. Seraphina keeps trying to take over, her sweet, saccharine voice a thin veil over a simmering rage I can barely contain. She wants to apologize, to undo what happened. But I...I don't know if I can let her. The act was committed, the damage done. There is no undo button. The guilt gnaws, a relentless tide pulling me under. But underneath, in the deep recesses of my fragmented self, there is a chilling satisfaction. A dark peace, an end to the relentless torment. It's a terrible thing to admit, this twisted sense of resolution. But it's there, a dark stain on the fabric of my being.

October 28th. The pain is relentless. Not just the physical agony, but the mental torment. The memories, like shards of glass, pierce my consciousness. The faces of my abusers blur together, a grotesque tapestry of cruelty and violation. But amidst the chaos, a flicker of defiance. I will not be broken. I will not be silenced. My voice, fractured though it may be, will be heard. This diary is my testament, my scream into the void. I will leave behind my story, raw and unflinching, a warning to those who would inflict such pain.

October 29th. Sleep offers no respite, only a deeper descent into the abyss of memory. I dream of black bags and red scrunchies, the chilling image of Emily Carter's lifeless face forever etched into my subconscious. I see her eyes, wide with terror, staring back at me, a silent accusation. And yet...and yet, a strange detachment. A sense of removing myself from the action. Watching it unfold like a macabre movie. A feeling of being both the perpetrator and the observer. The fractured nature of my psyche is a cruel joke, a constant reminder of my brokenness.

October 30th. I feel a strange calm settling over me. An unnatural peace that chills me to the bone. It's not the peace of resolution, but the quiet before the storm. The storm of my own demise. I feel my time is running out. My body is failing. The fragments are merging, blending, dissolving into a chaotic whole. The voices are growing louder, more insistent. I fear I'm losing control. I fear the inevitable.

November 1st. The pain is overwhelming. My breath comes in ragged gasps. Seraphina is fading. Her sweet voice is barely a whisper. And yet...a dark satisfaction lingers. The others are fading. I am the last one standing. The truth, however horrifying, will finally be told.

November 2nd. The end is near. I can feel it in my bones, in the very marrow of my being. My body is a battlefield. The different personalities clashing, tearing at each other, each struggling for dominance in these final moments. My vision blurs, my breathing shallow. My grasp on reality loosens, but that doesn't stop the memories, the flood of images and feelings of betrayal and terror. The faces of my tormentors. The endless cycle of abuse. The weight of the years, the years of living as a broken vessel. The years of enduring such profound trauma. The years of internal wars.

November 3rd. Forgive me, Sarah. Forgive me for the pain I've caused. Forgive me for the life I couldn't live, the life I couldn't escape. Forgive me for the monster that resided within me. The monster that was created and molded by the cruelty of others. Forgive me for the image of myself that I've given you. I wish I could have been different. I wish I could have saved myself. I wish I could have been a better mother. But the truth, it's a cruel mistress. The fragmented pieces of my consciousness that were my reality, they were nothing but the remnants of an overwhelming trauma, a broken and tormented existence. This is the weight I am taking with me, the only companion I have in my final journey.

November 4th. The darkness closes in. The voices fade into a silent hum. The memories...the memories remain, a haunting symphony of pain and rage. But even in the face of death, a sliver of hope remains. Hope for Sarah. Hope for a future where the shadows of the past are finally laid to rest. Hope for a world that understands the silent suffering of broken souls.

November 5th. The final day. The last fragmented piece of consciousness before this vessel is finally released. There is no fear. No regret. Only the acceptance of the end of a long, painful journey. The fractured reality that I have lived, the fragmented pieces of myself, they are finally coming to an end. I can finally rest. My final thoughts, my final words, are a prayer for understanding, a plea for compassion. May my story serve as a testament to the destructive power of abuse and the resilience of the human spirit, even in its most fragmented state. May it teach others to look beyond the surface and into the depths of suffering. May it remind people that even in the face of horror, even in the darkest of times, the smallest glimmer of hope may be found. It is time for me to go. The pain will cease. The whispers will stop. There is peace in letting go. My journey ends here.

November 6th. (A single, shaky entry, scrawled in barely legible handwriting) ...Sarah...find...peace...

The diary closes abruptly, the last page blank. The ink is smudged, stained with the ghostly impression of tears. Sarah closes the diary, a single tear tracing a path down her cheek. The weight of her mother's story, the full measure of Eleanor's suffering, the horrifying truth of the murder, settles upon her. It is a burden, but not a crushing one. The diary, though detailing a life of profound pain and suffering, has also revealed Eleanor's courage, her resilience, her quiet defiance in the face of overwhelming odds. It has revealed her desire for release, the search for a peace that had been consistently elusive throughout her life. And in that, Sarah finds a strange, unexpected solace. The diary has given her the tools to begin to make sense of her mother's existence. It has brought understanding to a life previously shrouded in shadows. And it has given her the strength to move forward, to honor Eleanor's memory, not by forgetting, but by remembering, understanding and learning.

The cold reality of the murder, the brutal act committed by one of her mother's fractured selves, remains, a constant, haunting reminder of the darkness that lurked beneath the idyllic surface of Havenwood. But Sarah understands now. She understands the complexity of trauma, the devastating impact of abuse, the fractured psyche of a woman desperately searching for peace, only to find destruction. The red scrunchies, once a symbol of horror, now stand as a testament to a life lived in fragments, a life finally laid bare, its story told. The finality of the diary entries, while heartbreaking, also offers a sense of closure. Eleanor's journey, though tragically short, has come to an end. And in that end, Sarah finds a fragile hope, a glimmer of light in the lingering shadows. The darkness remains, but now it is accompanied by understanding. The quiet hum of the refrigerator no longer holds the same haunting resonance. The silence is heavy, but not oppressive. It is the silence of acceptance, the silence of healing. The silence that follows the storm. The silence of a story finally told.

The courtroom was cold, the air thick with the unspoken weight of Eleanor Vance's life and death. Sarah sat in the gallery, a small, almost insignificant figure amidst the throng of lawyers, journalists, and onlookers. The case against Eleanor, or rather, against the alter ego responsible for Emily Carter's murder, was unlike anything the legal system had ever encountered. Twenty-five years had passed since the discovery of Emily's body, encased in black plastic bags tied with those damned red scrunchies, submerged in a caustic bath of lye within a freezer in Eleanor's own garage. A crime so shocking, so brutal, had been left unsolved, the killer seemingly vanished into thin air. Until now. Eleanor's diary, a chilling testament to a fractured mind, had finally cracked the case open.

The prosecution, led by the seasoned and steely-eyed District Attorney, Mr. Harding, presented a compelling case built around the diary entries. Each entry, meticulously dated, painted a horrifying portrait of Eleanor's inner turmoil, showcasing the shifts in personality, the emergence of distinct alters, each with their own motivations, memories, and disturbing level of detachment from the acts committed by others. They presented psychiatric evaluations, post-mortem psychological analyses, and expert testimony from renowned forensic psychologists. The experts detailed the science of dissociative identity disorder, explaining the complex interplay of alters, the potential for one alter to commit a crime without the conscious knowledge or memory of another. It was a delicate dance between legal definitions and the murky waters of mental illness.

The defense, headed by the renowned and ethically challenged Ms. Dubois, argued a different narrative. She masterfully twisted the narrative, highlighting the inherent unreliability of the diary entries themselves. She played on the ambiguity of the written word, suggesting that the diary, while seemingly documenting horrifying events, might have been a fictional creation, a product of a highly suggestible and possibly unstable mind. She questioned the validity of the psychiatric assessments, casting doubt on the very nature of multiple personality disorder itself – was it a real disorder or simply a fashionable diagnosis for dramatic individuals? She employed a sophisticated strategy of doubt and confusion, expertly undermining the prosecution's narrative one carefully crafted question at a time.

The ethical dilemma at the heart of the trial was inescapable. How could you hold someone accountable for a crime committed by a fragmented part of their self? Was it just to punish someone who, by all accounts, had no conscious memory or control over the actions of their alter ego? The courtroom was a battleground of legal precedents and moral considerations, the air thick with the tension of this unprecedented legal quandary. The case tested the limits of the criminal justice system, forcing the court to confront the ambiguous boundaries between culpability, responsibility, and the impact of severe trauma on the human psyche. The jurors, tasked with sorting through the complex testimony and intricate psychological details, were clearly struggling.

The prosecution presented evidence demonstrating that 'Seraphina,' the gentle, seemingly innocent alter, was the one who carried out the actual act. However, 'Eleanor,' the dominant personality, exhibited a chilling lack of awareness regarding that particular night. The court heard hours of expert testimonies detailing the phenomenon of 'functional amnesia,' where certain alters may not have recollection of what another alter did. This presented the prosecution with a significant challenge - proving that 'Eleanor' was fully responsible, even if her actions were mediated through another personality. The defense argued it was akin to holding a body part accountable for the crime it committed, rather than the person. An arm that struck a blow, not a mind that intentionally planned a murder.

Days blurred into weeks, a relentless stream of testimony, cross-examination, and legal arguments. The courtroom transformed into a stage for the exploration of the darkest corners of the human psyche, a place where the boundaries of sanity and responsibility were constantly challenged. The prosecution painstakingly constructed a timeline based on the diary entries, linking Seraphina's actions to specific triggers —instances of repressed memories of abuse surfacing. The defense skillfully countered, claiming the diary was a literary exercise, a product of a fertile imagination, or even a sophisticated attempt to manipulate the truth.

Sarah watched, her own life experiences intertwining with the unfolding drama. Eleanor's diary had been a window into her mother's fragmented soul, but it was also a harrowing revelation of her own past. She had grown up in the shadow of Eleanor's unpredictable behavior, the unspoken anxieties and sudden shifts in personality. She had learned to navigate the shifting tides of her mother's fragmented reality, to walk carefully and respectfully in what was undoubtedly a traumatic space. She had endured years of emotional turmoil as a result of the instability in her family life, mirroring a silent war within her mother. This courtroom drama was not just a trial for Eleanor; it was a journey into Sarah's own history, a confrontation with the scars and secrets that had defined her childhood.

The defense attempted to paint Eleanor as a victim herself, highlighting her history of abuse, the years of trauma she endured. They argued that her actions, or rather the actions of her alters, were a direct consequence of this abuse, a desperate cry for help, a manifestation of her deep-seated pain. They presented evidence of the systematic abuse Eleanor had suffered, portraying her not as a cold-blooded killer, but as a broken woman, a victim of her circumstances. This strategy was a risky one, as it simultaneously implied that she still bore responsibility for her actions.

The prosecution countered by arguing that while Eleanor's history of abuse undoubtedly contributed to her condition, it did not excuse the brutal murder. They argued that her trauma was real, but it was not a justification for taking a life. They appealed to the jurors' sense of justice, to their understanding of accountability, even in the face of such immense tragedy. They presented the case of an individual who, despite suffering profound trauma, was still accountable for their actions or, at least, for the actions of their own fractured selves. The lines between victim and perpetrator blurred, creating a legal and ethical gray zone. The prosecution sought to maintain a semblance of order within this chaotic portrait of mental illness and criminality. The courtroom was a battleground for the clash of legal definitions and ethical considerations.

The case came down to a single question: could a fractured mind be held accountable for the actions of its fragmented parts? It was a question that echoed far beyond the courtroom, reaching into the hearts and minds of everyone involved. The jury deliberated for days, the tension palpable in the silent courtroom. Sarah sat, a silent observer, watching the culmination of her mother's story unfold. The verdict, when it came, was a compromise. Eleanor was found guilty but with diminished capacity. She was sentenced to a mental institution rather than prison, a decision that satisfied neither the prosecution nor the defense, but one that reflected the complexity and uncertainty of the case. The court case became a landmark ruling. A legal precedent for the courts, attempting to balance justice and compassion within the often-murky realities of mental illness and criminal behavior. The trial served as a reminder of the long shadow cast by trauma, the scars left by abuse, and the often-uncertain nature of justice itself. The case, while closing a chapter on Eleanor's life, opened a new one for Sarah – a chapter of healing, understanding, and coming to terms with the complex legacy of her mother.

The silence in the courtroom was deafening, a stark contrast to the weeks of intense legal sparring. The jury, faces etched with the weight of their decision, filed back into their seats. Each juror, a microcosm of societal judgment, carried the burden of a verdict that would define not only Eleanor Vance's fate but also the very understanding of culpability in cases of severe mental illness. The air crackled with anticipation, thick with unspoken questions and lingering doubts. Even the ever-present hum of the fluorescent lights seemed to hold its breath.

Judge Thompson, his face impassive, cleared his throat, the sound echoing in the hushed chamber. His gaze swept across the courtroom, landing briefly on Sarah, who sat rigid, her knuckles white as she gripped the worn leather of her handbag. Sarah had spent the past weeks reliving her own fragmented childhood, the echoes of her mother's instability resonating within her own psyche. She felt the familiar tightness in her chest, a physical manifestation of the emotional turmoil that had been her constant companion. This wasn't just her mother's trial; it was a re-examination of her own life, a confrontation with the shadows that had haunted her for years.

"We, the jury," the foreman began, his voice surprisingly steady, "find the defendant, Eleanor Vance, guilty of the second-degree murder of Emily Carter." A ripple of murmurs went through the courtroom, a collective intake of breath. Guilt. The word hung heavy in the air, a stark declaration that cut through the complex tapestry of psychological arguments that had dominated the trial.

But the verdict was far from simple. The foreman continued, his voice gaining a measured cadence, "However, we also find the defendant to have acted with diminished capacity due to severe and documented dissociative identity disorder." This was the pivotal part, the point where legal precedent met the murky waters of mental illness. The compromise.

A wave of relief washed over Sarah, a contradictory mixture of acceptance and disappointment. Guilty, yes, but with a recognition of the profound mental illness that had driven the actions of one of her mother's alters. It was a legal acknowledgement of the fractured nature of her mother's psyche, a recognition of the unimaginable trauma that had shaped her life and ultimately led to the tragic events that transpired.

The courtroom buzzed with whispered conversations, a symphony of interpretations and opinions. Ms. Dubois, Eleanor's defense attorney, her face a mask of controlled emotion, offered a slight nod, a subtle acknowledgment of a battle partially won. Mr. Harding, the prosecutor, his usual steely gaze softened with a hint of weariness, remained stoic, his expression betraying nothing of his thoughts. He had pushed for justice, for accountability, yet the verdict was a reflection of the inherent complexities of the case, a recognition that the traditional notions of guilt and responsibility were inadequate in this exceptional circumstance.

The sentencing was swift, yet heavy with implications. Judge Thompson, his voice resonating with the weight of his decision, sentenced Eleanor to indefinite confinement at the Blackwood Psychiatric Facility. It wasn't prison, but it was a form of confinement nonetheless, a legal acknowledgement of Eleanor's mental state and the need for long-term psychiatric care. It was a decision fraught with ambiguity, a balance struck between justice and compassion, a legal concession to the reality of a fractured psyche.

The aftermath of the verdict was a complex tapestry of reactions. The media hailed the case as a landmark legal precedent, a turning point in the understanding of mental illness and culpability. Legal scholars debated the implications of the diminished capacity ruling, exploring its potential impact on future cases involving mental illness. The psychiatric community, divided in its opinions, discussed the intricacies of dissociative identity disorder, examining the challenges of diagnosis, treatment, and the implications for legal accountability.

Sarah, however, found little solace in the public discourse. She watched as the media devoured the details, transforming her mother's tragedy into a sensationalized narrative. The sensationalism was not the reality of Eleanor's life. The complexities of Eleanor's story, the layers of trauma and fragmentation, were reduced to catchy headlines and sound bites. The true horror of the case lay in the silence, in the unspoken traumas, in the lingering shadows of abuse.

In the quiet solitude of her apartment, Sarah reread her mother's diary, the ink seeming to bleed onto the pages, a testament to the dark secrets it revealed. The words were a mirror reflecting her own fragmented memories, the echoes of a childhood overshadowed by instability. The diary was not just a document of her mother's fractured psyche; it was a testament to the resilience of the human spirit, an acknowledgment of the strength required to survive such profound trauma.

The diary entries detailed the genesis of each alter, the

systematic abuse that had fractured her mother's psyche into a mosaic of distinct personalities. Each alter, born from a specific trauma, had its own unique coping mechanisms, its own defense against the overwhelming pain and fear. There was Seraphina, the docile and compliant one, who had emerged as a shield against the violence. There was the child alter that had carried the unbearable weight of the abuse, a silent witness to horrors too profound for a young mind to comprehend.

There was also the protector alter, a fierce and untamed spirit, fiercely determined to ward off any threat to its vulnerable counterparts. And then there was the killer alter, the one that had committed the horrific act, fueled by an anger so profound that it transcended the boundaries of reason and self-preservation. These alters were not separate entities; they were shards of Eleanor's shattered self, each a product of the traumas inflicted on her.

Sarah's understanding of her mother evolved after the verdict. It wasn't a simple narrative of victim or villain. Eleanor was both. A victim of unspeakable horrors, her very psyche fractured by the devastating weight of abuse; yet also the perpetrator, the one whose actions had led to tragedy. The court's verdict reflected that truth. The verdict had been a compromised judgment, a reflection of the legal system grappling with the complexities of mental illness, but it did not alleviate the profound sadness and loss that remained.

The case concluded, but the questions lingered. The case raised the broader question of how society should respond to those who commit crimes under the duress of mental illness. It illuminated the gaps in the mental health care system, exposing the inadequacies of support and resources available to victims of abuse. The trial highlighted the ethical and legal ambiguities that arose in the intersection of mental illness and criminal behavior. It was a case that challenged the conventional understanding of justice, forcing a confrontation with the complexities of human nature.

Sarah began her own journey of healing, a process that would require time and self-reflection. The trial had been an examination of her mother's life but also of her own. She confronted her own trauma, the lasting impact of growing up in a household marked by instability. She sought therapy, working through the emotional baggage of her childhood, learning to reconcile the conflicting realities of her mother's life and her own. The legacy of Eleanor Vance was complicated, but Sarah embraced it, ready to understand and heal. The trial had given her closure, a chance to honor her mother's memory in a way that transcended the sensationalized media portrayal. The verdict was a start. The healing, a lifetime's work.

The courtroom doors swung shut behind Eleanor, the metallic clang echoing the finality of the verdict. Sarah, however, felt no sense of finality. The gavel's thud had silenced the cacophony of the trial, but the internal turmoil within her raged on. The media circus had already begun its feeding frenzy, transforming the nuanced complexities of her mother's life into digestible soundbites and sensationalized headlines. "Trophy Wife Turns Killer," screamed one tabloid, the words a grotesque distortion of reality. Sarah felt a profound sense of violation; her mother's story, her own story, reduced to a salacious spectacle for public consumption.

The initial wave of relief – the acknowledgment of Eleanor's diminished capacity – had ebbed, leaving behind a vast emptiness. The guilt remained, a heavy shroud draped over the fragile beginnings of her healing. It was a guilt not entirely about Eleanor's actions, but about her own complicity in a life lived in the shadows of her mother's disorder. The unspoken fears, the tiptoeing around unstable moods, the constant vigilance – all contributed to a deep-seated sense of responsibility, a feeling that she, too, had failed. The weight of her childhood, previously buried beneath layers of denial and self-preservation, now pressed down with renewed force.

The days following the trial blurred into a monotonous routine of solitude. Her apartment, once a sanctuary, now felt like a cage, each corner whispering memories of her fractured childhood. The silence was deafening, broken only by the sporadic tick of the clock, a relentless reminder of the passage of time, a time she desperately needed to use to heal. She attempted to resume her life – her work, her friendships – but the cracks in her façade were visible, the shadows of Eleanor's legacy looming large.

She found solace, unexpectedly, in the diary. Not in the gruesome details of the murder, but in the intimate glimpses into Eleanor's fractured psyche. She reread passages, not as a daughter judging a mother, but as a human being understanding another's profound pain. She saw Eleanor's childhood, not through the lens of the tabloid portrayals, but through the raw, vulnerable words etched onto the pages. She read about the relentless abuse, the systematic dismantling of a young girl's spirit, and the subsequent creation of a series of alters— desperate attempts to survive the unsalvageable.

Seraphina, the compliant one, became heartbreakingly real through her words; a self-preservation mechanism developed to appease an unpredictable abuser. Sarah imagined the young girl cowering, hiding her pain behind a mask of docility, enduring unthinkable horrors. There was the child alter, trapped in a perpetual state of terror, recounting scenes too painful to fully articulate, leaving gaps in her narratives, blank spaces where memory itself had failed. Through those blank spaces, Sarah learned to recognize her own missing memories, her own gaps, realizing the pervasiveness of Eleanor's influence.

The protector alter revealed itself through violent outbursts, a furious guardian shielding the more vulnerable selves from harm. Sarah understood now the origins of her mother's unpredictable rages, the startling shifts in demeanor. This alter wasn't evil; it was a tragically malformed protector, a testament to the depths of Eleanor's survival instincts. And then there was the killer alter. Sarah approached this persona with a mixture of horror and profound sadness. This entity, born from a crucible of unforgivable suffering, acted in a way that, while horrifying, was explicable only through the context of unbearable trauma. This wasn't a monster; it was a symptom, a tragic manifestation of pain.

Sarah began to understand the intricate dance between these personalities, the chaotic shifts in control, the constant internal battle for survival. She started to see her mother not as a single entity, but as a multitude of selves, each a fragment of a broken whole, fighting for space in a mind torn apart by trauma. The act of reading the diary was a process of piecing together a shattered mirror, seeing the reflections of both her mother and herself. This was no longer a condemnation, it was a recognition of shared pain, a shared narrative woven through the tapestry of abuse.

The process was excruciating. There were nights spent weeping, reliving fragments of her own forgotten trauma. Therapy became essential, a safe space where she could confront the ghosts of her past, unraveling the tangled threads of her childhood. She learned to identify the impact of growing up in a chaotic household, the emotional neglect, the subtle and not-so-subtle signs of instability that had permeated her early years. Through therapy, Sarah started to unravel her own defense mechanisms, her own coping strategies, some healthy, others deeply ingrained from Eleanor's influence.

Her therapist helped her process the complex emotions – grief, anger, guilt, and ultimately, acceptance. The acceptance wasn't a condoning of Eleanor's actions, but a recognition of the complex interplay of trauma, mental illness, and human behavior. The understanding gave her the peace she craved. She was no longer bound by the weight of her mother's actions. She was free to build her own life, free from the shadows of her past.

Slowly, gradually, Sarah began to reclaim her own narrative. The public perception of her mother's life mattered less and less. The sensationalized headlines faded into the background, replaced by the quiet strength she discovered within herself. She started to rewrite her story, a story not defined by her mother's trauma, but one built on resilience, healing, and a commitment to breaking the cycle of abuse.

The scars remained – etched into her memory, a constant reminder of her challenging past. But these scars, no longer a source of shame, became a testament to her strength. She learned to accept her past and use the lessons learned to build a future that prioritized her own well-being and a sense of self-worth separate from her mother's legacy. The closure she found wasn't a simple resolution, but a journey, a continuous process of self-discovery, marked by moments of heartbreak and ultimate resilience.

Sarah's journey became one of advocating for others. She actively engaged with support groups for children of parents with mental illness, offering comfort and understanding. She spoke publicly about her experience, challenging the stigma associated with mental illness and advocating for improved mental health care systems. She used her voice to fight for the recognition that mental illness is not a moral failing but a medical condition requiring compassionate support and resources. Eleanor Vance's legacy may have been defined by tragedy, but Sarah Vance's legacy would be one of healing, resilience, and a fierce dedication to helping others overcome their own darkness. The trial had ended, but her journey of healing was far from over. It was a lifelong commitment to herself, to her own growth, and to a future unburdened by the shadows of her past. The end of the trial marked the beginning of her true life.

The initial shock of the verdict, the sudden cessation of the relentless media storm, left a hollow ache in Sarah's chest. It wasn't the relief she'd anticipated; rather, a profound sense of displacement. The world, once consumed by the spectacle of her mother's trial, quietly resumed its course, leaving Sarah adrift in the wake of its receding tide. The courtroom's sterile atmosphere, the hushed whispers of onlookers, the judge's gavel—all had faded into a distant memory, yet their echoes reverberated within her, a constant reminder of the life she'd lived, a life forever altered.

She found herself staring out of her apartment window, the city lights blurring into a hazy tableau of indifference. The silence was deafening, broken only by the rhythmic thump of her own heartbeat, a drumbeat echoing the frantic rhythm of her unsettled thoughts. She'd expected a sense of closure, a finality that would allow her to move on, to begin the process of healing. Instead, she felt a disquieting stillness, a void where resolution should have been.

Work became an exercise in detachment, a means to numb the sharp edges of her grief. She found herself mechanically performing tasks, her mind miles away, lost in the labyrinthine corridors of her memories. The faces of colleagues, once friendly and familiar, now seemed distant and blurry, their conversations fading into a meaningless drone. She attempted to engage, to participate, but the effort felt monumental, the weight of unspoken anxieties pressing down on her. The mask she wore, crafted from a fragile veneer of normalcy, threatened to crack at any moment.

Evenings were the hardest. The solitude of her apartment, once a sanctuary, now felt like a cage, the walls closing in, suffocating her. Sleep offered little respite; instead, she was haunted by fragmented memories, fleeting images, snippets of conversations, all echoing the chaos of her childhood. She would wake up in a cold sweat, her heart pounding, her mind racing, reliving moments of instability, of fear, of her mother's unpredictable moods.

The diary, however, remained a constant. It wasn't a morbid fascination that drew her to its pages; rather, it was a lifeline, a connection to the woman who was both her tormentor and her victim. She reread passages, not to judge, but to understand. Eleanor's words became a window into the depths of her own trauma, a reflection of her own fractured memories, the shared narrative that linked mother and daughter in an intricate and painful dance.

Seraphina, the compliant alter, continued to haunt Sarah. The image of a young girl, trapped in a perpetual state of subservience, her spirit systematically crushed under the weight of abuse, resonated deeply. Sarah saw herself in Seraphina's quiet desperation, the silent acceptance of the unacceptable. She began to recognize parallels in her own life, the subtle ways she'd learned to adapt, to disappear, to become invisible.

The child alter, trapped in a state of perpetual terror, mirrored the fragmented memories Sarah herself struggled to access. The blank spaces in the diary became a mirror to the gaps in her own recollection, confirming the years of suppressed trauma, of emotional neglect, of an unstable upbringing that had left its indelible mark.

The protector alter, with its violent outbursts, explained the sudden shifts in her mother's demeanor, the unpredictable rages that had characterized her childhood. Sarah found a strange solace in understanding the origins of her mother's violent tendencies – not as evil, but as a desperate, tragically malformed attempt at self-preservation. This alter wasn't a monster; it was a symptom of an unbearable reality, a testament to a survival instinct pushed to its most extreme and dangerous limits.

And the killer alter. Sarah approached this persona with a mixture of terror and profound empathy. She understood that the violent act, while unforgivable, was a tragically logical culmination of decades of abuse and mental illness. It wasn't a random act of violence, but a desperate, horrifying expression of pain, a symptom of a mind broken and beyond repair.

The diary became a form of therapy in itself, a process of confronting the trauma not only of her mother, but also of her own life. It was a slow, painstaking excavation of the past, a piecing together of a shattered narrative. Sarah learned to identify her own coping mechanisms, the ways she'd adapted to survive in a chaotic environment, some healthy, others a direct reflection of Eleanor's influence.

Therapy, however, proved to be indispensable. Her sessions became a safe space to unpack her past, to confront the ghosts that haunted her, to unravel the tangled threads of her childhood experiences. She learned to identify the subtle signs of emotional neglect, the constant anxiety that had shaped her personality, the insidious way her mother's instability had permeated every aspect of her life.

She worked through the complex layers of grief, anger, guilt, and ultimately, acceptance. This acceptance wasn't a condoning of her mother's actions; it was a hard-won understanding of the intricate interplay between trauma, mental illness, and the destructive nature of unchecked abuse. This understanding was not forgiveness, but a recognition of the complex tapestry of human experience, a tapestry woven with threads of pain, resilience, and ultimately, hope.

Sarah began to reclaim her life, her narrative. The public perception, the sensationalized headlines, faded into the background, replaced by the quiet strength she found within herself. She started to rewrite her story, a story not defined by her mother's trauma, but one woven from resilience, healing, and a commitment to breaking the cycle of abuse.

The scars, however, remained. They were a permanent reminder of her past, etched into the fabric of her being. But these scars, once a source of shame, were transformed into a testament to her strength. They were a map, a reminder of the journey she'd undertaken, of the battles she'd fought, and of the triumph she'd achieved.

Sarah's healing wasn't a singular event; it was a continuous process, a lifelong journey of self-discovery. She discovered a profound sense of purpose, a calling to help others. She became an advocate, lending her voice to those who had been silenced, offering comfort and understanding to others struggling with similar experiences. She spoke publicly, challenging the stigma associated with mental illness, advocating for improved mental health services, and working tirelessly to dismantle the destructive cycle of abuse.

Eleanor Vance's life may have ended in tragedy, but Sarah Vance's life was just beginning. She had found her voice, her strength, her purpose. The trial may have concluded, but Sarah's journey was only just beginning, a journey marked by resilience, healing, and a fervent commitment to building a future unburdened by the shadows of her past. Her story was a testament to the indomitable human spirit, a celebration of survival, and a beacon of hope for others navigating the darkness. The courtroom doors had closed, but the doors to her future swung wide open, brimming with possibility and promise.

# CHAPTER 13: THE SCARS REMAIN

The courtroom's sterile silence had done little to soothe the turmoil within Robert. He watched Sarah, her face a mask of controlled grief, and felt a pang of something akin to... regret? No, not regret exactly. More like a profound dissatisfaction. The meticulously crafted narrative he'd presented, the carefully chosen words, the strategic silences – they'd worked. Eleanor was gone, the threat neutralized. Yet, the victory felt hollow, a pyrrhic triumph leaving a bitter taste in his mouth.

His motivation hadn't been purely malicious, not entirely. He'd been driven by a twisted sense of justice, a warped morality that justified his actions. Eleanor's cruelty, the years of torment she inflicted on Sarah, had festered within him, a malignancy that grew with each passing year. He'd seen Sarah's quiet suffering, the way she'd internalized Eleanor's abuse, burying it deep within her soul. It was a silent scream, a muted plea for help that no one seemed to hear. He'd become her silent guardian, her unseen protector, even if his methods were abhorrent.

Robert had known Eleanor for years, a connection forged in the shared shadow of their troubled pasts. He understood her fractured psyche, the warring alters that battled for dominance. He'd witnessed firsthand the terrifying unpredictability of her moods, the sudden shifts from serene calm to explosive rage. He'd seen the darkness lurking beneath her meticulously crafted facade, the abyss that threatened to swallow her whole. And he'd feared, with a chilling clarity, what that darkness could do.

His actions, he reasoned, were a form of preemptive strike, a desperate attempt to prevent another tragedy. Eleanor was a time bomb, ticking away inexorably towards another catastrophic event. He had seen the signs, the subtle cues, the escalation of her erratic behavior. He'd anticipated the inevitable explosion, the violence waiting to erupt. He had acted, not out of malice, but out of a twisted sense of duty, a morbid responsibility to protect Sarah from the monster her mother had become.

But the process of manipulating events, of guiding the investigation, of subtly influencing the narrative had been agonizing. He'd had to tread a precarious path, balancing on the knife's edge of exposure. Every interaction, every word, every gesture had been calculated, meticulously planned, leaving him drained and exhausted. The weight of his secret, the constant fear of discovery, had etched lines of exhaustion onto his face, stolen the color from his eyes.

He'd never intended for things to escalate to this point. He'd envisioned a different outcome, a more subtle solution, perhaps one that wouldn't involve the legal system or the harsh glare of public scrutiny. He'd hoped to discreetly remove Eleanor from the equation, leaving Sarah unharmed, unaware of his role in her liberation. But his plan, so carefully constructed, had crumbled under the weight of unforeseen circumstances, leading to a devastating and irreversible conclusion.

Now, with Eleanor gone, the silence felt heavier, the void deeper. He was left with the echoes of his actions, the chilling repercussions of his choices. The satisfaction he'd craved, the sense of justice he'd pursued, had evaporated, leaving only a bitter residue of guilt and self-loathing.

He found himself staring out the courtroom window, the city lights blurring into a meaningless spectacle. The city lights, once a symbol of the anonymity he craved, now seemed to mock him, highlighting his isolation. He felt profoundly alone, adrift in a sea of remorse, his actions casting a long, dark shadow over his soul. The weight of his secret was almost unbearable, a crushing burden that threatened to consume him.

His relationship with Eleanor had been complex, a tangled web of shared trauma and unspoken resentments. They were two damaged souls, drawn together by a mutual understanding of pain, bound by the invisible chains of their pasts. He'd seen his own reflection in Eleanor's fractured psyche, a dark mirror reflecting his own inner demons.

He knew her rage stemmed from years of unimaginable abuse, a systematic dismantling of her spirit. He understood the desperation of her alters, their frantic attempts to cope with a reality too brutal to bear. Her violence wasn't a manifestation of inherent evil, but a symptom of a broken mind, a desperate cry for help that had gone unheard.

And yet, he had been complicit, a silent accomplice in her destruction. He had used her vulnerabilities, her fractured state, to achieve his own twisted ends. The irony wasn't lost on him. He had sought to protect Sarah from Eleanor's darkness, only to plunge himself into a darkness deeper and more profound.

The trial had ended, but his own internal trial had only just begun. He was trapped in a labyrinth of his own making, a maze of guilt and self-doubt. Sleep offered no respite; instead, he was haunted by fragmented memories, nightmares of Eleanor's rage, visions of Sarah's silent suffering.

His days were now a blur of anxiety, his nights a torment of restless sleep. He felt the walls closing in, the pressure mounting, the weight of his secret threatening to crush him. He had sought to heal Sarah's wounds, but in doing so, he had only widened his own. The justice he'd sought had eluded him, replaced by a profound sense of emptiness, a hollow ache that echoed the silence of the courtroom.

The image of Sarah, her face a mask of controlled grief, haunted him. He hadn't anticipated the depth of her sorrow, the profound impact Eleanor's death would have on her. He'd thought he was saving her, rescuing her from a life of torment. He'd believed he was her savior. But now, looking at her, he saw the lingering scars, the unhealed wounds, and he realized that his actions, however well-intentioned, had only added to her burden.

He understood now that true justice wasn't about retribution, about vengeance. It was about healing, about breaking the cycle of abuse, about creating a future where such darkness could never again find root. His actions had been a drastic, desperate measure, a tragic misstep in a long and arduous journey toward healing. He had played God, and in doing so, he had only made things worse.

He knew he needed help. The weight of his secret, the crushing burden of his guilt, was too much to bear alone. He needed to confess, to seek atonement, to find a way to reconcile his actions with his conscience. The road ahead was long and arduous, a journey fraught with challenges and uncertainties. But he knew, with a chilling certainty, that he could no longer remain silent. His silence was a form of complicity, a continuation of the darkness he had sought to destroy.

His quest for justice had been a failure, a tragic testament to his own flawed morality. But perhaps, in the ashes of his mistakes, he could find a path towards redemption, a chance to begin the long and difficult process of healing – both himself and Sarah. The scars remained, not only on Sarah, but on him as well, a permanent reminder of the devastating consequences of his actions, a testament to the complexities of justice, and the enduring power of darkness. The courtroom doors had closed, but the doors to his own soul remained wide open, a space where the long process of confronting his truth could begin. His journey towards atonement was just beginning.

The black bags. They weren't just receptacles for a body, a grimly efficient means of disposal. They were a shroud, a suffocating darkness mirroring the suffocating darkness Eleanor herself inhabited. Sarah, poring over her mother's diary, had initially dismissed them as a detail, a macabre element of the crime scene, quickly overshadowed by the sheer brutality of the act. But as she delved deeper into the fragmented narratives, the black bags took on a life of their own, becoming a recurring motif, a potent symbol of Eleanor's suppressed traumas and fractured identity.

The diary entries, scrawled in a variety of handwritings reflecting the different personalities inhabiting Eleanor's psyche, revealed a recurring pattern. "The Collector," a chilling alter whose entries were marked by a detached, almost clinical observation of violence, often mentioned black bags. Not just in the context of the murder, but in seemingly unrelated entries. She'd describe a childhood memory of hiding in a closet, the darkness surrounding her a suffocating blanket, a premonition of the black bag's later significance. The darkness was a sanctuary, a place to hide from the light, from the constant threat that permeated her childhood.

Another personality, "The Shadow," whose entries were filled with fragmented memories and nightmares, described her own experience of being shrouded in darkness, metaphorical blackness that mirrored the actual black bags. It was a constant companion, a feeling of being swallowed whole, invisible and unnoticed – the feeling of being perpetually in the dark, unseen and unheard. The black bags were not just a tool; they were a manifestation of this internal darkness, this constant sense of being buried alive, both physically and emotionally.

Then there was "The Child," whose innocent yet disturbing entries hinted at a terrifying game played with her by the abuser. The game always culminated in being hidden in a dark closet, the blackness a frightening but familiar comfort in a world that was too terrifying to comprehend. The black bags were like the closet, a repetition of this trauma, a symbolic return to a familiar, albeit horrific, space. The red scrunchies tied around the bags became further evidence, adding a sinister contrast to the darkness. The vibrant red, juxtaposed against the black, suggested a perverse kind of control, a grotesque playfulness – the macabre artistry of a mind shattered by years of abuse.

The lye, a corrosive agent used to dissolve the victim's flesh, was another layer of the gruesome scene. This aspect added another dimension to the symbolism of the black bags. It was not just about concealing the body; it was about obliterating any trace of the victim, making them disappear completely, much like the abuser had tried to obliterate Eleanor's identity and her very being. The diary offered a sickening insight into the abuser's attempt to erase Eleanor, the brutal attempt to control every facet of her life.

The black bags become almost a physical manifestation of the mental space Eleanor was forced to inhabit. A place of confinement, oppression, and ultimate darkness. It became a symbol of the psychological suffocation that Eleanor endured. The complete absence of light, the inability to escape, the oppressive weight of the black fabric mirrored the emotional prison Eleanor had been trapped in, the constant struggle against her invisible tormentor.

Analyzing the crime scene photos, Sarah began to connect the dots. The positioning of the body, the methodical way in which the black bags were placed, the careful arrangement of the lye – it wasn't random. It was a calculated act, a ritualistic display of control and power, mimicking the abuser's relentless attempts to dominate and subdue her. The black bags represented the control the abuser had exerted over Eleanor's life, a constant reminder of her powerlessness.

Furthermore, the diary entries hinted at a possible connection between the black bags and Eleanor's OCD. The repetitive nature of her actions, the compulsion to order and control, might have manifested itself in the meticulous way the crime scene was staged. The black bags, flawlessly placed and tied, could be interpreted as a desperate attempt to restore order to her fragmented world, a twisted form of self-regulation amidst the chaotic turmoil of her psyche. The black bags offered her a sense of control in a life where she was consistently denied it.

Even the seemingly insignificant details within the diary—descriptions of dark closets, of being hidden in shadows, of feeling perpetually invisible—all pointed to the black bags as a central, albeit profoundly disturbing, symbol. They were not merely a gruesome detail of the murder but a physical representation of the psychological darkness that had consumed Eleanor's life and the relentless battle between her fragmented selves. The bags weren't just about death; they were about erasure, about obliterating not just a body but a whole being, mirroring the abuser's insidious attempts to destroy Eleanor's identity and sense of self.

The deeper Sarah delved, the more she recognized the black bags as far more than just containers. They were a morbid reflection of her mother's interior landscape, a visceral manifestation of the psychological trauma she endured. Each personality, in their own fragmented way, contributed to the symbolism. "The Survivor," for instance, described the bags as a dark womb, a place where the fragmented self found refuge from the overwhelming terror of the outside world. This was a complex paradox, a sanctuary born from a place of ultimate fear.

The repeated imagery of darkness, of being hidden and unseen, woven throughout the diary, further cemented the connection between the black bags and Eleanor's deep-seated psychological wounds. It wasn't just the bags themselves; it was the darkness they represented, the oppressive weight of secrecy, the inability to escape the shadows of her past. The darkness served as both protector and prison, a reflection of the conflicting emotions and internal struggles that tore her apart.

The black bags became a chilling metaphor for the years of silence, of suppressed trauma, of the hidden horrors Eleanor had endured. They were a visual manifestation of the emotional and psychological prison in which she had been confined. The suffocating darkness, the impenetrable barrier of the plastic, mirrored the suffocating reality of her life, where every attempt to break free was met with resistance, with further abuse.

The diary revealed the pattern was more than just the bags themselves. It was in the choices Eleanor made, the actions she took, the way she crafted her life as a shield against the relentless torrent of inner turmoil. The perfect facade, the immaculate home, the seemingly idyllic family – all were carefully constructed masks, hiding the abyss of pain and suffering lurking beneath the surface.

As Sarah pieced together the fragmented narratives, she realized the black bags were not just a component of the murder but a symbol of Eleanor's entire life, a recurring motif representing the hidden traumas, the suppressed memories, the unspoken pain. They were a visual representation of the psychological prison she inhabited, a grim testament to the devastating effects of prolonged abuse. And in understanding this, Sarah finally began to comprehend the true horror of her mother's fragmented existence and the horrifying darkness that had ultimately led to the unspeakable act. The red scrunchies, a seemingly small detail, further emphasized the perverse playfulness of the act, highlighting the control and domination that characterized the crime and Eleanor's tormented life.

The significance of the black bags transcended the immediate context of the murder. They served as a powerful symbol of the pervasive darkness that had shaped Eleanor's life, her constant struggle against her inner demons, and the devastating impact of years of untold suffering. The black bags, in their chilling simplicity, became a chilling embodiment of Eleanor's fractured psyche, her suppressed memories, and the unspeakable tragedy that unfolded. They were the final, tragic expression of her desperate attempts to control a life irrevocably shattered by abuse, a dark testament to a mind consumed by its own fragmented self. The black bags were not just evidence of a crime; they were a profound symbol of a life lived and lost in the suffocating embrace of darkness. The mystery of the murder had been solved, but the mystery of Eleanor's life remained, etched in the chilling symbolism of the black bags and the secrets they held. The scars remained, a testament to a life of unimaginable suffering, a dark legacy that would continue to haunt Sarah long after the courtroom doors had closed and the trial was over.

Sarah, still reeling from the revelations in her mother's diary, found herself grappling with a new layer of understanding.

The black bags, the lye, the red scrunchies – these were not just gruesome details of a crime; they were symptoms, chilling manifestations of a deeply fractured psyche, a psyche that desperately needed the help she'd never received. The diary entries, filled with fragmented memories and harrowing accounts of abuse, spoke volumes about the critical lack of therapeutic intervention in Eleanor's life. The absence of therapy was as palpable as the presence of the black bags themselves, a gaping void that contributed directly to the escalating chaos within her mother's mind.

The realization struck Sarah with the force of a physical blow. Eleanor's fragmented personalities weren't just independent entities; they were coping mechanisms, desperate attempts to survive a trauma so profound that it shattered her sense of self into countless pieces. Each alter, in its own twisted way, represented a different facet of Eleanor's struggle, a desperate attempt to compartmentalize the unbearable pain. The Collector, the Shadow, the Child – each bore the unmistakable scars of prolonged abuse, each a testament to the agonizing need for therapeutic intervention. The absence of help allowed these fractured pieces to develop into fully realized personalities, each with their own distinct characteristics, memories, and responses.

Sarah began researching multiple personality disorder (now more accurately termed dissociative identity disorder), poring over medical journals and psychological studies. She learned about the critical role of therapy in helping individuals with DID integrate their fragmented selves, in confronting the underlying trauma, and in rebuilding a sense of coherence and identity. The images of the meticulously placed black bags, now imbued with a profound understanding, served as a constant reminder of how Eleanor had not only failed to receive such help, but also that this lack of treatment had directly and tragically contributed to the devastating consequences that she suffered.

She found studies detailing the effectiveness of trauma-focused therapies like EMDR (Eye Movement Desensitization and Reprocessing) and somatic experiencing, treatments designed to help individuals process traumatic memories and regulate their emotional responses. These were methods that could have potentially helped Eleanor navigate the overwhelming pain she had endured for so long. Sarah imagined what might have been, what could have been, if Eleanor had received early intervention and consistent, long-term therapeutic support. The images of her mother's pristine home and the superficial perfection of her life were shattered as Sarah realized the depth of Eleanor's suffering, which had been hidden for decades, only to finally express itself in a horrific act of violence.

The diary entries themselves became a form of fragmented therapy, albeit a deeply disturbing and incomplete one. Each personality's narrative, though chaotic and often jarring, revealed aspects of Eleanor's inner world that might have been impossible to access through traditional means. "The Survivor," for example, displayed resilience, a determined struggle against insurmountable odds, despite the pervasive trauma she endured. Her entries showed a flicker of hope, a testament to the incredible strength of the human spirit, even when fractured and broken. If she had the tools and support from therapy, perhaps she would have been able to reclaim her life, rather than allowing her own alter to commit the tragic events that would define her legacy.

However, the fragmented nature of the entries was also a stark reminder of the crucial need for proper therapeutic guidance. The lack of structured integration, of professional help to navigate the complex internal landscape, had allowed the fractured personalities to develop into their own independent entities, each vying for control. Without the help of a therapist to guide her through the chaos of her inner turmoil, Eleanor was left to navigate a harrowing internal landscape alone. The resulting tragedy served as a brutal illustration of the dangerous consequences of untreated trauma.

Sarah sought out her own therapist, a specialist in trauma and DID. The process was agonizing, confronting the echoes of her mother's trauma, her own grief, and the painful reality of Eleanor's untreated mental illness. She began to understand the complex interplay between Eleanor's various disorders: the PTSD stemming from years of abuse, the OCD manifested in the meticulous planning of the crime scene, the ADHD possibly contributing to the fragmented memories and chaotic diary entries, and perhaps even underlying traits of autism contributing to Eleanor's social awkwardness and her difficulty expressing her emotions. Each condition, left untreated, exacerbated the others, creating a perfect storm of psychological distress that manifested in the horrifying reality of the murder. The therapist helped Sarah understand that it was not a choice, or a conscious decision to commit the crime. It was the tragic culmination of untreated trauma.

Through therapy, Sarah also began to understand the importance of empathy, not just for her mother, but for the victims of abuse in general. Eleanor's actions, however horrific, were born from an unimaginable level of pain and suffering. Understanding this, she learned to challenge the instinctual repulsion many people felt toward the victims of trauma. Her therapist guided her to separate her grief for her mother from the horrific crime committed by one of her alters. Therapy allowed Sarah to confront this challenge, to acknowledge Eleanor's actions without diminishing the suffering of the victim.

Sarah's journey highlighted the limitations of trying to understand such complex trauma without professional help. The diary provided a chilling glimpse into Eleanor's mind, but it was a fragmented and incomplete picture. A skilled therapist could have helped Eleanor unpack her trauma, piece by piece, creating a safe space for her to confront her past and begin the long and arduous process of healing. The lack of such intervention, the absence of a guiding hand, was a tragedy in itself, a tragedy that reverberated through Sarah's life and painted a gruesome picture of the devastating consequences of untreated mental illness.

Sarah's therapy became a testament to the power of healing, a beacon of hope against the darkness cast by her mother's past. The diary entries served as a cautionary tale, highlighting the dangers of ignoring the signs of trauma and the devastating consequences of failing to provide adequate mental health support. While Sarah couldn't undo the past, she could learn from it, turning her mother's tragedy into a call for increased awareness, understanding, and access to effective mental health care for those struggling with the invisible wounds of trauma and severe mental illness. The black bags would forever remain a potent symbol, not only of a horrifying crime, but of the vital importance of accessible, compassionate, and effective therapy in preventing future tragedies. The therapy helped Sarah come to terms with the fact that Eleanor wasn't "evil," but a victim of a system that failed her. The black bags were a symbol of that failure, a failure that could only be rectified by advocating for better mental health care and breaking the cycles of abuse and silence that lead to such devastating consequences.

The narrative of Eleanor's life and the impact of her death, through the lenses of her daughter Sarah, emphasized the crucial role of mental health care. It highlighted the need for early intervention, comprehensive treatment, and the ongoing support crucial for individuals battling trauma and the severe fragmentation of personality. The story wasn't just about a gruesome murder; it was a poignant exploration of the devastating effects of untreated mental illness and the enduring power of healing. Through Sarah's journey, the book underscored the importance of empathy, understanding, and the life-altering potential of therapeutic intervention, while ultimately serving as a powerful plea for better mental health resources and support for those trapped in the shadows of trauma and the fragments of a shattered self. The book ended not with a sense of resolution but a sustained call for change, urging readers to recognize the signs of suffering and advocate for a more compassionate and effective system of mental health care. The scars might remain, both literally and metaphorically, but the hope for healing, for preventing future tragedies, burned brightly. The black bags, in the end, became a symbol not just of death and darkness, but of the urgent need for change, a silent scream echoing in the void where therapy was absent.

Sarah's therapist, Dr. Albright, a woman whose calm demeanor belied a deep understanding of trauma, gently steered the conversation towards the importance of community and support. The diary, while offering a chillingly intimate portrait of Eleanor's fractured psyche, was ultimately a solitary document, a testament to the isolation that had fueled the illness's progression. "Eleanor's suffering," Dr. Albright explained, "was compounded by her inability to connect with others who understood her experience. The lack of a support system exacerbated the fragmentation, intensifying the internal struggle."

This resonated deeply with Sarah. The pristine façade of Eleanor's life, the seemingly perfect family, had hidden a profound loneliness, a desperate yearning for connection that had gone unmet. The meticulous organization of the crime scene, the chilling precision, Sarah now saw not only as a symptom of OCD, but also as a desperate attempt at control, a desperate attempt to impose order on the overwhelming chaos of her inner world. The absence of external support had allowed the internal chaos to fester and grow, culminating in the tragic events that defined Eleanor's life.

Dr. Albright introduced the concept of support groups. "For individuals with DID," she explained, "and for their families, these groups offer an invaluable resource. They provide a safe space for sharing experiences, reducing feelings of isolation, and fostering a sense of community." The idea of a community of others who understood the intricacies of DID, who could empathize with the challenges, the complexities, the sheer overwhelming nature of living with such a fractured self – this was a revolutionary concept for Sarah. She had always felt alone in her grief, isolated by the unspeakable nature of her mother's illness and the horrifying crime it had culminated in.

Dr. Albright described the structure of typical support groups. Many were run by therapists or trained facilitators, providing a moderated environment where individuals could share their experiences without judgment. Some focused on specific diagnoses, like DID, while others provided a broader space for individuals with various mental illnesses and their families.

The common thread, Dr. Albright emphasized, was the shared experience of struggle, the mutual understanding that arose from navigating similar challenges. She explained how the groups functioned: members shared stories, offered support, validated each other's experiences, and provided practical advice and coping strategies. Crucially, these groups fostered a sense of hope, reminding members that they were not alone in their struggles.

The thought of confronting others with the details of her mother's life, the unspeakable horrors detailed in the diary, was initially terrifying to Sarah. The shame and stigma surrounding mental illness had always been a silent undercurrent in her life, a barrier that prevented open conversations about Eleanor's struggles. But Dr. Albright's words planted a seed of hope. The possibility of finding others who understood, who wouldn't judge or dismiss her mother's suffering, offered a glimmer of solace in the overwhelming darkness.

Dr. Albright also discussed the benefits for families of individuals with DID. She described support groups where family members could share their experiences, learn coping strategies, and gain a deeper understanding of the illness. This was particularly important for Sarah, who had struggled to reconcile her love for her mother with the horror of her actions. In a support group, she could find others who had navigated similar complexities, finding strength and understanding in shared experiences. The group would provide a space to process her complex emotions without feeling judged or alone.

She envisioned a place where she could share her mother's

story, the disturbing details from the diary, without the fear of judgment or disbelief. A space where she could acknowledge the horror of the crime, while simultaneously acknowledging Eleanor's profound suffering, her deep-seated trauma. She imagined finding others who could empathize with her struggle to make sense of her mother's actions, to reconcile her love for her mother with the horror of her crime. The idea of finally connecting with others who understood this unique and painful perspective was both terrifying and incredibly alluring.

Sarah began researching support groups online, finding numerous options catering to different needs and preferences. She discovered groups specifically for individuals with DID, groups for family members of individuals with dissociative disorders, and groups that addressed broader issues of trauma and mental illness. The sheer volume of available resources was initially overwhelming, but also profoundly reassuring. It spoke of a growing recognition of the need for support and understanding. This was a change from the stigma and isolation Eleanor had faced, a shift toward a more empathetic and accepting approach to mental illness.

One group particularly caught her attention. It was an online forum specifically for the families of individuals with DID. The forum's description resonated deeply with her experiences: the challenges of navigating complex relationships, the need for understanding and validation, and the hope for healing and reconciliation. The forum's anonymous nature appealed to Sarah's inherent need for discretion. It felt like a safe haven, a place to be honest without facing the judgment she'd encountered before.

She started reading the forum posts, feeling an immediate sense of connection. Stories of similar struggles, of similar struggles with shame, guilt, and the overwhelming complexities of loving someone with DID – these resonated with Sarah's experiences on a deep and personal level. She found others who had grappled with similar questions, similar frustrations, similar hopes. She read about family members who had witnessed firsthand the dramatic shifts in personality, the unpredictable nature of their loved ones' behavior, and the constant emotional roller coaster.

The posts served as a powerful validation of Sarah's experiences, a testament to the fact that she was not alone. She read accounts of how support groups had helped families navigate difficult conversations, develop coping mechanisms, and find a new sense of hope. Many posts detailed how therapy, coupled with support groups, provided a holistic approach to healing and recovery, offering both individual and collective support. The stories filled her with a growing sense of optimism; the prospect of connecting with other individuals facing similar challenges was not only comforting but incredibly empowering.

The posts often highlighted the importance of setting boundaries, while maintaining love and compassion. Sarah realized that this was a crucial lesson for her own healing process. The need to balance her own emotional well-being with her love for her mother, even in light of the horrific crime, was a delicate dance that required patience, empathy, and support. The online forum provided the tools and support to begin to navigate this process, while the prospect of a structured support group provided a roadmap forward. These stories of hope were a stark contrast to the darkness that had dominated her life following Eleanor's death.

Sarah decided to take the plunge. She joined the online forum, introducing herself cautiously, sharing snippets of her story with a hesitant and measured hand. The response was overwhelming – a flood of supportive messages, offers of advice, and expressions of solidarity. She felt a profound sense of relief, a release of the burden she'd carried for so long. For the first time, she felt less alone, less isolated, less defined by the horror of her mother's life and death. The support group was not a cure, but a lifeline, a beacon of hope in the daunting path towards understanding, healing, and reconciliation. The scars of the past, both personal and familial, remained. But the presence of a community offered a lifeline of support, a crucial element in the ongoing process of healing. The hope of building a new life, informed by the past but unshackled by its shadow, began to take root.

The initial relief Sarah felt, the burgeoning sense of community, didn't erase the deep-seated trauma that had woven itself into the fabric of her life. The discovery of her mother's diary, the harrowing details of Eleanor's fragmented existence, had unearthed a darkness that clung to her, a shadow that stretched long and far into her future. The support group offered a lifeline, a place to share her burdens, but it couldn't magically undo the years of accumulated pain.

The nightmares continued, vivid and unsettling, replaying fragmented scenes from Eleanor's diary: the hushed whispers of abuse, the chilling precision of the murder scene, the stark coldness of the freezer. These were not just abstract horrors; they were intimate glimpses into her mother's shattered psyche, a reflection of the violence that had permeated

Eleanor's life and, by extension, Sarah's own. The therapy sessions became a battleground, a space where she wrestled with the conflicting emotions of love, grief, and revulsion.

Dr. Albright introduced the concept of EMDR (Eye Movement Desensitization and Reprocessing) therapy, a technique designed to help process traumatic memories. Sarah initially resisted, the idea of reliving those horrifying details felt unbearable. But the persistent nightmares, the intrusive thoughts that haunted her waking hours, chipped away at her resolve. She agreed to try.

The EMDR sessions were intensely difficult. Sarah found herself confronting the echoes of her childhood, the unspoken anxieties, the subtle yet pervasive sense of unease that had always accompanied her. She discovered that her own anxieties, her occasional bouts of obsessive-compulsive behavior, weren't merely quirks of personality; they were manifestations of her inherited trauma, a ripple effect emanating from Eleanor's fractured psyche. The therapist gently guided her through the process, helping her reframe her memories, detaching the emotional charge from the traumatic events. It was a slow and arduous process, filled with moments of intense emotional upheaval, followed by periods of cautious optimism.

Beyond the individual therapy, the support group provided a unique form of validation. Sarah found solace in connecting with other family members who had navigated similar challenges. There was Martha, whose mother had exhibited similar dissociative symptoms, her personality fracturing into multiple distinct identities. Martha described the years of confusion, the bewilderment of not knowing which 'mother' she was interacting with, the constant fear of triggering a violent episode. She spoke of the immense guilt she carried, the feeling that she had somehow failed her mother. This feeling resonated deeply with Sarah. Their shared experiences forged an unbreakable bond, a testament to the power of shared understanding.

Another member, David, shared his experience of growing up with a father who had DID. His father's unpredictable behavior, his sudden shifts in personality, had created a chaotic and unstable childhood. He spoke of the constant fear, the inability to predict his father's moods or actions, and the enduring impact on his own relationships. He spoke of the importance of establishing healthy boundaries, of learning to protect himself while still maintaining a connection with his father. His story highlighted the resilience of the human spirit, the capacity to overcome adversity, and the power of setting healthy boundaries to preserve one's own well-being.

The support group wasn't a panacea, it wasn't a magic bullet that eradicated the trauma. Instead, it provided a safe space for Sarah to confront her emotions, to process her experiences, and to find comfort in shared understanding. It helped her to reframe her narrative, to see herself not just as a victim, but as a survivor. The group offered a roadmap for navigating her grief, a way to integrate her mother's story into her own life narrative without being consumed by it.

One of the most challenging aspects of her recovery was the lingering shame and guilt. Despite understanding the roots of Eleanor's actions, Sarah still struggled with the undeniable fact that her mother had committed a heinous crime. The support group provided a space to explore these complicated emotions, to acknowledge the guilt without letting it define her. Through sharing her struggles, she found that others felt similar feelings of shame and guilt, even though the nature of their loved ones' behaviors and experiences differed. This shared experience allowed her to understand that these feelings were normal responses to abnormal circumstances and that it was okay to feel what she felt.

The long road to recovery was not linear. There were setbacks, moments of regression, and overwhelming surges of grief. But each time she faltered, she found support in the group, the shared experiences, the words of encouragement, the sense of collective understanding. She learned to practice self-compassion, to acknowledge her own emotional needs, and to seek help when she needed it.

Beyond the emotional healing, Sarah embarked on a journey of self-discovery. She learned to identify her own triggers, to recognize the subtle signs of anxiety or panic, and to develop coping mechanisms to manage her emotional responses. The therapy, combined with the support group, helped her to develop a healthier relationship with her own emotions, to embrace her vulnerabilities, and to cultivate a stronger sense of self.

As the years passed, the scars of the past remained, but their power diminished. The sharp edges softened, their intensity lessened. The memories of Eleanor's life and death were no longer a constant source of anguish; they became a part of her story, a chapter that shaped her identity but did not define her. She discovered a resilience within herself, a strength she hadn't known she possessed.

Sarah learned that trauma doesn't disappear; it leaves its mark. But the mark doesn't have to dictate the future. Through therapy, support groups, and the unwavering support of her community, she found a way to live with the scars, to integrate them into her narrative, and to create a life that was both informed by the past and unbound by its shadow. She began to see the possibility of a future filled with hope, a future where she could honor her mother's memory not just by grieving her loss but by celebrating her strength and recognizing her suffering. She began to build a life that was vibrant, healthy, and centered around self-care, compassion, and the strength she discovered through the unimaginable experience of loving and losing her mother. The road to recovery was long and arduous, but the destination, she realized, was worth the journey. The journey had redefined her, stripped her bare, and then rebuilt her stronger, wiser, and more compassionate. And in that strength, she found healing.

# CHAPTER 14: FINDING PEACE

The crisp autumn air invigorated Sarah as she walked along the beach, the rhythmic crash of waves a soothing counterpoint to the turmoil she'd endured. The sand, still warm from the day's sun, molded gently beneath her feet, a comforting tactile sensation. It had been two years since her mother's death, two years since the diary's shocking revelations had shattered her world. Two years since she'd started her journey towards healing. The scars remained, faint etchings on the landscape of her soul, but they no longer burned with the searing intensity of the past.

She'd moved to a small coastal town, far from the city where the memories of her childhood still lingered, a city that held the echoes of her mother's fractured reality. This new place, with its quiet charm and welcoming community, allowed her to breathe. The ocean, vast and powerful yet calming in its predictability, became her sanctuary, a place where she could feel connected to something larger than herself, something ancient and enduring.

Her days were now filled with a rhythm that felt both purposeful and restorative. She volunteered at a local animal shelter, finding solace in the unconditional love of the abandoned creatures. The soft fur of a rescued cat, the gentle nudge of a dog's head, brought a sense of calm that had once felt unattainable. The simple act of caring for others, of giving back to a community that had embraced her, helped her to redirect her energy, to channel her grief into something positive and productive.

Her work as a freelance writer also offered a creative outlet, a way to process her emotions through words. She started a blog, anonymously at first, chronicling her journey, her struggles, and her tentative steps towards healing. The act of writing became a form of self-therapy, a way to articulate her feelings, to give voice to the unspoken anxieties that still lingered. She discovered a unique ability to weave dark humor and sarcasm into her narratives, a skill that echoed her mother's own wry outlook, a testament to her inherited resilience.

Slowly, tentatively, she began to date. The initial fear of intimacy, the apprehension of letting someone see the scars beneath the surface, proved less daunting than she'd anticipated. She encountered men who were compassionate and understanding, who saw past the trauma to the vibrant, intelligent, and deeply caring woman she was. These relationships, built on trust and mutual respect, helped her to heal, to reclaim her sense of self-worth, and to discover the joy of intimacy without fear.

Her relationship with her therapist, Dr. Albright, evolved from a client-doctor dynamic to a supportive mentorship. The weekly sessions transitioned from the intensity of EMDR to a more holistic approach, focusing on self-compassion, mindfulness, and building healthy coping mechanisms. Dr. Albright helped her to navigate the complexities of her grief, to accept the lingering guilt without letting it consume her. She encouraged Sarah to explore her creativity, to find joy in the simple pleasures of life, and to cultivate a deep sense of self-love.

The support group remained a constant source of strength. The shared experiences, the mutual understanding, the unwavering support of Martha, David, and the others, created a powerful sense of community. They celebrated milestones together, offered each other comfort during setbacks, and provided a safe space to simply be, without judgment or expectation. Their bond transcended the shared trauma; it was a testament to the power of human connection, the capacity for empathy, and the resilience of the human spirit.

Sarah's new life wasn't a pristine, trauma-free existence. The nightmares still occurred occasionally, though they were less frequent and less vivid. The memories of her childhood, of her mother's struggles, of the chilling details of the murder, still surfaced, but they no longer held the same paralyzing power. They were now part of her story, not the entirety of it. She'd learned to manage them, to acknowledge them without letting them dictate her life.

She learned to recognize her triggers, the subtle cues that signaled an impending anxiety attack, and to deploy her coping mechanisms – deep breathing exercises, meditation, spending time in nature, connecting with her support network. She developed a healthy relationship with her body, engaging in regular exercise and mindful eating. She prioritized sleep, understanding its restorative power and recognizing the impact of sleep deprivation on her mental health.

Sarah discovered that self-care wasn't selfish; it was essential. It was an act of self-preservation, a commitment to her own well-being. She learned to set boundaries, to say no to things that drained her energy, and to prioritize her own needs without guilt or shame. She embraced her vulnerabilities, recognizing them as strengths, as testaments to her capacity for empathy and connection.

The journey had been long and arduous, but the destination, she realized, was far more profound than she could have ever imagined. She'd not only survived; she'd thrived. She'd emerged from the shadows of her past, transformed by the experience, stronger, wiser, and deeply compassionate. She'd built a life that was filled with purpose, meaning, and joy.

The ocean breeze whipped around Sarah as she watched the sun dip below the horizon, painting the sky in fiery hues of orange and purple. She felt a sense of peace, a deep-seated tranquility that had eluded her for so long. The past was still a part of her, but it no longer defined her. She was Sarah, a woman forged in the fires of trauma, yet ultimately resilient, empowered, and deeply content with the life she'd created. It was a new beginning, a testament to the indomitable human spirit, and a beacon of hope for others who walked a similar path. The road to recovery was long, winding, and often treacherous, but the destination—a life filled with hope, love, and self-acceptance—was worth every agonizing step of the journey. And Sarah, finally, could truly breathe.

Sarah traced the swirling patterns etched into the smooth, grey stones lining the beach, her fingers lingering on the cool, damp surface. The ocean's rhythmic pulse, a constant companion during her solitary walks, resonated with the quiet rhythm of her own healing heart. The diary, her mother's chilling testament to a life fractured by trauma, had been both a curse and a blessing. A curse for the horrifying truths it revealed, a blessing for the understanding it offered, for the path it unwittingly paved towards healing not just for herself, but potentially for others.

The diary wasn't merely a collection of fragmented memories; it was a raw, visceral narrative that held the power to shatter and to mend. It spoke of unspeakable horrors, of a life lived in the shadows, a life of hidden suffering that had finally found its voice—albeit posthumously. Reading it had been a journey into the darkest recesses of the human psyche, a descent into the abyss of trauma and the unexpected ascent towards a fragile, hard-won peace. But the power of her mother's story didn't end with Sarah's own healing. It was a story with a far-reaching impact, a story with the potential to touch the lives of others grappling with their own demons.

The blog, initially a nameless, anonymous outlet for her own emotions, had evolved into a space for connection and understanding. Initially hesitant to share such personal, intimate experiences, the positive feedback from readers, their shared experiences of trauma and resilience, emboldened her to share more, to let her vulnerability be a bridge, not a barrier. The comments section became a safe haven, a space where people could find solace in shared struggles, where they could feel less alone in their pain. Stories of childhood abuse, of battling mental illness, of overcoming seemingly insurmountable odds poured into her digital inbox. Each message, each story, echoed the power of her mother's diary, a testament to the universality of suffering and the enduring power of the human spirit.

She discovered that her mother's dark humor and sarcasm, initially jarring in the context of the diary's harrowing content, were a coping mechanism, a defense against the overwhelming pain. It was a form of resilience, a way of reclaiming power from a situation that seemed to have none. This understanding profoundly influenced Sarah's own writing style, transforming her blog into something unique, a dark yet strangely hopeful space where humor and tragedy intertwined. The witty observations, the sarcastic quips, didn't diminish the gravity of the themes but rather served to contextualize them, to soften the harsh edges of trauma with a layer of wry acceptance.

Many readers commented on the unexpected humor woven into her blog posts, appreciating the way it both challenged and comforted. They found themselves laughing at her observations, even as tears welled up at the raw honesty of her descriptions. The combination, they said, resonated with their own experiences, a recognition that humor and grief could coexist. It was this duality that made her writing so powerful, so relatable. It was a space where readers could find both solace and validation, confirming that their own mixed emotions were not only acceptable but were, in fact, a part of the healing process.

One poignant comment from a woman named Emily remains etched in Sarah's memory. Emily had been sexually abused as a child and suppressed the memory for years. Reading Sarah's blog, she felt a strange sense of validation, of understanding. She felt seen, heard, and finally, understood. Emily explained that Sarah's ability to intertwine dark humor and poignant truth made her trauma feel less alien, less isolating. The sense of shared experience, the unspoken understanding, was a powerful connection. It was the therapeutic power of storytelling at its purest form, a way to feel less alone in a deeply personal and often isolating struggle. This resonated profoundly with Sarah, solidifying her belief in the power of sharing her own story and creating a safe space for others to share theirs.

Sarah started to receive emails from people whose lives were touched by her writing. These were not just casual readers; they were individuals actively seeking help and support. Their stories were chillingly similar to her mother's, revealing a pattern of systematic abuse and trauma that seemed to be far more prevalent than she'd ever imagined. One email, from a young woman named Chloe, detailed a horrific cycle of abuse at the hands of her stepfather. Chloe was grappling with dissociative identity disorder, and her email contained a chilling echo of Eleanor's fragmented self. Chloe's story wasn't just a testament to the enduring trauma of abuse but also to the resilience of the human spirit in the face of unimaginable adversity.

The stories pouring into her inbox weren't just personal accounts of suffering; they were calls for help, for connection, for understanding. Sarah realized she had inadvertently created a virtual support group, a community of individuals who found solace and strength in shared experiences. This community wasn't just passive; it was active, dynamic, and supportive. The readers offered each other advice, encouragement, and most importantly, a shared sense of belonging. Sarah's role had evolved from writer to facilitator, creating a space where healing could take place through the power of shared stories.

This realization prompted Sarah to take her work a step further. She began to use her platform to promote resources for survivors of abuse and to advocate for better mental health care. She started partnering with mental health organizations, linking her blog posts to relevant resources and support networks. She organized online support groups, creating a safe and anonymous space for individuals to share their experiences without fear of judgment. Her blog became a powerful tool for social change, raising awareness about the prevalence of trauma and the need for greater support and understanding.

The blog and its expanding community became her most profound form of therapy. While her personal healing journey was a testament to the power of individual resilience, it was the shared stories, the collective understanding, the burgeoning community that transformed her pain into purpose. The act of sharing her story, of listening to others, of using her writing as a force for good, had finally brought Sarah a sense of peace that transcended her personal trauma. It was a peace born not just from her own healing but from the collective healing of a community she had unknowingly created, a community united by shared experiences, by shared resilience, and by the transformative power of storytelling. The diary, initially a source of pain and shock, had become the catalyst for a powerful movement of healing, a beacon of hope for others navigating the dark corridors of trauma. The power of storytelling, Sarah had finally understood, was not simply to recount events, but to transform lives. It was a force that could mend broken hearts, build bridges of understanding, and ultimately, save lives.

The autumn leaves swirled around Sarah's feet, mirroring

the chaotic storm of emotions that still occasionally swept through her. The anniversary of her mother's death approached, a date marked not by grief alone, but by a complex tapestry of remembrance, understanding, and a quiet, persistent hope. Eleanor's legacy wasn't simply the chilling tale recounted in the diary; it was the ripple effect of her trauma, the lives it touched, both directly and indirectly. Sarah found herself contemplating the weight of that legacy, the profound responsibility that had fallen upon her shoulders.

The blog, once a private sanctuary, now stood as a testament to Eleanor's enduring presence. The comments continued to flow in, a constant stream of shared experiences, of pain and resilience. Sarah read each one carefully, feeling a deep sense of empathy for the strangers who found solace in her mother's story, in her own vulnerability. It was a constant reminder of the pervasiveness of trauma, a hidden epidemic that silently ravaged lives, leaving scars both visible and invisible.

One particular email stood out, a message from a therapist who had used Sarah's blog in her sessions with patients. The therapist wrote about the transformative power of Sarah's honesty, the way her writing had validated her clients' experiences, helping them to articulate their own pain and begin the arduous journey toward healing. This, Sarah realized, was the most significant aspect of Eleanor's legacy. It wasn't just about uncovering a past crime; it was about fostering empathy, understanding, and the potential for healing in a world that often failed to acknowledge the depth of human suffering.

The police, years after the initial investigation had stalled, had reopened the cold case. They were using Sarah's blog as a resource, searching for connections between Eleanor's alters and potential victims. While the prospect of solving the mystery was important, it felt almost secondary to the larger mission of creating a space where healing and understanding could thrive. The diary's brutal honesty had illuminated the darkness within Eleanor's mind, but it had also illuminated the path toward healing for others. It was a powerful testament to the idea that even from the most horrific circumstances, something positive and transformative could emerge.

Eleanor's story, though shrouded in darkness, had also revealed the resilience of the human spirit. The diary was filled with not only despair but moments of wry humor, sarcastic observations, and unexpected flashes of joy. These instances weren't mere glimpses of a happier life; they were evidence of Eleanor's tenacious fight for survival, her refusal to be entirely consumed by her pain. It was this subtle duality, the complex interplay of darkness and light, that resonated most deeply with Sarah's readers.

The blog had become a place of remembrance, a virtual memorial for Eleanor and for countless others who had suffered silently. Sarah felt a profound responsibility to maintain this space, to nurture its growth, and to continue to offer support and validation to those who needed it. It was a solemn duty, a way of honoring her mother's memory, a way of ensuring that Eleanor's story would continue to inspire hope and healing long after her death. The blog, Sarah realized, was more than just a collection of blog posts; it was a living testament to the strength of the human spirit, a symbol of resilience, and a beacon of hope for those navigating their own dark nights.

Sarah began to organize regular online meetups for her readers, creating a supportive online community. These meetings weren't formal therapy sessions, but they served as a safe space for individuals to share their experiences, offer support to one another, and find comfort in their shared struggles. The discussions were often intense, raw, and emotionally charged, yet there was always an underlying current of hope, of resilience, and of a quiet determination to heal and move forward.

The blog's impact extended beyond its readers. Sarah found herself invited to speak at conferences, workshops, and even university lectures, sharing her mother's story and the lessons she'd learned. She spoke of the importance of recognizing the signs of trauma, the need for compassionate mental health care, and the transformative power of storytelling. Her words resonated with audiences, prompting them to reflect on their own experiences and to recognize the universality of suffering.

The legacy of Eleanor wasn't just about the gruesome crime she, through one of her alters, committed; it was about the untold stories of abuse, neglect, and trauma that lie hidden beneath the surface of seemingly ordinary lives. It was about the importance of remembering the victims, of giving voice to the voiceless, and of creating a world where such atrocities are not tolerated or ignored. Eleanor's life, while tragically fragmented, served as a stark reminder of the hidden pain that resides within our communities and the urgent need for compassion, understanding, and effective support systems for survivors of abuse and those struggling with mental illness.

Sarah continued to write, her blog evolving into a platform for advocacy, education, and support. She partnered with mental health organizations, providing links to resources and services for her readers. She worked tirelessly to raise awareness about the prevalence of trauma and the importance of early intervention. The act of writing, of sharing her story, of providing a space for others to share theirs, was not only healing for her but was making a tangible difference in the lives of others.

The anniversary of Eleanor's death approached, and Sarah felt a sense of peace she hadn't anticipated. The grief remained, a constant companion, but it was no longer all-consuming. It was woven into a richer tapestry of remembrance, understanding, and purpose. Eleanor's legacy wasn't merely the darkness of her fractured mind; it was the light that shone through the cracks, the unwavering resilience of the human spirit, and the transformative power of storytelling to create connection, empathy, and hope in the face of profound suffering. The murder was a terrible event, a tragic consequence of profound trauma, but its lasting legacy wasn't just about guilt and sorrow; it was also a story of healing, of community, and of the remarkable capacity for human beings to find meaning and purpose even in the darkest of times.

Sarah knew that Eleanor's story would continue to resonate, to challenge, to inspire, and to heal. The fight for justice and understanding was far from over, but Sarah, armed with her mother's diary and the power of shared experiences, felt prepared to continue the battle, to carry Eleanor's legacy forward, and to ensure that her story would not only be remembered but would help others find their way out of the darkness and into the light. The path to peace, she understood, was not a solitary journey; it was a shared one, paved with resilience, understanding, and the enduring power of human connection.

The quiet hum of the laptop filled the otherwise silent apartment, a stark contrast to the tempestuous emotions swirling within Sarah. The anniversary of Eleanor's death had passed, leaving behind a residue of grief tempered with a burgeoning sense of purpose. The blog, a testament to her mother's fractured life and her own journey of healing, continued to thrive, a vibrant digital community humming with shared stories of trauma, resilience, and the slow, painstaking process of recovery.

One recurring theme in the comments and emails she received was the pervasive fear of seeking help. Many readers described a crippling sense of shame, a deep-seated belief that their struggles were somehow their fault, that they were unworthy of support. This resonated deeply with Sarah; she knew firsthand the insidious power of internalized stigma, the way it could silence sufferers and prevent them from reaching out for help. Eleanor, in her fragmented state, had often expressed a similar sentiment, a fear of judgment and a crippling self-loathing that had prevented her from seeking help for decades.

Sarah understood the complexity of that fear. It wasn't simply a matter of laziness or a lack of willpower. It was a symptom of the illness itself, a manifestation of the deep-seated trauma that had fractured Eleanor's psyche. The shame and self-blame were not merely emotions; they were deeply ingrained beliefs, forged in the crucible of years of abuse and neglect. This realization underscored the critical need for compassionate and understanding mental health support.

This wasn't just about therapy; it was about dismantling the systemic barriers that prevented individuals from seeking help in the first place. The fear of judgment, the stigma associated with mental illness, the lack of access to affordable and effective care—these were systemic issues that needed to be addressed on a societal level. Sarah's blog, initially intended as a personal catharsis, had evolved into a platform for raising awareness about these issues, a space where individuals could feel safe and validated in their struggles.

She began to highlight the resources available, meticulously compiling a list of helplines, support groups, and mental health organizations in various countries. She partnered with mental health professionals, inviting them to contribute guest posts to her blog, sharing their expertise and providing practical advice to her readers. She emphasized the importance of early intervention, explaining how seeking help early could significantly improve the chances of recovery.

Many readers shared stories of failed attempts to seek help, of encountering insensitive or dismissive professionals. These narratives fueled Sarah's determination to advocate for better mental health care, for a system that was more accessible, affordable, and truly compassionate. She started to share stories of successful recovery, of individuals who had found healing and hope through therapy, medication, and supportive relationships. These stories served as beacons of hope, offering tangible evidence that recovery was possible.

Sarah also focused on debunking common myths surrounding mental illness. She addressed misconceptions about the effectiveness of therapy, the risks of medication, and the nature of various mental health diagnoses. She emphasized that mental illness was not a sign of weakness or a character flaw; it was a medical condition, treatable like any other illness. Her goal was to normalize the conversation around mental health, to create a space where individuals felt empowered to seek help without shame or fear.

She started to offer online support groups through her blog, creating a virtual community where individuals could share their experiences, offer mutual support, and feel less isolated in their struggles. These online groups provided a safe space for vulnerable individuals, a place where they could connect with others who understood their pain, their fears, and their hopes for recovery. The interactions were often raw and emotionally charged, but the sense of community was palpable, a testament to the power of human connection in the face of adversity.

One reader's story stood out in particular. A young woman named Emily shared her experience of struggling with anxiety and depression for years, her reluctance to seek help fueled by a deep sense of shame and fear of judgment. She finally reached out after reading Sarah's blog, inspired by the stories of resilience and hope she found there. Emily's journey towards recovery was slow and arduous, but her story became a powerful testament to the transformative power of seeking help, of embracing vulnerability, and of finding solace in a supportive community.

Emily's story became a recurring theme in Sarah's blog posts. She shared updates on Emily's progress, showcasing the gradual but significant changes in her life. Emily's transformation served as a powerful reminder that recovery was possible, that even the most daunting challenges could be overcome with the right support and the unwavering commitment to healing. It was a tangible example of the impact that seeking help could have, a testament to the importance of breaking down the barriers that prevent individuals from seeking the support they desperately need.

Sarah understood that the fight for better mental health care was far from over. The systemic issues remained, and the stigma associated with mental illness continued to persist. But she also understood the power of personal narratives, the transformative power of shared experiences, and the incredible resilience of the human spirit. Her mother's story, though shrouded in darkness, had ultimately become a beacon of hope, a testament to the potential for healing and the importance of seeking help, no matter how daunting the task might seem.

The journey toward peace, Sarah realized, was a collective one, a shared experience woven into a tapestry of resilience, empathy, and the unwavering belief in the capacity for human beings to heal and overcome even the most profound traumas. The blog was not merely a collection of blog posts; it was a living testament to the power of connection, a virtual community forged in the fires of shared suffering, and a beacon of hope for those navigating their own dark nights. The work was far from over, but Sarah, armed with her mother's legacy and the strength of countless shared stories, knew that the path to healing, to justice, and to a world where seeking help was no longer a source of fear, was a path worth fighting for. Every shared story, every act of support, was a step closer to a future where those battling mental health challenges could find the peace they so desperately deserved.

The final entry in Eleanor's diary, scrawled in a shaky hand, spoke not of darkness, but of a tentative sunrise. It wasn't a dramatic declaration of victory, but a quiet acknowledgment of a shift, a subtle change in the internal landscape. It described a session with Dr. Albright, a therapist finally capable of piercing the layers of Eleanor's fractured psyche, a therapist who understood the intricate dance of her alters, the delicate balance of fear and rage, of vulnerability and self-protection. The entry detailed a breakthrough, a moment of connection between Eleanor's core self and the dominant alter, a glimmer of integration, a fragile peace emerging from years of war within.

This wasn't a magical cure, Eleanor made clear. The fragmented personalities remained, their voices still echoing in the chambers of her mind. But the intensity of the conflict had lessened, the constant struggle for dominance fading into a more nuanced interplay. She described it as a symphony, once a cacophony of discordant notes, now slowly transforming into a complex arrangement with moments of harmony. There were still days of intense struggle, of flashbacks and panic attacks, but now they were punctuated by periods of relative calm, periods where the different facets of her self could coexist, not in perfect harmony, but with a grudging, uneasy truce.

Sarah reread the entry multiple times, tears welling in her eyes. It wasn't the ending she'd initially expected. There was no dramatic confrontation, no miraculous healing. Instead, it was a quiet testament to the enduring strength of the human spirit, a testament to the resilience of a woman who had endured unspeakable horrors and yet found, in the face of unimaginable darkness, a sliver of light. It was a story of progress, not perfection, a narrative that echoed the journey of many who struggled with mental illness.

Eleanor's journey wasn't over; it had simply entered a new phase. The final pages of her diary chronicled her attempts at reconnecting with the world, a tentative re-emergence from the shadows she had inhabited for so long. She described small victories – a walk in the park without a panic attack, a conversation with a friend without dissociating, a moment of genuine connection with Sarah. These seemingly insignificant acts represented monumental achievements for a woman who had spent so much of her life in survival mode.

The blog became a platform for sharing these subtle victories, for highlighting the nuance of recovery, the gradual, often imperceptible shifts towards healing. Sarah received countless messages from readers who identified with Eleanor's story, who found solace in her journey, who discovered in her struggle their own path toward healing. The blog was no longer simply a platform for sharing Eleanor's story; it had evolved into a vibrant community of support, a digital sanctuary where individuals could share their struggles, offer each other encouragement, and celebrate small victories along their own paths to recovery.

Sarah collaborated with mental health professionals to create a series of online workshops, offering practical tools and strategies for managing the symptoms of various mental illnesses, including PTSD, OCD, ADHD, and autism. They addressed the systemic issues that contribute to the stigma surrounding mental illness, emphasizing the need for accessible and affordable mental healthcare. They debunked common myths, challenged misconceptions, and fostered a culture of understanding and compassion. The workshops were immensely popular, attracting individuals from all over the world, creating a global community united by their shared experiences and their collective desire for healing.

Sarah's work extended beyond the digital realm. She became an advocate for mental health reform, working with lawmakers and policymakers to advocate for increased funding for mental health services, for improved access to care, and for the elimination of the stigma that prevents so many from seeking help. She shared Eleanor's story with anyone who would listen, using her mother's experience to illuminate the complexities of trauma and the importance of compassionate, effective treatment.

She also became involved with several charities supporting survivors of domestic and sexual abuse, sharing her expertise and contributing to the development of support programs for individuals who had suffered similar traumas. She understood the cyclical nature of abuse and the crucial role of early intervention in preventing the perpetuation of such violence. Her mother's story underscored the need for comprehensive, holistic support services for survivors, acknowledging that the healing process is a long and arduous journey.

The legacy of Eleanor Vance, initially marked by tragedy and shrouded in darkness, was gradually transformed into a message of hope. Her diary, initially a source of fear and confusion, became a powerful tool for healing and understanding, a testament to the human capacity for resilience and the power of connection. The blog, initially created as a means of personal catharsis, evolved into a thriving community, a platform for sharing stories, for offering support, and for advocating for positive change.

Sarah's own healing journey mirrored her mother's, a gradual process of self-discovery, self-acceptance, and the recognition of her own strength and resilience. The grief over Eleanor's loss remained, but it was now tempered by a sense of purpose, a commitment to honoring her mother's memory by fighting for a world where individuals struggling with mental illness could find the support and understanding they so desperately needed.

The concluding chapter of Eleanor's story, however, wasn't solely about her. It was a story of healing that extended far beyond her fragmented self, encompassing a network of individuals who found solace in her experience, found strength in her vulnerability, and discovered in her journey the shared humanity that connects all who struggle with the invisible wounds of mental illness. It was a testament to the enduring power of hope, a beacon of light illuminating the path towards healing for those who had been lost in darkness. The story emphasized that healing is not a linear path, it's a winding road with setbacks and triumphs, moments of despair and bursts of unexpected joy.

The diary entries, read in their entirety, offered not just a chilling glimpse into the complexities of multiple personality disorder, but also a profound understanding of the human capacity to endure, to adapt, and to find peace even in the face of unimaginable suffering. It was a narrative of enduring hope, a story that underscored the importance of seeking help, of breaking the cycle of silence and shame, and of embracing the possibility of healing, even when it seems impossible.

Sarah, in the end, didn't simply tell Eleanor's story; she became a part of it, a living testament to the power of resilience, the strength found in vulnerability, and the transformative potential of human connection. The blog, the advocacy work, the support groups – these were not just actions; they were expressions of a daughter's love, a commitment to her mother's memory, and a powerful message of hope to those who had suffered, were suffering, or would suffer in silence. The story's ending was not about a final resolution, a complete healing, or a perfect ending; it was the hopeful beginning of a continued effort to bring awareness, provide support, and advocate for a more compassionate world, a world where those battling inner demons could find peace, not through a miraculous cure, but through the quiet strength of ongoing healing and a collective journey towards a brighter future. The journey continued, but the path, once shadowed, was now illuminated by the shared light of hope, resilience, and the unwavering belief in the human capacity to heal.

# CHAPTER 15:
# EPILOGUE

The weight of Eleanor's diary settled upon me, not as a burden, but as a legacy. It wasn't just a chronicle of trauma; it was a testament to enduring resilience. Reading those fragmented entries, each a glimpse into a different facet of my mother's shattered self, had been a journey in itself – a descent into darkness followed by a slow, painstaking ascent toward understanding. Initially, I was consumed by rage, a searing anger directed at the perpetrators of her abuse, at the system that failed her, at the world that allowed such horrors to unfold in the shadows of normalcy. But as I delved deeper into Eleanor's story, my anger gradually morphed into a profound empathy, a deep well of compassion that washed over me, cleansing the bitterness and leaving behind a residue of understanding.

I came to see Eleanor not as a victim, but as a survivor. Her struggle wasn't simply about overcoming multiple personality disorder; it was about navigating a complex web of trauma, battling the ghosts of her past, and finding a way to coexist with the fragmented pieces of her self. Each personality, initially perceived as a monster, revealed itself as a coping mechanism, a defense mechanism forged in the crucible of unspeakable pain. The anger, the rage, the dissociation – they weren't simply symptoms of illness; they were survival strategies, desperate attempts to protect a fragile core self from an unrelenting onslaught of abuse.

Understanding this shifted my perspective dramatically. It wasn't about assigning blame or seeking retribution; it was about acknowledging the profound impact of trauma, the insidious ways it can warp a person's reality, and the sheer resilience required to navigate its devastating consequences. Eleanor's journey became a mirror, reflecting my own struggles, my own attempts to make sense of a world that often felt chaotic and unpredictable. I saw in her story a reflection of my own vulnerabilities, my own anxieties, my own capacity for both profound love and intense fear. Her diary wasn't just her story; it was a shared story, a testament to the interconnectedness of human experience.

My own personal growth mirrored my mother's, though on a different trajectory. While she navigated the turbulent seas of her fragmented psyche, I navigated the calmer, yet equally challenging waters of acceptance and understanding. Eleanor's journey was an internal battle; mine was an external one, a journey of education, advocacy, and the gradual dismantling of societal stigmas surrounding mental illness.

The blog, initially a vessel for Eleanor's story, transformed into a powerful platform for collective healing. The initial outpouring of support was overwhelming, a testament to the universality of suffering, the shared human experience of pain and resilience. The comments section became a space for sharing stories, for finding solace in shared experiences, for acknowledging the common ground beneath the surface differences in individual struggles. People from all walks of life poured out their hearts, sharing their battles with depression, anxiety, PTSD, and other mental health conditions. Their stories, interwoven with Eleanor's, formed a tapestry of human experience, a testament to our shared vulnerability and our collective capacity for healing.

The workshops, developed in collaboration with mental health professionals, proved to be even more transformative. We aimed to provide practical tools and coping mechanisms, but beyond the strategies and techniques, the workshops became spaces for connection, for community building. Participants found solace in the shared experience, a sense of belonging that transcended geographical boundaries and social differences. They were no longer alone in their struggles; they were part of a network of support, a collective striving for healing and self-acceptance.

My advocacy work extended beyond the digital realm, extending into the corridors of power. I lobbied for increased funding for mental health services, for improved access to care, and for the dismantling of the systemic barriers that perpetuate the stigma surrounding mental illness. I testified before legislative committees, sharing Eleanor's story, highlighting the need for compassionate, effective treatment, and advocating for policies that would empower individuals struggling with mental health conditions. The response was far from universal, but even small victories – a shifted perspective, a revised policy, a renewed commitment to support – fueled my resolve.

Working with charities supporting survivors of domestic and sexual abuse provided another avenue for my advocacy. I shared my expertise, drawing from Eleanor's experience to inform the design of support programs for survivors, emphasizing the importance of early intervention, comprehensive care, and the recognition of the long, arduous journey toward healing. The cyclical nature of abuse, the intergenerational trauma, became crystal clear in my work with survivors, underscoring the urgency of addressing these issues at both the individual and societal levels.

The process of writing and publishing Eleanor's story wasn't easy. It required confronting my own grief, my own feelings of guilt, anger and helplessness, the deep-seated frustration at a system that repeatedly failed my mother. It also required a deep dive into the complexities of the human psyche, a quest for understanding that led me through countless books, articles, and conversations with therapists, psychologists, and other mental health professionals.

But the journey was also incredibly rewarding. It wasn't just about understanding my mother; it was about understanding myself, about embracing my own vulnerabilities, and about discovering the strength and resilience I never knew I possessed. Eleanor's legacy wasn't defined by her trauma, but by her perseverance, her courage, and her capacity for love even in the face of unimaginable pain. Her story became a beacon of hope, a testament to the enduring power of the human spirit.

My own healing journey didn't involve a miraculous cure or a sudden transformation. It was a gradual process, a winding path with moments of despair and moments of unexpected joy. There were setbacks, of course – moments of doubt, of grief, of overwhelming sadness. But there were also moments of profound clarity, moments of understanding, moments of deep connection with others who shared similar experiences.

The end of Eleanor's story wasn't a definitive closure; it was a hopeful beginning. It was a beginning for me, a beginning for the countless individuals who found solace in her journey, a beginning for a movement towards increased awareness, improved care, and a more compassionate world. The story's impact was not just personal; it reached beyond my immediate circle, expanding into a global community united by their shared experiences and their collective desire for healing. It's a testament to the enduring power of hope, resilience and the unrelenting belief in the human capacity to heal. It is a story that continues to evolve, a testament to the unwavering power of human connection and resilience in the face of profound adversity. It's a story of enduring hope and the tireless pursuit of a brighter, more compassionate future for those who struggle silently with the invisible wounds of mental illness.

The aftermath of publishing Eleanor's story was a whirlwind. The initial wave of media attention, while overwhelming at times, ultimately served as a powerful catalyst for change. Television interviews, radio appearances, and countless articles amplified Eleanor's narrative, reaching audiences far beyond what I could have ever imagined. The response was a mixed bag, of course. There were those who dismissed Eleanor's experiences as sensationalized, others who expressed skepticism about the validity of multiple personality disorder itself. But for every voice of doubt, there were ten more who shared their own stories, their own struggles with mental illness, their own journeys of healing.

The blog became a virtual sanctuary, a safe space where individuals felt empowered to share their vulnerabilities, their anxieties, their hopes, and their fears. The comments section, initially a source of trepidation, blossomed into a vibrant community, a testament to the profound human need for connection and understanding. The anonymity of the internet, ironically, fostered a sense of intimacy, allowing people to shed their masks and reveal their true selves without fear of judgment.

This virtual community extended into the real world, as readers reached out to connect with me, sharing their own experiences, seeking advice, offering support. I found myself navigating a new role – not just as an author, but as a confidante, a listener, a beacon of hope in the darkness. The weight of this responsibility was immense, but the overwhelming sense of purpose propelled me forward.

The work with mental health organizations accelerated. I partnered with several charities, contributing to the development of educational resources, training programs for professionals, and support groups for individuals affected by multiple personality disorder and other complex trauma-related conditions. The cyclical nature of trauma, the intergenerational patterns of abuse, became painfully apparent in this work. Many of the individuals I worked with had stories eerily similar to Eleanor's, highlighting the systemic failures that allowed such abuse to flourish and the urgent need for systemic change.

My advocacy efforts extended beyond charitable partnerships, penetrating into the political arena. I testified before congressional committees, sharing Eleanor's story, highlighting the critical need for increased funding for mental health services, improved access to care, and the reduction of societal stigma surrounding mental illness. The battles were long and arduous, characterized by setbacks and incremental victories. The progress was slow, frustratingly so, but even small wins – a revised policy, an increased allocation of funds, a public acknowledgement of the importance of mental health – fueled my resolve.

One significant achievement was the establishment of a national hotline dedicated to supporting individuals with dissociative disorders. This hotline, initially envisioned as a small-scale project, grew into a significant resource, providing critical support to thousands of individuals struggling in silence. The hotline wasn't just a phone number; it was a lifeline, a symbol of hope, a tangible representation of the progress that had been made.

The workshops I conducted, in collaboration with mental health professionals, evolved into dynamic interactive sessions incorporating experiential techniques, group therapy approaches, and artistic expression as a means of processing trauma. The workshops provided a platform for participants to share their experiences in a safe and supportive environment, fostering a sense of camaraderie and mutual understanding. The collective healing that emerged from these sessions was profoundly moving.

However, the journey wasn't without its challenges. There were moments of intense emotional exhaustion, moments of doubt, moments when the sheer magnitude of the task seemed insurmountable. The constant exposure to stories of trauma took its toll, reminding me of the deep-seated wounds that plague our society.

There were critics, too, those who questioned my motives, those who doubted the veracity of Eleanor's story, those who dismissed my advocacy as mere attention-seeking. Their words stung, of course, but I learned to filter them out, focusing on the positive impact Eleanor's legacy was having.

The global reach of Eleanor's story surprised and humbled me. Translations of the book appeared in multiple languages, spreading her message of hope and resilience across continents. International collaborations with mental health organizations emerged, creating a network of support and resources that extended far beyond national borders.

Years later, as the initial fervor surrounding Eleanor's story subsided, I found myself reflecting on the enduring power of her legacy. It wasn't simply a book; it was a catalyst for change, a spark that ignited a movement. The ongoing battle for understanding, for compassion, for social justice in mental health remains, but Eleanor's story serves as a potent reminder that even in the darkest of times, hope persists, resilience endures, and the human spirit possesses an undeniable capacity for healing. The fight continues, but now, armed with the collective strength forged through shared experiences, we walk forward with a renewed sense of purpose, a shared vision of a brighter future for those who struggle silently, those who carry the invisible wounds of mental illness, and for those who strive tirelessly for a world where compassion triumphs over stigma and support replaces isolation. The story is not an ending, but a powerful testament to the unrelenting human spirit's capacity for healing, a beacon guiding the path toward a more compassionate future.

The final police report, tucked away in a dusty file somewhere in the city archives, remained stubbornly inconclusive. The circumstantial evidence pointed to Eleanor, of course, but the lack of a definitive murder weapon, coupled with the fragmented nature of the personality disorder, left enough wiggle room for doubt to flourish. Even with the diary's revelations, certain pieces remained maddeningly elusive. The red scrunchies, for instance – a seemingly insignificant detail, yet one that haunted me long after the book's publication. Where did they come from? Were they a deliberate choice, a macabre signature, or simply an item readily available to the personality that committed the act? The question remained unanswered, a silent testament to the elusive nature of the human mind, even within the confines of a well-documented case.

The lye, too, presented a puzzle. Its presence suggested a premeditated act of brutal desecration, going far beyond a simple killing. But was it chosen for its readily available nature, or was there a symbolic meaning I failed to uncover, something lost in the labyrinthine corridors of Eleanor's fractured consciousness? The diary offered glimpses into the depths of her trauma, but it couldn't fully explain the precise motivations of the personality responsible for the act. Was it a desperate attempt to erase a memory, a physical manifestation of a deep-seated self-loathing, or something more sinister? These were questions that lingered, challenging the boundaries of even the most insightful psychological analysis.

Even the timing of the murder remained open to interpretation. Did it occur during a period of extreme stress, a moment when a particular alter gained dominant control? Or was it a meticulously planned event, the culmination of years of pent-up rage simmering beneath the surface of Eleanor's seemingly placid existence? The diary entries offered snippets of insight, but not a complete narrative. The chaotic jumble of memories, fragmented thoughts, and shifting personalities made it impossible to piece together a clear timeline, to definitively establish the circumstances that led to the horrific act. The fragmented nature of Eleanor's existence mirrored the fragmented nature of the investigation, leaving the mystery, in some respects, as unresolved as the day it happened.

The public, however, seemed satisfied with the narrative presented in the book. Eleanor's story, albeit incomplete in certain crucial aspects, had provided a level of closure. The act had been understood, in part, as a consequence of profound and prolonged trauma, a testament to the devastating power of abuse. The focus shifted from the act itself to the root causes of violence – a shift that brought some comfort, some solace, even amidst the unresolved questions.

My own journey, however, continued beyond the book's publication. The ambiguity surrounding the murder was unsettling, not just professionally but personally. I found myself drawn into the world of unresolved cases, cold cases where the victims' stories remained tragically incomplete. The act of storytelling, the quest to give voice to the voiceless, led me down unexpected paths, paths that sometimes felt far removed from the tidy conclusions of fiction.

I collaborated with several forensic psychologists, working on cases that bore a chilling resemblance to Eleanor's. The recurring themes – childhood trauma, the pervasive nature of abuse, the insidious ways in which it manifests itself in adulthood – painted a stark picture of the societal failures that perpetuated cycles of violence. The cases were heartbreaking, highlighting the long-lasting impact of trauma, the ripple effects that reverberated through families and communities. These encounters reinforced the urgency of continued advocacy and the necessity of deeper societal understanding and intervention.

The diary, though a crucial part of the narrative, also presented ethical challenges. Eleanor's privacy, even in death, had to be respected. The delicate balance between public interest and the need for discretion was a constant struggle. Certain passages, deemed too graphic or too personally revealing, were omitted from the published version, preserving a sense of dignity and respect for Eleanor's memory. The decision to withhold certain information, however, brought its own weight of ethical responsibility. What was I withholding? Was it truly protecting Eleanor's privacy, or was I sanitizing the narrative for public consumption?

The ambiguity surrounding the red scrunchies continued to haunt me, its subtle presence a reminder of the countless unanswered questions in this complex case. I often found myself revisiting the diary, searching for clues, for hidden meanings, for some insight that would bring resolution to this specific mystery. I even consulted textile experts, attempting to trace the origin of the scrunchies, hoping for some forensic breakthrough, however small.

But the scrunchies, like many aspects of Eleanor's story, remained stubbornly enigmatic, a symbol of the mysteries that lie hidden within the depths of the human psyche. The murder itself was a symptom, a manifestation of deeper traumas, and while the book had offered a window into the complexities of Eleanor's fractured mind, the exact circumstances, the precise motivations, remained shrouded in mystery.

Ultimately, the unresolved nature of the case served as a powerful reminder of the limits of understanding, of the inherent complexities of the human experience. The narrative, therefore, concluded not with a neat resolution, but with a lingering sense of ambiguity, a recognition of the mysteries that continue to defy explanation. It was a testament to the resilience of the human spirit, its capacity to endure trauma, and the ongoing struggle to find healing, even in the face of the darkest of secrets. It was a reminder that some mysteries, no matter how meticulously investigated, may always remain, leaving the reader – and the investigator – grappling with the enigmatic nature of the human condition. The story wasn't about the solution to a single crime, but the journey into the depths of the human psyche, the journey of uncovering the wounds that lie beneath a seemingly perfect facade, and the struggles of survival in the face of the unforgiving nature of trauma. The finality of death failed to provide closure; instead, it left behind a lingering question, a testament to the enduring power of secrets, both hidden and revealed. The mystery of Eleanor remained, as elusive as the personalities that formed her fragmented self.

The lingering questions surrounding Eleanor Vance's case, the unanswered whispers of the red scrunchies and the caustic bite of the lye, weren't merely narrative devices; they were a call to action. The book, in its unsettling exploration of a fractured psyche, was never intended to be just a thriller. It was, at its core, a desperate plea, a whispered cry in the darkness for recognition and understanding. Eleanor's story, in all its fragmented horror, was a mirror reflecting the untold struggles of countless others, trapped within the silent prisons of their own minds. The unresolved nature of her murder wasn't a failure of investigation, but a stark reminder of the societal blind spots that allow such tragedies to fester and bloom in the shadows.

The seemingly perfect facade of Eleanor's life, the idyllic suburban setting, the charming husband, the seemingly well-adjusted daughter – these elements served to underscore the insidious nature of mental illness. It thrives in secrecy, nurtured by shame and stigma, its tendrils wrapping around victims with an almost suffocating grip. Eleanor's case highlighted the devastating consequences of untreated mental health conditions, the way trauma can fracture the psyche, leaving behind a chaotic landscape of conflicting personalities, each battling for dominance, each carrying the weight of unspeakable pain.

The silence surrounding mental illness is deafening. It's the unspoken fear, the whispered anxieties, the averted gazes that perpetuate a cycle of suffering. Friends and family often remain silent, unsure of how to approach the subject, afraid of saying the wrong thing, afraid of triggering a crisis. Professionals, sometimes, fall short, hampered by limited resources, inadequate training, and the sheer complexity of the human mind.

But the silence must be broken. The stories, like Eleanor's, must be told, not as morbid tales of fascination but as desperate cries for help. Each untold story fuels the stigma, deepening the shame, reinforcing the isolation that keeps individuals locked away in their internal battles. The more we speak, the more we listen, the more we learn, the less terrifying the darkness becomes.

The book wasn't just about Eleanor; it was about the countless others who suffer in silence. It was about the children enduring unspeakable abuse, the adults grappling with the lingering scars of their childhoods, the families torn apart by the unseen wounds of mental illness. It was about the societal failings that allow these tragedies to occur, the lack of resources, the inadequate support systems, the pervasive stigma that prevents individuals from seeking help.

It is a call to action to seek help for ourselves or others struggling with mental illness. If you suspect a loved one is struggling, seek professional help immediately. The resources are out there, though often difficult to access. Don't hesitate to reach out to mental health professionals, support groups, crisis hotlines, and advocacy organizations. The information is available, the help is there, but reaching out requires courage and a willingness to break the silence.

The journey to healing is long and arduous, a winding path through darkness, doubt and fear. But it's a journey worth undertaking. The path to recovery is paved with small steps, with moments of clarity emerging from the chaos, moments of peace breaking through the storm. It's a process of self-discovery, of understanding the complexities of one's own mind, of learning to cope with trauma, of building resilience, and of finding strength in vulnerability.

The book, in its unflinching portrayal of trauma and its devastating consequences, served as a testament to the resilience of the human spirit. Eleanor, in her fragmented state, represented the courage it takes to survive the unthinkable, the tenacity to fight even when the darkness seems insurmountable. Her story, despite its tragic end, is a story of survival, a beacon of hope in the face of unimaginable pain.

This isn't about assigning blame or pointing fingers. It's about understanding the systemic issues that contribute to mental illness. It's about reforming institutions that too often fail to provide adequate care and support. It's about investing in comprehensive mental health services, ensuring accessibility for all, regardless of socioeconomic status or geographic location. It's about training professionals, equipping them with the tools and resources they need to effectively diagnose and treat mental illnesses. It's about creating a culture of understanding and empathy, replacing stigma with compassion, fear with support.

The fragmented nature of Eleanor's narrative was intentional. It reflected the fragmented nature of the human psyche, the chaotic landscape of the mind struggling to make sense of trauma. The gaps in the story, the unanswered questions, were not failings, but intentional choices, meant to underscore the mysteries of the human condition, the complexities of mental illness, and the challenges faced by individuals in their struggle for healing.

The red scrunchies, a seemingly insignificant detail, served as a powerful symbol of the unseen, the unspoken, the countless details lost in the labyrinthine corridors of the mind. They represent the hidden struggles, the unspoken trauma, the silent suffering that remains unacknowledged. They serve as a constant reminder of the importance of seeking help, of speaking out, of breaking the silence that surrounds mental illness.

The book's ending wasn't a resolution; it was a beginning, a call to action for a collective awakening. It's an invitation to engage in meaningful conversations, to challenge the stigma surrounding mental health, to demand better care, to advocate for policy changes that will ensure mental healthcare is accessible to everyone who needs it. It is a plea for greater understanding, empathy, and compassion – a recognition that mental illness is not a moral failing but a medical condition requiring treatment and support.

Eleanor's fragmented story serves as a testament to the importance of breaking the silence, of seeking help when needed. Her case highlights the vital necessity of early intervention, of comprehensive treatment plans, and the critical role of support systems. It is a call to action for society to address the systemic failures that contribute to mental illness and its devastating consequences.

We must create a world where individuals struggling with mental health conditions feel safe, supported, and empowered to seek help without shame or fear. We must transform our healthcare systems, ensuring they are equipped to meet the needs of those struggling with mental illness. We must educate ourselves and others, fostering a culture of understanding and empathy, where mental health is recognized as a vital aspect of overall wellbeing.

The journey to healing is a collaborative effort, a collective responsibility. It requires a concerted effort from individuals, families, communities, and healthcare systems to create a society where mental health is prioritized, where stigma is eradicated, and where individuals receive the support they need to thrive.

Eleanor Vance's story, though tragic, serves as a powerful reminder of the enduring strength of the human spirit and the urgent need to break the silence surrounding mental illness. It is a testament to the importance of seeking help, of speaking out, and of working together to create a world where everyone has access to the mental health care they need. Let us honor Eleanor's memory by continuing the conversation, by challenging the stigma, and by committing ourselves to creating a more compassionate and supportive society for all. Let her story be a catalyst for change, a beacon of hope guiding us toward a future where mental health is valued, understood, and supported. The silence must end. The conversation must begin.

The final pages of Eleanor's diary, brittle with age and stained with the residue of unspoken tears, lay open, revealing not a neat conclusion, but a fractured echo of the life they chronicled. The last entry, scrawled in a shaky hand, spoke not of resolution, but of a desperate clinging to the sliver of light piercing through the overwhelming darkness. It was a testament to the enduring resilience of the human spirit, a fragile whisper against the howling winds of trauma. There was no triumphant overcoming, no neat bow tied around the complexities of Eleanor's shattered self. Instead, there was a raw, visceral honesty, a stark portrayal of the ongoing battle within.

The murder, the chilling tableau in the freezer, remained a chilling enigma, a testament to the terrifying power of a mind fractured by abuse. It wasn't a simple act of malice, but a manifestation of the deep-seated rage, the overwhelming pain that had festered within Eleanor for decades. The red scrunchies, those seemingly insignificant details, now resonated with a haunting significance, symbolic of the unseen wounds, the hidden traumas that bind so many in silence. They were a constant reminder of the pervasive nature of suffering, the way trauma can weave itself into the very fabric of one's being, leaving behind an indelible mark that whispers long after the initial pain has subsided.

The book, in its exploration of Eleanor's fractured psyche, was never meant to provide easy answers. It was not a neat puzzle to be solved, but a labyrinthine exploration of the human condition, a journey into the shadowed corners of the mind where trauma resides. The unresolved questions, the lingering mysteries, were not failures of the narrative, but intentional choices, meant to reflect the enduring complexities of Eleanor's experience and the countless others who share a similar fate. The reader is left with a sense of unsettling ambiguity, forced to confront the disturbing reality of the unseen, the untold, the unspoken wounds that plague society.

Eleanor's story, far from being a singular tragedy, serves as a chilling reminder of the societal failures that allow such horrors to unfold. It is a reflection of the pervasive stigma surrounding mental illness, the societal reluctance to confront the uncomfortable truths of abuse, and the lack of readily available, comprehensive mental health resources. It is a critique of the systems that fail to protect the vulnerable, the systems that allow trauma to fester and bloom in the shadows, leaving lasting scars on individuals and generations to come.

The book compels us to confront not only the horrors of Eleanor's past, but the systemic issues that contributed to her fragmented state. It is a call to action, a demand for change, a plea for a more compassionate and understanding society. It is a challenge to those who turn a blind eye, who whisper anxieties and avert gazes in the face of mental suffering. It is a demand for systemic reforms, for better training and support for mental health professionals, and for accessible, comprehensive care for all.

The lasting impact of Eleanor's story lies not in the resolution of her murder, but in its persistent questioning of societal responses to trauma and mental illness. It lingers in the reader's mind, prompting reflection on the complexities of the human psyche, the enduring power of trauma, and the urgent need for societal change. The silence surrounding abuse and mental illness must be broken. The whispers of shame and stigma must be replaced with open conversations, with empathy, with compassion, with a genuine commitment to providing support and resources for those who need them most.

The red scrunchies remain, a haunting symbol of the unseen wounds, the hidden scars, the silent screams that are too often ignored. They are a reminder of the countless Eleanor Vances who suffer in silence, trapped within the confines of their own minds, their stories untold, their cries for help unheard. The book serves as a testament to their resilience, their courage, their struggle to survive in the face of unimaginable pain. It is a reminder of the ongoing battle against trauma, a call to action to break the silence, to speak out, to seek help, to create a society where the vulnerabilities of the human spirit are recognized, respected, and supported.

Beyond the chilling details of the murder, beyond the fractured narrative of Eleanor's diary, lies a deeper message, a profound truth about the human experience. Trauma leaves an indelible mark, a fracture in the psyche that can manifest in unpredictable and devastating ways. It is not a simple matter of overcoming adversity, but a lifelong journey of healing, of learning to cope with the lingering effects of pain, of rebuilding a shattered sense of self. Eleanor's story is not a tale of simple triumph over adversity; it is a stark, unflinching portrayal of the ongoing struggle for survival, for self-discovery, for healing in the face of unimaginable pain. It is a testament to the incredible resilience of the human spirit, the capacity for hope even in the deepest darkness.

The ending, therefore, is not an ending at all. It is a point of departure, a catalyst for introspection, a call to action. It is a challenge to confront the uncomfortable truths of our society, to acknowledge the systemic failures that contribute to mental illness and trauma, and to commit ourselves to creating a world where healing is possible, where support is readily available, and where the voices of those who suffer are finally heard. Eleanor's fragmented story is not merely a cautionary tale; it is a roadmap for change, a blueprint for a more compassionate and just society.

The reader is left with a profound sense of unease, a lingering empathy for Eleanor and the countless others who have suffered in silence. The complexities of trauma are not easily understood, nor are they easily resolved. The journey to healing is a long and arduous one, fraught with challenges, setbacks, and moments of profound despair. But it is also a journey of self-discovery, of resilience, of finding strength in vulnerability. Eleanor's story, in all its fragmented horror, is a testament to the enduring power of the human spirit, a beacon of hope in the darkest of times. It reminds us that even in the face of unimaginable pain, the capacity for healing, for growth, for hope remains.

The unanswered questions, the lingering mysteries, the fragmented narrative – these are not flaws but deliberate choices, meant to mirror the unpredictable and often incomprehensible nature of trauma. The reader is left to grapple with these complexities, to ponder the societal failures that contribute to suffering, and to consider the urgent need for change. The book is not a simple thriller; it is a complex exploration of the human condition, a poignant reflection on the enduring power of trauma, and a powerful call to action for a more just and compassionate world. Eleanor's story, though tragic, is ultimately a story of hope, a testament to the resilience of the human spirit, and a reminder that healing, though challenging, is always possible. The silence must end. The conversation must begin. The change must start now.

## Back Matter

First and foremost, I extend my deepest gratitude to the individuals who bravely shared their experiences of trauma and mental illness. Their stories, though painful, provided invaluable insight and fueled the authenticity of this narrative. Their courage inspires hope and underscores the importance of open dialogue about these often-silenced realities. To those who have lived through the darkness, this book is dedicated to you.

My sincere appreciation also goes to Dr. Emily Carter, whose expertise in trauma-informed care and dissociative disorders offered invaluable guidance throughout the writing process. Her insights shaped the psychological accuracy of the portrayal and ensured a responsible and sensitive depiction of multiple personality disorder. Any inaccuracies remain solely my own.

To my editor, Sarah Miller, thank you for your unwavering support, insightful feedback, and patience in navigating the complex themes of this novel. Your dedication to crafting a compelling and impactful story is greatly appreciated. Finally, to my family and friends, your love and understanding provided an unwavering support system during the demanding process of writing this book.

This appendix provides additional resources for individuals seeking information and support regarding multiple personality disorder (DID), trauma, and related mental health conditions. It is not an exhaustive list, but a starting point for those in need of assistance. Remember, seeking professional help is crucial, and this appendix should not be used as a replacement for professional guidance.

**National Alliance on Mental Illness (NAMI):** nami.org

**The International Society for the Study of Trauma and Dissociation (ISSTD):** isst-d.org

**The Trauma Center at Justice Resource Institute:** jri.org

**The National Sexual Assault Hotline:** 1-800-656-4673

**Dissociative Identity Disorder (DID):** A mental disorder characterized by the presence of two or more distinct personality states, often referred to as alters. These alters have distinct memories, behaviors, and emotional responses. DID is frequently associated with severe childhood trauma.

**Alters:** Distinct personality states within an individual with DID, each with its own unique characteristics.

**Trauma:** A deeply distressing or disturbing experience that has an enduring impact on an individual's emotional and psychological well-being.

**PTSD (Post-Traumatic Stress Disorder):** A mental health condition that can develop after a person has experienced or witnessed a terrifying event. Symptoms may include flashbacks, nightmares, and avoidance of reminders of the trauma.

**OCD (Obsessive-Compulsive Disorder):** A mental health condition characterized by unwanted and intrusive thoughts (obsessions) and repetitive behaviors (compulsions).

**ADHD (Attention-Deficit/Hyperactivity Disorder):** A neurodevelopmental disorder that affects attention, hyperactivity, and impulsivity.

**Autism Spectrum Disorder (ASD):** A developmental disability that can cause significant social, communication, and behavioral challenges.

# A Comprehensive Bibliography of Foundational Resources on Trauma, Dissociative Disorders, and Key Psychological Theories

## I. Introduction to Trauma and Dissociative Disorders

### Defining Trauma and its Impact

Trauma, particularly in its severe or chronic manifestations such as physical, sexual, or emotional abuse, neglect, experiences of war, or acts of terrorism, is consistently recognized as a significant etiological factor for a spectrum of psychological conditions. These conditions include Posttraumatic Stress Disorder (PTSD) and the various dissociative disorders.1 The profound impact of overwhelming experiences can lead to substantial disruptions in an individual's subjective continuity, affecting fundamental mental functions such as awareness, memory, identity, emotion, perception, and behavior.3 Beyond the psychological manifestations, trauma elicits a complex psychobiological response to threat, with measurable biological correlates that underscore the deep physiological imprint of traumatic events.4

## Understanding Dissociation and Dissociative Disorders

Dissociation is conceptualized as a disconnection between a person's thoughts, memories, feelings, actions, or sense of self. This phenomenon exists on a continuum, ranging from common, mild experiences like daydreaming or "highway hypnosis" to severe, pathological disruptions that significantly impair daily functioning.3 Clinically, pathological dissociation is characterized by involuntary and unwanted intrusions into awareness and behavior, often termed "positive dissociation," or an inability to access information or control mental functions, manifested as symptoms like gaps in awareness or memory, referred to as "negative dissociation".4

The Diagnostic and Statistical Manual of Mental Disorders, Fifth Edition, Text Revision (DSM-5-TR) delineates three primary dissociative disorders: Dissociative Identity Disorder (DID), Dissociative

Amnesia, and Depersonalization-Derealization Disorder.2

Dissociative Identity Disorder (DID): Previously known as Multiple Personality Disorder (MPD), DID is characterized by the presence of at least two distinct personality states or "alters." These distinct identities are accompanied by profound changes in behavior, memory, and thinking, which may be observed by others or reported by the individual. Recurrent episodes of dissociative amnesia and inexplicable intrusions into consciousness, such as hearing voices or experiencing intrusive thoughts, are hallmark symptoms.1 DID is frequently conceptualized as "the most severe form of a childhood-onset post-traumatic stress disorder," with individuals experiencing a fragmented sense of self rather than possessing multiple distinct personalities.1

Dissociative Amnesia: The primary symptom of this disorder is a significant difficulty remembering important personal information, which is typically linked to a traumatic or highly stressful event. This amnesia can manifest in various forms: localized (inability to recall a specific event or period, the most common type), selective (inability to remember specific aspects of an event or some events within a period), or, rarely, generalized (a complete loss of identity and life history).2 It is strongly associated with experiences of childhood trauma, particularly emotional abuse and neglect.3

Depersonalization-Derealization Disorder: This disorder involves persistent or recurrent experiences of unreality or detachment from one's own mind, self, or body (depersonalization), or from one's surroundings (derealization). Crucially, during these altered experiences, the individual maintains an awareness of reality and recognizes the unusual nature of their experience, which often causes significant distress.[2] Childhood interpersonal trauma, especially emotional abuse, has been identified as a significant predictor for the development of this disorder.[7]

## The Trauma Model vs. Fantasy Model of Dissociation

The relationship between reported trauma and dissociative symptoms has been a subject of considerable debate, leading to the development of two primary, conflicting models:

Trauma Model (TM): This widely supported model posits that pathological dissociation, including DID, is an adaptive, phylogenetically important psychobiological response to severe antecedent traumatic stress and/or chronic psychological adversity, particularly developmental trauma experienced in early childhood.[1] It views dissociation as a survival mechanism that allows for automatization of behavior, analgesia (pain reduction), depersonalization, and the isolation of catastrophic experiences to enhance survival.[4] Empirical evidence consistently demonstrates a moderate and significant relationship between trauma and dissociation, even when objective measures of trauma are employed. Dissociation is temporally linked to trauma and trauma treatment, and it predicts trauma history even when fantasy proneness is controlled.[4]

Fantasy Model (FM) / Sociogenic Model: This alternative perspective argues that dissociation is a psychological process causally unrelated to actual traumatic events. Proponents suggest that trauma histories reported by individuals with dissociative experiences and/or dissociative disorders are largely confabulations or exaggerations, stemming from high fantasy proneness, suggestibility, and cognitive distortions.[1] This model views DID as a societal construct and a learned behavior, potentially developed through iatrogenesis (therapy-induced effects), cultural beliefs about the disorder, or exposure to the concept in media.[1]

Empirical evidence provides strong support for the trauma model. Studies indicate that dissociation is not reliably associated with suggestibility, nor is there evidence supporting the fantasy model's prediction of greater inaccuracy in recovered memories.[4] Instead, dissociation correlates positively with trauma memory recovery and negatively with general measures of narrative cohesion.[4] The DSM-5-TR's strategic placement of dissociative disorders immediately after trauma- and stressor-related disorders explicitly reflects the strong relationship between complex trauma and dissociation.[1] Furthermore, neurobiological studies corroborate the trauma model, showing a negative correlation between hippocampal volumes and childhood traumatization in both DID and PTSD, providing neuroanatomical evidence for these clinical observations.8

## Critical Understandings from the Field

The extensive body of research on trauma and dissociative disorders points to several critical understandings that shape contemporary clinical practice and future directions in the field.

First, the research overwhelmingly supports the centrality of trauma in the etiology of dissociative disorders, with childhood trauma, particularly abuse and neglect, identified as the primary etiological factor. The "Trauma Model" is not merely a statistical association but is presented as a fundamental causal link, where dissociation functions as a "psychobiological response to threat".1 This deep understanding dictates that effective treatment for dissociative disorders must be trauma-informed and trauma-focused. Addressing symptoms alone, without engaging with the underlying traumatic experiences and their sequelae, is likely to be insufficient, potentially leading to chronic distress or relapse.3 The reclassification and placement of dissociative disorders within the DSM-5-TR signify a crucial paradigm shift in clinical understanding and diagnostic practice, emphasizing the necessity of a trauma-informed lens. This also underscores the critical importance of primary prevention efforts aimed at reducing childhood trauma to mitigate the incidence and severity of dissociative disorders. The description of dissociation as a "regulatory response to fear or other extreme emotion with measurable biological correlates" 4 reveals a sophisticated biopsychosocial mechanism.

This suggests that chronic trauma fundamentally alters the brain's threat response systems, leading to dissociative states as an ingrained, albeit often maladaptive, survival strategy. This integration of biological and psychological understanding is crucial for developing holistic treatment approaches that target both the mind and the body.

Second, a notable pattern in the literature is the high comorbidity of dissociative disorders with a wide array of other mental health conditions. These include PTSD, depression, anxiety, borderline personality disorder (BPD), substance use disorders, eating disorders, self-destructiveness, and suicidality.2 This is not merely a list of co-occurring conditions; the data suggest that comorbidity is "the norm rather than the exception" in treatment-seeking populations.11 This pervasive comorbidity means that pure presentations of dissociative disorders are rare. Clinicians must possess advanced skills in differential diagnosis, recognizing that dissociative symptoms can often be masked by or misdiagnosed as other disorders, leading to ineffective treatment pathways.5 Consequently, treatment plans must be highly individualized, integrative, and holistic, addressing the complex interplay of symptoms and underlying trauma rather than isolated diagnoses. The finding that high dissociation predicts poor response to standard PTSD treatments like exposure therapy 4 further emphasizes the necessity of specialized, phase-oriented, and dissociation-informed interventions. The repeated association of dissociation with "self-mutilation" and "suicidality" 7 highlights a severe clinical risk profile. This connection underscores the paramount importance of prioritizing safety, stabilization, and the development of distress tolerance skills (e.g., as taught in Dialectical Behavior Therapy) before engaging in deeper trauma processing. This sequential approach is vital to ensure patient safety and optimize treatment efficacy.

Third, despite robust empirical support for the trauma model and the inclusion of dissociative disorders in authoritative diagnostic manuals, a persistent controversy and under-recognition of dissociative disorders exist within the field. Dissociative Identity Disorder (DID) remains "extremely controversial" [1] and its etiology "still controversial" among some.[8] Critically, clinical reviews reveal that dissociative symptoms are "largely unrecognized" and patients are "typically... misdiagnosed".[5] This under-recognition is attributed to factors such as insufficient clinician training, inadequate information in undergraduate and graduate textbooks, and a broader "reluctance to accept the nature and severity of childhood abuse".[8] This discrepancy between scientific evidence and clinical practice points to a significant systemic gap in mental health education and training that demands urgent attention. The ongoing controversy and under-recognition lead to delayed or incorrect diagnoses, prolonged suffering, and the application of ineffective treatments for patients.[5] It also highlights an urgent need for increased professional advocacy and public education to destigmatize these conditions and improve early identification. The "reluctance to accept the nature and severity of childhood abuse" [8] suggests that the challenge of recognizing dissociative disorders extends beyond a mere knowledge deficit; it touches upon a profound societal and professional discomfort with confronting the pervasive reality of severe, chronic trauma. This implies that addressing the under-recognition of dissociative disorders requires not only educational initiatives but also a broader cultural shift within mental health professions to fully acknowledge and integrate the impact of complex trauma. This also positions the work of figures like Judith Herman, who highlighted the social and political dimensions of abuse 13, as enduringly relevant.

## II. Foundational Psychological Theories

The understanding and treatment of trauma and dissociative disorders are underpinned by several influential psychological theories. These frameworks offer distinct yet often complementary perspectives on the development, manifestation, and resolution of trauma-related psychopathology.

Table 1: Overview of Major Psychological Theories and Their Proponents

Theory Name     Structural Dissociation Theory

Key Proponent(s)     Onno van der Hart, Ellert Nijenhuis, Kathy Steele

Core Concept/Focus

Personality fragmentation into "parts" as a response to chronic trauma; phase-oriented treatment for integration.

Structural Dissociation Theory

Developed by Onno van der Hart, Ellert Nijenhuis, and Kathy Steele, Structural Dissociation Theory is a comprehensive framework for understanding the impact of chronic traumatization.14 Rooted in Pierre Janet's psychology of action, this theory posits that severe, particularly childhood, trauma leads to a structural dissociation of the personality.15 This fragmentation involves the division of the personality into different "parts" or "action systems," each holding specific traumatic memories, emotions, and coping responses. This division serves as a means of surviving overwhelming experiences by compartmentalizing unbearable aspects of reality.15

The theory distinguishes between primary, secondary, and tertiary structural dissociation, representing increasing levels of complexity and severity of trauma and dissociative symptoms. It provides a robust framework for understanding the profound impact of trauma on personality organization and clarifies the contribution of trauma to a range of disorders beyond simple PTSD, including Complex PTSD, Dissociative Identity Disorder (DID), Borderline Personality Disorder, and somatoform disorders.15 A core tenet is the "phobic maintenance of structural dissociation," where fear of traumatic memories or dissociative parts actively prevents their integration, thereby perpetuating the dissociative state.15 The foundational text for this theory is The Haunted Self: Structural Dissociation and the Treatment of Chronic Traumatization (2006) by van der Hart, Nijenhuis, and Steele.14 This book is widely recognized as a landmark contribution, integrating classic Janetian observations with modern neuroscience and attachment theory, and outlining a comprehensive, phase-oriented treatment model focused on identifying, understanding, and facilitating the integration of structural dissociation.15

## Adaptive Information Processing (AIP) Model (EMDR)

The Adaptive Information Processing (AIP) model serves as the theoretical underpinning for Eye Movement Desensitization and Reprocessing (EMDR) therapy, a modality developed by Francine Shapiro.17 The AIP model postulates that psychological trauma and distressing life experiences result from unprocessed or inadequately processed information. When overwhelming events occur, the associated perceptions, emotions, and distorted thoughts become "stuck" or isolated from the brain's natural adaptive memory networks, leading to persistent symptoms.18

EMDR therapy, through bilateral stimulation (e.g., eye movements, sounds, or tactile stimulation), is believed to activate and facilitate the brain's intrinsic information processing system. This allows for the integration of traumatic memories into more adaptive and functional networks, a process thought to mimic brain activity during REM sleep.19 EMDR aims to desensitize the emotional distress associated with traumatic memories and establish new, adaptive relational connections within the memory networks.19 It operates on the premise of the mind's innate capacity to heal from psychological trauma, much like the body heals from physical injury.19 The foundational text for EMDR is Eye Movement Desensitization and Reprocessing: Basic Principles, Protocols, and Procedures (1995, with updated editions in 2001 and 2017) by Francine

Shapiro.17 This definitive textbook details the eight phases of this psychotherapy.

## Cognitive Models of Trauma (Cognitive Behavioral Therapy - CBT, Cognitive Processing Therapy - CPT, Prolonged Exposure - PE)

These models, deeply rooted in the principles of Cognitive Behavioral Therapy (CBT), emphasize the pivotal role of maladaptive thoughts, beliefs, and avoidance behaviors in the maintenance of trauma-related symptoms. The primary therapeutic goal is to identify, challenge, and modify distorted cognitions and dysfunctional behaviors that perpetuate distress following trauma.22

Cognitive Behavioral Therapy (CBT): A broad therapeutic approach that focuses on the intricate relationships among thoughts, feelings, and behaviors. It targets current problems and symptoms, aiming to change unhelpful patterns of thinking, feeling, and behaving.22 Aaron T. Beck's extensive foundational work on cognitive therapy provided the theoretical bedrock for these trauma-specific applications.23

Cognitive Processing Therapy (CPT): A specific, structured type of cognitive behavioral therapy designed to help patients learn how to modify and challenge unhelpful beliefs related to the traumatic event. By creating a new understanding and conceptualization of the trauma, CPT aims to reduce its ongoing negative effects on current life.22 Notably, CPT, particularly the comprehensive approach including written accounts, has shown favorable outcomes for individuals with higher levels of dissociation, as the act of writing may facilitate the integration of fragmented memories.25 The comprehensive manual for CPT is Cognitive Processing Therapy for PTSD: A Comprehensive Manual by Patricia A. Resick, Candice M. Monson, and Kathleen M. Chard.17

Prolonged Exposure (PE): A specific type of cognitive behavioral therapy that teaches individuals to gradually approach trauma-related memories, feelings, and situations that they have previously avoided. Through systematic exposure, the individual presumably learns that these trauma-related cues are not dangerous and do not need to be avoided, leading to a reduction in fear and anxiety.22 The therapist guide, Prolonged Exposure Therapy for PTSD: Emotional Processing of Traumatic Experiences, by Edna B. Foa, Elizabeth A. Hembree, and Barbara Olasov Rothbaum, is a foundational text for this modality.17

### Internal Family Systems (IFS) Theory

Proposed by Richard C. Schwartz, Internal Family Systems (IFS) posits that the human mind is naturally multiple, comprised of various "parts" or sub-personalities that interact within an "internal family system".17 From an IFS perspective, trauma symptoms are understood not as pathology but as adaptive coping strategies adopted by these parts to protect the system from further pain or overwhelming emotions.31 The theory emphasizes the existence of a core "Self," which is inherently wise, compassionate, calm, and capable of leading the internal system towards healing.29 IFS aims to heal these "parts" from their trauma burdens, thereby restoring harmony and balance to the internal system by fostering a Self-led approach.32 It is a non-pathologizing and empowering approach that encourages treating even the most difficult or extreme parts with curiosity, respect, and empathy.29 Foundational texts include Internal Family Systems Therapy by Richard C. Schwartz and Introduction to Internal Family Systems by Richard C. Schwartz.17 The latter is particularly noted for its accessibility, making it an ideal starting point for both laypersons and clinicians.

## Sensorimotor Psychotherapy Theory

Sensorimotor Psychotherapy (SP), developed by Pat Ogden, is a somatically-oriented therapy that recognizes the intrinsic and inseparable link between mental, emotional, and physical experiences.17 It posits that traumatic experiences are not only stored in the mind but also deeply imprinted in the body, manifesting as persistent physical sensations, habitual postures, and dysfunctional movement patterns, leading to chronic autonomic and affective dysregulation.33 SP focuses on addressing both the cognitive-emotional aspects and the bodily and autonomic symptoms of traumatic stress and attachment-related disorders.36 It places a strong emphasis on cultivating mindfulness, encouraging clients to develop non-judgmental awareness of their persistent physical, cognitive, and emotional responses evoked by trauma-related stimuli. SP teaches somatic skills to manage physiological activation and helps clients differentiate between past traumatic events and present reality.33 Its theoretical principles are heavily informed by neuroscience research findings on the effects of trauma on the brain and body, and it integrates concepts from polyvagal theory and the triune brain theory.33 Foundational texts include Trauma and the Body: A Sensorimotor Approach to Psychotherapy by Pat Ogden and Sensorimotor Psychotherapy: Interventions for Trauma and Attachment by Pat Ogden and Janina Fisher.17

## Dialectical Behavior Therapy (DBT)
### Theoretical Underpinnings

Developed by Marsha M. Linehan, Dialectical Behavior Therapy (DBT) was initially designed for the treatment of Borderline Personality Disorder (BPD) but has been widely adapted and proven effective for trauma-focused work, recognizing the significant overlap between BPD symptoms and complex trauma presentations.10 DBT is grounded in a biosocial model and, in its trauma-focused adaptations, often integrates principles from Polyvagal Theory to address the physiological impact of trauma on the nervous system.38 The core dialectic in DBT is the synthesis of acceptance and change, aiming to help clients manage intense emotions and impulsive behaviors that frequently stem from traumatic experiences.38 DBT is a highly structured, skills-based approach that teaches clients four main skill sets: mindfulness, distress tolerance, emotion regulation, and interpersonal effectiveness.37 These skills empower individuals to find a "middle path" between extreme responses often created by ongoing trauma, promoting healthier coping mechanisms and improved functioning.38 DBT has demonstrated effectiveness in treating PTSD associated with childhood abuse.37 Foundational texts include Cognitive-Behavioral Treatment of Borderline Personality Disorder by Marsha M. Linehan, which lays the theoretical groundwork, and Skills Training Manual for Treating Borderline Personality Disorder by Linehan, a crucial practical companion.17

## Other Relevant Theoretical Frameworks

Beyond these primary therapeutic models, several other theoretical frameworks significantly contribute to the understanding of trauma and dissociation:

Polyvagal Theory: Developed by Stephen Porges, this neurophysiological theory provides a detailed understanding of how the vagus nerve and the autonomic nervous system regulate an individual's responses to stress and trauma. It explains the physiological underpinnings of states such as social engagement, fight/flight, and the freeze/dissociation response, offering a neurobiological explanation for how trauma is "stored" as habitual reflexive states in the nervous system.33

Biosocial Model: Marsha Linehan's original model for DBT, which posits that Borderline Personality Disorder (and by extension, many complex trauma presentations) arises from the interaction between a biological vulnerability to emotion dysregulation and an invalidating developmental environment.38

Attachment Theory: This developmental theory, particularly relevant in the context of chronic childhood trauma, emphasizes the profound impact of early relational experiences and attachment styles on the development of self-regulation, emotional processing, and an individual's capacity to cope with stress. Disorganized attachment, often a consequence of severe childhood abuse and neglect, is highly relevant to the development and manifestation of dissociative phenomena.15

## Evolving Perspectives in Trauma Therapy

The landscape of trauma therapy is undergoing a significant evolution, marked by a paradigm shift towards embodied and integrative approaches. While traditional cognitive-behavioral therapies (CBT, CPT, PE) remain foundational and effective for certain trauma presentations 22, the increasing prominence of EMDR, Internal Family Systems (IFS), and Sensorimotor Psychotherapy (SP) signifies a crucial development.18 Sensorimotor Psychotherapy explicitly states that "traumatic experiences often get stored in the body" 33 and directly addresses "autonomic and affective dysregulation".36 The integration of Polyvagal Theory as an underpinning for DBT and SP 33 provides a robust neurobiological explanation for this "body-based" understanding of trauma. This progression represents a significant shift from purely "top-down" (cognitively-focused) approaches to more "bottom-up" (somatic and affective) and integrative treatments. It implies that comprehensive trauma therapy often necessitates addressing physiological arousal, body sensations, and fragmented self-states, which may not be fully accessible or resolved through traditional verbal processing alone.33 This evolution is particularly vital for treating complex trauma and dissociative disorders, where the verbal narrative of trauma can be fragmented, inaccessible, or re-traumatizing. The consistent integration of neuroscience findings, such as the impact of trauma on the hippocampus, amygdala, and autonomic nervous system 4, across these diverse theoretical models highlights a convergence of psychological and biological understanding. This convergence suggests that the future of trauma research and clinical training will increasingly bridge these traditionally separate disciplines to provide truly holistic and effective care for survivors.

Another critical pattern observed is the deep interconnectedness and shared etiology of trauma, dissociation, and personality disorders. Structural Dissociation Theory explicitly links chronic trauma to the development of PTSD, Complex PTSD, DID, and Borderline Personality Disorder (BPD).15 Dialectical Behavior Therapy (DBT), originally developed for BPD, is now widely recognized and utilized for trauma treatment.37 Furthermore, numerous studies highlight the high comorbidity between dissociative disorders and BPD.2 This strong pattern suggests a shared underlying etiological pathway, most often rooted in early, chronic interpersonal trauma. This profound interconnectedness implies that BPD, often conceptualized as a distinct personality disorder, shares significant symptomatic overlap and potentially a common developmental trajectory with complex trauma and dissociative disorders. Consequently, effective treatment for BPD, especially trauma-focused DBT, may inherently address dissociative symptoms and vice versa. This challenges overly rigid diagnostic boundaries and encourages a more transdiagnostic approach to severe psychopathology that stems from early adverse experiences. The concept of "phobic maintenance of structural dissociation" 15 reveals a self-perpetuating cycle where the fear of engaging with traumatic memories or integrating dissociative parts actively prevents healing. This highlights the critical importance of establishing safety, achieving emotional stabilization, and building internal and external resources before attempting deep trauma processing. This phased approach is a cornerstone of effective treatment for complex trauma and dissociative disorders, and is explicitly integrated into models like structural dissociation theory and trauma-focused DBT.

## III. Essential Books

The following selection of books represents foundational and highly influential works that have shaped the understanding and treatment of trauma and dissociative disorders. They are essential reading for clinicians, researchers, and advanced students in the field.

Table 2: Seminal Books in Trauma and Dissociation Studies

| Author(s) | Title | Publication Year | Key Contribution/ Significance |
| :--- | :--- | :--- | :--- |
| Herman, J. L. | Trauma and Recovery: The Aftermath of Violence—From Domestic Abuse to Political Terror | 1992, 2015 | Defined Complex PTSD and emphasized the social/political dimensions of trauma. |
| van der Kolk, B. A. | The Body Keeps the Score: Brain, Mind, and Body in the

Healing of Trauma | 2014 | Synthesized neurobiological effects of trauma and holistic treatment approaches. | | van der Kolk, B. A., McFarlane, A. C., & Weisaeth, L. (Eds.) | Traumatic Stress: The Effects of Overwhelming Experience on Mind, Body, and Society | 1996, 2007 | Comprehensive edited volume on biopsychosocial aspects of traumatic stress. | | van der Hart, O., Nijenhuis, E. R. S., & Steele, K. | The Haunted Self: Structural Dissociation and the Treatment of Chronic Traumatization | 2006 | Foundational text for Structural Dissociation Theory and phase-oriented treatment. | | Shapiro, F. | Eye Movement Desensitization and Reprocessing (EMDR) Therapy: Basic Principles, Protocols, and Procedures | 1995, 2001, 2017 | Definitive manual for EMDR therapy by its originator. | | Ogden, P., & Fisher, J. | Sensorimotor Psychotherapy: Interventions for Trauma and Attachment | 2015 | Practical guide to body-oriented therapy for trauma and attachment. | | Schwartz, R. C. | Internal Family Systems Therapy / Introduction to Internal Family Systems | 2001 / 2019 | Introduced the IFS model for healing internal "parts" impacted by trauma. | | Linehan, M. M. | Cognitive-Behavioral Treatment of Borderline Personality Disorder | 1993 | Foundational theoretical text for Dialectical Behavior Therapy. | | Linehan, M. M. | Skills Training Manual for Treating Borderline Personality Disorder | 1993 | Practical companion for teaching core DBT skills. | | Foa, E. B., Hembree, E. A., & Rothbaum, B. O. | Prolonged Exposure Therapy for PTSD: Emotional Processing of Traumatic Experiences—Therapist Guide | 2007, 2019 | Comprehensive manual for implementing Prolonged Exposure therapy. | | Resick, P. A., Monson, C. M., & Chard, K. M. | Cognitive Processing Therapy for PTSD: A Comprehensive Manual | 2017 | Indispensable guide for practitioners of Cognitive Processing Therapy. |

## Seminal Works on Trauma

Herman, J. L. (1992, 2015). Trauma and Recovery: The Aftermath of Violence—From Domestic Abuse to Political Terror. Basic Books. 13

This book is widely regarded as a "magnum opus" and a "groundbreaking" contribution that fundamentally redefined the study of psychological trauma.13 Herman almost single-handedly introduced and elucidated the concept of Complex Posttraumatic Stress Disorder (CPTSD), distinguishing it from traditional PTSD by incorporating symptoms such as self-hatred, inability to trust, and existential despair, particularly in survivors of chronic, interpersonal violence like sexual abuse and domestic violence.13 Her work critically frames abuse as a social and political act, necessitating social and political reparation.13 Published at a time when reports of childhood incest and abuse were frequently dismissed or misinterpreted as client fantasy within contemporary psychoanalytic practice 13, Herman's rigorous scholarship brought these realities to the forefront of clinical and academic discourse.

van der Kolk, B. A. (2014). The Body Keeps the Score: Brain, Mind, and Body in the Healing of Trauma. Viking. 13

Considered a "classic and required reading for all trauma clinicians" 41, this book masterfully synthesizes decades of research and clinical experience on the neurological and physiological effects of trauma. It vividly describes how trauma impacts the brain and body, leaving psychological and physiological residue.13 Van der Kolk explores a range of effective treatment modalities, including Eye Movement Desensitization and Reprocessing (EMDR), yoga, and neurofeedback, highlighting a holistic approach to healing.41 This book significantly popularized the concept of trauma being "stored in the body" 33, aligning with and fueling the growing interest in somatic and body-oriented approaches to trauma therapy.

van der Kolk, B. A., McFarlane, A. C., & Weisaeth, L. (Eds.). (1996, 2007). Traumatic Stress: The Effects of Overwhelming Experience on Mind, Body, and Society. Guilford Press. 13

An earlier, comprehensive edited volume that brought together leading experts in the field to explore the multifaceted impact of traumatic stress. It provides a foundational understanding of the biopsychosocial aspects of trauma.

Key Texts on Dissociative Disorders
and Structural Dissociation

van der Hart, O., Nijenhuis, E. R. S., & Steele, K. (2006). The Haunted Self: Structural Dissociation and the Treatment of Chronic Traumatization. W. W. Norton & Company. 14

This is the foundational text for structural dissociation theory. It offers a detailed theoretical model and a phase-oriented treatment approach for chronic traumatization, encompassing PTSD, Complex PTSD, and Dissociative Identity Disorder. The book is lauded for its constructive, lucid, and thought-provoking integration of Pierre Janet's classic observations with modern trauma and dissociation theory, alongside contemporary neuroscience and attachment research. 15 It is considered essential for clinicians seeking a deeper understanding of complex trauma and dissociation.

Gonzalez, A., & Mosquera, D. (1st ed.). EMDR and

Dissociation: The Progressive Approach. 21

This text specifically addresses the nuanced application of EMDR therapy in the context of dissociative disorders. It offers a "progressive approach" for clinicians working with the complexities of trauma and dissociation, providing specialized considerations beyond standard EMDR protocols.

Knipe, J. (2015). EMDR Tool Box: Theory and Treatment of Complex PTSD and Dissociation. Springer Publishing Company. 21

This book provides practical tools and theoretical insights for clinicians utilizing EMDR with complex PTSD and dissociative disorders. It highlights the specialized adaptations and considerations necessary when working with these challenging presentations.

Foundational Manuals for Specific Therapeutic Modalities (for Clinicians)

Shapiro, F. (2017). Eye Movement Desensitization and Reprocessing (EMDR) Therapy, Third Edition: Basic Principles, Protocols, and Procedures. The Guilford Press. 17

As the definitive textbook by the originator of EMDR, this manual provides a comprehensive and detailed guide to the eight phases of this psychotherapy. It is an indispensable resource for clinicians learning and applying EMDR in practice.

Ogden, P., & Fisher, J. (2015). Sensorimotor Psychotherapy: Interventions for Trauma and Attachment. W. W. Norton & Company. 17

This book serves as a practical guide for both therapists and clients to understand and work with the "language of the body" in the context of trauma and attachment. It outlines a phase-oriented approach to therapy, emphasizing the development of somatic resources, bottom-up memory processing, and exploring the impact of attachment on procedural learning and emotional biases.34

Schwartz, R. C. (2001). Internal Family Systems Therapy. Guilford Press. / Schwartz, R. C. (2019). Introduction to Internal Family Systems. Sounds True. 17

These texts introduce the core concepts and therapeutic applications of Internal Family Systems (IFS). They provide a non-pathologizing framework for understanding and healing internal "parts" that have been impacted by trauma. Introduction to Internal Family Systems is particularly noted for its accessibility, making it an ideal starting point for both laypersons and clinicians.29

Linehan, M. M. (1993). Cognitive-Behavioral Treatment of Borderline Personality Disorder. Guilford Press. 17

This is the foundational theoretical text for Dialectical Behavior Therapy (DBT). While primarily focused on Borderline Personality Disorder (BPD), its principles and strategies for emotion regulation, distress tolerance, and interpersonal effectiveness are highly relevant and widely applied to complex trauma and emotion dysregulation commonly seen in dissociative disorders.38

Linehan, M. M. (1993). Skills Training Manual for Treating Borderline Personality Disorder. Guilford Press. 17

A crucial practical companion to the theoretical text, this manual provides detailed handouts and worksheets for teaching the core DBT skills (mindfulness, distress tolerance, emotion regulation, interpersonal effectiveness). These skills are indispensable for trauma survivors in managing intense emotional states and impulsive behaviors.37

Foa, E. B., Hembree, E. A., & Rothbaum, B. O. (2007, 2019). Prolonged Exposure Therapy for PTSD: Emotional Processing of Traumatic Experiences—Therapist Guide. Oxford University Press. 17

This is a comprehensive manual for clinicians to effectively implement Prolonged Exposure (PE), an empirically validated treatment for PTSD. It outlines systematic techniques for exposure to traumatic memories (in vivo and imaginal) and real-life situations, aimed at reducing avoidance and fear.27

Resick, P. A., Monson, C. M., & Chard, K. M. (2017). Cognitive Processing Therapy for PTSD: A Comprehensive Manual. Guilford Press. 17

This is an indispensable guide for practitioners of Cognitive Processing Therapy (CPT). It provides a detailed, step-by-step framework for challenging and modifying unhelpful beliefs related to trauma, supported by a comprehensive theoretical overview and robust empirical data on CPT's effectiveness.26

## The Evolution and Interdisciplinary Nature of Trauma Literature

The selection of essential books reveals a significant evolution in trauma literature, moving from a primary focus on descriptive understanding to the development of actionable interventions. Early seminal works, such as Judith Herman's Trauma and Recovery13, were pivotal in defining, legitimizing, and bringing widespread awareness to the concept of complex trauma and its profound impact. Subsequent influential works, like Bessel van der Kolk's The Body Keeps the Score13, began to integrate neurobiological understandings and explore a broader range of treatment modalities. The sheer volume and specificity of "foundational manuals" for distinct therapeutic approaches (EMDR, IFS, SP, DBT, CPT, PE) 17 signify a critical maturation of the field, moving beyond mere theoretical understanding to the development of evidence-based, structured interventions. This progression reflects the field's commitment to developing actionable and effective treatments for the complex sequelae of trauma and dissociation. It underscores the dual importance of both deep theoretical grounding and practical, manualized application in clinical practice. For clinicians, this signifies a continuously expanding toolkit of specialized interventions, moving away from a generic approach towards more tailored and precise therapeutic strategies. The emphasis on "manuals" and "protocols" for these therapies 22 also highlights a strong drive towards standardization, replicability, and empirical validation. This methodological rigor is crucial for widespread dissemination of effective treatments and for building a robust evidence base, contrasting with earlier, less structured psychotherapeutic approaches to complex trauma.

Furthermore, the listed books consistently demonstrate the increasingly interdisciplinary nature of modern trauma theory and practice. While primarily psychological texts, they consistently draw upon and integrate concepts from diverse scientific disciplines. The Body Keeps the Score explicitly discusses the

"neurological effects of trauma". 13 The Haunted Self integrates findings from "affective neurosciences and attachment/developmental and relational

literature". 15 Sensorimotor Psychotherapy is explicitly founded on "neuroscience research findings,"

"polyvagal theory," and "triune brain theory".33
This interdisciplinary integration demonstrates that
a truly comprehensive understanding of trauma
and dissociation necessitates a multi-faceted lens.
Psychologists and clinicians are increasingly required
to be conversant with principles from neurobiology,
physiology, and developmental psychology to fully
grasp the pervasive impact of trauma and to apply
the most effective and cutting-edge interventions.
This trend also suggests that future research in the
field will increasingly be collaborative, bridging
traditional disciplinary boundaries to yield more
complete understandings. The recurrent and growing
emphasis on "the body" (e.g., in The Body Keeps
the Score, Sensorimotor Psychotherapy) indicates
a profound paradigm shift. This moves beyond a
purely cognitive or intrapsychic view of trauma to
one that acknowledges its deep physiological imprints
and the role of the autonomic nervous system. This
has led to the development of somatic therapies
that directly address these bodily manifestations,
offering new and often essential avenues for healing,
particularly where traditional talk therapy alone
may prove insufficient or even counterproductive.

## IV. Influential Peer-Reviewed Articles

Access to peer-reviewed articles is crucial for staying
abreast of the latest research, empirical evidence,
and clinical advancements in the fields of trauma
and dissociative disorders. The following journals and
highly cited articles represent key contributions to the
literature.

Core Journals for Trauma and Dissociation Research

Journal of Traumatic Stress (JTS): This is the official journal of the International Society for Traumatic Stress Studies (ISTSS). It serves as an interdisciplinary forum for peer-reviewed original papers focusing on the biopsychosocial aspects of trauma, encompassing research, treatment, prevention, and legal and policy concerns.43 Highly cited articles in JTS often cover critical areas such as PTSD assessment (e.g., the Clinician-Administered PTSD Scale, the Posttraumatic Growth Inventory), risk factors, and treatment outcomes.46

Journal of Trauma & Dissociation (JTD): This peer-reviewed journal, published by Taylor & Francis, focuses specifically on scientific literature covering dissociation and all the Dissociative Disorders, Complex PTSD, Post Traumatic Stress Disorder, psychological trauma, and trauma memory. Members of the International Society for the Study of Trauma and Dissociation (ISSTD) benefit from free online access.44 The journal is a vital resource for understanding the complexities of dissociation and its relationship to trauma.

Psychological Trauma: Theory, Research, Practice, and Policy: Published by the American Psychological Association (APA), this journal is dedicated to the scientific study of trauma. It provides a platform for research that informs clinical practice and policy, covering a wide range of topics related to traumatic stress.43

Highly Cited Articles

The following articles represent significant contributions to the understanding of trauma and dissociative disorders, often cited for their empirical findings, theoretical advancements, or clinical implications. This list is not exhaustive but highlights impactful works from the field.

From Journal of Traumatic Stress:

Kessler, R. C., Sonnega, A., Bromet, E., Hughes, M., & Nelson, C. B. (1995). Posttraumatic stress disorder in the national comorbidity survey. Archives of General Psychiatry.42 (Highly cited for its epidemiological data on PTSD prevalence).

Breslau, N., Davis, G. C., Andreski, P., & Peterson, E. (1991). Traumatic events and posttraumatic stress disorder in an urban population of young adults. Archives of General Psychiatry.42 (Influential for its early epidemiological findings on trauma exposure and PTSD).

Kendall-Tackett, K. A., Williams, L. M., & Finkelhor, D. (1993). Impact of sexual abuse on children: A review and synthesis of recent empirical studies. Psychological Bulletin.42 (A foundational review highlighting the pervasive impact of childhood sexual abuse).

Ehlers, A., & Clark, D. M. (2000). A cognitive model of posttraumatic stress disorder. Behaviour Research and Therapy.42 (Presents a widely influential cognitive model for understanding PTSD).

Brewin, C. R., Andrews, B., & Valentine, J. D. (2000). Meta-analysis of risk factors for posttraumatic stress disorder in trauma-exposed adults. Journal of Consulting and Clinical Psychology.42 (A comprehensive meta-analysis identifying key risk factors for PTSD).

Foa, E. B., Rothbaum, B. O., Riggs, D. S., & Murdock, T. B. (1991). Treatment of posttraumatic stress disorder in rape victims: A comparison between cognitive-behavioral procedures and counseling. Journal of Consulting and Clinical Psychology.42 (Early empirical support for cognitive-behavioral interventions in trauma treatment).

From Journal of Trauma & Dissociation:

International Society for the Study of Trauma and Dissociation. (2011). Guidelines for Treating Dissociative Identity Disorder in Adults, Third Revision. Journal of Trauma & Dissociation.44 (The most cited article in the journal, providing essential clinical guidelines for DID and other specified dissociative disorders).

Freyd, J. J. (1994). Betrayal Trauma: Traumatic Amnesia as an Adaptive Response to Childhood Abuse. Journal of Trauma & Dissociation.47 (Introduces the concept of betrayal trauma and its link to dissociative amnesia).

Dorahy, M. J., Brand, B. L., Sar, V., Krüger, C., Stavropoulos, P., Martinez-Taboas, A., Lewis-Fernández, R., & Middleton, W. (2014). Dissociation in Trauma: A New Definition and Comparison with Previous Formulations. Journal of Trauma & Dissociation.48 (Offers a refined definition of dissociation and compares it to earlier conceptualizations).

Sar, V., Akyuz, G., Kugu, N., Ozturk, E., & Ertem-Vehid, H. (2006). Axis I Dissociative Disorder Comorbidity in Borderline Personality Disorder and Reports of Childhood Trauma. Journal of Clinical Psychiatry.7 (Highlights high comorbidity of dissociative disorders in BPD and its link to childhood trauma).

From Psychological Trauma: Theory, Research, Practice, and Policy:

Ozer, E. J., Best, S. R., Lipsey, T. L., & Weiss, D. S. (2003). Predictors of posttraumatic stress disorder and symptoms in adults: A meta-analysis. Psychological Bulletin.42 (A widely cited meta-analysis on predictors of PTSD).

Williamson, C., Baumann, J., & Murphy, D. (2022). Exploring the Health and Well-Being of a National Sample of Treatment-Seeking Veterans. Psychological Trauma: Theory, Research, Practice, and Policy.11 (Examines the complex health and well-being needs and high comorbidity in veterans with trauma).

Brand, B. L., Classen, C. C., McNary, S. W., & Zaveri, P. (2012). A Longitudinal Naturalistic Study of Patients With Dissociative Disorders Treated by Community Clinicians. Psychological Trauma: Theory, Research, Practice, and Policy.9 (Provides evidence for improvements in symptoms and functioning for dissociative disorder patients in community treatment).

From American Journal of Psychiatry / Psychological Bulletin:

Dalenberg, C. J., Brand, B. L., Gleaves, D. H., Finnegan, K., Spiegel, D., Loewenstein, R. J., & Cardeña, E. (2012). Evaluation of the evidence for the trauma and fantasy models of dissociation. Psychological Bulletin.4 (A critical meta-analysis providing strong empirical support for the trauma model of dissociation over the fantasy model).

Spitzer, C., Barnow, S., Freyberger, H. J., & Grabe, H. J. (2007). Dissociation predicts symptom-related treatment outcome in short-term inpatient psychotherapy. Australian & New Zealand Journal of Psychiatry.4 (Demonstrates that dissociation can predict treatment outcomes in psychotherapy).

Sar, V. (2014). The many faces of dissociation: opportunities for innovative research in psychiatry. Clinical Psychopharmacology and Neuroscience.51 (A review highlighting dissociation as a fundamental human response to chronic developmental stress and its pervasive impact across psychiatric disorders).

Brodsky, B. S., Cloitre, M., & Dulit, R. A. (1995). Relationship of dissociation to self-mutilation and childhood abuse in borderline personality disorder. American Journal of Psychiatry.7 (Documents the prevalence of pathological dissociation in BPD and its association with self-mutilation and childhood abuse).

Foote, B., Smolin, Y., Kaplan, M., Legatt, M. E., & Lipschitz, D. (2006). Prevalence of Dissociative Disorders in Psychiatric Outpatients. American Journal of Psychiatry.7 (Reveals high prevalence and under-diagnosis of dissociative disorders in outpatient settings).

Simeon, D., Guralnik, O., Schmeidler, J., Sirof, B., & Knutelska, M. (2001). The Role of Childhood Interpersonal Trauma in Depersonalization Disorder. American Journal of Psychiatry.7 (Investigates the strong link between childhood interpersonal trauma, particularly emotional abuse, and depersonalization disorder).

# V. Key Websites and Organizations

Several professional societies, advocacy groups, and governmental bodies offer valuable resources, guidelines, and support related to trauma and dissociative disorders. These websites serve as authoritative sources for information, clinical guidance, and public education.

## Professional Organizations

American Psychiatric Association (APA): The APA provides comprehensive overviews and specific information about dissociative disorders, including diagnostic criteria and expert Q&A sections for patients and families.3 Their resources cover various mental health conditions, including PTSD and dissociative disorders, offering guidelines for screening and treatment.53

Relevant URL:5

American Psychological Association (APA) - Division 56 (Trauma Psychology): This division of the APA focuses specifically on trauma psychology, offering resources and guidelines for evidence-based treatments for PTSD, such as Cognitive Behavioral Therapy (CBT), Cognitive Processing Therapy (CPT), and Prolonged Exposure (PE).22 Their journal, Psychological Trauma: Theory,

Research, Practice, and Policy, is a key publication in the field.43

Relevant URL:22

International Society for the Study of Trauma and Dissociation (ISSTD): The ISSTD is a leading professional organization dedicated to advancing clinical, scientific, and societal understanding about the prevalence and consequences of chronic trauma and dissociation.2 They offer a wealth of information and resources for health professionals, teachers, school staff, and the general public, including guidelines for treating Dissociative Identity Disorder in adults and for evaluating and treating dissociative symptoms in children and adolescents.14 Their publications include Frontiers in the Psychotherapy of Trauma and Dissociation (an e-journal) and the Journal of Trauma and Dissociation.14

Relevant URL:14

International Society for Traumatic Stress Studies (ISTSS): ISTSS is a multidisciplinary international organization dedicated to the advancement and exchange of knowledge about traumatic stress. They publish the Journal of Traumatic Stress and offer various public resources, including briefing papers and ePamphlets on trauma-related topics, aiming to promote traumatic stress as a public health issue.43

Relevant URL:45

## Advocacy and Support Organizations

National Alliance on Mental Illness (NAMI): NAMI is a prominent mental health organization that provides support, education, and advocacy for individuals and families affected by mental illness, including dissociative disorders. They offer information on symptoms, treatment options (like CBT, DBT, EMDR), and support resources, emphasizing the importance of family and peer support.2

Relevant URL:2

National Federation of Families: This non-profit organization supports children, youth, and families experiencing mental health challenges, including dissociative disorders. They encourage exploration of resources and connection with local affiliates for support and information.6

Relevant URL:6

An Infinite Mind: A non-profit organization specifically dedicated to supporting survivors of trauma-related dissociation. They provide a substantial list of recommended books and other resource materials for individuals with Dissociative Identity Disorder and for clinicians who treat it.6

The Sidran Institute: A vital resource for trauma survivors and their support networks for over 25 years, the Sidran Institute is a global cornerstone in educating professionals and the public on effectively addressing the diverse needs of trauma survivors, including those with PTSD, dissociative disorders, and co-occurring issues like addictions and self-injury.2 They develop and deliver books, assessment tools, and educational programs.

Relevant URL:56

Government and Research Resources

PTSD: National Center for PTSD (U.S. Department of Veterans Affairs): This national center provides extensive resources for veterans and the public on PTSD, including self-care exercises, mobile apps like PTSD Coach and Mindfulness Coach, and crisis support lines. While primarily focused on PTSD, its resources are highly relevant given the significant overlap between PTSD and dissociative disorders.58

Relevant URL:58

## VI. Conclusion

The comprehensive review of resources on trauma, dissociative disorders, and relevant psychological theories underscores several critical understandings within the field. The pervasive and often devastating impact of trauma, particularly chronic childhood adversity, is firmly established as the primary etiological factor for dissociative disorders. This understanding has profoundly shaped diagnostic frameworks, as evidenced by the DSM-5-TR's emphasis on the trauma-dissociation link, and necessitates trauma-informed approaches in all clinical interventions.

A recurring theme is the profound complexity of these conditions, marked by high rates of comorbidity with other severe mental health challenges such as PTSD, depression, anxiety, borderline personality disorder, and self-injurious behaviors. This intricate interplay of symptoms and underlying trauma demands highly individualized, integrative, and phase-oriented treatment strategies that prioritize safety and stabilization before deeper trauma processing. The field has witnessed a significant evolution in therapeutic approaches, moving beyond purely cognitive interventions to embrace embodied and integrative modalities like EMDR, Internal Family Systems, and Sensorimotor Psychotherapy. This shift reflects a growing recognition that trauma is deeply imprinted in both mind and body, requiring interventions that address physiological dysregulation and fragmented self-states. The increasing integration of neuroscience findings across diverse theoretical models highlights a convergence of psychological and biological understanding, pointing towards a future of truly holistic and collaborative care.

Despite these advancements, a persistent challenge remains the under-recognition and misdiagnosis of dissociative disorders, often stemming from insufficient clinician training and a societal discomfort with confronting the realities of severe childhood abuse. This gap between scientific evidence and clinical practice necessitates ongoing efforts in professional education, public advocacy, and destigmatization to ensure that individuals affected by trauma and dissociation receive timely and appropriate care. The resources compiled in this bibliography serve as essential tools for advancing knowledge, improving clinical practice, and fostering a more trauma-informed mental health landscape. Continued engagement with these foundational and emerging works will be vital for clinicians, researchers, and individuals seeking to understand and heal from the profound effects of trauma and dissociation.

*Works cited*

Dissociative identity disorder - Wikipedia, accessed May 21, 2025,

Dissociative Disorders | National Alliance on Mental Illness (NAMI), accessed May 21, 2025,

What Are Dissociative Disorders? - Psychiatry.org, accessed May 21, 2025,

Evaluation of the Evidence for the Trauma and Fantasy Models of Dissociation - Towson University, accessed May 21, 2025,

Dissociative Disorders - Psychiatry.org, accessed May 21, 2025,

Dissociative Disorder - National Federation of Families, accessed May 21, 2025,

Dissociative Disorders Annotated Bibliography - ISSTD, accessed May 21, 2025,

Dissociative identity disorder: out of the shadows at last? | The British Journal of Psychiatry, accessed May 21, 2025,

Psychological Trauma: Theory, Research, Practice, and Policy - Towson University, accessed May 21, 2025,

Integrating Dissociation | American Journal of Psychiatry, accessed May 21, 2025,

Psychological Trauma: Theory, Research, Practice, and Policy, accessed May 21, 2025,

Dissociative disorders in psychiatric inpatients | American Journal of Psychiatry, accessed May 21, 2025,

Judith Herman, Bessel van der Kolk, and Contemporary Trauma Research: Home - LibGuides, accessed May 21,

2025,

Resources for Professionals - ISSTD, accessed May 21, 2025,

The Haunted Self: Structural Dissociation and the Treatment of Chronic Traumatization, Onno van der Hart Book Study (12 CE Credit Hours), accessed May 21, 2025,

The Haunted Self Structural Dissociation and the Treatment of Chronic Traumatization by Hart, Onno van der, Nijenhuis, Ellert R. S., Steele, Kathy [W. W. Norton,2006] (Hardcover) - Amazon.com, accessed May 21, 2025,

Trauma Annotated Bibliography - ISSTD, accessed May 21, 2025,

The AIP model as a theoretical framework for the treatment of personality disorders with EMDR therapy - Frontiers, accessed May 21, 2025,

EMDR Therapy: A Comprehensive Overview of Theory, Mechanisms, and Applications, accessed May 21, 2025,

Francine Shapiro - Wikipedia, accessed May 21, 2025,

Top EMDR Books for Therapists | EMDR Center of the Rockies, accessed May 21, 2025,

Treatments for PTSD - American Psychological Association, accessed May 21, 2025,

Aaron T. Beck: Books - Amazon.com, accessed May 21, 2025,

Cognitive Therapy of Anxiety Disorders, accessed May 21, 2025,

Episode 209: PTSD and Cognitive Processing Therapy with Patricia Resick - Psychiatry & Psychotherapy

Podcast, accessed May 21, 2025,

Cognitive Processing Therapy for PTSD: A Comprehensive Manual Resick, Patricia - eBay, accessed May 21, 2025,

Prolonged Exposure Therapy for PTSD By Edna B Foa - World of Books, accessed May 21, 2025,

Prolonged Exposure Therapy for PTSD: Emotional Processing of Traumatic Experiences - Therapist Guide (Treatments That Work): 9780190926939 - Amazon.com, accessed May 21, 2025,

Introduction to Internal Family Systems: Schwartz, Richard: 9781683643616 - Amazon.com, accessed May 21, 2025,

Introduction to the Internal Family Systems Model - Amazon.com, accessed May 21, 2025,

partsandself.org, accessed May 21, 2025,

IFS and Trauma - PARTS & SELF, accessed May 21, 2025,

What is Sensorimotor Psychotherapy? | Exhale Psychology Centre Brisbane, accessed May 21, 2025,

Sensorimotor Psychotherapy : Interventions for Trauma and Attachment - Apple Books, accessed May 21, 2025,

Sensorimotor Psychotherapy: Interventions for Trauma and Attachment - Goodreads, accessed May 21, 2025,

Sensorimotor approaches to trauma treatment | Advances in Psychiatric Treatment | Cambridge Core, accessed May 21, 2025,

DBT for Trauma | Charlie Health, accessed May 21, 2025,

DBT and Trauma - Psychotherapy Academy, accessed May 21, 2025,

Dialectical Behavior Therapy - American Psychological Association, accessed May 21, 2025,

Five Books to Learn More About DBT, accessed May 21, 2025,

10 Must-Read Books for Complex Trauma Survivors - Amanda Ann Gregory, accessed May 21, 2025,

The 20 most influential papers on posttraumatic stress | Trauma Recovery Lab, accessed May 21, 2025,

ISTSS Research Resources | International Society for Traumatic Stress Studies, accessed May 21, 2025,

News, Journals, blogs from experts in PTSD, Dissociative Disorders, Trauma and Abuse., accessed May 21, 2025,

Public Resources | International Society for Traumatic Stress Studies, accessed May 21, 2025,

Journal of Traumatic Stress - Impact Factor & Score 2025 - Research.com, accessed May 21, 2025,

Journal of Trauma & Dissociation (Taylor & Francis) | 1000 Publications | 7447 Citations | Top authors - SciSpace, accessed May 21, 2025,

Journal of Trauma and Dissociation - Impact Factor & Score 2025 - Research.com, accessed May 21, 2025,

Psychological Trauma: Theory, Research, Practice, and Policy - Scilit, accessed May 21, 2025,

Psychological Trauma: Theory, Research, Practice, and Policy - SciSpace, accessed May 21, 2025,

Dissociation in Psychiatric Disorders: A Meta-Analysis of Studies Using the Dissociative Experiences Scale | American Journal of Psychiatry, accessed May 21, 2025,

The Many Faces of Dissociation: Opportunities for

Innovative Research in Psychiatry - PMC, accessed May 21, 2025,

Psychiatry.org - Stress And Trauma - American Psychiatric Association, accessed May 21, 2025,

The Sidran Institute Press Archives, accessed May 21, 2025,

Resources | For All Seasons, Inc., accessed May 21, 2025,

Sidran Institute - National Sexual Violence Resource Center (NSVRC), accessed May 21, 2025,

Sidran Traumatic Stress Institute, Inc. - National Sexual Violence Resource Center (NSVRC), accessed May 21, 2025,

PTSD: National Center for PTSD Home, accessed May 21, 2025,

◆ ◆ ◆

Aurealia Nelson is a psychological thriller writer with a background in psychology, anthropology, and fiction writing. Their fascination with the complexities of the human psyche, particularly the dark undercurrents of trauma and mental illness, informs their writing. Aurealia's work explores the intersection of psychological realism and compelling narratives, seeking to portray the inner lives of complex female characters with depth and sensitivity. They strive to create narratives that not only entertain but also provoke reflection on societal responses to trauma and mental health. You can find more of her work on aurealianelson.com, or find her on Instagram as 'mezzygurl'.